Judgment
CALLS

Alafair Burke

St. Martin's Paperbacks

First published in the United States by Henry Holt and Company.

JUDGMENT CALLS

Copyright © 2003 by Alafair Burke.
Excerpt from *Missing Justice* copyright © 2004 by Alafair Burke.

Cover photograph by Kazuo Ogawa/Photonica

Library of Congress Catalog Card Number: 2002192175

ISBN: 0-312-99720-5
EAN: 80312-99720-5

Printed in the United States of America

Henry Holt and Company hardcover edition published 2003
St. Martin's Paperbacks edition / May 2004

St. Martin's Paperbacks are published by St. Martin's Press, 175 Fifth Avenue, New York, NY 10010.

10 9 8 7 6 5 4 3 2

For my loving parents,
James Lee and Pearl Chu Pai Burke

1

A February morning in Portland, Oregon, and it was still dark outside when I walked into the courthouse, the air thick with the annoying drops of humidity that pass for rain in the Pacific Northwest. No surprises there. What did surprise me was finding a Police Bureau sergeant waiting in my office.

I'm a deputy district attorney for Multnomah County, making me about one percent of the office that prosecutes state crimes committed in the Portland area. Since I took this job three years ago, I've gotten used to having voice mail and e-mail messages waiting for me on Monday mornings. People just don't seem to realize that government law offices aren't open on weekends. It's unusual, though, and rarely a good sign, to find a cop waiting for you first thing in the morning.

At least I knew this one.

"Hey, Garcia, who let you in?" I said. "I thought we had some security around here."

Sergeant Tommy Garcia looked up from the Oregon State Bar magazine he had lifted out of my in-box. He smiled at me with those bright white, perfectly straight teeth that contrasted beautifully with his smooth olive skin. That smile had led me to believe he was a nice guy when I met him for the first time three years ago, and I had been right.

"Hey, Sammie, what can I say? I love reading the part at the back that tells about all the bad lawyers and what they did to get disbarred or suspended. Gives me a sense of justice. You should be careful about giving me such a hard time, though. I might start to think you're like the rest of the DAs around here, with a stick up your ass."

Tommy's in charge of the bureau's vice unit, so I know him well. As a member of the eight-lawyer team known as the Drug and Vice Division, I talk to Tommy almost weekly about pending cases and see him at least once a month at team meetings.

"You must want something from me big and bad, Garcia, to be buttering me up like that. What is it," I asked, "a warrant?" The local judges won't even read an officer's application for a search warrant unless it is reviewed and approved first by a deputy DA. In a close case, the cops tend to "DA shop."

Garcia laughed. "You're too smart, Kincaid. Nope, no warrant. I do need your help on something, but it's a little more complicated." He reached behind him to shut the door, looking at me first to make sure I didn't mind.

"MCT picked a case up over the weekend, thinking it would be an attempt murder. The suspects are bad, bad guys,

Sammie. Two of them grabbed a girl out of Old Town. One of them started to rape her, but couldn't get it up, so he beat her instead, and then the second guy finished what the first couldn't. When they were done, they left her for dead out in the Columbia Gorge.

"I don't know all the details, but apparently the initial investigation was a bit of a cluster fuck. It sounds like everything's on track now, but O'Donnell was the riding DA and got pissed off at some of the early mistakes. So he's planning on kicking it into the general felony unit for prosecution. You can pretty much figure out what's gonna happen to it."

The general felony trial unit is a dumping ground for cases that aren't seen as serious. The trial DDAs often have extremely limited time to spend on them, and the overwhelming majority plead out to reduced charges and stipulated sentences during a fast-paced court calendar referred to as "morning call." It's the criminal justice system's ugly side. Tim O'Donnell was a senior DDA in the major crimes unit. If he bumped a Major Crimes Team case down to general, he knew it was gone.

"Sounds bad, but it also sounds like MCT's beef is with O'Donnell."

"Yeah, well, O'Donnell's mind's not an easy one to change, and I think there's another way to go here because of a vice angle. The victim's a thirteen-year-old prostitute named Kendra Martin. Unlike most of 'em, she doesn't try to look any older. Wears schoolgirl outfits like that one girl used to wear on MTV before she got implants and started running around naked. What's her name? My daughter likes her. Anyway, she looks her age, is my point.

"Turns out her injuries weren't as bad as they first looked, so the MCT guys know it'll be hard to get attempted murder to stick. But they kept working the case, even after they realized that they could've handed it off to precinct detectives. This case is under their skin."

Any reluctance on the part of the Major Crimes Team to hand over a case to precinct detectives was understandable. In theory, regular shift detectives are perfectly good investigators, but in reality, disappointed precinct detectives who were passed over for the elite MCT frequently drop the ball, deciding their cases must not be sufficiently "major" to warrant good investigations.

"I don't doubt their earnestness, but I still don't see why they'd come to DVD with this, let alone to me. I've never even handled an MCT case."

"They figured because of the vice connection that someone in DVD might take the case from O'Donnell and run with it on something more serious than a general felony. And I've been watching you since you got here, Kincaid. You're good, and this could be a case for you to show what you can do when given the chance."

"Don't think you can play me like that, Garcia. I know an ego stroke when I see it." Of course, recognizing the stroke for what it was didn't prevent me from succumbing to it. The truth was, he was right. I'd been eager to get my hands on a major trial. It's a no-win situation: DVD cases aren't sexy enough to prove yourself to the guys running this place, yet you're supposed to prove yourself before you can try victim cases. Garcia was dangling a way for me to beat the system.

I wasn't about to sign on for this, though, without knowing the details.

"I don't think there's much I can do about it, but I'm willing to talk. Have someone call me?" I asked.

"I can do better than that," he said. "I got two MCT detectives waiting for you down the street."

Garcia must've known he'd be able to work me. He had told Detectives Jack Walker and Raymond Johnson to wait for us at the cafeteria in the basement of the federal building. Created to provide subsidized meals to low-level government workers, the cafeteria had found a cultlike following among the city's law enforcement crowd. A three-dollar tray of grease dished out by lunch ladies in hairnets had a certain retro appeal.

I exercised some moderation and got a bowl of oatmeal while Garcia waited for his plate to be loaded up with bacon and home fries. After he'd paid for our meals, he led me to a corner table.

"Jack Walker, Raymond Johnson, this is Samantha Kincaid."

I shook their hands. Jack Walker was a beefy man in his fifties, starting to lose his hair, with a full mustache. His short-sleeved dress shirt stretched tight across his belly, the buttons pulling in front. His grip was almost painfully firm, and his palms were rough. He looked like a cop, through and through.

Johnson was a different story altogether. A tall well-built African American in his mid-thirties, Raymond Johnson looked and dressed like a *GQ* model. He wore a collarless shirt with a three-button charcoal suit. His hair was close-cropped, and he wore a diamond stud in his left ear. He shook my hand and held it just a little longer than necessary, which was fine with me.

"It's nice to meet you both," I said. "I've seen you around the courthouse, but I don't think we've ever actually met."

Jack Walker spoke first. "Yeah, likewise. I've been hearing a lot of good things about you from Tommy, here, and Chuck Forbes says you guys go way back."

Suddenly, Johnson's handshake made a little more sense. To say that Chuck Forbes and I go way back is to sanitize the situation considerably. I didn't think Chuck would tell all to his cop buddies, but I wouldn't be surprised if he had said something in a certain way with that grin of his that would clue a guy like Raymond Johnson in to the gist of his reminiscing.

I hoped I wasn't blushing. "Well, I don't want to disappoint you, but it's a long shot that I'll be able to help." I asked them to tell me about the case from the beginning, and Johnson took over.

"We got the call around three on Sunday morning. A group of high school kids went out near Multnomah Falls to party. They were all pretty drunk, and a couple of them hiked into the forest to get it on. The girl tripped over what she thought was a log. Turns out the log was Kendra Martin."

He explained the facts in detail; I could see why he enjoyed a reputation among the DDAs as one of the bureau's best witnesses. "She was wearing a bra and a skirt pulled up over her hips, nothing else. No purse, no ID. Real beat up, finger marks on her neck, blood coming out of her bottom." I looked down, trying to hide my discomfort. Johnson continued. "The kids called police and medical. Looking at her, everyone assumed the worst. Her pulse was slow, she wasn't moving or talking, her face and body were covered with blood. The med techs took her straight to Emanuel Legacy, and patrol cops called in MCT. We page O'Donnell and tell him what we have, and he says we don't need a DA to come out. We don't have a suspect in custody yet, and the scene where we found the vic, even if it turns out to be the crime scene, is already fucked up by the high school kids. He tells us to keep working and to page him if we get a suspect or if anything big comes up over the weekend."

This was promising to be a long meeting if Johnson didn't speed it up, so I broke in. "How'd you guys split up the investigation?"

"Chuck and his partner, Mike Calabrese, supervised patrol in securing the scene, and Jack and I went to Emanuel to follow up with the vic. By the time we arrive, she's been there almost an hour and doing a lot better. The ER doc told us that most of the blood was from the anal tearing and a single large laceration on her face. She was out of it and had a slow pulse because she was on heroin. To be on the safe side, the doctor gave her Narcan to knock the heroin out of her system and keep her from ODing. She was bruised up pretty bad, but she was basically OK by the time we got to the hospital."

"So that's when you realized it wasn't a Major Crimes Team case after all," I said, letting them know that Garcia had already filled me in on the jurisdictional problems.

Jack Walker responded. As the senior detective he probably felt the need to justify the decision to keep the case with MCT. "Depends on how you look at it. Yeah, if patrol had known at the scene what the vic's actual injuries were, they probably wouldn't have called us out. But once we got involved, we had a teenage vic saying that a couple guys pulled her into their car and raped and beat her. She told the doc she didn't know how heroin wound up in her system; that they must have injected her during the assault without her realizing it. It looked like a straight stranger-to-stranger kidnap, doping, rape, and sod of a little girl. It didn't seem right to bump the case down to shift detectives."

"What charge did you use to hang on to the case, attempted murder?" I asked.

Walker nodded. "Yeah, we decided we had enough. Actually, it's an attempted agg, since the girl's under fourteen."

Intentionally killing a person under fourteen is aggravated murder, which can carry a death sentence. Luckily, Kendra Martin didn't die, so the defendants would at most be charged with Attempted Aggravated Murder.

"So what did you do after you decided to keep the case?" I asked.

Johnson answered. "We go in to talk to her, and I'm telling you the girl was a real piece of work, cussing us out, calling us every name in the book. Accusing us of keeping her there against her will when there was nothing wrong with her so SCF would make her go home." Runaways were notoriously distrustful of the state's Services for Children and Families department.

"She wasn't making a lot of sense, so we had to explain to her that we were there to investigate her statement to the doctor. That calmed her down a little. Still pretty bitchy, though." Johnson caught himself and looked over at Garcia for a read on his choice of words. I assured him his candor was fine and asked him to continue as I pulled a legal pad from my briefcase.

"Anyway, the vic initially said she was walking in Old Town around ten on Saturday night, on her way to Powell's Books, when Suspect One comes up from behind and pushes her into the backseat of what she called a"—he looked down at his notebook—" 'some big, seventies, four-door, loser shit box.' Said it was a dark color. Suspect One gets in back with her while Suspect Two drives to a parking lot somewhere in southeast Portland.

"She says Suspect One acted like the one in charge. He starts getting real rough with her in the backseat, saying a lot of dirty stuff and pulling her clothes off. Thing is, right when she thinks he's about to rape her, she realizes there's nothing there. The guy can't get it up. So he just goes off and starts beating the shit out of her, then penetrates her vaginally and anally with a foreign object, she can't tell what. The doctors say it was probably some kind of stick—they found splinters. Anyway, they left the parking lot and got onto I-84 going east. She remembers passing signs to the airport. After they stopped—we're guessing they were out by Multnomah Falls at this point—Suspect One tells Suspect Two to take a turn at her. She thinks he penetrated her vaginally and remembers Suspect One telling him to finish off in her mouth. Her memory of what happened toward the end was pretty hazy. She also thinks they must've taken her purse, because she had it with her when they pulled her in the car."

I felt sick. It's bad enough that people like these men walk on the same planet as the rest of us. The fact that they manage to find one another and work together is utterly terrifying.

"Could she describe the suspects?"

Ray Johnson nodded. "Nothing helpful, just that she'd know them if she saw them again. We figure it's a long shot but go ahead and pull some mug shots off X-Imaging of guys on supervision for child sods and stranger-to-stranger rapes."

One of PPB's newest toys, X-Imaging is a computerized data system that stores all booking photos taken in the state.

By using the computer to select booking photos correspond-
ing to certain MOs, an officer is more likely to get a success-
ful identification from a witness than by dumping several
hundred booking photos in front of her. I could tell from
Johnson's voice that in this case, the strategy had hit pay dirt.

"She's flipping through the printouts and hones right in
on one guy, Frank Derringer. I swear, it was one of the best
mug-shot IDs I've ever seen. I mean, you've seen how it goes;
with that many pictures, most wits start to get confused. This
girl is just flipping through 'em left and right and then—
bam!—she nails it. One hundred percent certain. 'That's
him,' she said. Pointed right at Derringer's mug."

Johnson was getting excited now. "We get even more
worked up when we see that Derringer's the guy we pulled
who was just paroled last summer on an attempted sod of a
fifteen-year-old girl. Unfortunately for Derringer, this girl
had just started a kick boxing class. As he was pushing
her down, she popped up and landed a roundhouse kick
straight to his Adam's apple and got away. He only served a
year because it was an attempt, but it shows the guy's got it
in him.

"We called O'Donnell at that point and told him what we
had. He gives us the OK to pick up Derringer. We picked him
up last night around seven. His parole officer, Dave Renshaw,
went out there with us. The plan was to arrest Derringer on
a parole violation for having unsupervised contact with a
minor child, then write paper to search the apartment."

I interrupted. "Does Derringer have any cars registered
to him?"

Johnson nodded. "That would've been too easy. We ran
him. Only car registered to him is an 'eighty-two Ford Escort.

It was his associated vehicle until a couple years ago, probably when he went to the pen. Since then, it comes up as associated with one of Derringer's pals. Guy's gotten three DUIs in two years in that same car."

"You know how these guys are," Walker said. "They sell their pieces of junk to each other and never bother notifying DMV."

"So, is that all you had when you went out to the house? The victim's ID?"

Walker appeared to share my frustration. "Yeah, that's about it, but I don't know what more we could've gotten before we went out. They did a rape kit at the hospital, but, according to the victim's version, there's probably no semen to get a sample from. Derringer never did her. Even if the other guy left behind some pre-ejaculatory liquid or they get something from the oral swab, it can take about a week for a PCR analysis."

"What about blood?" If the victim drew any blood fighting, the hospital could identify the blood type in a matter of minutes.

Johnson shook his head. "Nah. The vic was too doped up to put up a fight, so she didn't have any evidence under her fingernails or draw any blood from them. We did have a couple things to corroborate her story. As luck would have it, Calabrese found the victim's purse in a trash can by the road about a half mile from where they dropped her. He and Forbes were thinking the bad guys maybe dumped the stick on the way out. Good thinking, but no luck. But finding the purse showed that Martin was remembering at least some details accurately."

My face must have revealed my skepticism. "I don't want

to sound like I've made up my mind, but that's pretty weak corroboration, Detective. It just shows Kendra was robbed; it doesn't say anything about who did this to her. Were there any prints on the purse?"

"We don't know yet. We've got it down at the lab being looked at with the rest of the girl's clothes."

"OK, so what you guys are telling me is that, at least so far, this case turns entirely on Kendra Martin's identification of Derringer. Do we all agree on that?"

They all nodded.

"So when you went out to Derringer's apartment with his PO, did this case manage to get any better?"

The second the words came out, I regretted them. Seasoned cops like Jack Walker and Raymond Johnson no doubt were well aware of the differences between their approach and a district attorney's. Cops just need to make the arrest. The DA is the one who has to prove the case to a jury beyond a reasonable doubt afterward, who has to deal with a defense attorney gnawing at every argument and challenging every piece of evidence. Trying a weak case can feel like getting poked in the eye for two weeks.

Cops learn to live with the difference in perspective. But they don't like being talked down to. And I was pretty sure I had done just that.

"No confession, if that's what you're looking for. Damn it, Garcia, I thought you said this girl was willing to try a close case. We're not even done giving her the facts, and she's already shutting us down." Jack Walker was clearly pissed off.

I chalked up the "girl" comment to generational differences and swallowed my pride. No use alienating these guys over a careless comment, even one that irritated the hell out of me.

"Detective, I'm sorry if my tone suggested that I was criticizing your investigation, but to be honest I'm a little frustrated by what I am beginning to perceive as an attempt to portray the evidence as stronger than it really is. Look, if the case is a real dog, I'll figure that out, whether or not you lead it to me barking. If it's a gimme, I'll notice that too. But I want to decide on my own. With that said, I apologize for my smart-ass comment. I should have said exactly what I was thinking, and now I have. I hope you haven't made up your mind about me, just as I haven't formed a final decision about your case."

The table was quiet as Garcia and Johnson waited to see if I had managed to make things worse. Then Jack Walker shook his head and smiled. "Well, that was definitely direct. And you're right. I guess we were kind of hyping the case up a little." He glanced over at Johnson, not so much with a look of blame as like a child who peeks over at his partner-in-mischief when he realizes the teacher has figured them out but good.

Walker then looked directly at me, and I could tell we'd entered a spin-free zone. "Look, the truth is, the biggest thing we've got right now is the girl's ID of Derringer. Derringer denied everything. He says he was over at his brother's watching a basketball game and then stayed for *Saturday Night Live* and some beers. The brother's name is Derrick Derringer, if you can believe it. Anyway, so far Derrick's corroborating his brother, but he's got three felony convictions, so there you go."

"So did you arrest Derringer at his house?" I asked.

Walker shook his head. "Not us. Renshaw hooked Derringer up on a parole violation based on Kendra's ID and took him down to the Justice Center for booking. We figured the parole detainer would at least hold him overnight, when O'Donnell could decide what charges to file."

"And what did O'Donnell make of all this?"

Detective Walker slumped back in his chair, the excitement draining from his face. "That's where this whole thing fell apart on us. After we had Derringer hooked up, we went back to central to meet Chuck and Mike. They had finished processing the scene and were working on the warrant. Just as we're finishing up, O'Donnell shows up—in a fucking suit—to review the warrant. He's reading it, just nodding the whole time, not saying squat. Then he says, 'What about this girl?' So Ray and I explain how she started out like a pill but then was a complete ten on the ID. O'Donnell didn't like it; said the case rested entirely on the girl. Then he asks whether we've run her."

"You'd finished the warrant and still hadn't run her?"

Walker pursed his lips and shook his head. "I know, we fucked up. We'd been up all night, running around. We assumed she was straight up when she picked a sick fuck like Derringer. We forgot about running her. It was a rookie mistake."

Johnson continued with the bad news. When they ran the victim, they found a few runaway reports and an arrest for loitering to solicit. Worse, the cop who made the loitering pop found a syringe in the girl's purse with heroin residue on it. Furious that the detectives had miscalculated their victim, O'Donnell had tried to bully her into coming clean, but his tough approach only made her dig her heels in deeper.

Walker had to smooth things over with her, and she eventually admitted to a nine-month heroin habit that she worked the streets to support.

"So it's basically a trick gone bad?" I asked.

"No," Walker said. "At least we don't think so. She admits she was walking Old Town, looking for a trick. She'd just finished one up and had scored some horse on the street. She figured she'd keep working while she was high. Anyway, these two guys pull up and offer her fifty bucks if they can high-five her."

"OK, I've been working vice a few years now, but I still don't know what a high five is."

I knew it had to be bad when Walker and Johnson looked to Garcia for help and raised their eyebrows. Garcia averted his eyes while he told me. "It's when a girl gets on all fours and one guy does her from behind while she blows the other one." I was about to ask why the hell it was called a high five until I got a mental image of two naked guys on their knees giving each other a high five.

I rolled my eyes in disgust. "So they ask her to work for both of them, basically, and she goes with them?"

Walker eagerly accepted the invitation to change the subject. "Not according to her. She says she told them to meet her in the parking lot of the motel at Third and Alder. She rents a room there when she works. She assumes they've got a deal and starts walking to the hotel. That's when Derringer pulls her into the backseat.

"The rest of it happened pretty much like she said originally. When the car was stopped and Derringer was undoing his pants, she tried getting out but the guy in front pushed her back in. They told her she wasn't going anywhere and she may as well shoot up what was left in her purse, so she did. Thing is, she says it never dawned on her they were gonna kill her until Derringer started to choke her out. But, my thinking is, she knew it at some level when they pulled her back into the car. She was just trying to get it over with. She said she injected so much horse, the assault didn't hurt that bad, and this guy really worked her over."

Ray Johnson shook his head. "Man, you should've seen O'Donnell. I don't know if you guys are tight, but he can be one tight-sphinctered prick. He got all moralistic and lectured the entire team about our obligation to be 'cautious wielding the stern hand of the law.'" Johnson's nerdy white guy impersonation pretty much nailed Tim O'Donnell.

"Anyway, it was bullshit," he continued. "O'Donnell had us clean up the warrant to include the new information and then signed off on it, saying he was gonna kick it out of major crimes territory if we didn't find anything that changed his mind. We found some porn, but nothing damning. So, he's planning on filing it today as an Assault Three and assigning it to precinct detectives for general follow-up before grand jury."

I couldn't believe it. All you had to prove for assault in the third degree was that two or more defendants acted together to injure another person. It didn't begin to portray the savage acts that had been committed against Kendra Martin.

"Assault Three? That's it?" I said.

Johnson nodded. "I know, ridiculous. He says the ID's weak, plus the defense can say the whole thing was a consensual trick, that the girl cried rape so her mom wouldn't find out she was turning tricks for smack. Said he was only issuing the assault because of Derringer's prior. He basically called the girl a piece of trash."

"And you guys don't think she is. You think she's telling the truth?"

Walker looked at me and tilted his head slightly. "Ms. Kincaid, I really do. It's almost in her favor that she lied to us at first. Shows she still knows that working's shameful, not just a matter-of-fact thing to her. Maybe that logic doesn't make any sense to you, but I think she's basically still a pretty good kid. We pissed O'Donnell off by not reading the case right, but he's taking it out on the case, and this Derringer dirtbag is going to get the benefit."

"I agree that Derringer needs to be done, but I'm not sure how I can help you."

I wasn't surprised that Sergeant Garcia had a suggestion. He had the respect of his fellow officers because he was a smart cop and a good guy. In a bureau where most black and Latino officers stall out at the front line of street-level enforcement, administrative staff promoted him because he had a political savvy so smooth that its targets never even knew they'd been had.

"The way I see it, this girl could be a good link for Vice. She's young and probably knows a circle of working girls we don't have access to. If we can earn her trust, she might be able to lead us to some of the pimps we haven't been able to latch on to, the guys who are turning out the real young ones.

"I'll call O'Donnell like I don't know much about the case but think it might have potential with Vice, then ask if he minds me getting MCT's OK to approach the vic as a potential informant. At that point I can sell him on letting a DVD attorney take the case, so they have a head start if the vic winds up developing other contacts for us. And then I'll seal the deal. 'Unless,' I'll say, 'you want to keep the case yourself and help me flip any vice contacts I work.' "

Johnson was impressed. "Tommy, my man, you oughta run for president. That is slick. You in, Kincaid?"

"I don't mind taking the case, but here's the problem: it still needs major help. The rape kit's not back, the victim's clothes are still at the lab, Derringer's alibi needs work, and we still don't have the driver. If this case is filed as an Assault Three, it's outside MCT jurisdiction. You know the precinct detectives aren't going to do the follow-up that's needed."

Garcia was a step ahead of me. "I'll make another call to O'Donnell, telling him that you want to file the case as a major crime so MCT can keep working on it, but that MCT understands it might get bumped back down later on."

I hate this kind of crap. The four people at the table agree what needs to happen and are willing to put in the work, but have to plot how they can even start without bruising a fragile ego.

I was skeptical. Garcia was good, but I still thought O'Donnell might see right through it and blame me when he wound up looking like a chicken shit. It would have been so easy to blame O'Donnell for the bad decision and say there was nothing I could do.

Apathy is grossly undervalued and never there for me when I need it. I was already sucked in. I'd broken up some escort services and prosecuted a few pimps, but I'd never had a chance to handle a case like this one. And, to my mind, with scum like Derringer, it was better to issue the case and lose than let him walk away up front.

"Alright, let's give it a try," I said.

| 2 |

Raymond Johnson was right. Tommy Garcia should run for office. Around nine o'clock, Tim O'Donnell popped into my office to give me a heads up that Tommy Garcia might be calling about an assault that happened over the weekend. I feigned ignorance. According to O'Donnell, the victim was a strung-out Old Town Lolita who acted surprised that a trick might want rough sex.

By ten, O'Donnell told Garcia he didn't care what charges were filed if someone from DVD agreed to pick it up. Once I got the word from Garcia, I called O'Donnell to be sure he was aware I'd be filing Measure 11 charges against Derringer. I didn't want him getting ticked off later.

Oregon joined the growing ranks of "tough on crime" states a few years ago when voters passed Ballot Measure 11 by a landslide. The law requires mandatory minimum sentences for the most violent felonies. Not surprisingly, once

Measure 11 defendants figured out they were facing long minimum sentences upon conviction, whether they pled out or not, they stopped pleading guilty and started rolling the dice at trial. As a result, the DA's office stopped filing charges that fell under Measure 11 unless the bureau's investigation was flawless. In response, PPB formed the Major Crimes Team. The precinct detectives weren't too happy about what they understandably viewed as a demotion.

In theory, the DA's office chose carefully which cases to file under Measure 11, because the consequences of a conviction are profound. But when it became clear that pissed-off precinct detectives were slacking on their general felony cases, the DAs started looking for creative ways to justify filing cases under Measure 11 so MCT would be responsible for the follow-up. Once the work was complete, they'd threaten the defendant with the mandatory minimum sentence in order to get him to plead guilty to whatever he should've been charged with in the first place. And now I had to pretend I was doing exactly that so a loser like Tim O'Donnell would give up a case he didn't even want.

I could hear laughing in the background when O'Donnell picked up the phone. As usual, the rest of the boys in the major crimes unit were huddled in his office for mid-morning coffee and a round of "No, *I've* got the raunchiest big-tit joke."

"Hey, Tim. It's Samantha Kincaid. You were right. Garcia did call me about that Derringer case. I agree it's a solid Assault Three, but MCT won't do the follow-up unless we file it under Measure Eleven."

"Listen, Kincaid, if you want to do the work on it, that's fine with me. I don't know why you'd want to. I talked to the vic at the hospital—she's a white trash junkie liar, no matter what those MCT guys tell you. The case is a loser."

"Yeah, you're probably right, but Garcia seems to think she might be able to get us some good vice cases."

"Tell me the truth, Kincaid. Do you actually give a shit about those whores?" More laughter in the background. I tried to control my anger as he put the phone on speaker.

"Alright, seriously, you guys. Who in this room really cares if some sack teaches a drug addict from Rockwood how to sell it to support her junkie habit?" When no one said anything and the guffawing started again, he said, "See, Kincaid? That's why you get all those vice cases. Ask me, we should give those guys a medal. Without them, those girls would be breaking into houses and stealing to get the money."

When he realized I wasn't joining in the festivities, he tried to cover. "We're just giving you a hard time, Sam. You know that, right? Sure you do. Hey, here's a good one. What does a Rockwood girl say right after she loses her virginity? 'Get off me, Daddy, you're crushing my smokes.' "

I'd love to be one of those people who could throw off the perfect zinger. The kind with the optimal amount of sting, but with enough of the funny stuff to keep you from looking like a freak. But in my experience, those perfect zingers never leap to mind at the right time.

"Funny, O'Donnell. Hey, hold on a sec." I set the phone down on my desk and rushed down the hall to his office. Standing in the doorway, I could see their wee brains straining to figure out how I could be in O'Donnell's office and on the phone at the same time. "There's nothing funny about the Derringer case, and there's definitely nothing funny about some guy getting over on his daughter. You say

something like that to me again, and it'll feel like someone
stretched your sad little ball sack up over that big empty head
of yours."

I stormed back toward my office before I could make
things worse. Behind me, I heard O'Donnell yell out, "Real
nice, Kincaid," over the other guys' laughter. I hadn't meant
it to be funny, but if they were going to take it that way,
so be it.

I had to hand it to O'Donnell. He could be a Grade A jerk,
but at least the guy could take it. As I slammed down the
phone in my office, I could hear his laugh above all the
others.

I waited for my pulse to return to normal, then called over
to the jail to make sure Derringer was still in custody. The
Multnomah County holding center's under an order from a
federal judge for overcrowding. If the cells get full, the sher-
iff's office is required to start releasing prisoners according to
a court-created formula. In theory, a sex offender in on a
parole hold should be one of the last to be released, but I'd
stopped being surprised by MCSO's decisions a long time ago.

I finally got connected to a Deputy Lamborn.

"You calling about Frank Derringer?" he asked. "Because
I've been trying all morning to figure out who to call, and I'm
getting ready to come off shift. Can't read the PO's signature
for shit."

"What's going on?" I asked.

"Well, we noticed something I thought the PO should
know about. When we bring the prisoners in for booking,
they've got to strip down out of their street clothes and put
on their jail blues. Anyway, when Derringer was changing,
one of the guys noticed that Derringer doesn't have any
pubic hair."

"Come again?" I said.

"Yep, all gone down there. So, anyway, we assumed he had crabs or something and were joking around about what lucky prisoner was gonna have to share a cell with him. But then I noticed Derringer had a parole hold for an Attempted Sod One and figured a sex offender might have a more sinister reason for getting rid of the short and curlies. Thought someone should know about it."

That someone was me. I wrote down Lamborn's information so I could add him to my witness list. Then I cut the call short so I could call Derringer's parole officer to see if he knew anything else.

He picked up the phone on the first ring. "Renshaw."

I introduced myself to Dave Renshaw as the DA who was going to pick up the Derringer case, then passed along Deputy Lamborn's observation.

"Well, I don't like what he had to say about my penmanship, but the boy was certainly using his noggin, wasn't he?"

"I'd say so. Unless Derringer's got some explanation, it looks like he knew he was going out for a victim and didn't want to leave any physical evidence behind. I was calling to see if you had anything in your file that might help. Derringer hasn't been out on parole for long, so if we could show that no one ever noticed anything unusual about Derringer's appearance when he was in prison—"

Renshaw cut me off. "Oh, I can do better than that. One of Mr. Derringer's parole conditions is that he submit to plethismographic examination." My silence told him I didn't know what that was. "Standard for most sex offenders. A counselor hooks the guy's private parts up to an EKG and then shows slides of various sexual images. By monitoring what gets someone like Mr. Derringer hot, the counselor can see whether the parolee's preferred fantasy images are changing with treatment or whether he's still perverted."

"Are you about to say what I hope?"

"Yes, ma'am. Derringer was in—let's see, I've got his file right here—yep, just last week for his initial examination, and I was there for it."

"And everything was normal down there?"

"I don't know about that, but, yes, I definitely would've noticed if he had shaved that area, and I didn't see anything out of the ordinary."

"And what were the plethismograph results?" I asked.

"Oh, the doctor would tell you that Derringer was responding to treatment. Derringer's pulse got pretty fast during some of the violent porn and stayed flat and steady during what most of us would consider straight porn, but his johnson stayed limp the whole time. The doctor thought Derringer's pulse raced out of nervousness that he *might* get caught getting off on the violence. But with what I know so far about this new case, I think Derringer was getting turned on but just wasn't responding downstairs."

Definitely possible. We were wrapping up the call when Renshaw said, "Now this is interesting. I was flipping through the file while we were talking. I usually get the facts of my guys' cases straight from the police report, but intake typed in something that must've come from the prosecuting attorney's file. The notes say that Derringer's brother, Derrick, had offered himself as Derringer's alibi witness."

"This is on Derringer's old case?"

"Right, the Attempted Sod," Renshaw clarified. "I didn't realize that Derringer ever tried to go with an alibi, but it says here that Derrick was scheduled to testify that Frank was with him when the girl said she was attacked. Then our Mr. Derringer turned around and changed his defense. Instead of saying it wasn't him, he argued the whole thing was consensual rough sex, trying to get the case bumped down to statutory rape. In the end, Derringer pled guilty as part of a plea bargain, but that doesn't stop him from telling me at every opportunity that the girl consented. Everyone I supervise is innocent, don't you know."

I thanked him profusely for all the information and assured him I'd be calling him as a witness. For now, I had other work to do.

Renshaw had lodged a detainer against Derringer based on probable cause that he'd had unsupervised contact with a minor, a violation of his parole conditions. Derringer was booked over the weekend, so his case would be called in the Justice Center arraignment court this afternoon for a release hearing. Technically, a parole detainer is enough to hold a parolee for up to sixty days pending a hearing. I would have liked to keep Derringer in custody on the violation and wait for MCT to finish the investigation before I decided what charges to file.

The problem was that the allegation underlying Derringer's violation was essentially an allegation of new criminal conduct. In these circumstances, most local judges won't hold the parolee in custody unless the State actually files new charges. So I needed to have a charging instrument ready in a few hours or the court might cut Derringer loose.

One alternative was to issue the lowest-level charges, like assault, kidnapping, and rape. That would be enough to hold Derringer until MCT was finished. Once the grand jury heard the complete evidence, I could come back with an indictment for Attempted Aggravated Murder. I'd been burned by this method before, though. A smart defense attorney can convince a defense-oriented judge that upping the charges on a defendant after he has been arraigned on the initial complaint is prosecutorial misconduct. Under the law, it's not, but that doesn't stop a court from doing what it wants.

This case would turn on Kendra Martin. Before I made up my mind about charges, I wanted more than Walker and Johnson's opinion about her. During my stint in DVD, I'd dealt with a few street girls. Most of what Walker and Johnson said about Kendra sounded right. I wasn't surprised that she would lie about the work and about her habit. And, if she was street smart, I believed she didn't get into that car on her own. What bothered me was her initial response to Walker and Johnson. Detectives with their experience are used to the typical rape victim response. It's normal for rape victims to be defensive and to direct their anger at police. But this girl, a thirteen-year-old, sounded like a nightmare. If I was going to go all out and guarantee myself a tough trial, I didn't want to spend the next few months fighting with a teenage sociopath.

I went to the law library and pulled a copy of the *Physicians' Desk Reference*. The emergency room had injected Kendra Martin with Narcan to prevent her from overdosing. According to the *PDR*, the active ingredient in Narcan was naloxone, which reverses the effects of opiates and induces immediate withdrawal. Even for a relatively new user like Kendra Martin, the shock to her system would be enough to create a very unhappy camper.

The effects of heroin last longer than the effects of naloxone. As a result, once the naloxone wears off, the person might have a short period where they're still under the influence of the opiates. Those effects gradually wear off, and the person returns to their normal state.

If Walker and Johnson were right about Kendra Martin essentially being a nice girl, the mix of Narcan and heroin would explain her initial crankiness, followed by a period of indifference.

Having satisfied my main point of doubt, I decided to go with my gut. Walker was right. Derringer and his buddy got a thirteen-year-old girl to shoot up a boatload of heroin, then beat her, choked her, sexually assaulted her, and left her to die in the woods. The case would be tough to prove, but it was looking better now with the information from the jail and Renshaw. There was enough for an attempted aggravated murder indictment and enough to get it to the jury. And even if a jury didn't go for the attempted agg, it could still convict on the kidnap, assault, and sex charges.

I spent the next couple of hours reviewing the reports that had been written on the case so far. I was impressed. Most of the time, if you read a cop's reports after the case has been described to you, the reports and the verbal summary don't quite match up. Either something was omitted from the conversation or, more commonly, left out of the written reports. MCT's good reputation appeared to be well deserved. I was pleased to see that everything I already knew, and nothing else, was in the reports. And I was irritated that I couldn't stop myself from paying special attention to the quality of Chuck Forbes's work.

Chuck had joined the bureau after college and had wound up on the fast track into MCT after he obtained a murder confession that eventually led to one of Oregon's first capital sentences. I took a special interest in Chuck Forbes for more personal reasons: He had taken my virginity from me in high school (OK, I kind of gave it to him), and we had continued our bad behavior on and off throughout our youth. We bickered constantly back then, and we still argue today. However, I'd made a vow to stop mixing wild sex with the fighting almost a decade ago, the summer after my college graduation. Once I make a vow, I stick with it.

We lost touch when I started law school in California, and my visits to Portland had dwindled and then stopped. But then the New Yorker I called my husband at the time took a job here, so I moved back. My friendship with Chuck and the accompanying spark had reignited when he showed up to testify as the arresting police officer in my first trial as a DDA. And now here I was, divorced and long past high school, trying to read his police reports without reminiscing.

Deciding I needed to take a break, I put on my coat and walked over to the Pit for lunch. Tourists might assume that the Pioneer Place mall's food court owed its nickname to its basement location, but they'd be wrong.

My usual Pit selection is Let's Talk Turkey, the only downtown deli that uses turkey from the bird instead of the pressed stuff. The good stuff you get on Thanksgiving beats slimy slabs of processed turkey food, hands down. However, healthy just wasn't going to cut it today. I decided a corn dog on a stick and a chocolate milkshake promised the perfect balance of sugar and fat. It had been awhile since I'd indulged my weakness for food on a stick, but I soon remembered why I always felt guilty when I did. The poor girl working at Food on a Stick wore the same uniform that the unfortunate employees had been subjected to when I was in high school: short shorts, a scoop-necked tank top, and a hat that can only be described as phallic. Like the generations of Food on a Stick girls that preceded her, she had long flowing hair, thin arms and hips, and breasts that didn't look like they wanted to stay in that little top. How does such a big company get away with never hiring a man?

The floor of the food booth was elevated and surrounded on three sides by mirrors. She was bent over at the waist, bobbing up and down as she pumped the juice from a bucket full of lemons for the nation's most famous fresh-squeezed lemonade. She seemed grateful to have a break from the thrusting to get my corn dog.

As I walked away, I saw a group of prepubescent boys sitting on a bench by the escalator, enjoying the view of the resumed lemon-pumping. I knew they weren't the first group of boys to cut class to hang out and watch a Food on a Stick girl at work. Hell, it was practically a rite of passage in America's suburbs. That said, I still couldn't help myself when I heard one of them speculate what the girl could do on his stick.

Introducing myself as a deputy district attorney for Multnomah County, I flashed my badge to make sure they appreciated the enormity of my clout. "You all better get back to school or I'm going to have to page a police officer from the truancy unit to have you picked up." The kids hightailed it up the escalator faster than you can say there's-no-such-thing-as-a-truancy-officer-anymore.

Feeling good about my lunch and my good deed, I headed back to the courthouse to draft the complaint about Derringer.

A criminal complaint is the initial document used to charge a defendant with a felony in Oregon. It's simply a piece of paper, signed by the prosecuting district attorney, notifying the defendant of the charges that have been filed. Once the defendant is arraigned on the complaint, the State has a week to present evidence to a grand jury and return an indictment. Without an indictment, the complaint will be dismissed and the defendant will be released from the court's jurisdiction.

I drafted a complaint charging Derringer with Attempted Aggravated Murder, Kidnapping in the First Degree, and Unlawful Sexual Penetration in the First Degree. I also included charges of Rape in the First Degree and Sodomy in the First Degree, since Derringer could be held responsible as an accomplice for the sex acts of the other suspect, even if the second suspect was never caught. Finally, just so O'Donnell wouldn't think I had completely disregarded his opinion, I added the Class C felony of Assault in the Third Degree.

I walked the complaint over to the Justice Center so I could get a look at Derringer and argue bail myself. The Justice Center is a newer building two blocks down from the county courthouse. It houses PPB's central precinct, a booking facility, holding cells for prisoners with upcoming court appearances, and four non-trial courtrooms, used for routine preliminary matters like arraignments, pleas, and release hearings.

I took the stairs to JC-2, the courtroom where Derringer's case would be called on the two o'clock arraignment docket, and handed the court clerk a copy of the complaint, a motion for continued detention of the defendant, and a supporting affidavit summarizing the facts. The JC-2 DA looked relieved when I told her I'd handle the Derringer matter myself. She was a new lawyer I'd met a few weeks ago at a happy hour. I suspected she was just getting used to the monotony of calling the misdemeanors and petty felonies that comprise most of the JC-2 docket. God help her if she had picked up the Derringer file to find an Attempted Agg Murder complaint.

Judge Arnie Weidemann was presiding over the docket today. It could have been worse. Weidemann was a judge who truly stood for nothing. He was neither a state's judge nor a liberal. He didn't write law review articles expounding on either judicial activism or conservative restraint. He was interested in neither outcome nor analytical process.

If he felt strongly about anything, it was keeping his courtroom moving. Quick from-the-hip decisions during the juggling of a crowded docket were his forte. Weidemann, therefore, was a terrible judge to draw if you had a complex legal issue that required sophisticated analysis. He wasn't bad, though, for what I needed today. A superficial take on Derringer's case would weigh in my favor on pretrial issues like release and bail.

When it was time for Derringer's matter, I took a moment to look over at him while the MCSO deputy accompanied him to the defense table. His hair was shaved down to a shadow not much darker than the one left on his face from the night in jail. A tattoo of a vine of thorns hugged the base of his skull. Everything about him looked chiseled except for the acne scars cratering his cheekbones. His strong jaw was clenched, his lips a cold slit. His eyes appeared to register nothing as he stared straight ahead, seemingly unfazed by his current circumstances.

Then his head turned slightly as I approached, and I realized he was watching me out of the corner of his eye. It was unnerving, but I went ahead and called the case. "The next matter is *State of Oregon v. Franklin R. Derringer*, case

number 9902-37654. Samantha Kincaid appearing for the
State. The defendant is in custody on a parole detainer for
having unsupervised contact with a minor. Based on the
same incident underlying the parole violation, the State now
charges him with Attempted Aggravated Murder and other
substantive crimes in a six-count complaint that I have for-
warded to the court. The State requests that the defendant
be held without bail."

An audible snort from Derringer revealed his disdain. He
had already filled out an affidavit of indigency, requesting
the court to appoint a state-paid attorney on his behalf. The
court now made a finding that Derringer qualified for court-
appointed counsel. Then a hard case got even tougher. The
judge appointed Lisa Lopez to represent him.

Public defenders generally fall into one of three different
camps. There's no diplomatic way to describe the first bunch.
They're bad attorneys who wind up in the public defenders'
office by default. Whether they're devoted to a specific client
or to the larger cause of criminal defendants' rights is, in
practical terms, irrelevant. Even at the top of their game, the
performance of these lawyers is dismal—so pathetic, in fact,
that most prosecutors will admit it takes the fun out of
winning.

A second crop of public defenders consists of what I call
the straight shooters. These attorneys have been around long
enough to understand the realities of the system, and axiom
number one is that the overwhelming majority of criminal
defendants are guilty. The straight shooters review discovery
materials early on and decide whether the client even stands
a chance. If he doesn't (and most don't) the defendant will
soon get a heart-to-heart from his attorney. The straight

shooter will explain the way things work to his client and then negotiate the most favorable plea deal possible.

If the client has a serious defense, or if there is a real possibility of having material evidence suppressed, the straight shooter will take the issue to court and do a good job trying it. He or she will always deal honestly with the prosecuting attorney.

The second camp of defense attorneys is my favorite. Lisa Lopez was not, however, among them. She belonged to the third group, the true believers. Card-carrying members of this crowd represent the most naive demographic still in existence. It doesn't matter how long they've been around trying cases, these attorneys are fundamentally incapable of distrusting their clients. Don't misunderstand me: There's plenty of distrust to go around for police, victims, witnesses, and prosecutors. But they always believe their clients.

Lisa Lopez was the truest of the true believers. Everyone knows that police sometimes make mistakes, overstep their bounds, and even engage in grossly unethical and illegal acts of malice. Yet somehow these relatively rare instances of misconduct happened to transpire in 95 percent of Lisa Lopez's cases. And, of course, all her mistreated clients were also innocent.

Lopez stepped forward and obtained the court's permission to meet with Derringer and review the complaint and affidavit before she argued the release motion.

For the next fifteen minutes, I pretended to review the file while I looked at Lopez and Derringer huddled together like teammates on a high school debate team. I determined he was articulate, because Lisa was scribbling frantically on her legal pad. In a crunch, most attorneys will cut the client off when it's obvious the time would be better spent reviewing documents.

Lisa was impressive. When the judge took us back on the record, you would've thought she'd had the case for a week.

"Your honor, this case is grossly overcharged. Ms. Kincaid's affidavit lacks any direct evidence that anyone attempted to kill the alleged victim in this case. Moreover, Mr. Derringer shouldn't even be here. They've got the wrong guy. My client cooperated with police. He told them he was at his brother's house at the time of the incident. His brother has corroborated that information. Finally, Mr. Derringer is not a flight risk. He was born and raised in southeast Portland, and his family still lives here. There simply is no basis to hold him without bail. We ask that he be released on his own recognizance."

"Ms. Kincaid?"

The key is to establish a good reason to hold on to the defendant without showing more cards than you need to. "The defendant poses a risk to the public that cannot be overstated. He is a paroled sex offender who is only four months out of prison. His prior offense was an attempt to sodomize a fifteen-year-old girl. In this case, he is charged with kidnapping a thirteen-year-old girl, violating her with a foreign object, and then directing his unidentified accomplice to rape and sodomize her. According to his parole officer, the defendant's only employment since his release from prison has been through temporary agencies. If released, he is not only a flight risk, he also poses an enhanced safety risk to the community."

"Alright, I've heard enough. How 'bout I split the baby on this one. I'll make him eligible for release on enhanced bail of four hundred thousand dollars. *If* he posts bail, he will be released to Close Street Supervision."

"Your honor, the State also requests that you grant our motion to withhold the victim's name, telephone number, and address from the defense." Oregon's discovery laws require the State to notify the defense of every potential witness's name and location information, unless the court finds good cause to withhold discovery. "She is a child witness, and the nature of this offense makes her vulnerable to intimidation. The risk of contact with the victim is aggravated in this case, where an unknown and unindicted co-conspirator remains at large."

Nothing was ever easy with Lisa. "I object to the State's motion, Judge. The prosecution's entire case rests on this girl's identification of my client. Obviously, I need to know who she is and what her history is. I also have a right and an obligation to contact her to see if she'll talk to my investigator."

The docket was crowded today, and Weidemann was taking a typically Solomonic approach to keep it moving. The problem with this was that it prompted sneaky lawyers like me and Lisa Lopez to argue for more than what we actually wanted so we'd get a bigger chunk of the pie.

All I really wanted was to keep Kendra Martin's address from Derringer. I've never seen a case where the court protected the victim's identity. And Lisa had been around long enough to know that no judge was going to hand over the victim's home address once a DA had argued that she might be at risk. Yet here we were, arguing.

The result was predictable. "The State will disclose the victim's identity to the defense. As for the victim's location information, reasonable information will be provided to Ms. Lopez so she can prepare for trial. She will not, however, be permitted to divulge the location information to Mr. Derringer."

Once the contested issues were addressed, Lopez recited the usual waivers and invocations of rights for the record. Derringer invoked his Sixth Amendment right to counsel, meaning we couldn't question him without Lopez's presence. And he waived his speedy trial rights. Technically, there's a statute that gives defendants the right to be tried within thirty days unless they're released on their own recognizance. No one wants to go to trial that quickly, so defendants routinely waive their speedy trial rights at arraignment once the pretrial release decision has been made.

I made the appropriate notes in my file, picked up the paperwork from the court clerk, and left, satisfied. With that high a bail, Derringer would need to post $40,000 cash to get out. Even if his family was willing to put up their own money for him, I doubted they had it. Worst case was that he'd be out on Close Street Supervision. If I called in a favor, they'd use electronic monitoring to put him on house arrest pending trial. It would also be some consolation that we could watch the house and get a phone tap to try to find the second guy.

Lisa caught up with me on the stairs outside the courtroom and gave me a thumbs up. "Thanks for the case, Samantha. My alibi versus your heroin-shooting prostitute? Looks like a winner."

"I'm sure your client will be happy to have served as trial practice for you when he's serving twenty years with a reputation as a child molester who can't even get it up. Just a tip, but you might want to check out Derringer's brother before you hang your hat on him."

I was going to have to tell her about the problems with Derringer's alibi witness eventually, so I might as well do it now to knock her down a few pegs. As is the case with most bluster, I didn't know if it would work, but it was worth a shot. Lopez was right. The case would be tough without additional evidence. I walked back to the courthouse praying that MCT would find me something more.

Spending the first seven hours of my day on a case I hadn't even known about until this morning had taken its toll. By the time I got back to my office, I had fourteen voice mail messages, a stack of police reports to review, and a flashing message on my computer screen announcing I had mail. If people would just behave themselves, my job would be so much easier.

Still, I managed to leave the office in time to make my dinner reservation in the Pearl District. Until a few years ago, no one distinguished between the Pearl District and Old Town. Growing up, we defined Old Town as the entire area north of downtown, between the Willamette River and I-405. Other than the train station and a few restaurants Portlanders called China Town, there weren't many legitimate reasons to go to Old Town back then. Those three square miles harbored the majority of the city's homeless population, a thriving drug trade, and cheap bars with underground behind-the-counter needle-exchange programs. Most of the buildings in the area were abandoned warehouses.

But life north of Burnside changed in the early 1990s,

when Portland's economy began to experience its current boom with the help of Nike, its nationally recognized ad agency, and more high-tech companies than you could shake a stick at. Portland became the sought-after new address for thousands of upwardly mobile young professionals.

To uprooted Californians and to Easterners like my ex-husband, a move to Portland was supposed to represent a dedication to a new way of living, a clean slate, a commitment to a simpler lifestyle that balanced work, play, and family. Their office walls were lined with photographs of them hiking in the Columbia Gorge and skiing Mount Hood, and they bought life memberships in the Sierra Club. But they also drove Range Rovers and Land Cruisers that got eleven miles to the gallon and had never actually been muddied by off-road use.

One upside of the Yuppie Takeover, however, was the development of the Pearl District. A group of savvy developers foresaw the desire of this new crowd to live in upscale housing close to downtown. They purchased entire blocks of warehouses on the west end of Old Town and refurbished them as loft apartments and townhouses. Buildings you used to be afraid to walk by now boasted million-dollar apartments. Along with the housing had come a slew of chic restaurants, retail shops, hair salons, interior decorators, and every other business that might make the life of some thirty-year-old millionaire a little more comfortable.

Some of the old-timers, artists who had used the warehouses as inexpensive studio space, complained about the gentrification. But most Portlanders, like me, were happy to have a neighborhood close to downtown where they could go after work for dinner and a drink.

Tonight's dinner was at Oba, my favorite Pearl District

spot. The bar in the front of the restaurant was, at least for now, the beautiful people's place to see and be seen. And, although I didn't have first-hand knowledge, Oba enjoyed a reputation as a good place to find a companion for the rest of the night. I came for the food.

Grace was already there when I arrived. Despite the throngs of people packed into the bar, my best friend had managed to procure a seat at a table of young and painfully attractive men. One of them was returning from the bar with her favorite drink, a Cosmopolitan. And, of course, all of them were laughing. Grace Hannigan is one of the funniest people I know.

I worked my way over to the table and leaned over so Grace could hear me. "You been here long?"

"Hey, woman. I didn't see you come in. I just got here a little bit ago."

One of the men at the table got up and offered his chair.

I could barely hear Grace over the noise. She leaned in. "This one on my right is a client. He saw me walk in and waved me over. He's a computer programmer. The rest of them are with him." She leaned in even closer and said in my ear, "The blond one's got potential. He's coming in next week. I made room on my calendar."

Grace cuts hair. It's a good thing she's got the kind of job where a guy can make an appointment to see her on a risk-free basis, or she would probably never get a date. You know how actresses and models say that guys never ask them out? You're supposed to infer that they're so beautiful that men are too intimidated to risk rejection. I wouldn't have believed it unless I had a best friend like Grace. She has collagen-free pouty lips, bright white teeth, and flawless skin that's alabaster in winter and bronzed in summer. Her hair looks different every time I see her, but her natural curls always frame her face just right. And she can eat all the junk she wants and never get fat. I'm so glad I know her, or I'd probably hate her.

Despite Grace's looks, men who are obviously attracted to her rarely ask her out. Instead, they make appointments for haircuts. Eventually, they get around to asking her if she has time to grab a drink or dinner afterward, but they always use the haircut as the way in. Grace says she can never tell whether a man's appointment is a pre-date formality or if he just wants his hair cut, but I keep telling her that any man willing to pay $60 for a haircut is probably looking for a date. A nice shag. A good bang. A first-rate bob.

I ordered a Bombay Sapphire martini, but we didn't last at the bar for long. We were eager to talk about the week that had passed since we'd last seen each other, and the noise was too much, so we moved to our table.

I let her go first, because her news was always more fun. Most of her week this time was spent working on the set of a movie being filmed in the area. Grace's business had been thriving in town for years, but in the last couple of years she had developed a strong reputation as an on-set stylist for the increasing number of film productions that were coming to Portland.

As much as Grace enjoyed the new field of work, what she really seemed to love was the dish. Grace had always acted as part-time therapist to clients who trusted her with their life's secrets, and she actually refrained from passing these tidbits on to others. However, she felt no such loyalty toward pretentious thespians and spoiled prima donnas. Working regularly on production sets satisfied Grace's lust for good, spreadable dirt.

Tonight's topic was the disagreeable side of America's most beloved actress. Physically, she was as perfect as Grace had expected. But after working with her for three days, Grace now believed her to be one of the ugliest people she'd met.

"This girl was *killing* me, Sam. She likes to tell all those magazines that her famous hair just looks that way on its own? Well, God let me make it through the weekend so I could tell you otherwise. She must've stopped shooting six times a day, yelling at me, 'It's drying out, it's drying out. Can't you see I need a mist?' Then I'd have to stop what I was doing and spray her head with a mixture of moisturizer and Evian water. She says regular water leaves a 'residue.' Then everyone had to sit there and wait while I scrunched her hair with my fingers until it dried, to lock in what she says are natural curls.

"So, during a break, when I was touching her up, I mentioned in passing that shooting schedules can be hard on the hair. You know, all that blow drying, crimping, curling, and whatnot really takes its toll. Truth is, her hair's toast, beyond saving. I pulled her hair up around her shoulders and told her she'd look just as beautiful with a short cut if she wanted a change after this movie's done. The girl wigged."

Grace lifted her head and affected a slight southern accent. " 'I'm not some housefrau who needs a frumpy easy-to-manage hairdo. With all due respect, you're not being paid to think. You're being paid to make sure I look good. And this hair is what looks good, what has put me on the cover of hundreds of magazines, and what makes me worth twenty million dollars a film.' It was all I could do not to cut that shit right off her head. Add the fact that she picks her teeth and reeks of garlic, and I don't see her as America's little sweetheart anymore."

People judge others by their professions, but the reality is that Grace, in addition to being funny and extremely good at what she does, is incredibly smart. She always has been. In high school, the two of us were always neck and neck at the top of the class. Although we started to lose touch a few years into college, she was the first person I called when I moved back to Portland, and we picked up the friendship right where we'd left off.

As much as I was enjoying Grace's comic relief, I couldn't get the Derringer case out of my mind. I laid out everything I knew so far.

She shook her head. "I don't know how you handle a job where you have to think about that kind of stuff. There must be some happy medium between those sick subjects and the superficial junk I have to deal with all day."

"Maybe we should both hang it up and become accountants."

"Nah, too boring," she said. "We'll just have to keep trying to balance each other out."

"Seriously, it's not just that it's hard, Grace. I've gotten used to dealing with unpleasant subjects at work. I'm scared I'm going to *lose*. These are the most serious charges I've ever filed against anyone, and part of me's excited about it. But if it falls apart, I won't just look bad at work, I'll feel like shit for letting this dirtbag go free."

"Sam, you've got to put it in perspective. If it weren't for you, this guy would already have won. Tim O'Donnell would've issued that chippy assault charge against him. What could he get for that?"

"With his record, maybe two years at most after conviction. He'd be out in eighteen months, maybe even nine if he pled guilty," I said.

"See? And, even in a worst-case scenario, you'll still get that, right?"

"I think so. Even if the case falls apart, I think Lopez would plead Derringer out to assault to avoid going to verdict on the attempted murder."

"So what are you worrying about? Sounds to me like you saved the day just by getting involved, no matter what happens. This way, the police are still working on the case, so they might even catch the second guy. You need to look at it from that perspective. You may win. But even if you don't, you haven't really lost anything."

She was right. I should feel good about what I did today. It was time to put aside the serious stuff and talk to her about the personal side of this case.

"Oh, and I may have neglected to fill you in on the identity of one of the main investigators."

"Why would I care? Is he a cutey?" She feigned enthusiastic curiosity and gave me a wink.

"Um . . . No! Well, I mean, yeah. I don't really know. Look, what I mean is that for once this man actually has something to do with me and not you."

"Excuse me for assuming. I've gotten used to you never being interested. It's been two years since your divorce, and you still act like men don't get to you anymore, except . . . oh, lord, Sam, you're not actually going to try working with Lucky Chucky, are you?"

It's been more than fifteen years since Chuck Forbes's football buddies had come up with that nickname. Two of them had barged into Chuck's house carrying a keg one weekend when his parents were out of town. I guess we didn't hear them over "Avalon." For the rest of high school, Chuck was Lucky Chucky. They finally stopped calling me Been-laid Kincaid at the end of senior year.

"Can't we move a little bit past that, Grace?"

"It's not that there's anything wrong with Chuck. It's what's wrong with the two of you. When are you going to realize that he makes you crazy? You either need to write each other off or lock yourselves in a room together until you get it out of your systems. You have this twisted love-hate, only-happy-when-you're-not-getting-together kind of relationship. And every time you see him, you dwell on it for the next two weeks but won't let yourself follow through. I am driven crazy by osmosis. Please don't do this to me. Is that why you took this case?"

"Oh, please. No, I swear, Grace. I would've taken it anyway, for all the reasons we talked about. But I don't know how I'm going to handle this. Just reading the police reports, I find myself poring over every word of his, admiring what a good cop he's become. I guess I'm just going to have to deal with it."

"Deal with it? You've only ever had one way of dealing with Chuck Forbes. You decide you can keep the relationship platonic. You start hanging out, kidding around, watching games on the weekends, all the things that friends do. But then the chemistry kicks in and the next thing you know you get scared and back off, he gets mad, and you both go off into your separate corners and pout until you once again trick yourselves into believing that you can make the friendship thing work and the whole damn cycle begins again. Did it ever dawn on you that Roger might have felt a little left out?"

I stared at her. Roger's my ex-husband. We met at Stanford Law School. Dad thought Roger was too much of a blueblood, but Mom and I thought he was perfect: a grown-up who knew what he wanted and how he was going to get it. Smart, good-looking, and ambitious, Roger had wanted to marry me right out of law school so we could start our perfect life together back in New York. We moved into the Upper East Side apartment his family bought us as a wedding present, him working toward partnership at one of the country's biggest firms, me working as an Assistant U.S. Attorney.

The perfect life didn't last long. Roger landed a job as in-house counsel with Nike, so we wound up moving to Portland after only a couple of years in New York. A few months later, I discovered that my husband had taken literally his new employer's ad slogan encouraging decisive, spontaneous, self-satisfying action. We both thought I would be working late preparing for a trial set to start the following day, but the case had settled with a last-minute guilty plea. My intention was to surprise Roger by coming home early with dinner and a movie in hand.

Instead, I found him doing it with a professional volleyball player on top of our dining room table. I got the house and everything in it, but I made sure he got the table.

Now Grace and I rarely referred to my former husband as anything other than Shoe Boy or for any reason other than comic. We definitely never insinuated that I was somehow responsible for his infidelities.

"That's totally unfair, Grace. You know that Chuck and I have been nothing more than friends since I came back to town. Unlike some people, I took my marriage vows seriously."

"Come on, Sam. I'm not saying Roger was justified to whore around. I'm just saying he might have been bothered when you and Chuck started spending time together again. Roger thought leaving New York was going to change things, but you were still putting in the same kind of hours and running thirty miles a week. Then you started making time for Chuck. Say what you want about only being friends, but to Roger it was more than that, even if you weren't technically cheating. He had to have seen the chemistry; everyone does. You drop that hard-ass force field of yours with me and with Chuck, but you never dropped it with Roger. And if he was bothered by it, the next guy will be too. So, unless you want to be alone for good, you need to decide where Chuck Forbes fits into your life. You're not in high school anymore, honey."

I didn't know what to say.

"You pissed?" she asked.

"No, just surprised."

"I know. I get sucked in by you two also, but I worry about you, is all. This isn't college, when you could sleep with Chuck on breaks and then run back to Cambridge. Make sure you know what you're doing." She smiled. "Don't get me wrong. I *have* noticed how good he looks in that uniform of his."

I returned the smile and said, "At least I'm not writing Mrs. Charles Landon Forbes, Jr., in my notebook anymore."

We quickly changed the subject, but the conversation nagged at me throughout the rest of the meal. Roger used to accuse me of being ambivalent about our relationship; now Grace was suggesting the same thing about my feelings for Chuck. The way I'd always seen it, my job was hard enough; the personal stuff should take care of itself.

| 3 |

Work returned to a normal pace the next day.

I had left several messages on Andrea Martin's machine the day before but hadn't heard back from her. This morning, she picked up.

"Ms. Martin, my name is Samantha Kincaid. I'm a deputy district attorney for Multnomah County. How are you?"

"Could be better, under the circumstances and all."

"I left a few messages for you yesterday," I said.

"Yeah, I didn't get 'em till late. I wait tables at the Hotcake House at night. I was planning on trying to call you back later."

"My understanding is that the police have talked to you about what happened over the weekend. Is that right?"

"Yeah. One of 'em, Mike somebody, called me in the middle of the night Saturday. Told me Kendra was in the hospital. I'd just gotten off work, but I would've come down anyway. I guess Kendra didn't want me there, though."

"Where is Kendra now?"

"I think she's in her room. I'm just heading out for my day job at Safeway."

"Did you know where Kendra was on Saturday night when this happened?"

"No. She runs away so much I've stopped calling the cops on her. She just gets mad at me when they pick her up. I'm to the point I just want her to come home every night. I figure I got a better chance if I give her her freedom. The other way sure wasn't working."

"So she came home on Sunday afternoon then?"

"Yeah. She didn't want to. I don't know what's so bad around here that she'd rather be out on the street. But the hospital wouldn't let her go unless she came here or agreed to foster care. At least she picked here."

"She's been through a lot. She might want your help right now."

She laughed. "Miss . . . what'd you say your name was again?"

"Samantha Kincaid. Call me Samantha."

"Well, you obviously don't know my daughter. She don't want help from no one. Always been that way, too. It's like she decided when she turned ten or something that she was grown."

"Did Detective Calabrese explain what Kendra's lifestyle has been while she was on the street?"

"I wouldn't call it much of a lifestyle. But, yeah. That guy and his partner—a blond guy, real young—came by the Safeway on Sunday to break the news to me. They told me Saturday night she was assaulted. Guess they wanted to say the other stuff in person."

They probably wanted to watch her response. Kids who run away are often the victims of abuse by their parents. If anything would set a parent off, it would be learning that their kid has been shooting up and turning tricks. They wanted to make sure she didn't seem the type to take her anger out on Kendra physically.

"How has Kendra been doing since she's been home?"

"Alright, I guess. Like I said, she don't really talk to me."

"Well, I was calling mainly to introduce myself and to let you know I'm handling the case. The police have arrested one of the suspects. His name is Frank Derringer. He's in jail for now, but we have to take the case to a grand jury within a week, and Kendra's going to need to testify for that. I've got it scheduled for Friday. Assuming the grand jury indicts Derringer, the court will schedule the case for trial. Most cases don't actually go to trial, but if this one does, it will probably be in a couple of months and Kendra will need to testify. Do you have any questions for me?"

"Do you know when the cops are going to give Kendra her stuff back? Her keys were in her purse, and I don't know whether to get a new set cut."

"I'm not really sure, Ms. Martin. It can take the crime lab a few weeks sometimes to finish working on evidence. Depending on what they find, we may need to keep the evidence sealed for trial. I can find out about her keys for you, if you'd like."

"Whatever. I can get a new set cut at the store tomorrow. Am I going to have to come to any of these things? I can't afford to take time off work."

"You're certainly welcome to come with Kendra as support, but I don't think you'll need to testify until the trial. I'll make sure Kendra has transportation to the courthouse when she needs to come down here."

"Alright, then. I better be going. You need anything else?"

"Would it be OK if I dropped by your home tonight to meet Kendra?" I asked.

"You'll have to talk to her about that. You want me to get her?"

"No, that's OK, I'll try talking to her later." If Mom didn't care, I'd rather just drop in on Kendra unannounced. Wouldn't want her running off anywhere. "Feel free to call me if you have any questions. Let me give you my direct line."

"Um, I can't find a pen right now. If I need anything, I can look it up, right?"

I told her that she could, even though I knew she wouldn't.

I devoted the rest of my day to the routine drudgeries of the drug section of the Drug and Vice Division. The DA assigned me to DVD because I used to prosecute drug cases when I was in New York. I accepted the assignment because I wanted to keep working as a prosecutor when Roger and I moved, and the Portland U.S. Attorney's Office wasn't hiring. In most people's eyes it was a step down: I went from handling cases involving nationwide distribution conspiracies and literally tons of dope to prosecuting sad-sack hustlers for dealing eight-balls of methamphetamine and as little as a single rock of crack cocaine.

But while I may have lost the prestige of a federal prosecutor's office, I had developed a niche as part of the vice section of DVD, prosecuting the monsters who lure, coerce, and force women into prostitution. The less-experienced DVD attorneys shied away from those cases because they were hard to prove, hard to win, and hard to take. The career prosecutors who handled the major felony person crimes didn't want them because they were viewed as less important than murders and other violent offenses. But I felt more rewarded by those cases than I'd ever felt prosecuting even complex federal drug conspiracies.

Today, however, my plate was full of drug charges. No surprise, the grand jury returned indictments on all four of the cases I presented. Most drug-related cases are pretty much the same. The only variation tends to be in the type and degree of stupidity involved.

Usually it was a matter of poor strategy. My daily caseload is full of tweekers who agree to let the police search them, even though they're carrying enough dope to land them in the state pen for a couple of years. Apparently, an undocumented side effect of dope is a gross overestimation of one's own intelligence. Dopers become convinced they've hidden their stash so well a cop won't find it. They're always wrong.

But sometimes it goes beyond poor strategy to straightout stupidity. In one of today's cases, two men did a hand-to-hand drug deal standing two feet from a Portland police officer. What stealth tactic had this shrewd officer used to avoid detection? He was part of the city's mounted patrol unit, which covered a downtown beat on horseback. When the men were arrested, one of them said to the officer, "Dude, I didn't even see you up there, man. I just thought it was cool that a horse had found its way to the park." It hadn't dawned on them to look up and see whether someone might have accompanied the savvy equine.

Despite all the talk about the modern "war on drugs," the truth is that most police don't go out of their way to

investigate minor drug offenses. They don't have to. There is
so much dope out there, and the people taking it are so dense,
that the cases literally fall into the cops' laps, whether they
want them or not. The upside is that it makes my job easier.

When I was done getting my cases indicted, I called MCT
to see if a detective could drive out to Rockwood with me to
interview Kendra. I wanted to talk to her tonight, before she
got antsy and ran away again. Grand jury was Friday, and I
needed to know what to expect from my star witness.

I try to have a police officer or DA investigator with me
whenever I talk to someone who will be testifying in one of
my cases. If the witness ever went south on me, I'd want
a person present who could testify about the witness's
statement, since lawyers are not allowed to testify in their
own cases.

Someone picked up after four rings. "Walker."

"Detective Walker, it's Samantha Kincaid at the DA's
office. I'm calling about the Derringer case."

"Sure. What can I do you for?"

I told him what I'd found out the day before from Deputy
Lamborn and Dave Renshaw.

"Oh, hang on a sec. The rest of the guys have got to hear
this." I heard him put me on speaker. "You want to tell 'em
or should I?"

Figuring I was more likely than Walker to keep the conversation on track, I repeated the information about Derrick
Derringer's previous offer to serve as an alibi witness for his
brother and then got to the part about Derringer's body hair.

Walker couldn't help himself. "Can you believe what a
fucking waste of time and money that is? Everyone knows
these guys never change. They just get off having someone
watch them watch that smut. But the system manages to find

the money to pay some doctor to handle these guys' johnsons, when it could use the money to keep them in the pen where they belong."

I heard Ray Johnson nearby. "How many times I gotta tell you that you make my workplace hostile when you call something like that a *johnson*, man? So, Kincaid, what's the doctor say about Derringer's broken pecker?"

I certainly didn't know what it meant. "Look, five different shrinks could probably come up with five interpretations. What's important is that we know Derringer shaved within a few days of the attack. That's big. Any news on that end?"

"No," Walker replied. "The lab's still working the rape kit and the other evidence. No leads on who this second guy is. Ray's looking at Derringer's known associates from before he went to the pen, but nothing yet. So far, Derringer's only calls from the jail have been to his brother. He's playing it cool."

"Alright, let me know if you get anything new. Also, I need one of you to come out to Kendra Martin's with me tonight. Grand jury's on Friday, and I want to prep this girl while she's still on board."

"Geez. I really want to help you out on this one, since you're going out of your way for us. But my anniversary's tonight. The wife's got the whole night planned: dinner, some dance thing. She'll kill me if I cancel on her."

"Don't let me mess up your marriage. It doesn't really matter who goes. I just need a witness."

"Hold on. Hey, Ray. Can you run out to Rockwood with Kincaid tonight to interview the Martin girl? She wants to get her ready for grand jury on Friday, and she needs a witness."

"Depends what you mean, can I go? I *can* go, if it needs

to be done. But Jack, you know my mama flew up from Cali today. She's probably at my house waitin' on me as we speak. What kind of boy am I to go on OT while my mama's in town? Can I go out with her tomorrow, or does it have to be tonight?"

I heard another voice farther in the background. "Go home to your mama, Ray. I'll go."

Uh-oh. I knew that voice. "That's alright, Jack," I said hastily. "It's probably better to go out there with someone who's already met Kendra. It can wait until tomorrow."

"It's up to you, but Chuck can go. He's met the Martin girl too. He and Mike went to talk to the mom on Sunday and stopped by the house to check on Kendra." He yelled into the background, "Hey, Chuck. You get a pretty good rapport with the girl?"

I heard something; then Ray came back on the line. "Yeah, he says things went real good. He took over some CDs that were donated by the rape victims' advocates."

There was no easy way out of this one. I wanted to talk to Kendra tonight, and Chuck made as much sense to take along as anyone. "If he's willing to go, that works for me. Can you ask him to meet me in front of the Martin house at seven?"

He was waiting for me with a Happy Meal in one hand. He held the box up as I got out of my car in front of Kendra Martin's house. "Mommy Martin didn't strike me as the type to make sure there was a pot roast on the table by suppertime. I figured Kendra might want something to eat. I would've picked up something for you, but then I pictured you trying to run it off at midnight."

"Very funny." Call me an extremist; I have a tendency to couple large meals with monster runs. It had been two months since we'd seen each other, and he was already trying to pull me into our flirtatious rhythm. I was determined to make this quick, but as I started walking to the front door, I realized he wasn't following.

I turned around and walked back to where he still stood with a grin on his face. "What the hell's so funny, Forbes?"

"Oh, so it's Forbes now?"

"Hey, you've always called me Kincaid."

"Yeah, well, you've always called me Chuck. Am I supposed to call you something different now too?"

"You can call me whatever you want, as long as you keep your smart-ass comments to yourself while I interview Kendra Martin."

"They teach you those manners at Hah-vud?"

"Give me a break. Last time I checked, that little park we call the waterfront was still named after your daddy."

"Yeah, and look at all the good that being the governor's son has done me. Driving fifteen miles out of my way on my night off for *your* interview, standing here with a McMeal for *your* witness. The last time I checked, Kincaid, you and I were still friends. Would it kill you to at least say hi to me before we head in for work?"

I closed my eyes and took a deep breath. "No, it wouldn't. You're right. Hi. Hi, Chuck. It's nice to see you. Now can we go do my interview?"

"Yes. And it's nice to see you too."

I rang the doorbell. I could hear obnoxious music, the kind that started to sound like noise when I turned thirty, blaring from inside. I rang the doorbell again and then banged on the door. I felt him standing behind me while we waited on the porch in silence. When I heard the music get lower and footsteps approach the door, I looked at him over my shoulder. "That was nice of you. To bring her some dinner, I mean."

"Thanks."

I couldn't tell what Kendra Martin looked like when she answered the door, because her face was obscured by a big pink gum bubble. It popped to reveal a thin pale girl with doe eyes and full lips. Her wavy, dark hair stopped right below her shoulders. She wore an Eminem sweatshirt and a pair of jeans that looked like they'd fit my father. So far, she seemed like a typical thirteen-year-old.

She looked past me at Chuck. "What're you doing here?"

"I came by to see whether you listened to anything I told you on Sunday. What did I tell you about looking out the window to see who's here before you open the door to anyone?"

She shifted her weight all the way to one leg and swung her hip one direction and tilted her head in the other. "I guess I forgot this time. Anyway, it was you, so it's OK, right?" She twisted a lock of hair with her fingers. Obviously Chuck Forbes's magnetism was not lost on this new generation of teenage girls.

"OK, we'll treat that as a test run. But I mean it: From now on, you have to look before you open that door. If it's someone you don't know, you don't answer. Got it?"

"Yeah, I got it. Whaddaya doin' here?"

"I brought someone over who I want you to meet. This is Samantha Kincaid."

Kendra looked at me without saying a word. Then she smiled at Chuck and popped her gum. "She your girlfriend?"

Chuck looked at me and raised his eyebrows. "No, she's

not my girlfriend. But she is a really good friend of mine, and she's a DA. She's going to be handling your case."

I held out my hand to her. She shook it but looked down at the floor while she did it.

"It's nice to meet you, Kendra. I've heard a lot about you. Detectives Walker and Johnson tell me you did a real good job helping them at the hospital last weekend."

"That's funny. They told Chuck and Mike I acted like demon spawn."

"They might've mentioned something like that to me too. But they also said you were very helpful. Do you mind if we come in?"

She looked at the box in Chuck's hand. He said, "I thought you might be hungry. The fries are still hot."

"Come on in." She took the box from Chuck. "Thank you."

"Don't mention it. It was Sam's idea, anyway."

"Thank you," she said to me.

I looked at Chuck. "It wasn't a problem. Really."

The Martin house wasn't what I expected. I had braced myself for the worst. Unfortunately, I'd gotten used to the fact that an entire segment of the population raises its children in filthy homes that don't look like they could possibly exist in the United States. Last year, police went to an apartment on a noise complaint and found nine children alone in a one-bedroom apartment. They all slept on the same bare, stained mattress on the bedroom floor. The carpets were soaked with cat urine and feces. The kids had been alone for a week and were living off of dry cat food and some candy bars that the oldest child, an eight-year-old boy, had been given to sell for the school choir.

Their mothers, two sisters in their early twenties, had left on a meth binge. As they later told police, they lost track of time and never meant to leave their kids alone. It turned out that maternal neglect was the least of the kids' problems. By the time the investigation was over, police learned that all of the children had been sexually assaulted. Their mothers had accepted drugs and money in exchange for permitting various men to take the children of their choice into the apartment's bedroom alone.

From what I'd heard about Kendra Martin's troubles and her mother's parenting style, I had expected their house to be a hellhole. I had jumped to the wrong conclusion. The house was cleaner than my own and reflected the efforts of someone trying to do her best without much to work with. A crisp clean swath of blue cotton was draped over what I suspected was an old and tattered sofa. In the corner, a thirteen-inch television sat on a wooden tray table. In a move that Martha Stewart would envy, someone had made a lamp base out of an old milk jug.

"Kendra, I don't want to tell you things you already know, so let me start by asking you whether you have any questions about what a DA does."

"Not really."

"What do you think my job is?"

"You're kind of my lawyer, right?"

"Well, technically my client is the State. But in this case, my goal is to help prove who did this to you and then convince the court to put them in prison for a long time. When we do go to court, I'll be the one who asks you most of the questions. So in some ways it will be like I'm your lawyer. Have you ever testified before?"

"No. I got in some trouble after Christmas." She looked at Chuck. "She knows about that, right?"

"Yes, I know you were arrested on Christmas."

"Well, I went to juvie on that, but no charges were filed so I didn't have to talk or anything."

"You're going to need to testify this Friday, but you don't need to worry about that. Friday's going to be in front of a grand jury: it'll just be me, you, and seven jurors. The man the police arrested won't be there, and there's no defense attorney or judge. I'll ask you questions, and the grand jurors will listen to your answers. Then they'll decide whether to charge him. Assuming he's charged, there might be a trial later on, and that's more like what you see on TV. Does that sound OK?"

"I guess."

"How are you feeling?" I asked.

"Not so good."

"You staying clean?"

"Yeah, so far. I didn't really think it would be this hard, though."

I could tell she was having problems. She wasn't as bad off as older addicts I've seen withdrawing in custody, but it wasn't going to be easy for her. I suspected the only reason she wasn't out using again was that she didn't have any money and was scared shitless to hit the street again.

"Is it alright if we talk about what happened?"

"I guess so. Is it OK if I go ahead and eat?"

I hadn't noticed she'd been holding off. "Go for it."

She opened the box tentatively and ate the fries one by one, taking small bites and chewing slowly.

"Had you ever seen either of these men before?"

"Unh-unh."

"So you don't think they were ever customers of yours or knew you from somewhere before?"

"I don't know where they'd know me from. They didn't look familiar or anything like that."

I couldn't tell if she was avoiding my question about prior customers or if she believed she'd already answered it.

"So, you're sure they weren't customers?"

"Yeah. I'm pretty sure I would've recognized 'em if they were. I haven't done it *that* many times."

Poor girl. She probably justified what she did by telling herself that she wasn't really a prostitute if she didn't do it often and stopped before she was older.

"Was there anyone else around when they were talking to you or when you got pulled into the car?"

"No. When they stopped the car, I looked around to make sure no one was watching before I started talking to them. I didn't want to get caught again after what happened on Christmas. I think there might've been one homeless guy sitting on the corner, but he looked really out of it."

I looked over at Chuck. "We canvassed the area and didn't find any witnesses," he said. "We found a guy who usually sleeps on that corner, but he didn't see anything."

"Kendra, the police have already told me what they know about what happened. But, if it's alright with you, I'd like you to tell me in your own words. I need you to be completely honest with me, even though parts of it might be embarrassing. No one here is going to be mad at you or get you in trouble for anything you say."

She started from the beginning and told me everything. I never needed to prompt her, and she continued talking even when she was clearly very upset about what happened. Her statement was consistent with what she told Walker and Johnson the night of the assault. She would make a great witness, but unfortunately she did not reveal anything I didn't already know. I'd been hoping for some new avenue of investigation.

I told her I understood why she initially kept some information from Detectives Walker and Johnson at the hospital, but that I'd be asking her to explain it to the grand jurors.

"I don't even remember much about when they first came into the room. Whatever that doctor gave me had me feeling really sick. I just remember being mad."

"What do you remember telling them?"

"Well, I said I was on Burnside to go to Powell's. You know the real reason I was there. I just didn't want to tell them, is all. It's embarrassing, and I could get in trouble for it."

"Do you remember telling them you didn't know how heroin got in your system?"

"Not really, but then later on, when they came back with that lawyer guy, he told me he knew I'd lied about it. So I figured I must've said it. I didn't want to get in trouble, is all."

"Is that the only reason you lied?"

"I don't know. It's hard to explain. It's like, I guess I was pretty sure they wouldn't arrest me or anything since I was in the hospital and all. But I thought if they knew what I'd been doing, they wouldn't believe me about what happened. Or maybe they'd believe me but not really care, since I, like, you know, kind of got myself in that situation. And I wanted them to believe me and go out and find who did it. So I told the truth about what they did to me, but I didn't tell them the parts I figured didn't matter as much. Does that make any sense?"

"It makes a lot of sense. Are you still doing that? Are you still leaving things out that you think aren't important?"

"No. Detective Walker said he'd work on my case even if it turned out that I had been doing something bad before it happened."

"Good, because he meant it. I think you're a very smart young woman and you've been brave to tell the truth."

She stuck her chin out, rolled her eyes, and tried hard to hide a smile. "Thanks." She probably wasn't used to compliments.

"I know you don't know us very well, but can you tell us why you don't like living here?" I asked.

"It's actually OK right now."

I'd forgotten how frustrating it is to try to talk to a kid. "Why do you run away?"

"Last time I left was because I was going crazy here. I felt really sick and wanted to get some horse. The doctor says I've gotten to where my body wants it, even if I don't think I do."

"Is that why you started in prostitution?"

"I wouldn't really call it prostitution. I mean, I guess it's gotten to that, but that's not how it started. It was just like I'd hear about somebody who was, like, holding and then I'd find them and try to get some. But most of the time I didn't have any money. At first, I'd offer to go to the Kmart and, like, shoplift something in return. That was working OK, but then all the stores around here started telling me not to come in anymore.

"So then, last summer, some guy told me he'd give me the stuff if I'd—you know, if I'd, like, let him put it in my mouth. And that seemed like a way for me to get what I wanted without getting caught stealing or anything. Once I started getting it that way, I started to, like, use even more of it."

"When did you start using heroin?"

"The middle of seventh grade, so like maybe a year ago?"

"Do kids at your school do that already?"

"No. Some of the kids smoke pot and stuff."

This was like pulling teeth. "So how did you wind up using heroin in the seventh grade?"

"If I say, are you gonna tell my mom?"

"Not if we don't have to."

For a second, I thought that wasn't going to be good enough for her. Kendra looked down at Eminem on her sweatshirt and started rubbing out a blob of ketchup that had fallen out of her hamburger onto his pecs. It was like she forgot we were there. Without raising her head, she said, "Mom already feels real bad that I'm, like, the way I am. She thinks it's her fault or something for not being with me more. If she knew how it started, she'd, like, really freak out and blame herself and stuff."

"You're very considerate to be concerned about your mom. I know she works hard to keep everything going around here, and I won't tell her things that you tell me unless the law requires me to."

She thought about that for a moment. "It started a while ago. My dad doesn't live with us. I don't know him, actually. Mom works all the time, so I'm usually here alone. I don't really mind. But every once in a while, she has a boyfriend start living here. I don't know why she dates these loser guys who don't even have jobs and stuff when she works so hard.

"Anyway, last year this guy named Joe was staying here with us. He said he was a contractor, but he like never left the house or anything. I guess one day while I was at school, he went nosing through my stuff in my room. I had a little bag of pot hidden in my dresser. I'd only smoked it once. Me and my friend got it from this guy at school, just to try it.

"So anyway, when I got home, he's sitting on the couch holding this bag. He said he was gonna tell Mom unless I could keep a secret about him. And then he goes into Mom's room and brings out his gym bag. He had a bunch of pot in there, but he had heroin too. He told me he didn't tell my mom or anything 'cause of how she feels about drugs, but he'd let me use some. I didn't want to, 'cause that seemed like way more major than pot. But Joe said popping wasn't really like shooting up or anything and wasn't as big of a deal. And he said if I didn't try it, then I wouldn't be in on his secret, and he'd tell Mom mine. So I tried it."

"Is that the only time you used heroin with him?"

"Yeah, right. He wanted me to do it with him again like a week later, then it was more and more, until he was waiting for me almost every day after school."

"Kendra, did Joe ever touch you or do anything sexual to you?"

"Not really. He'd like touch my hair and stuff when we were high. Gave me the heebie-jeebies. He was totally gross. After a couple months, I guess Mom found his stash and kicked him out. I was happy he was gone, but then I didn't have any way to get the heroin."

I didn't know what to say. This poor girl had destroyed herself out of fear that she would create one more source of stress in her overworked mother's life. Now, even after all she'd been through, she still worried more for her mother's well-being than her own. I hoped Andrea Martin deserved the concern.

"Before you started being with men in order to get the heroin, had you ever engaged in any other sexual activity?"

She blushed and looked down at the floor. "Just kissing and stuff with a couple boys at school."

"No older boys?"

"Unh-unh."

"Not Joe?"

"I said no."

"None of your mother's other boyfriends ever tried to touch you in a bad way?"

"No. I'd tell you. How come you're so sure someone tried to get over on me?"

I knew I had strayed from the open-ended style of questioning used with child sex abuse victims, but it seemed unlikely that Kendra hadn't been victimized before she began selling herself for drugs. It was possible, but the vast majority of women who become prostitutes were molested as children.

If she wasn't molested, my guess is that watching her mother's own relationships with men had left her vulnerable to abuse before this Joe person ever came into the house and began grooming her. Pedophiles often take their time developing a relationship of trust with the child, sharing secrets and breaking barriers. Once the abuse begins, the child chooses to permit its continuance rather than lose the abuser's affection. After spending two months using heroin with her mother's boyfriend, Kendra's next step was almost guaranteed.

"I'm not sure about anything, Kendra. I just wanted to make sure you weren't keeping anything from me, to protect them or maybe your mother."

"Well, I'm not. If it's like you're thinking someone must've done something to me for me to be this way, you're wrong. I guess I'm just screwed up."

"You're not screwed up, and it's not your fault. Do you know that? What happened to you is not your fault."

"That's what the advocate person said, too. Mom thinks it's my fault."

"I bet she doesn't." I wasn't so sure about what Andrea Martin thought, but I knew what Kendra needed to hear.

"She keeps saying I shouldn't have been out there."

"Well, she's right. It's good that you're acknowledging that you made a mistake to put yourself in a risky situation. But that doesn't make this thing your fault. You see the difference?"

"I guess so."

"Say it's not your fault."

She looked at Chuck, then me, then down at her feet. "That's kind of dumb."

"It's not dumb," Chuck said. I was glad he jumped in. I was used to working with women who couldn't listen to anyone but a man, and thirteen wasn't too young for it to start. I needed some help.

She sighed. "It's not my fault," she said quietly.

"Now, look me in the eye," I said, "and say it louder."

She looked at me this time, only at me. "It's not my fault."

This time, she sounded like maybe she meant it.

"Good girl. You're going to think this is silly, but whenever you start to doubt that, I want you to look in the mirror and see how pretty and smart you are. Then I want you to say that out loud to yourself and see how confident and strong you look, OK?"

She rolled her eyes, but she smiled. "Man, every time one of you guys comes over, I get some new thing I'm supposed to remember to do. Look out the window, talk to myself in the mirror. Next time, you're gonna have me standing on my head and singing the Backstreet Boys."

I smiled back at her and then asked why she worked out of the Hamilton, the motel at Third and Alder. She explained that she met a group of teenage girls at Harry's Place, a shelter for street kids. When it became clear that Kendra was picking up spare money the same way the others were, they told her she should work out of the Hamilton. Apparently, the management there didn't care about what went on, and enough girls were turning tricks out of the motel that it provided something of a support network. The girls would watch out for each other and pass along tips they'd pick up on the street.

Kendra explained that she worked sporadically enough that she'd managed to avoid hooking up with a pimp. "They're definitely out there, though. Haley, this girl I know the best out of that group—she's older than me—anyway, Haley said she did what I did for about a year before she couldn't get away with it anymore. The other girls were telling her she wasn't safe out there by herself, and she got beat up a couple times pretty bad. So she was giving half of her money to some man, but he was supposed to watch her back and make sure she stayed safe."

I'm sure this guardian was a real gentleman.

Kendra's face lit up as she told me about the girls she'd met on the street, at Harry's Place, and at the Hamilton. I could tell she missed them, even if she wasn't missing the lifestyle yet.

"Do you want to see pictures of them?" She hopped up from the sofa and disappeared into the back of the house. She returned with a miniature backpack in the shape of a panda bear and fished out two envelopes.

"I love taking pictures. I don't have a camera, but we used

to, like, pitch in our money to get a disposable one some-times. We'd take turns carrying it around until the film was gone. It would take awhile for them to actually get devel-oped, since no one ever had enough money. But I took these in last week."

She handed the pictures to me one by one, flipping through most of them quickly, explaining that she hadn't taken them and didn't know most of the people in them. I tried not to reveal my shock. One group of pictures showed girls in their bras and panties frolicking on the lap of a hard-bodied shirtless man with a tattoo of the Tasmanian Devil on his right pec. The photographs didn't reveal his face, but he was obviously an adult, and, from the looks of things, he was about as carnivorous as the notoriously frenzied cartoon character emblazoned on his chest.

"Those were taken when someone else had the camera," Kendra said, by way of explanation.

Kendra seemed to have an eye for photography. When she finally got to the three pictures she had taken, I could see that she'd managed to capture a youthful, playful side of these girls that was nowhere to be seen in the other photos. Three of them were sitting outside in Pioneer Square, mak-ing funny faces and forming peace signs with their fingers over each other's heads.

"That's my friend Haley," Kendra said, pointing to an attractive teenage girl who was crossing her eyes and sticking out her tongue at the camera. Of Kendra's friends, she looked the most like a prostitute. I recognized her from the Tas-manian Devil pictures.

"Kendra, would you mind if I borrowed these pictures?" I sensed that she wanted an explanation. "Chuck and I work with a man named Tommy Garcia. He's been trying to figure out who's been making girls like Haley and your other friends give them a portion of their money."

After some negotiation, we decided that she'd hang on to the three pictures of her friends and I'd take the rest to Garcia.

When Kendra went to the kitchen to throw out the empty Happy Meal box, Chuck pulled me aside.

"I was thinking about the investigation while you two were talking. Kendra told Ray and Jack she'd know the place those guys drove her to if she saw it, but they never took her out. Probably thought it was too much of a long shot. But I want to drive her around a little over there and see if she recognizes anything. We can canvass for witnesses. Maybe someone called in a suspicious car or something. You never know."

"Sure, sounds good." I was surprised that he wanted my input. "You don't need my permission to do stuff like that."

He squinted in mock disbelief. "Don't flatter yourself, Kincaid. I need you to drive us."

It was my turn to feign misgivings. "Something wrong with that ride of yours? Since when do you need me to schlep you around?"

"Why do you always have to bag on my car? You have to admit, it's pretty sweet."

Chuck loved cars. As long as I'd known him, he had always driven some old car that he had poured his heart, soul, and wallet into to fix. For the last few years, it had been a magnificent ruby-red 1967 Jaguar convertible.

"You know I love that car. I just think it would look a lot better around someone else. Me, for example."

"In your dreams, Kincaid."

"So if I can't have your car, what do you need me and my little Jetta for?"

"Department GO says we don't put civilians in our personal vehicles while we're on the job. I don't want to go all the way downtown for a duty car. Let's just take yours."

I looked at my watch. It was a quarter after eight. "And what makes you think the DA's office doesn't have a general order saying the same thing?"

"Because you guys don't need GO's. Only reason cops have them is to cover our asses now that police are getting sued left and right after Rodney King and Abner Louima. You lawyers are so fucking political, you can CYA without any stupid policies."

"Nice language. You kiss your mother with that mouth?"

"No, but I don't remember you having any problems with it."

"Knock it off, or you and that little smirk can drive to Texas alone for all I care."

"Leave the tough act for the courthouse. You forget how well I know you. We both know you care, so fish out the keys to that tin can of yours so we can go to work."

Once again, I was left yearning for the perfect zinger. I settled for my keys.

| 4 |

It took some doing to convince Kendra to come with us, but when I explained how helpful she could be, she relented. She paused on the porch as she was pulling the front door shut behind her. "Oh, hold on a sec. I don't have any house keys. Mom's supposed to get a new set made at the store tomorrow."

I'd forgotten about that. "Can we go by your mom's work and pick up her keys on the way home?"

"Um, her boss gets real mad if she does personal stuff at work. I'm not supposed to bug her or anything when she's there. The store's a lot nicer."

Chuck did a quick overview of the house and came up with a solution. We placed a full cup of water on the floor a few inches in front of the back door, and stuck several pieces of masking tape from the door to the doorframe. We left the

door unlocked and walked out of the front door, locking it
and pulling it shut behind us on the way out.

Kendra looked puzzled until Chuck explained that any
unusual event at the beginning of a break-in usually spooks
the burglar enough that he leaves. In a worst-case scenario,
we'd at least know someone had been there when we got back
if the water was spilled and the tape unsealed.

As responsible adults, we should have consulted Kendra's
mother before taking her daughter and leaving her home
unlocked. But by now Chuck and I had surmised that this
was no typical mother-daughter relationship. If it was OK by
Kendra, Andrea Martin would assume it was for the best.

When she saw the cars parked in front of her house, Kendra had a clear preference. "Cool car! Are we taking it?"

Her eager look up at me spoke volumes. I turned my head
to smile back at Chuck. "I told you it was a chick car."

"It's not a chick car. You know how much power that
thing has? She was complimenting you. Probably figured a
highbrow lawyer like you would drive something with a little
more style."

Kendra tried to hide her disappointment. "Your car's nice
too, Miss Kincaid."

"Thanks. And you call me Samantha, or I'm going to start
calling you Miss Martin."

She laughed. "OK, Samantha."

Chuck hopped in the backseat so Kendra could ride up
front. I headed south and then west on Division, toward
southeast Portland. Rockwood was on the outskirts of Portland, straddling the east border of the city and the west
border of suburban Gresham. It marked the end of approximately 140 consecutive blocks of east Portland, inhabited
by white welfare families who were seldom acknowledged by

either the liberal elite who occupy the central core of the city or the more conservative soccer-mom families who make up the suburbs.

The only landmark Kendra could give me was Reed College. She remembered seeing it while they were driving. The school was located just a few miles southeast of downtown, on Woodstock Boulevard. It was a fitting name for the location. The college was a bastion of leftist politics and had proudly carried the motto ATHEISM, COMMUNISM, AND FREE LOVE since the 1950s. Some student in the eighties had made a mint selling parody T-shirts saying NEW REED: THE MORAL MAJORITY, CAPITALISM, AND SAFE SEX.

Students arrived on campus looking like regular kids who just got out of high school, but by Thanksgiving they'd all stopped bathing and had torn holes in the L. L. Bean and J. Crew clothing their parents had shipped them off to Oregon with. When I was in high school, the slur "You smell like a Reedie" was used whenever someone got a little ripe in gym class.

Although the school was recognized nationally for its stringent academic requirements, Kendra, like most Oregonians, had described it to me as "that hippie school."

Chuck was trying to help her narrow our search. "Would you say you stopped pretty soon after you saw the college, or did you see the college closer to the beginning of the drive?"

"It was maybe a little bit after halfway."

"Did they get on a freeway after you saw the college, or did they drive on residential streets?"

"Well, after, they took the freeway out to where they left me, I guess. But I think they were just driving on regular streets before that."

Old Town to Reed College was about a ten-minute drive.

If they didn't get on a freeway or a major arterial, then they hadn't driven all the way out to the far end of the city. Still, what seemed like a long shot when Chuck thought of it in Rockwood seemed even more ridiculous now that we were in the car.

We needed more. "Do you remember anything else? Any stores? Gas stations? Strip malls?"

"I'm sorry. I wasn't looking at stuff like that. I just remember driving in front of the college. I looked to see if maybe there were some people walking around who might see me if I tried to get out, but it was really dark."

"So if you had passed an open store, do you think you would've remembered it?"

"Um, yeah, I guess. Because I was looking for a place with a bunch of people."

"When they stopped, were you near houses? Or was it more industrial?" The police report said that Kendra had described being in a parking lot, but I hadn't formed an impression of what type of lot.

"It was a big parking lot, but there weren't, like, any other cars or anything. And there was, like, one real big building but then nothing else, just like a park or something. But it wasn't a park I'd ever seen or anything."

I was at a loss. I headed toward Reed College until I could think of a better plan.

"Oh, wait, I remember something. After they stopped, before I tried to run away, I remember I couldn't hear what they were saying to each other. They were, like, having to yell to talk because a train was going by."

Now we were getting somewhere. Portland doesn't have much in the way of train tracks. There's the Max, a light rail that's part of the city's public transportation. It runs east to west across the entire county on a single track. Then there are the railcar tracks. The east-west tracks are close to the Max rails along Interstate 84. The north-south tracks are roughly adjacent to Highway 99. "Like a Max train or a big train?"

"Louder than the Max. A big train."

The east-west train tracks didn't seem likely. They were on the north side of the city. I didn't think Kendra would confuse any neighborhood along the tracks with southeast Portland. But the north-south tracks ran right through close-in southeast Portland, just a half a mile or so west of Reed. There were a few neighborhood parks within earshot of the tracks.

I drove past Reed College and headed to the Rhododen-dron Gardens. The front parking lot and small information booth fit Kendra's description at least roughly. When I pulled into the lot, she said, "No, this isn't it. It was a bigger lot, and there wasn't a fence like this. It just went right into the park area and then there was a bigger building."

Westmoreland Park had a larger parking lot without a fence, but I didn't recall any kind of building, and sure enough there wasn't one.

"Does this even look like the same neighborhood?" I asked.

"Yeah, it does. I don't think I've ever been here or any-thing. But, yeah, it was like this. Like with a lot of trees and stuff. And when we passed houses, they were big like these."

We were in the middle of a pocket of upscale houses in southeast Portland. The Sellwood-Moreland neighborhood, like my own in Alameda, was made up of turn-of-the-century homes. It was the most recent central neighborhood to have been taken over and colonized by yuppies. Considered a hippie enclave when I was a kid, the place was now overrun by coffee shops, chichi bakeries, and antiques stores. Area residents now actually golfed at Eastmoreland, a municipal course that rivals many private country clubs.

Sometimes my disjointed pattern of thought actually pays off. It suddenly dawned on me that the last time I went to Eastmoreland to use its covered driving range, I sliced the hell out of a ball because a train had come barreling by at the top of my backswing. The parking lot is enormous and surrounded by thick hedges on two sides and the golf course on the others.

I felt a rush, but I tried to hide my excitement. I didn't want to coach Kendra into a specific answer. I took a few side streets through Westmoreland and then turned into the Eastmoreland lot.

Kendra knew immediately. If her ID of Derringer had been this solid, I could see why she'd earned Walker's and Johnson's confidence.

"Samantha, this is it. I remember, I remember! That's the big building, and over there's the park. Are we near train tracks? This is totally it. They drove me right over there, around the side of the building."

I knew that around the corner from the clubhouse, a strip of asphalt led to the driving range. I parked there whenever I came to hit balls, but it had never dawned on me how dangerously isolated the area would be when the course was closed. Acres of greens surrounded the lot on the north, east, and south. To the west, thick hedges, train tracks, and a six-lane freeway separated the parking lot from the nearest house.

From the backseat, Chuck patted Kendra on the shoulder.

"Good memory, kiddo. Good job, Kincaid, for thinking of this place. You two didn't even need me here."

I knew he was attempting to hide his disappointment. The odds of finding a witness were slim. He would check with the golf course in the morning, but he wouldn't find anything.

I tried to look on the bright side. At least I could prove that the crime had taken place in Multnomah County, so Derringer couldn't weasel out on a technical argument over jurisdiction. Also, the golf course was only a few minutes from Derringer's house, which at least added a piece of circumstantial evidence. At this point, anything helped.

I decided to drive by Derringer's apartment before heading back to Rockwood. It would be nice to know the exact distance for trial, and I might as well get it while I was down here.

I took a right onto Milwaukee Avenue and made a note of my odometer reading. Milwaukee is the primary commercial road running through Sellwood. It was also one of the only places where you'd find low-rent, high-crime apartments in this pocket of southeast Portland.

Frank Derringer's apartment building was on Milwaukee and Powell, which I learned was exactly 1.7 miles from the Eastmoreland Golf Club. I pulled into the small parking lot in front of the building, turned on my overhead light, and jotted down the odometer reading on a legal pad I pulled from my briefcase.

"Sorry for the stop, guys, but I wanted to make sure I made a note in the file about our find at the golf club while it was still fresh in my mind."

Chuck realized where we were but didn't say anything. He

apparently agreed there was no need to inform Kendra that
we were sitting just a few feet from her assailant's home. She
didn't seem like the pipe-bomb-building type, but you never
can tell.

I added a short note for the file, summarizing Kendra's
statement at the golf course. As I was returning the pad to
my briefcase, Kendra opened her car door, got out, and
began walking across the street.

"Where the hell's she—"

Before I could finish the question, Chuck was out of the
car too. It wasn't hard for him to catch up. Kendra stopped
by an old tan Buick on the corner across the street from the
complex. When I got to where she and Chuck stood, Chuck
was saying, "What? What is it? Kendra?"

Kendra was ignoring him, entranced by this remarkably
unexceptional car. Then she said, "He must've painted it."

"Who? Who painted what?"

Kendra spoke as if thinking aloud. "The car. He must've
painted it. It was dark before. Now it's tan."

"Kendra, what are you saying?"

"I'm saying that this is the car. This is the car they pulled
me into. I remember it. But it was dark before."

Chuck and I traded skeptical looks. This wasn't good. Witnesses were notoriously bad at identifying cars, especially
when, like Kendra, they knew nothing about them. And this
particular identification seemed especially suspect, given
that the car was an entirely different color from what Kendra
had described after the attack.

The viability of the case against Derringer rose or fell on
Kendra Martin's credibility. Not just her honesty but also her
memory would be the key to convincing a jury to believe her
testimony. If Kendra made an assertion of fact that we later

determined to be incorrect, I would have an ethical obligation to tell Lisa Lopez about the mistake. The case would be over.

A couple of years ago, I had a robbery case where the clerk described the robber with as much detail as if he had been looking right at him. The cops picked up the defendant just a few blocks away, sitting at a bus stop where someone happened to have stuffed a sack full of marked bills behind a nearby bush. The man matched the teller's description in every way, except his tie was blue and not green.

A lazy cop could have written a report saying the teller gave a verbal description, the defendant fit that description, and the teller then ID'd the guy in a line-up. Open and shut. But the rookie on the robbery had been fastidious, submitting a detailed fifteen-page report. The defense lawyer cross-examined the teller for four hours, and three jurors eventually voted not guilty, leaving me with a hung jury. My guess is that the eager officer now has a habit of glossing over certain facts in his reports.

How much Chuck Forbes lets slide in his reports I didn't know, but the point was moot. I was standing right here, falling into the hole that Kendra Martin was digging deeper with her every word. The line between changing her statement and leading the investigation would be thin. Chuck and I needed to be sure to stay on the right side of it.

He spoke first. "Kendra, if you're not sure, why don't we come back in the morning when it's light out and you've had the chance to sleep on things." We both looked at her, hoping the message might translate.

But thirteen-year-old ears are deaf to subtlety. "I don't need to come back. This is the car. It's just not the right color."

It was my turn to try. "So, are you saying that this is a

similar *kind* of car to the one they had, but that the one they were driving was a different color?"

"No. I mean, this *is* the car they had. Someone must have painted it."

Struggling to hide my frustration, I said, "Kendra, a lot of cars look like this one. You're too young to remember, but when Chuck and I were your age, almost every car made in America looked just like this. Sad, isn't it?" She wasn't laughing. "Maybe it's better if we take Chuck's advice and come back and look at it when it's light out before you make up your mind for sure."

"I don't want to come back tomorrow. What if it's gone? I don't need to see it again anyway. I'm sure this is the one. I couldn't remember it enough to, like, describe it out loud at the hospital, but now that I see it, I recognize everything about it. See, it's got a ding in the door over here where the driver sits. And the front hubcap is different than the back hubcap. Then I ran over here to look at it better. When I looked inside, I remembered it too. The dash is all freaky, like a spaceship. I don't know how to say it. It's just the same. But it looks like they did stuff to it. It's like way cleaner inside and it's a different color."

It was possible. The car was, after all, parked outside of Derringer's building, and people have been known to paint their cars.

Chuck was busy taking a closer look at the Buick. "She might be on to something, Kincaid. For such a piece of . . . um, junk, this baby's paint's looking real good. So's the interior."

It made sense. We knew already that Derringer was willing to go the extra mile to hide physical evidence. If he'd shave his body to avoid leaving hair samples, he might rework his car to dispose of any incriminating evidence.

"I don't think we can get a warrant with what we've got. Kendra says it's the same car, but the fact that it's a different color's going to kill us. Is there some way to tell for sure if the paint is new?"

"Sure. I'll just chip a little bit off." He reached in his pocket for his keys.

"No! Stop. Don't touch the car."

Chuck held his hands up by his face. "I wasn't going to open it or anything."

"It doesn't matter that you weren't going to open it. Looking beneath the paint still constitutes a search. If you chip that paint off, whatever you see underneath will be inadmissible. And if we get a warrant based on what you see, anything we find as a result of the warrant will also be thrown out. Is there some way to tell if the paint's new without touching the car?"

"Depends how good a job they did. If it was a quickie, they might not have gotten beneath the bumper and the lights. The cheap way to do it is to tape those areas off and paint around them. If he got it done after Saturday night, I doubt they did a thorough job. Problem is, I can't tell anything in this light."

"I've got a flashlight in my trunk. I'll go get it."

When I got back, Kendra said, "How come he can use a flashlight but can't chip some of the paint off?"

"He's allowed to look at anything in open view. Flashlights are fine. Some courts even let you use stuff like night vision goggles without getting a warrant."

"Hey, I've got something here."

Chuck waved us over. He was crouched down by the back bumper, supporting his weight with one hand and aiming the light with the other.

"It looks like this light tan stops right here at the edge of the bumper." He was talking slowly, the way people always seem to do when they're squinting. "Hard to tell exactly what color's behind there. Dark brown, maybe. But it's definitely a lot darker than the new stuff. Look over at the edge over here. It looks like they were kind of sloppy taping the bumper here. There's a thin line of paint on the metal right at the lip there. Can you see it?"

"Barely, but it's enough. So the paint job must've been done recently."

"Definitely. Even if no one ever washes the thing, normal wear and tear from the weather would at least break down that line a little bit. That's real new paint, with a clear edge left from the tape."

That was enough for me. "Alright, we need to run the plates and make sure it doesn't belong to some priest down the street. Assuming we don't get something on the plate that changes our minds, let's order a tow and get paper on it." The law permits police to tow a vehicle and secure it while they apply for a search warrant. I asked Chuck, "What's the best way to do this?"

"I don't have my phone with me. It's back in my car."

He was looking at me like I could change that. I'd proudly avoided buying a cell phone for years. "You know I don't have one of those things."

"Let's drive up the street to the gas station, and I'll call Southeast Precinct to have a patrol officer come out and sit with the car until a tow comes. What'll work best is if you drop me off at the Justice Center. I'll start the warrant application while you drive Kendra home, then you can swing back by Central to review the warrant. Up to you whether you want to stick around for the search."

It must've been a slow night for crime. It only took a few minutes for a patrol officer to meet us at Derringer's. Kendra and I dropped Chuck off at the Justice Center, where Central Precinct is located. Then I hopped onto I-84 and headed back out to Rockwood.

I walked Kendra to the front door, then remembered Chuck's contraption. We went around back, and I pushed on the back door hard enough to pull off the tape, holding the knob tightly so the door wouldn't swing open. Reaching my hand in at the bottom of the crack, I pulled out the glass of water. It was still full.

"Are you going to be OK here by yourself, Kendra?"

She nodded. "Uh-huh. I'm used to it since Mom started working nights."

"What time does she normally get home?"

"A little bit after eleven."

I looked at my watch. Kendra would only be alone for about an hour.

"OK. Make sure you tell her that's Chuck's car out front. He'll probably have a patrol car drop him off so he can pick it up, so don't get scared if you hear him leaving in the middle of the night."

"Alright."

"It was really nice meeting you, Kendra. You're a very strong girl to be doing so well after what happened to you. I want you to know that all of the police and I are extremely impressed and very proud of you."

She was smiling with her lips together, which I suspected was as close to beaming as Kendra got. "Thanks."

"One of the MCT detectives will come by Friday morning and pick you up for grand jury, but I want you to know you can call me before that if you want." I wrote my direct line on the back of one of my business cards for her and then waited at the back door until I heard her lock it.

Once I saw lights coming on inside the house, I pulled out of the driveway. My car was racking up more miles tonight than it usually saw in a month. I got back onto I-84 and drove into downtown. Cones of red and green rippled on the Willamette, reflecting the lights of the Hawthorne Bridge. I grabbed a parking spot on the street across from the Justice Center and took the elevator to the MCT offices on the fifth floor.

Chuck was sitting at his desk, his attention focused on his computer screen. He didn't hear me, and I paused a moment to take a good look at him. I suddenly realized that for years I hadn't been seeing him clearly. In my mind, he still looked like he had in 1978; he had simply exchanged his football uniform for a badge and a shoulder holster. But the twenty extra pounds of bulk he'd carried as a kid were gone. His face was thinner, and lines had begun to mark his forehead and the corners of his eyes, just as they had mine.

Working as a cop wasn't this year's sport. Whether he entered law enforcement initially for the thrill, to rebel against his family, or out of sincere dedication, he was in it now for real. With his father's contacts, he could have taken any career path he wanted in this city. But here he sat fifteen hours into his workday, at a metal and corkboard cubicle, in front of an outdated monitor, waiting for his first lover to review his warrant so he could prove that a dirtbag like Frank

Derringer had brutalized a thirteen-year-old heroin addict and prostitute in a Buick built while we were still making out under the Grant High School bleachers.

For the first time, I was seeing Chuck Forbes as a man, not as an icon of a glorious time in my life that was over. I felt tears in my eyes, blindsided by the sad realization that Chuck and I were no longer kids and by the profound honor I felt upon finding myself walking a common path with him as adults.

I hate that I get so sappy when I'm tired.

I must have made a noise, because Chuck stopped reading and looked over his shoulder. Swinging his chair around, he said, "Hey, you, what's the matter? Did something happen when you were with Kendra?"

I swallowed and got ahold of myself. "No, everything's fine. Just zoning out."

"Good job with her tonight," he said. "It was nice to see you act like yourself with someone on the job. Seemed to work, too."

"How's the warrant coming?"

I'd ignored his comment, and he had the good sense to pretend not to notice. "Good. I'm done and just went over it again. If it's alright with you, I incorporated by reference all the affidavits from the warrant for Derringer's place, then I drafted a quick affidavit containing all the new info we got tonight."

"That should be fine. Does the warrant authorize removal of the seats and carpet if that's what the crime lab needs to do to look for blood?"

"Yeah, it's got the works. The car will be in pieces by the time the lab's done with it."

"What did you find out about the registration?"

"Plate comes back to a guy named"—he grabbed a computer printout from his desktop—"Carl Sommers. Last time it was registered with DMV was a couple of years ago. The tags expire next month. Anyway, Sommers filed a statement of sale with DMV about seven months ago saying he sold the car to a guy named Jimmy Huber."

"What's a statement of sale?"

"It's just a piece of paper from the registered owner saying he doesn't own the car anymore. It's a CYA thing in case the buyer doesn't re-register the car. Anyway, Sommers's sheet is clean, and it looks like this Huber guy never did register the car."

"What do we know about Huber?"

"Hold your horses, now. I'm getting there. I ran Huber in PPDS. He looks like a shit. Couple of drug pops and a bunch of shoplifting arrests and domestic beefs. He just checked into Inverness in December to do a six-month stint for kicking his girlfriend in the head in front of their baby."

"Nice guy. What's his car doing on Milwaukee?" The Portland Police Data System is a fountain of data derived from police reports.

"That's the good part. Looks like he knows Derringer's brother, Derrick. PPDS shows Derrick and Huber together as custody associates on a dis con last summer at the Rose Festival."

Your average drunken delinquent has at least a few downtown arrests for disorderly conduct. For a certain type of man, the party hasn't begun until you're screaming and puking your guts out in an overnight holding cell.

As I looked over the PPDS printouts for Huber and Derrick Derringer, something was bothering me, but I couldn't put my finger on it. I started thinking out loud. "So, Huber knows Derringer through his brother and sold him the car. But Derringer was still in prison when Huber got hauled off to Inverness."

"Right, but he could've given the car to the brother, who then gives it to Frank when he gets out. The exact mechanics don't really matter. The point is we can tie the car to Derringer through his brother."

He was right. In my exhaustion, I was losing sight of the big picture and, as usual, convincing myself that I was missing something. "No, you're right. It's good. You put that in your affidavit?"

"Yeah. I think I'm done with it. You want to read it and get out of here? You look tired."

"I am. I don't know how you guys pull these crazy shifts. I'm about to fall over."

"It's all about the adrenaline, baby." Chuck does a mean Austin Powers. "You want me to rub your shoulders while you read?"

Grace's masseuse says I have a bad habit of storing stress in my shoulders. Funny, I think I store it in my ass along with all the food I pack down when I'm freaking out. But I do get big knots in my deltoids after a long day, and Chuck's back rubs were heavenly. Turning one down was painful. "Um, I don't think that's a good idea. We're at work and everything."

"Your call. If it makes you feel any better, the bureau has a woman come in once a month to do chair massages. It's just a relaxation thing, not foreplay."

"I know. Thanks anyway."

I finished reviewing the warrant. It was a quick read, since

we were reusing the affidavits MCT wrote to get the warrant
to search Derringer's house. The only new material was the
information Chuck had added about the car.

"Looks good," I said, as I signed off on the DA review line
of the warrant. "Who's on the call-out list tonight?" The
judges rotate being on call to sign late-night warrants and
put out any fires that might arise.

"Lesh and Hitchcock."

Lawrence Hitchcock was a lazy old judge who smoked
cigars in his chambers and pressured defendants to plead out
so he could listen to Rush Limbaugh at eleven and then close
up shop early to play golf. I'd rather swallow a bag full of
tacks and wash them down with rubbing alcohol than risk
waking up Hitchcock at eleven at night.

David Lesh was the clear preference. He'd been a prosecutor for a few years after law school, then jumped ship to
the City Attorney's office to work as legal advisor for the
police department. He was a couple of years older than I was
and had been an easy pick for the governor to put on the
bench a few years back. He had a good mix of civil and criminal experience and was known throughout the county bar
for being as straight-up and honorable as they come. Best of
all, he hadn't changed a bit since he took the bench. He still
worked like a fiend and went out for beers with the courthouse crowd every Friday. Lawyers missed talking to him
about their cases, but we were better off having him as a
judge.

"Call Lesh," I advised Chuck.

"No kidding. I had that lazy fuck Hitchcock on the Taylor
case, remember?"

I always forget that cops know as much about the lives of
judges as the trial lawyers do. I suspected they gossiped

about the DAs as well. In this specific instance, Chuck had good reason to know about Hitchcock. He'd presided over the very complicated trial of Jesse Taylor, a case that had landed Forbes on the MCT. Taylor's sixty-five-year-old girl-friend, Margaret Landry, confessed to Forbes that she and Taylor had killed a girl.

When I started at the DA's office, Landry was the big talk around the courthouse. The local news covered the case's every development. Most stories started with the phrase, "A Portland grandmother and her lover. . . ." Headlines spoke of MURDEROUS MARGARET. If you asked them, most people who followed the case would tell you they were fascinated that a sixty-five-year-old grandmother and hospital volunteer eventually confessed to helping her thirty-five-year-old alco-holic boyfriend rape and then strangle a seventeen-year-old borderline-intelligence girl named Jamie Zimmerman.

Forbes had stumbled into the case fortuitously. Landry initially told Jesse Taylor's probation officer that she read about Jamie Zimmerman's disappearance in the *Oregonian* and suspected her boyfriend's involvement. At the time, Chuck was working a specialty rotation, helping the Depart-ment of Community Corrections track people on parole and probation. If not for the cooperation agreement between the bureau and DOCC, Taylor's PO might never have told the police about Landry's suspicions, because Landry used to call him at least weekly to try to get Taylor revoked. Her claims were always either fabricated or exaggerated.

Despite his hunch that Landry was at it again, the PO mentioned the tip to Chuck because this was the first time Landry had accused Taylor of something so serious as a murder. Chuck and the PO had followed up with several vis-its, and each time Landry changed her version of the events leading up to her accusation. The two men kept returning in an attempt to get her to admit that she was lying. But then she threw them for a loop: The reason she was sure Taylor had killed Zimmerman, she said, was that she helped him do it.

The continuing amendments to Landry's story after she was arrested only served to whet the public's appetite. She subsequently retracted her confession and accused Forbes of coercing the statements from her. But after she was convicted by a jury, Landry confessed again and agreed to testify against Taylor to avoid the death penalty. When Taylor was convicted and sentenced to die in one of Oregon's first death penalty cases, she once again recanted.

By then, however, common sense had prevailed, the hype died down, and people realized that Margaret Landry's confession spoke for itself. The grandmother who looked like Marie Callender was as deviant and sadistic as any man who comes to mind as the embodiment of evil. Last I heard, both Taylor and Landry were maintaining their innocence, and Taylor still had appeals pending.

At the time, the public interest in the Jamie Zimmerman murder was chalked up to tabloid curiosity. I didn't see it that way; in my opinion, people were riveted because Margaret Landry scared them. When they saw her interviewed, they saw their aunt, the woman down the block, or the volunteer going door-to-door for the Red Cross. If she could abduct, rape, and murder a young woman, then locking our doors, moving to the suburbs, and teaching our children to avoid strange men would never be enough to protect us.

Chuck's mind clearly had wandered in a different direction. "I had a hard enough time swallowing a death sentence on a case I worked on, but when it comes out of the courtroom of some ass like Hitchcock, I almost hope it does get thrown out."

After decades without a death penalty, the Oregon legislature had approved one in 1988. The relatively gentle jurors of Oregon had delivered capital sentences to only a handful of people, and most people assumed that those defendants would die natural deaths in prison before Oregon's courts would permit an execution to be carried out.

Despite the unlikelihood of an Oregon execution, handling murder cases in what was now theoretically a death penalty state still bothered Forbes and other people in law enforcement with mixed feelings about the issue. Like me, Chuck could not definitively align himself with either side of the debate. Unlike most knee-jerk opponents, he recognized that an execution could bring a kind of closure to a victim's family that a life sentence could not. But he continued to be troubled by the role of vengeance and the inherent discrimination that too often lay at the heart of the death penalty's implementation.

"Where is that case anyway?" I asked.

"Last I heard, Taylor hated prison so much he'd fired his attorneys and waived his appeals, but the State Supreme Court was still sitting on it. I almost hope they throw the sentence out. As long as the conviction stands, it's still a win for us."

Maybe Chuck had finally taken a position on the issue after all.

"Hey, enough of this. Why don't you head on home?" Chuck suggested.

"No, I'll stay here. I'm OK."

"You've got less sense than a thirteen-year-old. Do I have

to talk to you like you talked to Kendra?" He counted the multitude of reasons I should go home on his fingers. "I probably won't even do the search tonight. There was a shooting a couple hours ago up in north Portland, so the night-shift crime lab team is probably tied up out there. The car's in the impound lot, so it's not going anywhere. Go home. Vinnie misses you."

Vinnie is my French bulldog. He moved in with me a couple of years ago, the day my divorce was finalized. He gets upset when I stay out late.

Chuck wrinkled up his face and pulled out his ears, like a mean-looking pug with bat ears. In other words, he looked like my Vinnie. "I can picture him right now. He's going, 'Mmm, these curtains taste good. This carpet looks a lot better soaked with a huge puddle of French bulldog piss.' " For whatever reason, Chuck had decided that if Vinnie could speak he'd sound like Buddy Hackett.

"You're right. I'm going home. And the search can wait until tomorrow. Don't you work too late either," I said.

"Aye-aye," he said, waving his hand in a quick salute.

I stopped as I was walking toward the door. "Will you be able to get your car OK?"

"Yeah. I'll get a patrol officer to take me out there."

I turned around again at the door. He was making copies of the warrant. "Hey, Chuck."

"Huh?"

"You're really good at what you do."

His face softened, and his eyes smiled at me. "Thanks. Back atcha, babe. Now go home. You're only this sweet when you're tired."

I drove home smiling.

| 5 |

By the time I got home, it was almost midnight. Vinnie was waiting for me at the door, very disappointed. In my head, I heard Chuck's Buddy Hackett impersonation, scolding me for being out so late.

I threw off my coat, picked him up, made all sorts of embarrassing cooing noises, and scratched him ferociously behind those big goofy ears. When the snorts began, I knew he'd forgiven me.

Vinnie's basic needs are met when I'm gone. He has his own door in back that goes out to the yard. An automatic feeder keeps him portly. He's even capable of entertaining himself. I'm pretty sure he thinks his rubber Gumby doll is his baby. But at the end of the day, he's a momma's boy and needs me to talk to him.

Between work, keeping in touch with the few friends who are willing to put up with me, and trying to burn off all the crap I eat, I have just enough time left for my chunky little pal. I have no idea how other people manage to be needed by whole other tiny little individual people and still maintain their sanity.

I went into the kitchen and checked the level on Vinnie's feeder to be sure he ate. He had. He takes after me that way. Every little meat-flavored morsel was gone. I was sorry I missed it. Vinnie's so low to the ground that he has to reach his neck up over the bowl and then plop his whole face inside to eat. Then he picks out all the soft and chewy nuggets from his Kibbles 'N Bits. When those are gone, he eats the dry stuff. When he really gets going, he breathes fast and loud like an old fat man.

I must've been really hungry, because that mental image actually made me think of food. I was torn between the refrigerator and my bed.

I was leaning toward the latter when I noticed the message light flashing on my machine. I knew if I tried to sleep now, I'd be lying in bed wondering who called. I hit the Play button and unpeeled a banana that was turning brown and spotty on the counter.

"Sammie, it's your old man. Are you there? I guess not. Glad to see you're out and not sitting at home alone reading a book with that rodent you call a dog. Hi, Vinnie. You know I'm only kidding. You can't help being ugly, little man."

I love it that my father laughs louder at his own jokes than anyone else. I wonder if he knows the people doubling up around him when he talks are enjoying Martin Kincaid's contagious delight with life and not the substance of what he's saying.

"Anyway, baby, I hope you're doing OK. You got a hot date or something? I was going to come by today and mow your lawn if it was dry again, but old Mother Nature, she had other plans. I went and saw a movie instead. I tell you, that Kevin Spacey is something else. You have to see this picture. OK, I don't want to take up your whole machine. You've probably got all kinds of men trying to call you. Some real winners from down at the courthouse. I'm just giving you a hard time, Sammie. You know I'm proud of you. You're a top-notch human being. Give me a call tomorrow if you've got some time. 'Bye."

I'd finished my banana by the time he hung up. The length of my father's phone messages correlates directly with how lonely he is in his empty house. My mother died almost two years ago, just seven months after doctors found a lump in her right breast. As much as I wish I had never married my ex-husband, the marriage had at least brought me back to Portland, so I was here for my mother's last few months.

In retrospect, it was quick as far as those things go, but at the time it seemed like an eternity. Mom was as tough a fighter as they make, but in the end the cancer was too much even for her. People like to say that my father and I are lucky that she passed quickly, once it was clear that treatment was futile. Maybe I'm selfish, but I don't agree.

Since Mom died, I'd spent more time with my father as he adjusted to life as a widower. He was doing as well as could be expected under the circumstances. He retired from federal employment as a forest ranger last year, so he has a good pension and reliable benefits. Without a job to go to, he now finds comfort in his routine. He goes to the gym, takes care of the yard, watches his shows, goes target shooting, and plays checkers with his ninety-year-old next-door neighbor.

I see my dad at least every weekend. We usually catch a

movie and then wind up talking for a few hours afterward. Grace comes with us sometimes. So does Chuck, when we're getting along. I think it makes Dad happy to see me with friends he's known and liked since I was a kid. He never did like Shoe Boy and thinks most of my lawyer friends are snobs. Too bad I didn't inherit his good judgment.

It was much too late to call him back, so I got ready for bed, snuggled into the blankets, and picked up a mystery I'd started the week before. Vinnie followed me into bed, lying by my feet on his stomach with all four legs splayed out around him like a bear rug. I only made it through a few pages before I nodded off and dropped the book on my face. There's a reason I only read paperbacks.

The sun shining through my bedroom window woke me the next morning before the alarm. It was a nice change from a typical Portland February, when the excitement of the holidays is over and the endless monotony of dark, wet, gray days makes it hard to get out of bed. It was just after six o'clock, leaving me enough time for a quick run before work. I hopped out of bed, pulled on my sweats and running shoes, and brushed my teeth before setting out on a four-mile course through my neighborhood.

For the first time since October, I was able to look around clearly at my neighborhood rather than squint through a steady fall of drizzle. As I ran past the coffee shops, bookstores, and restaurants along the tree-lined streets of my historic neighborhood in northeast Portland called Alameda, the brisk dry air stung my cheeks and filled my lungs. Running clears my head and helps me see the world in a better light.

I finished up my fourth mile about a half hour later, and hung on to my good mood while I listened to a block of "Monday Morning Nonstop Retro Boogie" in the shower. One of the benefits of living alone is that you can belt out the entire *Saturday Night Fever* sound track in the shower if you feel like it, and no one complains, even if you sing like me.

Grace had recently convinced me to trade in my usual shoulder-length bob for a wispy little do. When she dried it at the salon, my hair looked like it belonged on one of the more glamorous CNN anchors. When I tried it at home, I ended up looking like a brunette baby bird. It wasn't too bad today, so I spruced it up with gel and slapped on some blush and eyebrow pencil. I caught a quick look in the mirror. At five-eight and through with my twenties, I still have good skin and a single-digit dress size. Not bad. By the time I was done, I had time to catch my regular bus in to work.

Southwest Fifth and Sixth Avenues constitute Portland's bus mall, carrying thousands of commuters from various communities within the metropolitan area through downtown Portland. I hopped out at Sixth and Main and walked the two blocks to the Multnomah County Courthouse on Fourth, stopping on the way to fill my commuter's mug at Starbucks with my daily double-tall nonfat latte.

I was running a few minutes shy of the time the District Attorney liked us to be here. But I was well ahead of the county's newest jurors—all summoned to appear for orientation at 8:30 A.M.—and the county's various out-of-custody criminal defendants scheduled for morning court appearances.

I'm not sure which way it cuts, but I have always found it odd that the criminal justice system throws jurors and defendants side by side to pass through the courthouse's metal detectors and to ride the antiquated, stuffy elevators. In either event, I beat the crowd and didn't have to push through the rotating throng that would be huddled outside the doors of the courthouse for the remainder of the day trying to suck down a final precious gasp of nicotine before returning to the halls of justice.

I made my way through the staff entrance, took the elevator up to the eighth floor, tapped the security code into the electronic keypad next to the back entrance, and snuck into my office without the receptionist noticing I was a little late.

My morning and what was supposed to be my lunch hour were consumed by drug unit custodies—the police reports detailing the cases against people arrested the previous night. The Constitution affords arrestees the right to a prompt determination of probable cause. The Supreme Court seems to think forty-eight hours is prompt enough, meaning an innocent person might have to sit in jail for a couple of days until a judge gets around to checking whether there's any evidence against him. In Oregon, we only get a day, so we have to review the custodies and prepare probable cause showings before the 2 P.M. JC-2 docket. If we don't get them arraigned by the afternoon docket, they get cut loose.

Around two o'clock, just as I was getting antsy about not having heard anything about the warrant, my pager buzzed at my waist. It was the MCT number.

Chuck picked up on the first ring.

"How much do you love me?" he asked.

"Only men I love right now are Vinnie and my daddy. But you can tell me what you've got anyway if you want."

"I'm not sure I believe you, but I guess it'll have to wait for another day. Lesh signed off on the warrant last night, but like I thought, we couldn't get the lab folks out here until this morning. You're not gonna believe it. Not only did Derringer put a new coat of paint on that P.O.S., looks like he had it completely overhauled. New carpet, new upholstery, the works."

"How do we know it's new?"

"Stupid bastard must've forgotten to check his car when the work was finished. We found the shop work order under the front passenger floor mat. Got it done Sunday morning at some shop over on Eighty-second and Division. Paid eight hundred dollars—cash."

"So we don't have any blood evidence," I said.

"Nope. The tech guys had a lot of fun ripping out all of this asshole's new stuff, but it doesn't look like any blood soaked through to the cushions. But come on, Sam. What's a loser like Derringer doing pouring that kind of cash into a thousand-dollar car? Didn't you say the guy does temp work?"

"That's what his PO says. I didn't say it wasn't good. I just thought the news would be better since you seemed so excited."

"I'm not done yet. I was giving you the bad news first. The lab called me this morning." He paused to make me wait for it.

"DNA?"

"Damn, Sam. You're shooting a little high there."

"So no DNA," I said.

"No. What'd you expect? Kendra said the guy did it in her mouth. Hardly ever get anything from that."

"Unless it happens to fall on some intern's navy blue dress, right?"

"Yeah. Bill definitely caught a bad break on that one. Anyway, we don't have any DNA, but there *is* good news. They found a latent print on the strap of Kendra's purse. They matched six points to Derringer."

"Is the tech willing to call it on that?" I asked.

"Yes. I called her back to be sure. It's Heidi Chung. You know her?"

"Yeah. She comes in on drug cases sometimes. Seems pretty good."

"She's a ten. Anyway, Heidi says Derringer's got some kind of broken ridge on his right index finger that's pretty unusual."

Experts quantify the similarity between an identifiable latent print left at the scene with a suspect's print based on the number of points that match. When I was back at the U.S. Attorney's Office, the FBI usually wouldn't call a match until they had seven points. But a match can be called with fewer points when the ones that are there are especially rare. Luckily, Derringer's prints were as screwy as he was.

"OK, now that rocks. You just made my day."

"I knew you'd be happy. Not quite love, but I feel appreciated."

"It's huge," I said. "Good job finding that purse in the first place. We've got that little shit."

We went over everything we had. Kendra's ID of Derringer, the proximity of Derringer's apartment to the crime scene, the shaving of his body hair, the car work, and now his fingerprint on Kendra's purse. It felt like someone had pulled a sack full of rocks off my shoulders.

The talk about Kendra's purse reminded me of my conversation with Mrs. Martin. "Oh, speaking of Kendra's purse, we should probably get her keys back to her. Her mom was going to get a new set made, but there may be other things she needs."

"What keys?"

"Her house keys were in her purse. Remember? We had to leave the door unlocked for her last night?"

"No, Sam, I don't remember. She said she didn't have keys and her mom was getting a set made. I just assumed she didn't have any because she hadn't been living there. Shit!"

"What's the difference? Just get the keys back."

"The difference is that there weren't any keys in the purse, Sam. Fuck!"

Why hadn't I checked with him? I had just assumed. I replayed last night in my head. When I drove Kendra home, I made sure that the back door hadn't been tampered with, but I hadn't gone in with her. "Did you call her? Have you talked to her today?" I said.

"No," he said. "I was going to as soon as I got off the phone with you."

"Oh my God. What have I done?"

"Calm down, Sam. She's probably fine." He was talking fast now. "Think. Is there any way Derringer or his buddies could get Kendra's address from the court case?"

"No. No, the judge ordered the defense attorney to withhold the address from Derringer, and Lisa wouldn't violate that. They know her name, though."

"What about the mom's name? Do they have that?" he asked.

I thought through all of the filings in the case. "No. It's not in there. Just Kendra's." Luckily, Martin was a common surname, so the phone book wouldn't do them any good.

"OK. It's OK. Ray and Jack checked with her after we found the purse to make sure she didn't have anything in there with her mom's address on it. I was out there this morning for my car, and everything looked normal. You stay calm. I'll call you right back."

I tried to calm down. She should be OK. If something had been wrong when Andrea got home from work, we'd know by now.

Despite all the logical reasons not to worry, it was hard to concentrate, so I distracted myself by checking my bottomless voice mailbox. Along with the usual stuff, there was a message from O'Donnell. "Hey, Sam, O'Donnell here. I waited around in your office awhile, but I guess I missed you. Hope you're not still riled up about the other day. The guys and I were just having some fun. Anyway, I hear you did a number on the Derringer indictment. Since it was my dog to start with, I thought I'd call in and see if you have anything new. I assume you're going to have to plead it out at some point, right? Those Measure Eleven charges aren't gonna stick. Give me a call when you've got a chance and let me know where things stand."

For the same reason I always eat the vegetables on my plate first, I went ahead and called him. Better to get it over with.

I gave him a quick rundown on where we stood.

"Shit, Kincaid. With only a six-point latent on the print, you're toast without DNA. It's your case, but I'd plead it out quick if I were you. Case like this, you might be able to squeak out a decent deal before the guy realizes you're shooting blanks."

"I'll take it into consideration. Thanks. Anything else?"

"How's that vice angle going? Didn't Garcia say something about trying to use the vic to get some intel on pimps?"

"Yeah, Tommy thought it might pan out. Turns out the girl hadn't been working long. And what she did, she did on her own. I've got some pictures she took of some other girls, but it doesn't look that promising."

"Yeah, I saw those on your desk when I was in there earlier. Didn't realize the connection. It's not too late to pull out, you know. You could still dump the mandatory minimums and send it down to general trial," he said.

"I'll keep that in mind." I got off the phone before I said something I'd regret and turned back to my computer. Nothing could take my mind off Kendra. I checked the time so I'd know when I'd waited long enough to check in with Chuck.

After a long 78 seconds, Tommy Garcia popped his head into my office.

"Hey, Sammie. ¿Qué pasa?"

I sighed. "The Derringer investigation's on hyperspeed. It's coming together, though. How about you?"

"I'm just over here for a grand jury. Got here a little early, so I thought I'd check in on you. See how your vic's doing."

"Kendra. Yeah, seems like a pretty decent kid, actually." I didn't see any reason to alarm Tommy with the problem of the keys. "Speak of the devil, though, I've got something for you." I found the photographs Kendra had given me and handed them to him. "You might be interested in these. Kendra's clique from the Hamilton."

He flipped through once and then went through them more methodically. "A couple of these girls look real familiar." He leaned toward me and pointed at one of the girls rubbing against the faceless man with the Tasmanian Devil tattoo. I recognized her as Kendra's friend, Haley. "This one's a real piece of work. Holly or Halle or Haley or something."

"I think it's Haley."

He rolled his eyes, clearly tired of the indistinguishable trendy names found among today's kids. "Anyway, she's one of the hard-core street kids. She's about sixteen. Been on the streets at least four years and lives the life in every aspect. Hates the police, caseworkers, anything that's legitimate."

"Sounds like she'd have good information for vice."

"Man, are you kidding? She's like a matriarch out there. She knows the kids, but she also knows who's plucking them off the buses and streets to get them into it. Problem is, a girl like that ain't easy to flip. She's convinced herself that her life is the one she wants, not just what she got stuck with. She wouldn't take the road out even if it were open to her."

"Well, she and my vic were pretty tight. I got the impression that this girl sort of watched Kendra's back."

"I don't know, Sam. From what I can tell, this girl's all about survival, so unless your vic had something for her . . ." He faded out. "Hell, I guess it can't hurt to take a shot. Use your case as the in with her?"

"It's up to you. I thought the pictures might help you out, but don't take it as an indication that you need to do anything with them." Most detectives would be offended if a DA tried to tell them to initiate an investigation, but Tommy was worried about letting me down.

"Yeah, I might give it a shot. I'll let you know. You need these back?" he asked, holding up the photographs.

"Nope. Hold on to 'em as long as you want."

As Garcia left the office, I snuck a look at the clock. Thirteen minutes now. Why hadn't Chuck called?

Just as my self-imposed fifteen minute deadline was about to expire, the phone rang.

Chuck knew to get to the important stuff first. "She's at home, and she's fine." He could hear my relief. "I shouldn't have even mentioned it to her. I think it scared her mom. She's saying some things are out of place. I'm sure she's just getting used to having Kendra around all day again. But she's still spooked."

"But there's nothing else suggesting anyone was in the house?"

"No. Look, it's fine, Sam. Even if they took the keys, I don't see how they'd know where Kendra lives, and it doesn't make any sense for them to go there just to poke around. I called one of the community safety liaisons out in Gresham, to be safe. He's leaving the department as we speak to relock the house on the city's dime. I'm just pissed that I didn't put it together sooner."

"It's my fault. I'm the one who Andrea talked to about getting the keys out of the purse. I should've made sure they were in there."

"No use blaming anyone now. Luckily it turned out OK." With our temporary panic out of the way, he moved the conversation back to the new evidence. "So, you happy about the case now?"

"Happy doesn't begin to describe it. I'm ecstatic."

"You want to grab a bite tonight? Celebrate the good news?"

"I was going to stop by Dad's tonight."

"Alright, some other time." He sounded disappointed, and I was surprised to find myself feeling the same way. When we didn't want to kill each other, I truly felt at home with Chuck. We'd known each other so long that we were comfortable together in a way we didn't feel with anyone else. At least, I didn't. From what I'd heard, Chuck was never lonely for company in the evenings, but given how often his name passed through the rumor mill, it didn't seem like he'd kept anyone around long enough to get serious.

"You want to come with me? Dad always likes seeing you,

you know." The words were out of my mouth before I reminded myself that, when it came to me and Chuck, there was a cloud for every silver lining.

"Sure. Sounds great. Pick you up at seven?"

"Only if I get to drive the Jag," I said. If I was going to play with fire, I may as well get some warmth out of it.

Just as I hung up the phone, it rang again. Maybe it was Chuck, having second thoughts too.

"Kincaid," I said.

It was Judge Leeson's clerk. Maria Leeson had the unfortunate privilege of being the presiding judge for the Multnomah County Circuit Court, meaning she had to deal with all the miscellaneous shit that none of the other judges had time for.

"The judge wants to know why you're not down here," she said.

"Because I'm here. And not there."

"You better get down here."

"What's going on?" I asked.

"You've got a case on the docket. State v. Derringer."

"For what?"

"Call," she said. Cases were on the call docket when they were about to go to trial. Before a judge and courtroom were set aside, the parties were supposed to show up and report the status of plea negotiation and whether they were ready to go to trial. We usually sent one DA to the call docket to report information for the entire office. Poor Alan Ritpers was the current call DA.

"I gave all my trial information to Ritpers. The Derringer case just got arraigned the other day," I said.

"Yep, and that's why you need to get down here," she said. "Lopez called yesterday to have the case added to the docket, and Ritpers is clueless. The judge wants you down here. Now."

I headed straight down, skipping the antiquated and over-stressed elevators for the four flights down to Judge Leeson's courtroom. Lisa was waiting near the defense table and rose when I entered the room.

"My apologies, your honor," I said. "I wasn't aware of the appearance."

"Check your docket, Ms. Kincaid." Maria Leeson peered down at me over the top of her half-moon glasses. "Alright, Ms. Lopez, now that we've got a DA here who's heard of your client, tell me again what you're asking for."

"Thank you, Judge Leeson. My client is currently in custody, unable to meet bail imposed by Judge Weidemann during the arraignment. He wants a speedy trial, and I'm requesting the earliest available trial date."

Leeson pointed her glasses down at me again. "Ms. Kincaid?"

"The defendant waived his speedy trial rights at arraignment, your honor. In light of that waiver, the State requests a trial date in the usual course." Translation: let the defendant rot for a year while I finish getting the goods against him.

"Did you waive at arraignment, Ms. Lopez?" Leeson asked.

"Only because of the limited ability to consult with my client, your honor. I was appointed to the case at arraignment and only had so much time before the case was called. Ms. Kincaid was requesting a no bail hold, so, as you can imagine, my initial discussion with my client focused on the release issue. Once that was decided, I didn't have much choice other than to make the usual stipulations. Since then,

I've spoken further to Mr. Derringer. He can't make bail, and he wants a speedy trial."

I did my best to argue that Lopez should've preserved all rights at arraignment if she had any doubts, but we all knew that's not how it works.

"Alright," Leeson said. "I'm allowing the defendant to withdraw his waiver of speedy trial rights, meaning he gets his trial within thirty days." Leeson held a hand up to the court reporter, indicating her wish to go off the record. "You sure about this, Lisa?"

Invoking speedy trial rights was incredibly short-sighted. The requests usually only came from newbies who'd never been in custody before. I was surprised to hear that Derringer couldn't stick it out while his attorney prepared for trial.

Lopez shrugged. "I've advised Mr. Derringer against it. What can I do?"

Leeson arched her eyebrows and signaled for the court reporter to go back on record. "Alright then, let's set a date. I got a bunch of judges out for spring break in late March, so . . . that means Judge Lesh two weeks from Monday."

No way. "Your honor, this is an attempted murder case. There is physical evidence that still needs to be tested. The state needs more than two weeks."

"Too bad, Ms. Kincaid. I don't have anything else. If you can't proceed when the case comes up for call before trial, Mr. Derringer will be recogged."

I had to be ready for trial in two and a half weeks, or else Derringer would be released on his own recognizance. Lopez's strategy was a risky one. She was betting that we had only the evidence in the initial police reports. Too bad for her; she placed the bet without the benefit of the new evidence Chuck gave me. A quick trial date was fine with me.

The change in schedule gave me a good excuse to revoke the dinner invitation I had extended to Chuck. I broke the bad news to Dad and worked late instead.

My pager buzzed the next day around one as I was inhaling fish tacos at my desk. I could tell from the prefix that it was a bureau cell phone.

"Garcia."

I recognized Tommy's voice. "Tommy, it's Samantha Kincaid. You page me?"

"Yeah. I was out riding with patrol checking on hot spots, when whaddaya know; your vic's friend, Haley Jameson, is sitting with a bunch of the other street urchins outside Pioneer Courthouse."

At any given time, you could find a pile of homeless kids hitting people up for money by the Max tracks on the north side of the federal appellate courthouse, next to fountain pools decorated with stone beavers, Portland's unofficial mascot.

"If you've got the time to walk down here, I thought your connection with the vic might help me get a rapport with this girl. Otherwise, I'm left saying that I know someone who knows someone."

I looked at the clock. "I've got time. Tell me where to meet you, and I'll be right down."

Tommy met me at the southeast corner of the Pioneer Courthouse.

"So tell me about this girl," I said. "She been through the system?"

Garcia shook his head. "Nothing serious. Couple RJVs, loitering pops. Spent a few nights at juvie, went through LAP a couple times."

I'd seen plenty of them before. Street kids rarely got picked up for anything more severe than runaway juvenile violations, even though they were often at the fringes of more serious crimes like robberies and assaults. If they had any experience in the system at all, it was usually for curfew violations, public drunkenness, loitering, or runaway juvenile pops. Typical arrests for those kinds of offenses resulted in a night at juvie, a trip back home or a foster placement, and maybe a little court-ordered counseling. LAP stood for Learning Alternatives to Prostitution. The probation department developed the program a few years ago. Participants were supposed to learn legitimate job skills and enough self-worth to stop seeing the sale of sex as a good deal. It might be a good program for someone serious about getting out of the life, but, like most court-ordered counseling, it was treated as a joke by the people forced to go through it to avoid jail.

"So what's the plan?" I asked.

"OK, here's how we need to play it. If we single her out of the group, she's going to use us as a way to get props from her friends. We've got nothing on her, so once she calls our bluff, it's over. I'll play it nice and tell the group they need to stop blocking the sidewalks. Get them to move on. Maybe we'll have a shot then at talking to her alone. You act like you're my partner."

It was the last part I couldn't go for. I was pretty sure my boss wouldn't approve of one of his deputies impersonating a police officer. When Tommy was through teasing me about always following the rules, we agreed I'd fall back while he tried to break up the group.

He wasn't in uniform, so a couple of the less savvy kids didn't realize Tommy was a cop as he approached them. "Hey, man, spare some change?" one of them asked.

"Not today, dude." Tommy flashed his badge. "But I do have a tip for you. Mounted patrol should be coming by in a few minutes. Why don't you guys hightail it out of here before they give you a hard time."

The one I was pretty sure was Haley piped up. "What do you care?"

"Honestly? I don't care whether you go to juvie or not. But the officers doing the rounds today are coming up on reporting time, and I got a bet with a buddy at the precinct that their unit's not going to meet their enforcement quotas this month. Listen to me or not. It's up to you."

That did the trick. The kids slowly started getting up, collecting their blankets and bags, and walking in separate directions in smaller groups. Haley started to cross the street to Pioneer Square. "Haley, hold up," Tommy called after her.

She swung around toward us, throwing a large handbag over her shoulder and placing her hands on her hips. "I knew you guys were full of shit. Give me a break. Alright, man?"

Tommy held his hands up in mock surrender. "We're not here to hook you up on anything. We wanted to see if you could give us some help with something."

Hands still on her hips, she rolled her eyes and laughed to let us know that the notion of cooperating with the police amused her. She nodded in my direction. "Yeah, and what's she here for, fit me for my Girl Scout uniform?"

I had some damn good tacos going soggy on my desk. The last thing I needed was for some twit to patronize me, but I did my best to keep the anger out of my voice. "I'm Deputy District Attorney Samantha Kincaid. Sergeant Garcia and I were hoping you could talk to us about something that happened Saturday night to a girl you might know, Kendra Martin. Take a minute with us, and we'll buy you some lunch. You could probably use a bite to eat."

She raised her eyes toward Tommy with anticipation. He picked up on the cue. "Twenty bucks to hear us out. Up to you whether you stay after that."

The cash worked. We sat with her on one of the brick steps in Pioneer Square and explained that we were investigating the assault on Kendra Martin and thought she might have heard something on the street about it. We didn't tell her that Kendra had told me that they were friends or that I had pictures of her getting it on with the Tasmanian Devil guy. She stared at us through hard eyes, lips pressed into a straight line, as we described the violence inflicted upon Kendra. I thought I saw her take a quick downward glance and a small swallow when Tommy told her that a man named Frank Derringer had been arrested and charged.

Tommy made a soft play to get information from her. "Anyway, I've asked around the patrol officers and they tell me you know about as much as anyone does about what goes on with the kids down here. If you can give us anything on this guy Derringer, or any other guys who might be into doing this kind of thing to a girl, we'd keep your name out of it."

"I don't believe you, but since I don't know nothing about it, it don't make a difference, does it?" Haley pulled the twenty bucks Tommy'd given her from her front pocket and shook it in front of her as she stood to face us. "Thanks for the twenty bucks, though. Losers." She made the shape of an L on her forehead with her thumb and forefinger, just in case we missed her point.

We didn't try to stop her as she walked away. It was clear that we didn't have whatever it might take to get Haley Jameson to betray the life she'd committed herself to.

"Lost cause"—Tommy sighed—"but, hey, at least we gave it a shot. I'll flag it in PPDS for someone to call me if she gets popped for anything down the road."

"Tommy, I know we were only using the case to get a conversation going with her about vice, but I got the impression she knew something."

He shrugged his shoulders. "Possible. Guy like Derringer might get around. But if there's something there, we're not getting it from that girl."

| 6 |

I usually spend the day before a trial at my dining room table, reviewing the entire file and practicing my open. I broke from habit for Derringer. The case centered around Kendra Martin, and anything I could do to boost her confidence on the stand would do far more for us than a review of the file.

Everything had gone well in front of the grand jury. I got the indictment in less than an hour, and Kendra did a good job with her testimony. Afterward, to prepare her for the actual trial, I had shown her a courtroom and even put her in the witness chair to run through her testimony. But to make her feel as comfortable as possible tomorrow under the circumstances, I wanted her comfortable with me.

It was an unusually warm day for the beginning of March in Portland, so I decided to take Kendra to the zoo. I invited Grace, too. Kendra seemed a little skittish about leaving her house, but she and Grace seemed to hit it off from the start, and it was hard not to enjoy the warm sun after months of chilling rain.

The Portland zoo is a natural habitat zoo. The advantage is obvious: Instead of being confined in concrete bunkers surrounded by metal bars, the animals get to roam freely on acres of land designed to replicate their environments of origin. The downside is that the animals use their oasis just as any reasonable person would if given the option: to avoid any unnecessary contact with meddlesome humans.

As a result, our visits to the giraffe and lion areas were unproductive. After staring at a boring mound of rocks for fifteen minutes without a single indication of a lion's presence, I was ready to pack it in to visit lizards, snakes, anything that was stuck in a cage the old-fashioned way so that stupid humans could gawk at it, whether it liked it or not.

Something passed through my field of vision, and I felt the hair on the back of my neck rise. Turning around, I saw a man on a cell phone standing outside the rain forest building. He wasn't looking in our direction, but I realized I had seen him earlier at one of the other exhibits and, come to think of it, he'd been alone then too.

I gave Kendra some money to buy us all red-white-and-blue ice pops shaped like rockets. As I watched her walk over to the concession stand, I lowered my voice. "Don't make it obvious that you're looking, Grace, but you see that guy by the rain forest? On the phone?"

She snuck a little peek. "Sweetie, you *do* need to get yourself a man if you're stooping that low."

I looked at the guy again. "Grace, no. Yuck. It's just—isn't it a little weird for a man to be at a zoo by himself?"

"Maybe his family's inside, and he left to make a call."

"I saw him earlier, though, and I think he was alone then too. It didn't stand out at the time, but now I think he was looking at us over by the lions."

"What lions?" She laughed.

"I'm not kidding, Grace. Maybe he's a little pervert who's at the zoo to watch all the kids."

"Or maybe he's just some suburban dad who's trying to keep up with the office while he's on daddy duty at the zoo, and he was looking at us because we aren't so hard on the eyes." She slipped into a Mae West routine.

"Hey, knock it off. I'm serious."

"No, Sam, you're paranoid. You've got crime on the mind, and you're especially uneasy about Kendra today. If you're really worried, we can go say something to security. Tell them to keep an eye on him."

I thought about it. "Nah, you're right." I looked back at the guy. He was putting his phone away and walking into the rain forest. "I'm sure he's harmless."

We polished off the rocket pops and headed toward the polar bears. Grace and I were entranced, as usual, by Portland's swimming polar bears, but I noticed that Kendra seemed a little distracted.

"You holding up OK, kiddo?" I asked.

She looked at me like I'd offered her broccoli, and then spoke extremely slowly in the event I'd suddenly become extremely stupid. "Um, yeah. Unless I'm missing something, the zoo's not exactly a high stress kind of thing, Samantha."

She was playing tough, but I knew the trial was weighing on her mind at least as much as on mine. "Very funny, wiseacre. Last time I checked, I was going to be picking a jury tomorrow, and you were scheduled to testify in a couple days. Do we need to talk about that?"

"No. I understand how everything will go. I'll be OK."

I was worried. I'd prepped her, but the trial would be her first face-to-face with Derringer since the assault, and I suspected that she had no idea of what was coming. I'd advised her that Lisa Lopez would cross-examine her. She knew that Lopez undoubtedly would ask her about her drug use and prostitution. We ran through a mock cross together, but I couldn't bring myself to get rough with her on the issues of drug use and promiscuity. I was hoping Lisa would pull her punches on these issues. If she did hit Kendra hard, the jury might hold it against the defense.

I gave Kendra's arm a little squeeze and said goodbye. "You take it easy this week, OK? You're going to be fine." Grace was going to give Kendra a ride home, but first they were going to make a stop at Lockworks, Grace's salon.

It would be good for Kendra to see other women in careers more satisfying than her mother's, and Grace has all the stuff good role models are made of. She graduated magna cum laude with a business degree from the University of Oregon. About two years into a marketing job with a big company in town, she foresaw that Portland was attracting a more cosmopolitan population than the city was capable of servicing. She had been cutting her friends' hair since high school, she had a great mind for business, her taste had always been impeccable, and people had always been drawn to her. She took out a loan, bought part of an old warehouse, and opened Lockworks in the Pearl District. She lured the best stylists in the city by offering them good benefits and a piece of the profits, and used her contacts to recruit customers while she went to cosmetology school at night.

Lockworks is now the swankiest salon in town, and

customers wait weeks to get an appointment with Grace. Luckily, she still cuts my hair like she did in high school, in her kitchen while we eat raw cookie dough.

As I pulled out of the parking lot, I noticed the cell phone dad leaving, too. Except he still didn't have anyone with him. And he was driving a brown Toyota Tercel. Did they let dads drive those things? As he left the lot, I dug through my purse for a piece of paper. Normally my bag's full of old receipts, but I'd just cleaned it out. I pulled out the edge of a dollar from my wallet and scribbled down the guy's plate number before I lost sight of him. Maybe I'd run it later to make sure he wasn't a fugitive pedophile.

I had just enough time to drive back downtown to make the meeting I'd scheduled with MCT. Immediately before a trial, I like to get the principal investigators together to run through all the evidence and review what we can expect from the defense. It was a practice I'd followed in the federal system, where the agents support the case all the way through the trial. Unfortunately, the local police are so busy that it's hard to get investigative time on a case once it's been indicted by the grand jury.

Lisa had given me a copy of her witness list just a few days ago. In an ideal world, I would have asked the police to interview each of the potential defense witnesses so we could lock in what they might say at trial. All I was hoping for in the real world was an idea of who each person was. From there, I would have to guess what the purpose of their testimony would be.

I had finally broken down and bought a cell phone, and I

was still in that phase every new cell phone owner goes through, finding reasons to use my fancy new gadget. On my way to central precinct, I called MCT to make sure everyone was assembled as planned.

It took awhile for an answer. "Walker."

I had to raise my voice to be sure he heard me over all of the whooping and hollering in the background. "Detective Walker, it's Samantha Kincaid. I just wanted to make sure we're still on for today. Any news?"

"Hell, yeah, we've got news. Haven't you heard?"

I obviously hadn't, so he continued. "Oregon Supreme Court ruled in a special session this morning that the State can stick the big needle to Jesse Taylor. I wouldn't have thought those libs had it in them, but we're finally gonna have an execution around here."

I said something about the state court being just the beginning. Even though Taylor had waived appeals, his prior attorneys would still try to go to federal court on their claim that Taylor was incompetent to fire them and waive his rights. But, as the words came out, I could think only of Chuck, having to nod politely as the rest of the guys cele-brated the ruling that brought a man he had investigated one step closer to state-sanctioned death.

It probably didn't help that this was the case that got Chuck onto MCT. After Margaret Landry confessed to Forbes, the police brought in MCT, but Chuck stayed involved in the investigation. They must've liked him, because they added him to the team about a year later.

At least he didn't need to worry about whether the police got the wrong man. And it wasn't as if the defendant was possibly a redeemable guy who made a split-second mistake during some robbery-gone-bad. Both Taylor and Landry were unrepentant sadists. When Landry finally confessed to Forbes, she admitted that she and Taylor wanted to find a woman for a three-way. Taylor went to a biker bar and picked up Jamie Zimmerman, whom Landry described as "a 'tard of some sort, but a hot piece of ass." Back at their house, Taylor got rough with both women and then began strangling Jamie with his belt. Landry helped him by holding Jamie down while she was fighting. After Jamie was dead, Landry performed oral sex upon her while Taylor masturbated. Then they wrapped her body in their shower curtain and dumped her near the Gorge.

And, despite Margaret's subsequent statement that she fabricated the entire story to get her abusive boyfriend in trouble, I had no doubt that she and Taylor were guilty. Her confession contained accurate details that she couldn't have known unless she was involved somehow.

She had tried to explain the details away by saying that Chuck had coerced her confession and had fed her the details she was missing. But the jury had seen that the son of a former governor didn't need to set up innocent grandmothers to get a good job in the bureau.

Although Landry never repented for Zimmerman's murder, she had avoided the death penalty by agreeing to testify against Taylor after the jury convicted her. She depicted herself as a do-gooder who volunteered teaching ceramics at hospitals and treatment centers. She claimed that she would've remained a law-abiding grandmother if it weren't for her abusive younger boyfriend.

Jesse Taylor, on the other hand, had little to say in his defense. A chronic alcoholic who suffered frequent blackouts, Taylor said he couldn't remember anything he'd done that night, but didn't think he ever met Jamie Zimmerman and didn't think he would ever kill anyone. But he didn't think he'd pass up a chance at a three-way either. Great defense.

That said, the certainty of Taylor's guilt and the pure viciousness of the crime apparently were of little comfort to Chuck. When I arrived at the Justice Center, he was waiting with Jack Walker, Ray Johnson, and Mike Calabrese. The celebration over the Supreme Court's Taylor ruling had died down, but Chuck still looked unnerved. I wanted to say something about the news but had to settle for an empathetic glance that I hoped he caught before I launched into new business.

"Hi, guys. Thanks for making time to go over the case. It helps me if we're all on the same page before we start the trial."

Mike Calabrese shook his head and told me with a wave of his hand that he wasn't bothered. He was a New York transplant, and eleven years in Portland hadn't changed the accent a bit. "Listen, Sammie, I can't speak for these guys, but me? I say there's no one better than you. I'm tired of these DAs who stick us up there on the stand and assume we know how it's gonna go. Most of them don't want to take time away from their weekend, so me? I appreciate it, is what I'm sayin'."

I pulled out my trial notebook. "I thought we could start by running through the evidence that each of you will be covering. Then we'll go over the likely defense theories. You can help me out by making sure I know who these defense witnesses are. Any questions before we start?"

Jack Walker held up a hand. "Yeah. I don't mind or anything, but our LT was a little peeved about all four of us being out to testify. Usually they just have one from each pairing go to court."

The bureau has to pay cops time and a half for all off-duty work, so this meeting wasn't cheap. "I want all of you to testify for a couple of reasons. One advantage to this approach is that, subconsciously, we'll defeat any kind of Who Cares attitude the jurors might have in the back of their mind. Remember, they're not going to hear about Derringer's prior unless he testifies, so they'll be seeing him on his best behavior, in a suit, leaning over and writing notes to his attorney. And, as much as we all like Kendra, some jurors might see her as getting what a girl should expect when she's turning tricks for dope. By having all of you testify, we'll be telling the jury that the bureau cared about this case and put a lot of resources into it to get a thorough investigation.

"By having each of you testify about a separate aspect of the case, we're also distributing the credibility of the police investigation among all four of you. If no single detective is seen as the lead, Lopez can't get any mileage out of ripping one of you guys a new one. If she tries doing it to all of you, the jury will see that it's dirty."

Walker nodded. "Got it. I'll tell the lieutenant so he gets off our backs."

"As far as the order of your testimony goes, I'll be spreading your statements out around Kendra's, so she will be the highlight of the show. But I don't want to end with her testimony just in case she winds up taking a beating on cross.

"The first witnesses will be the two kids who found Kendra in the Gorge. That'll set the scene for the jury. Then I'm going to call Mike." Calabrese would cover Kendra's condition when they got to the scene and the processing of the crime scene.

The fingerprint on Kendra's purse would be a critical piece of evidence. To get it before the jury, I'd need to show that the purse examined by the crime lab was the same one Mike found near the crime scene. We went through the purse's chain of custody. Mike placed it in a sealed and marked bag at the Justice Center and then brought it to the crime lab without opening it. Later, Heidi Chung would explain that she removed the purse from the sealed bag that had been marked by Officer Calabrese. It's the kind of testimony that puts jurors to sleep, but, unfortunately, lawyers have to jump about six evidentiary hurdles to get to the good stuff.

After Mike, I'd call the EMTs who drove Kendra to the hospital. They'd help show how bad Kendra looked at first. Then we'd get into what actually happened to her.

I was especially concerned about Kendra's initial lies to the police about why she was in Old Town and whether she used heroin. I walked them through how I was planning to deal with this. First, Ray would testify about the initial interview with her. The bar against hearsay would keep him from repeating most of Kendra's statements, since they weren't made in court. But I could ask him about statements that were eventually determined to be *false*. Out-of-court statements are only hearsay if offered for their truth. He could also testify about Kendra's demeanor.

I'd follow Ray with the ER doctor. If the jury didn't understand Kendra's explanation for why she lied, they might hang their hats on the Narcan if an MD explained the effects of the drug.

After the doctor, Jack Walker would testify about the second interview with Kendra. I wanted him to talk about the change in Kendra's demeanor from the first interview to the second and what he said to Kendra to get her to open up with him. "Explain it to the jury just as you did with me," I told him. "If they're going to understand why she was initially dishonest, it's going to come from you, followed directly by Kendra."

After Kendra, I'd call Andrea Martin to describe Kendra's recovery since she'd been home. Then Deputy Lamborn and Dave Renshaw would testify about Derringer's shaved body hair, followed by Chuck's testimony about the car overhaul.

"Chuck, be ready to go over the contents of the work order from the Collision Clinic." The only bone Lopez threw me was on that order. The document was admissible under a hearsay exception for business records, but technically I should bring in an employee to establish the foundation. I'd included the shop's custodian of records on my witness list just in case, but Lisa had agreed to stipulate to admissibility. Stipulating for business records was the usual professional courtesy, but with Lisa it could've gone either way.

After Chuck, I'd call Heidi Chung, closing on the strength of the fingerprint evidence.

When I'd finished, the detectives were clearly impressed.

Ray Johnson nodded his head. "Man, that's classy, Kincaid. You've got him smack down, girl."

"Hey, you guys did all the work. I just put it together in a way that gets it all in front of a jury."

"You think he's going down on all counts?" Walker asked.

"To be honest, I'm not so sure. If Derringer were smart, he'd abandon this whole identity defense, especially since we got that fingerprint. If he'd focus on the actual legal charges instead of denying identity, he could beat the attempted murder and try to get out from responsibility for the sex acts of Suspect Number Two. But the jury's likely to get so pissed off by his lame-ass alibi defense, they're not going to split the legal hairs in his favor. They'll convict him of the whole damn thing once they decide he was the one who did it."

Mike Calabrese liked that possibility. "Why shouldn't the loser get smacked for lying his ass off? Would be nice for a jury to call something in our favor for once."

We turned to the defense witnesses next. Lisa had given me the bare minimum, names and addresses. She had even listed the five witnesses in alphabetical order so I wouldn't know who was most important.

Jack Walker started with the top. "Well, you know who Derrick Derringer is. He's the scumbag's brother slash alibi."

"Last time we talked about him, we hadn't found anything to prove they weren't together. I'm assuming that hasn't changed."

Walker said, "All we got is that he's lied for his brother in the past and is no stranger to the system himself."

"Yeah, but is the jury going to hear about that?" Ray Johnson asked.

I nodded my head and popped open a can of Diet Coke that Calabrese tossed me from the MCT mini-fridge. "The priors for sure. As soon as a person takes the stand, all his felony priors come in to impeach. I'm sure the jurors will be real impressed that big brother's got a robbery and two forges. As far as his statement backing Derringer on the last beef, I filed a motion to get it in. Have to wait and see. If the jury hears about it, Derringer's toast. They'll not only know that the alibi's bullshit, but they'll also figure out that Derringer's done this kind of thing before."

Mike's beefy hands looked awkward opening a tiny snack pack of chocolate pudding that I imagined his wife packed in his lunch every day. I tried to ignore the fumbling and focus on what he was saying. "I say they're taking a big risk

putting the brother up there. They can't possibly think anyone's gonna buy this alibi deal. I mean, what about the fucking print on the purse, for Christ's sake? I mean, don't you
think I'm right on this, Samantha?"

"All the way. Like I said, Lisa'd be better off arguing reasonable doubt on the legal elements of the most serious
charges, instead of going with this alibi defense. I still can't
figure out why she's doing it. It's got to be coming from Derringer. Probably figures that, with the prior attempted sod,
the judge will tee up on him even if he beats the attempted
murder and the accomplice charges. Figures if he's going
down for the count anyway, he may as well roll the dice and
try to beat the whole thing."

Chuck pushed his palms against the edge of his desk,
rolled his chair back a couple of feet, and crossed his arms.
"He must have some loaded fucking dice, because I don't see
him beating a damn thing with this weak-ass witness list."

It's a fundamental truth that the number and density of
cuss words increases exponentially as the number of cops
and DAs in a room goes up.

"I'm glad you're so confident," I said. "I recognized the big
brother, and I knew Lisa'd be calling Jake Fenninger. He's
the cop who popped Kendra on Christmas. But I don't have
a clue on the other three. Enlighten me?"

"Well, let's start with Geraldine Maher and Kerry Richardson. Know what they have in common?" Chuck raised his
eyebrows, daring me to guess. When I continued to stare at
him, he said, "They work at Lloyd Center."

I felt my eyes widen. "The shopping center? What does a
fucking mall have to do with my attempted murder case?"

"I wouldn't have put it together except for the last name
on the list, Timothy Monrad. Rad was a new recruit for the

bureau last summer. Works northeast neighborhood patrol, including—you guessed it—Lloyd Center."

"Nice of Lisa to let me know that one of her witnesses is a cop," I said.

"Don't freak out. It's not a big deal," Chuck said with confidence. "See, Kerry Richardson comes up in PPDS as a complainant over and over up at Lloyd Center. Turns out he's what they call a 'loss prevention officer' at Dress You Up, that discount department store down at the end by the movie theater?"

I nodded to let him know I recognized the name.

Chuck continued. "OK, so when I saw Rad's name on the list too, I was psyched. I figured there might be some connection through Lloyd Center. So I ran all of Rad's arrests at Lloyd Center and cross-referenced them with Richardson's PPDS records. I found a report from January where Rad was the arresting officer on a trespass that Richardson called in. The trespasser was Andrea Martin."

"That's right. I remember. I ran Andrea's record in February as background. She had no convictions, but I did see a real recent arrest for trespass somewhere." I didn't pursue it, because even if I called Andrea to the stand, misdemeanor trespass is not the kind of crime that can be admitted into evidence against a witness. And her case hadn't even been issued; it was just an arrest.

Chuck continued. "The somewhere was Lloyd Center. I pulled the arrest report. Back in November, Kerry Richardson thought he saw Andrea shoplifting in the store. He went and got the manager, Geraldine Maher, and the two of them stopped Andrea outside in the mall. She had receipts for the things in her bags, but Richardson insisted he'd seen her sneak something. They figured she must have stashed whatever she stole somewhere right outside of the store. They didn't call police, but they did eighty-six her from the store. Richardson must have some memory, because when Andrea came back into the store in January, he recognized her and called police. Rad made the arrest. Andrea told Rad she just assumed that the eighty-six from the store had ended by then."

"I'm not surprised we didn't issue that. Sounds like she never should've been excluded in the first place."

Ray Johnson was laughing. "So that's it? The whole defense is that the vic's a whore, her mom's a trespasser, and Derringer's scum brother says they were watching TV?"

I was just as bewildered. "I don't know what the hell Lisa's thinking. The jury's going to hear about Kendra's background from me. I'll go over it during voir dire, opening, and Kendra's direct, so Lisa doesn't get any mileage by calling Fenninger. She can't get in those Lloyd Center witnesses to impeach Andrea. And even if she did, who would care?"

Mike Calabrese gave me a thumbs-up. "Lock and load, baby. That's what I say."

I love it when a plan comes together.

I left the detectives at the Justice Center and walked over to the courthouse to review my trial notebook one last time. I had already outlined the topics I wanted to discuss during jury selection and had written my opening statement, the direct examinations of the state's witnesses, and the cross-examination of Derrick Derringer.

I no longer carried the anxiety I'd been shouldering all

week about Lisa Lopez's list of defense witnesses. She was desperate if she was trying to get Kendra and Andrea's prior arrests into the record. No wonder she'd been pretty quiet about the case when I'd seen her around the courthouse lately. I had to admit a certain level of smug satisfaction. If it hadn't been for her initial bravado, I'd feel sorry for Lisa. She was going to spend her next two weeks stuck with a major barker at trial, all for a scumbag sex offender who wanted his free lawyer to present a preposterous defense that he and his dimwit brother cooked up. But after Lisa's attempts to get under my skin at arraignment, I was going to enjoy handing her a solid trouncing at trial.

I called Chuck around seven to see if he was ready to go. We had finally gotten around to rescheduling dinner with my dad. He agreed to meet me at my car; I was uncomfortable letting the other MCT detectives know that we were spending time together outside of work.

Dad opened the door before we could knock. "You sure the city can make it through the night without you guys? I tell you, with the two of you working together, the bad guys had better watch their backs." Dad always found creative and not so subtle ways of letting me know that in his view Chuck and I belonged together.

Dad was making his specialty, steak on the grill. Dad's like a lot of men of his generation. Wouldn't think of putting together a full meal in the kitchen, but sees cooking an entire dinner outside as one of the great manly traditions, like hunting, fishing, or teaching a kid to bat.

Dad took Chuck out to the deck to show him his new Weber while I poured us some wine. Watching them crouched by the grill reminded me of the summer the two of them built the deck. It was right after our college graduation, mine from Harvard, Chuck's from the University of Oregon. Chuck had decided not to leave the state for college, a decision his parents had harangued him for until they realized it would be bad form for the governor and his wife to suggest their son was too good for the state's best public university. By the time Chuck graduated, the former Governor Forbes spoke at commencement of the pride he felt when his son turned down the Ivy Leagues for U of O.

That summer was also the summer I told Chuck he had to fish or cut bait. I had vowed not to bifurcate my life anymore between him and everything else. At Harvard, I missed out on things that other kids experience when they go away to school, because my heart had stayed with Chuck back in Oregon. When other kids took summer internships on the Hill or in Manhattan, I had faithfully returned to Portland, four years in a row. I decided law school would be different.

So I'd begged Chuck during our senior year to live up to his potential and apply to graduate programs around the country. He was accepted into Stanford Business School and put down his deposit over Christmas break when I sent my acceptance to the law school. By spring break, he was saying that he hadn't gotten used to the idea of himself in business school, and, by summer, he was thinking of pulling out.

So I told him to choose.

Of course, it wasn't as easy as that. I cried for two hours and told him that I loved him and wanted to be with him and couldn't picture my life without him in it. I said that moving to Stanford with him would make me happier than I'd ever been, and *then* I told him to choose.

He chose to cut bait. He didn't know what he wanted to do, but he knew he didn't want to go to California, and he

knew he didn't want to go to business school. He was thinking of becoming a cop.

I didn't handle it well. I laughed at him and asked what it
would be next: astronaut or firefighter. I told him he'd never
grow up and would never amount to anything. I pointed out
that he'd been given every advantage in life—privileges other
people actually had to work for—and took it all for granted.
When my tirade finally ended, he went outside, finished up
the last coat of stain on the deck, and walked out. I didn't
see him again for six years.

I'd heard he'd joined the bureau, of course. I'd actually
considered turning down the job at the DA's office because
of it. But I had no interest in the alternatives I'd been given
at the city's big firms, and Roger knew it. There's no good
way to tell your husband that you're making employment
decisions based on an old boyfriend, even if it is to avoid him.
So, instead, I'd played the odds that I could avoid one of the
county's two thousand cops, at least for a while.

When I saw his name on the police reports for my first
trial, I tried to ready myself. I prepared the speech in my head
and went over it again and again in the shower that morning,
the way I should have been rehearsing my opening statement. I was going to apologize for all the venom that came
out of me that day. Then I would laugh as I said it all worked
out for the best in the end, since he'd accomplished what he
wanted, and I was so happy with Roger.

None of it was ever said. He walked into my office with
his patrol partner, handed me a cup of coffee, and said,
"Jason Hillard, meet Samantha Kincaid. Kincaid and I went
to Grant High together. So what's the game plan?"

I'd prepped them for the trial, but the case turned into a
bench warrant when the defendant no-showed. Two years

later, looking at Chuck with my father, I realized I'd still never apologized to him for how I behaved that summer, nor had I thanked him for saving me from having to do it when I wasn't ready that day in my office two years ago.

They came back into the kitchen with the steaks, and Dad started heaping mass quantities of food onto three plates. I set the table, blinking away tears before any could roll down.

"I was just telling Chuck about the damage you did last weekend at the target range," Dad said.

My entire life, my father has enjoyed gun collecting and target shooting. Cursed with having a daughter as his only child, he had tried repeatedly to spark some interest from me, but to no avail.

To his initial chagrin, I eventually learned to use a gun only when my ex-husband insisted on keeping one in our New York apartment. If he was going to keep a loaded handgun in an unlocked nightstand, I figured I sure as hell better know how to use it. So some of the agents took me to the ATF firing range and taught me how to load, aim, fire, and reload just about every weapon available, legally and otherwise, in the United States. As irrational as gun ownership is as practiced by the most hard-core of American gun lovers, I'm a good enough shot and get sufficient shooting practice that I find a sense of security in the .25 caliber automatic that I keep taped to the underside of my nightstand drawer.

Chuck took his attention away from his steak long enough to say, "I never would've believed it if someone had told me back in high school that Sam would grow up to be a beef-eating gun toter who likes to put bad guys in prison."

"Remember when she decided to be a vegetarian her junior year?" Dad was laughing so hard I thought he was going to choke. "God, she tried. Decided eating meat was so barbaric."

Chuck was nodding his head in agreement. "Right. But, in the end, she hated the idea of being hypocritical even more, and, try as she could, she couldn't live a one-hundred-percent animal-friendly lifestyle."

That's why I've always felt so at home with Chuck. He got me. He could take the traits that other people see as so inconsistent and understand that they make me who I am. I eat like a pig, but I run thirty miles a week. I despise criminals, but I call myself a liberal. I'm smart as hell, but I love TV. And I hate the beauty myth, but I also want good hair.

To Chuck, it somehow all made sense, so I never felt like I was faking anything. Dad has never quite figured me out, but he sure enjoys making fun of me. "Poor girl drove me and her mother crazy trying to avoid leather, animal fat, anything that might make her seem like a hypocrite for telling everyone else how mean we were for eating meat."

I had to laugh too, remembering my mother's face when she opened her Christmas gift one year to find the hideous macramé purse I'd triumphantly presented as an alternative to her tried-and-true tasteful brown leather handbag.

"Does rubbing my face in my youthful attempts to be a good person make you guys feel good?" I said. "OK, you win. I love the smell of leather. I like being at the top of the food chain. I eat thick slabs of beef, still pink in the middle. Vegetables are what my food eats. Are you happy now? Maybe we should talk about the time Chuck joined the feminist center in college so he could scam on women. Or how about, Dad, when you got a CB radio and grew a mustache after you saw *Smokey and the Bandit*? What was your handle again, the Rocking Ranger?"

We continued like that, recalling our most embarrassing moments—at least the ones clean enough to tell in front of my dad—until the high-pitched beeping of a pager broke through our laughter. By instinct, Chuck and I both immediately hit the "stop making that wretched noise" button on the right side of our waists and looked down at the digital display. "It's me," I said. "Grace. I better get it."

Grace was calling to let me know that she'd dropped off Kendra and to wish me luck with trial the next day. She also told me that when she went inside with Kendra, Kendra had played the answering machine in front of her. Apparently, her old friend Haley was looking to get back in touch with her, had heard that she was living at home again, was wondering what she was up to, that sort of thing. It was hard not to be furious as I remembered my only encounter with the girl.

I tried to keep cool as I dialed Kendra's number.

"Hey there. How you holding up?"

"Alright, I guess. I just want the trial to be over with."

I said what I could to relieve the anxiety. In the end, there's nothing you can say to comfort a victim who senses the system's potential to fail.

I raised the phone message from Haley with caution. "Grace mentioned that Haley is trying to get in touch with you. I didn't realize you had stayed in contact with her."

"I haven't. She called, that's all."

"She give you any idea what she wanted?" I said.

The distinctively teenage sulk came through loud and clear over the phone. "Will you please, like, not freak out? She was just wondering how I was doing."

I didn't like the idea that Haley might be working her way back into Kendra's life, so I said what I could to discourage her from returning the call. I knew in the end she'd do what she wanted.

I'd been looking forward to curling up with a book and going to bed early when I got home. That's not what happened.

I should've known something was wrong as soon as I put my key in the lock. Vinnie usually runs to the front door to welcome me home. OK, so it's more of a waddle. The point is that he comes to the door when he hears my keys. This time, I could hear Vinnie barking, but he wasn't at the door.

I remember the noise behind me in the dark as I bolted the front door. And I think I remember feeling the crack against my head that quickly followed, but maybe I fabricated that memory later with the help of blinding head pain and a lump the size of a golf ball.

When I came to, the clock told me I'd been out for an hour. My house was a wreck. Cupboards were open, cushions were thrown, drawers were emptied. And I could still hear Vinnie's muffled barks from somewhere in the back of the house.

As much as I wanted to run to him, I'd watched enough scary movies to know what to do if someone might be in your house. What you don't do is creep around in the dark silence. That's how you wind up skewered by some guy in a bad mask.

Instead, I went to my car, started the engine, and used my cell phone to call 911. And my dad. And then Chuck. And then I realized I could call everyone I knew, and it wouldn't get the first of them here any faster.

So I waited and watched. Even when I could hear the sirens, still no sign of life. Whoever tore the place apart must have left after knocking me out.

Two patrol officers swept through the house while the EMTs finished checking me out in the ambulance. No concussion, just assurances that I'd have a brutal headache for the next forty-eight hours.

The police cleared me to enter after I showed them my ID and assured them I knew how to handle a crime scene. A pane in the back door had been smashed to gain entry.

Chuck and Dad showed up around the time I was freeing Vinnie from the kitchen pantry. Knowing Vinnie, he'd made a valiant effort, but it doesn't take much to kick a French bulldog into the nearest closet. He put up a brave front when I picked him up, but I could feel him shaking.

Dad kept on eye on me, while Chuck pulled rank to make the patrol officers page out a technician to search for prints. PPB doesn't dust every home burg, so I was getting special treatment. Must have been the nasty knock to the head.

When he was done with immediate business, Chuck came into the kitchen where my dad was fixing me a drink and monitoring the ice pack on my head. "You doing OK?"

"Yeah, I guess."

"How's the mutt?" he said, smiling as he flipped one of Vinnie's ears over.

"Seems to be getting over it. Dad's going to take him to the vet for me tomorrow just to make sure he's alright."

One of the young patrol officers walked in and gave the kitchen a cursory lookover. "Man, they really did a number, didn't they?"

I looked around and took in just how bad the place looked. And then I took it out on the patrol officer. "Better call off the crime scene team. McGruff the Crime Dog here has got the whole thing figured out. Yep, they really did a number on the place. I hadn't picked up on that, Mr. Sensitivity. Jesus Christ, get yourself a copy of Policing for Idiots before you go out on any more calls." I put my hands against the kitchen table, pushed my chair back, and stormed over to the sink to look out the window.

Dad came to my side and patted my shoulder while I fought back tears and tried to regain my composure. When I'd gotten myself under control again, Chuck suggested that I look around when I was ready to see if anything was missing. As I started to leave the kitchen, the patrol officer said, "Just make sure you don't touch anything, ma'am."

I didn't turn around, but I heard Chuck say, "You got a death wish or something, Williams? Use your fucking head."

The only valuables I own are some jewelry I inherited from my mother, and I'd be surprised if anyone ever found those. If every old house has some irregularity that invites fantastic stories, mine is an old wall safe that someone had built into the baseboard of my bedroom. The day I was entrusted with my mother's jewelry, I locked it inside that safe and moved my solid maple headboard directly in front of it.

The bed was right where I'd left it. In fact, nothing seemed to be missing, making me wonder why someone had bothered.

We were throwing around theories in the kitchen, with me desperately searching for one that didn't involve any further mortal danger. First I floated the typical teenage thrill burg. Wanna-bes get a high off being in another person's house, going through their stuff, and trashing the place. But they probably wouldn't have slugged me in the noggin.

My next front-runner was a small-time junkie thief who broke in and then went nuts and trashed the place when he realized I didn't own the kinds of things that small-time junkie thieves steal, like CDs, DVDs, and other small items that are easily resalable to those who live in the modern world.

That theory just might have stuck, at least for the night, if I hadn't decided I needed a beer.

I opened the fridge to find my twelve-inch chopping knife prominently displayed on the top shelf. It secured a note that said, *Next time we slice up you and your dog. It's that easy.*

So much for a theory that didn't scare the shit out of me.

| 7 |

Like any other crime victim, I could do nothing about the intrusion into my home and assault upon my person except wake up in a messy house with a pounding headache.

PPB had assured me that they'd do what they could to find prints, but I knew there wouldn't be any. And I assured PPB that I'd go over my files to identify anyone who might want to scare me, but I felt in my gut that it had something to do with Derringer. Unfortunately, Derringer currently enjoyed the greatest protections a defendant can enjoy. Lopez had served me and the police department with written notice that he was invoking his rights to counsel and to silence, which meant that, while his trial was pending, the police couldn't question him about anything, even suspected new crimes.

The truth is that prosecutors are rarely threatened. Some speculate that it's because they are feared, but the real reason prosecutors are generally safe from the scum they prosecute

is that they're replaceable. You take out your prosecutor and
nothing changes. The same witnesses bring the same evidence to the same jurors, only with a different mouthpiece
coordinating the show.

Unfortunately, an occasional defendant is too stupid to
see that reality, and I suspected Derringer was one of them.
Now I had to go into trial with yet another reason to feel sick
whenever I looked at him.

The first day of trial was mercifully quick. Judge Lesh had
reviewed all the written motions in advance and was ready
to rule on them without holding an evidentiary hearing. Even
though the appearance took only a few hours, I still found
Derringer's presence disconcerting. I'd almost hoped he'd
throw me a look to confirm my suspicion that he was behind
the ransacking. His seeming indifference only served to foster the combination of rage and fear that I'd been nursing
since the previous night. I tried to use it to fuel my concen-
tration on the pending motions.

I was nervous about Lopez's motion to exclude the false
alibi Derrick Derringer had volunteered for his brother the
last time around. It was my position that this was relevant
in determining whether Derrick was telling the truth now.

Lisa argued that the evidence was too prejudicial to provide to the jury. Or, as she put it, "Your honor, Ms. Kincaid
knows full well that, under the Rules of Evidence, my client's
prior conviction is inadmissible. By framing this evidence as
impeachment of Derrick Derringer, she's trying to find a way
to get my client's prior conviction through the back door."

Lesh went off the record. "Ms. Lopez, you're doing a good

job for your client, but if I were you I would avoid using the term 'back door' when referring to his prior conviction, which I see is for attempted sodomy."

David Lesh was one of those people who could say the most inappropriate things and yet somehow never offend anyone. A legendary story holds that when Lesh was still a prosecutor, one of the female judges and her law clerks saw him leaving the building wearing shorts. The judge jokingly commented that the DAs were letting their dress standards lapse a bit. Lesh's response? "I don't mind telling you, judge, that these legs are under a court order from the National Organization for Women. I cover these beauties, and those fanatical broads at NOW will have me arrested." The clerks held their breath, sure that their judge was about to unleash. Instead, the story goes, she laughed and said, "Well, in that case, counselor, you should at least get out in the sun periodically. You could blind someone with those things." My guess was that Lesh had so much going for him on the stuff that mattered that people were almost reassured by his irreverence.

Proving once again that he was a complete professional where it counted, Lesh went back on the record and made what I believed to be the right ruling. The jury should be allowed to consider Derrick's previous lie for the limited purpose of judging his credibility as an alibi witness in this trial. The problem was that if the jury knew the whole story, including the nature of Derringer's previous conviction, the unfair prejudice to the defendant would be overwhelming. So Lesh carved out a fair compromise.

"Here's what we're going to do, folks. First of all, the State can't get into any of this until after the defendant's brother has taken the stand and offered testimony to exonerate the defendant. Until he does that, Ms. Kincaid, the evidence you want to use is irrelevant.

"Even after the evidence becomes relevant, I am concerned about the potential for unfair prejudice. Ms. Kincaid, the only facts you really need to get to the jury are that Derringer—Derrick Derringer, I mean—provided an alibi for the defendant in the past and that the defendant, contrary to the proffered alibi evidence, eventually admitted that he was, in fact, at the scene. I assume you can find a way to put those facts into evidence without revealing the underlying charge to the jury or whether the defendant was ever actually convicted."

I nodded in agreement, but then said yes aloud so the court reporter could transcribe my answer.

"Alright, then, that's the plan. And, Ms. Kincaid, I cannot emphasize this enough. The facts that I just mentioned are all I want to hear from your witnesses on this matter: Brother supplied alibi for defendant, but then defendant later admitted he was there." He counted off the points on his fingers. "If I hear one other word—one mention of sodomy, or kidnapping, or a teenage girl victim, or the fact that a jury found the defendant guilty of something—I will declare a mistrial. And I may even declare a mistrial with prejudice. So I warn you to proceed with caution and make sure your witnesses understand the rules we're playing by. Do we understand each other?"

I assured him that we did, and he moved to the rest of Lisa's motions.

Lisa had filed a motion to suppress the evidence regarding Derringer's pubic hair. She tried to argue that the plethismographic examination and the jail booking process constituted unlawful searches in violation of Derringer's Fourth Amendment rights. But once she agreed that both processes were part of the normal corrections process and not intended to produce evidence of a crime, Lesh quickly denied the motions.

In the alternative, Lisa asked the court to prohibit Derringer's parole officer from testifying that he had seen Derringer without his pants at the plethismographic examination. She argued that the evidence was overly prejudicial because it revealed the fact that Derringer was on parole for a sex offense.

In the end, Lesh decided to permit Renshaw to testify that he was Derringer's parole officer and had occasion to see him without his clothes. The jury would not hear about the setting or circumstances. I didn't like it, because I thought the jurors might come up with their own oddball explanations as to why a parole officer would see a client naked. But I decided there was no other way to get Renshaw's observations in without letting the jury know about the prior sex offense, which surely would lead to a reversal on appeal.

"Alright," Lesh said. "Now, before I call a jury panel up here, let's see if my rulings on these motions change anything about whether we need to have a trial. I assume from the fact that we're here that the two of you have had plea negotiations on this case by now."

Lisa and I sat silently.

"Nothing?" the judge asked. He told the court reporter to go off the record. "What the hell are you two doing? Now, before I say what I'm about to say, Mr. Derringer, I want you to understand that my comments have nothing to do with my opinion about your guilt. I haven't heard the evidence, so I don't have an opinion at this point. And, in any event, that's going to be a decision for the jury, not me. But I've been involved in a lot of trials, both as a lawyer and a judge. And I've read the papers filed in this case, and I have some idea of what's coming around the corner."

He turned his attention back to me and Lisa. "I'll be frank with both of you. From what I've read in the motions and the warrants, Ms. Kincaid, you've charged the hell out of this case. Frankly, I'm surprised you chose to present this to the grand jury as an attempted murder."

Lisa was never one to pass up an opportunity to ingratiate herself with the court. She jumped in to thank Lesh for telling me what she'd been saying all along.

He stopped her cold. "Not so fast, there, Ms. Lopez. I've got even more for you. You may not have noticed, but your client's alibi rests on the word of his convicted felon brother who by all appearances has lied for the defendant before. Your client also is on parole for an offense that is strikingly similar to the one for which he now stands trial. I hope you have advised him that he is gambling in a very big way. I can tell you right now, if he loses, he won't be looking at a year in the pen this time. He's looking at a very long sentence, with a parole board that will remember that he burned them the last time."

Having reminded both of us of our weaknesses, Judge Lesh wanted to hear our offers. I offered to dismiss the attempted murder and other charges if Derringer would plead to the kidnapping and sodomy, with a ten-year minimum sentence. I offered to reduce that to seven if he'd flip on Suspect Number Two. Lisa wouldn't hear it. She wanted Assault Three with eighteen months—no cooperation. Lesh gave up when it became clear we'd never agree, and the clerk called up a jury panel.

*   *   *

Picking a jury can be the most difficult part of a trial. Most people can be convinced of just about anything, and one dud can sway enough of these sheep to yield very bad results.

One of my first trials in Oregon was a slam-dunk controlled buy. An undercover used marked money for the drug buy; then the surveillance officers who watched the deal followed the suspect, keeping track of him by his distinctive two-tone spectator loafers. When the defendant was popped in the men's room of a nearby restaurant, the marked drug money was in his pocket. The dummy blew any theoretical chance at an acquittal when he showed up on the second day of the trial wearing the same two-tone spectator loafers that every police witness mentioned the previous day when describing the suspect.

After three days of deliberations, the jury hung, 7 to 5, in favor of guilt. The judge was so incredulous that he broke from the usual procedure and permitted the lawyers to question the jurors before they were dismissed. Turns out that one particularly headstrong guy convinced four of the others that the defendant must be innocent, because no one would be stupid enough to wear those shoes to court under the circumstances. The four sheep found it difficult to defend the decision, saying repeatedly, "We just don't think he did it." When I asked the leader about the marked drug money, all he could say was, "Now, that was a problem for him. I'll admit that." The seven sane jurors looked like their heads were going to explode after spending three days trying to argue with that kind of logic.

My case against Derringer was strong, but I needed to weed out any jurors who might cut him loose on the most serious charges, thinking that the victim deserved what she got. In the end, Lisa bumped two retired women who looked at Derringer like they were already afraid of him. I bumped two men with previous assault arrests and two who said they were surprised that a person could be charged with raping a prostitute. The worse of the two said it sounded more like theft, then suppressed a chuckle. I was glad he said it, not only because I knew to bump him but also because I saw one woman flinch in revulsion. Lisa apparently didn't see it, because she left her on the panel. A definite keeper for me.

By the end of the day, we had picked our jury.

Deciding that personal safety required me to navigate even further into the twenty-first century, I bit the bullet and had a top-of-the-line home security system installed that night. I could tell by the way the installation guy eyed my trashed house that he didn't think I'd be needing it. I didn't bother explaining.

Just knowing that the system was there helped. I fell asleep the minute I hit the bed and didn't wake until the alarm clock advised me it was time to go to work. At least I'd be rested for the second day of trial.

I walked into Lesh's courtroom prepared for my opening statement. On the way in, I checked to make sure that my witnesses were there: Mike, the EMTs, and the kids who found Kendra were subpoenaed for the morning. I figured there was no way we'd get through opening statements and all those witnesses before lunch.

I had decided not to ask Kendra to attend the entire trial. Her mother could not miss enough work to accompany her, and I thought that the sight of Kendra sitting without a parent would feed the impression that she was something other than a victimized child.

Fortunately, Derringer wasn't going to be getting an upper hand in the sympathy arena by packing the halls with loving supporters. The only people in the spectator seats were a few curious court-watchers and Dan Manning, a young reporter for the *Oregonian* who was always trying to branch out beyond his normal neighborhood beat by picking up crime stories that otherwise wouldn't get covered.

I liked Dan. He tried to give potential future sources— people like me—good press as long as he could do it and still give the straight story. He stopped me as I was walking in. "Do you have a few seconds for a quote? I'm thinking about using this trial as a centerpiece for a larger special-interest article about the dangers faced by teen prostitutes. You know, hoping to ride the coattails of the renewed interest about the Jamie Zimmerman murder, now that Taylor's back in the news."

I prefaced my answer by explaining that the Rules of Professional Responsibility prohibit prosecutors from going very far in their statements to the media. I was relieved when he nodded; he knew the drill. For a prosecutor, media interviews are like navigating a minefield. Stay too safe within the lines, and your typical nitwit reporter looking for a story will make it sound like you don't believe in your case. Go too far, and you're looking at sanctions from the court and the bar.

I told Dan I'd be happy to talk to him if he would assure me that he wasn't going to print Kendra's name. He agreed, reminding me that the *Oregonian* was one of the few papers that had not abandoned its policy of withholding information about the victims of sexual offenses after the William

Kennedy Smith rape allegation triggered sensationalist paper-selling headlines.

I gave Dan a few canned quotes about the trial and also plugged DVD as an aggressive, proactive unit working to prevent girls from entering the world of prostitution and to arrest and prosecute the adults who lure them into it.

When it was time for opening statements, I delivered mine from memory, without notes.

"Good morning. In case you don't remember, my name is Samantha Kincaid, and I'm a deputy district attorney for Multnomah County. I represent the State of Oregon.

"I want to start this morning by thanking you for your candor when we spoke yesterday during the jury selection process. It is because of your honesty during that process that the twelve of you have been chosen to hear this case. And I am thanking you ahead of time, because I think you will find the next week or so to be a difficult one. It will be difficult because the process changes now. We don't get to talk to each other like normal people, the way we did yesterday. You are now jurors, and the rules of our trial system require a formality unlike any other setting in our society. You are entrusted with a profoundly important decision, but the rules require you to sit here passively, listening, without asking questions or even talking to one another about the case until all the evidence is closed and you begin your deliberations. I do not envy your task, but I promise to do my best to anticipate the issues you might find most important and to focus on them.

"But I think you will find this week to be difficult for reasons other than those faced by any person fulfilling a citizen's responsibilities as a juror. You face an especially daunting task because this particular trial will force you to focus on the sadistic acts of the man sitting over here, Frank Derringer."

I had their attention now. A few of them shifted in their chairs to move forward.

"You are going to hear facts about what Frank Derringer did to a thirteen-year-old girl named Kendra Martin—the kind of facts that most people go a lifetime without ever having to contemplate. This man"—I pointed to Derringer—"pulled Kendra Martin from the street, dragged her into a car driven by an accomplice, and drove her to an isolated parking lot with every intention of beating and raping her. And as he brutalized her face and body with his fists and forced her legs apart to take him, something happened that made Frank Derringer's already horrific violence escalate and turned this crime into something I wish I didn't have to tell you about.

"At the pivotal moment when Kendra Martin thought the defendant was going to force himself inside of her, the defendant found himself flaccid, unable to fulfill his intentions. So Frank Derringer found a different way to take out his rage against the scared thirteen-year-old girl who was pinned beneath him in the backseat of his car. He took a stick and rammed it repeatedly between Kendra Martin's buttocks. From the degree of tearing, doctors estimate that the stick was at least an inch and a half in diameter. They know it was made out of wood, because they found splinters inside Kendra Martin's anus. And when Kendra lay bleeding from the defendant's torture, Frank Derringer still didn't stop.

"The defendant told his accomplice to do what he couldn't do himself and then watched while this second man raped and then sodomized Kendra Martin, now barely conscious. And when the whole thing was over, these two men drove

Kendra to the Columbia Gorge and dumped her like a bag of garbage to die.

"You're going to learn that Kendra Martin hasn't lived the kind of life that most thirteen-year-old girls get to live. She's going to get on the witness stand and tell you very personal facts about her home life and her background. And she'll tell you that she's not proud to admit that when the defendant kidnaped, raped, and sodomized her and then left her to die, she was a runaway girl engaging in prostitution to support a growing heroin addiction. She'll also tell you that she initially tried to tell the police what Frank Derringer did to her without admitting her own troubles.

"But I believe that when she explains to you why she initially withheld some information from police, you will understand. You will also understand, and you'll determine from the rest of the evidence and from your own common sense, that Kendra Martin did not deserve what Frank Derringer did to her. She never consented to be tortured and left to die near Multnomah Falls.

"You will hear evidence that Frank Derringer plotted this crime in advance and then took extraordinary steps to avoid detection." I gave them a detailed preview of the evidence that Derringer had shaved his pubic hair during the days before the attack and then painted his car and replaced its interior the next day.

"You'll also hear from Detective Mike Calabrese. He'll tell you that he found Kendra Martin's purse in a trash can about a mile away from where the defendant and his accomplice dumped Kendra to die. An expert in fingerprint technology with years of training in this type of evidence will testify that a fingerprint left on the strap of the purse belongs to Frank Derringer."

I paused and looked across at the face of each juror to make sure that the jury realized the impact of the fingerprint evidence.

"After you've heard from all these witnesses and experts, I'll have a chance to talk to you once again. At that time, I think you'll find that the State's evidence is going to measure up to the strong case I've outlined for you here. And based on that evidence, I'm going to ask you to return verdicts of guilty on all counts. I'm confident that once you hear the horrendous facts of this case, and the overwhelming evidence establishing Frank Derringer's culpability, returning that verdict will be the easiest part of this entire trial for you."

Legal strategists say that jurors make up their minds about a case by the end of opening statements. At the end of mine, I felt like I had them. I took my seat at the state's counsel table, closest to the jury box.

When Lesh nodded to Lopez to indicate she should proceed, she rose from her chair, put her hands on Derringer's shoulders, and said, "Members of the jury, Frank Derringer would like nothing more than for you to hear the truth about what happened in this case right now, because he is an innocent man who wants to go home. But, your honor, as his attorney, I have decided to withhold my opening statement until the State has put on its case."

Lisa apparently had even less confidence in her case than I thought. I wondered if she had reserved opening to delay locking in her defense until she knew for certain what we had.

But Lisa had gone a little further than that, insisting that Derringer was innocent. Most attorneys go out of their way not to use that word; all they really want to hear is "not guilty," and in a courtroom "not guilty" is a far cry from innocence. If I wanted to be a stickler, I could argue that she made an opening statement by referring to the merits of the case. But what did I care? Better for me to put on a one-sided show.

I'd be putting on my witnesses earlier than I thought. So far, so good.

My first witnesses were Brittany Holmes and Parker Gibson, the high school students who found Kendra in the park and called the paramedics. With their preppy good looks, they could have been a couple of teenagers you see sailing and splashing water on each other wearing hundred-dollar khakis in those mail-order catalogs. But they were polite and articulate, so they were good witnesses.

The kids described their terror when they realized that they had tripped not over a log but over the bloodied and unconscious body of a young girl. What came across unmistakably was that when they saw Kendra, they saw a girl just like one of their friends or little sisters. They showed no judgment.

The EMT's testimony went just as well. Whether it was seen from the fresh outlook of a shocked teenager or through the lens of a skilled professional experienced in dealing with violence, this crime was a serious one. The people who were there to witness her condition firsthand all agreed that Kendra had been treated horrifically.

Mike Calabrese was up next, to explain how he and Chuck supervised the crime scene. He summarized the basic mechanics: marking off a perimeter, keeping a log of everyone who entered and exited, collecting and maintaining anything that looked like it might be physical evidence. That kind of stuff impresses juries.

Around the time they finished processing the crime scene, they got word from the hospital that the suspects had sodomized Kendra with some type of stick. "We didn't find anything in the immediate crime scene that could've been the weapon, and we couldn't search the entire park for a stick. But my partner, Chuck Forbes, noticed that the park put garbage cans along the side of the road. We decided to look in the cans along the road on the way out of the park on the long shot that the suspects threw the weapon in one of them."

"Did you locate anything in any of the garbage cans that might have been used to sodomize Kendra Martin?"

"No, ma'am, we did not." Mike's rough edges were barely detectable when he testified, I noticed.

"Did you find anything that you deemed to be relevant to your investigation?" I asked.

"We did," he answered.

"And what was that?"

Calabrese turned his head toward the jury box and answered. "Approximately a mile from the crime scene, I found a black leather purse on top of the garbage in one of the containers."

I cut in. "At this point in your investigation, Detective, were you aware that the suspects had taken Kendra Martin's purse from her?"

"No, ma'am, I was not."

"OK. So what did you do when you found the purse?" I asked.

"I wasn't sure whether it was related to our case or not, but it was suspicious in any event. I've been trained that discarded property is considered abandoned under the Constitution, so I'm permitted to search it without a warrant. I removed the purse from the garbage and opened it."

As long as he actually gets it right, I like it when an officer tells the jury the basis for conducting a search. It's not actually the jury's job to decide whether evidence was obtained lawfully. That's for the judge to determine. But you never know when you're going to get some wise-ass wanna-be ACLU'er on the jury who decides to convince the rest of them that some constitutional violation has occurred. "OK. And did you use your bare hands to remove the purse from the garbage and open it?"

"No, ma'am. I was wearing police-issue latex gloves during my search." He looked at the jury. "It wasn't much fun poring through that stuff even with the gloves." Some of the jurors laughed quietly, and he continued speaking to me. "Once I saw the purse, I removed the gloves I had been wearing and replaced them with a new pair. I was wearing those when I picked up the purse and opened it."

"And what did you find in the purse when you opened it?"

"Things that looked to me just on first appearance like they might belong to the victim, given her age. She had some gum in there, a tube of lip gloss, a change purse with a Hello Kitty sticker on it. Turned out to be empty. There was no official identification in the purse. The victim's just a kid, so there wasn't going to be a driver's license or the standard type of ID. I did find one of those wallet inserts that have the see-through plastic pockets to put pictures and credit cards in. It had a few pictures in there that looked like school photographs of some little kids. Some of the kids had written messages on the back of their pictures. They were addressed to

Kendra. I figured at the time that must've been the victim's name, but I subsequently confirmed that information with other detectives."

"Once you determined that the purse belonged to Kendra Martin and was involved in your investigation, what did you do?"

"My intention was to preserve the purse as I found it, so a crime technician could process it for fingerprints or anything else of evidentiary value. I took a plastic evidence bag from my car and, still wearing my gloves, I placed the purse in the bag, sealed it, and marked it with the date and my initials."

"And, detective, why did you mark the bag like that?"

"Whenever we seize physical evidence, we seal it in an evidence bag to protect it from tampering, then mark the bag with our initials and the date and time. The bag isn't opened until it gets to the crime lab. It's a way for us to make sure that what the crime lab gets is what we actually seized in the field."

In the same tedious question-and-answer format, we made our way through Mike's link in the chain of custody. He brought the bag with the purse inside of it back to the precinct and put it in the evidence locker. Luckily, he was the person who had "lab run" duty the next day, so I didn't have to bring in an extra witness to vouch for the walk from the Justice Center to the crime lab. Mike delivered it to Heidi Chung personally.

I spent the rest of the morning continuing to work step by mechanical step through my trial outline. I was running the show in the courtroom, since Lisa appeared to be doing little in the way of cross-examination. Of Brittany Holmes, Parker

Gibson, and the EMTs, she asked one question: "Do you have any personal knowledge to suggest that my client was one of the people who assaulted Kendra Martin?" Of course, they all said no. She didn't ask Calabrese a single question.

My guess was that she was saving the heavy stuff for Kendra.

| 8 |

Ray Johnson and Jack Walker were waiting on a bench outside of Lesh's courtroom when I got down to the fifth floor after the lunch break. I started having my witnesses meet me outside the courtroom soon after I became a DDA. That way, when the judges invariably start late, I can make use of the time by preparing my witnesses in the hallway. An added bonus of the practice is that it keeps the dirtbag informants in my drug cases out of my office and away from my stuff.

I assumed that the man sitting alone on a separate bench farther down the hall was Dr. Preston Malone, the emergency room resident who treated Kendra at the hospital. Anyone who's had a shower and hasn't ingested illegal narcotics within a couple of days stands out on a bench in the courthouse. Unless, of course, you can tell the guy's a cop, either from the uniform or the other sure signs—beer gut, bad tie, big gun, those kinds of things. In Preston Malone's case, the medical journal he was reading gave him away.

When Ray and Jack spotted me, they both opened their mouths to speak, but I rushed past them with one finger up to let them know I'd be right back. I wanted to touch base with Dr. Malone first. Typical of most physicians, he hadn't found time in his schedule to prepare his testimony with me. And, although I had Kendra's medical records for the grand jury, Dr. Malone hadn't appeared personally to testify. In other words, I had no idea what I was getting.

When he realized I was approaching him, he stood and offered his hand. From a distance, the guy looked really good. But standing close to him now, I could see that his profession was taking its toll. He hadn't shaved, his eyes were bloodshot, and his hair was a mess. Tell you the truth, I'm not sure that his eyes were completely focused. Coming out of ER like that? Scary.

He apologized for not being able to meet with me before trial.

"With the schedules we get at the hospital, it's pretty much impossible to keep an outside appointment. I have to admit, I was happy to get a subpoena. Thought maybe I could catch a nap while I was waiting. But when I was walking out, the attending physician gave me this medical journal and asked me to summarize the articles for him when I got back."

"You have to go back when you're done here? You'll probably be here until the end of the day."

He smiled. "Not the way a hospital defines the end of a day. I went in yesterday at six in the morning. I'll get home around ten tonight."

I vowed inwardly never to complain again about my workload.

I ran through the trial outline in my head. "Actually, I could put you on first so you don't have to wait around here."

"Um, thanks, but if it's the same to you, I'll wait as long as possible. I'm almost done with this journal, then I'm gonna crash right here on this luxurious wooden bench."

"I guess with your residency, you don't really need a suite at the Four Seasons to sleep," I said.

"No, but the thought is pure ecstasy."

I could tell he was about to nod off at the idea, so I got my trial prep in quickly. Malone's job would be to describe Kendra's demeanor and injuries. I hoped the nap would refresh him before his testimony.

I left him there, lying on the wood bench, and walked back to where Walker and Johnson waited.

"Pretty good kid, isn't he?" Walker said, nodding his head toward Preston Malone.

"Seems like a hard worker. You guys ready?"

"Let's roll, girl." I could tell Johnson was getting into witness mode.

After Lesh took the bench and brought the jurors back in, I rose and said, "The State calls Detective Raymond Johnson."

When he stood to walk to the witness seat, I noticed Claudia Gates, the heavyset middle-aged black woman on the jury, sit a little straighter in her chair and let her eyes follow Ray to the front of the courtroom.

For her sake, after I asked Ray to state his name, age, profession, and some other general background information, I added, "Are you married, Detective Johnson?" I'm not above playing to a juror's weaknesses.

Whether he knew why I was asking or whether he just has a natural charm, Ray Johnson gave the perfect answer: "Not yet, Ms. Kincaid. So far, the only woman in my life's my momma, but I'm still trying."

I thought I actually heard Claudia Gates's blood rush, but it was more likely the courtroom's crappy radiator.

I know. I'm a hypocrite. As much as I hate it that a good portion of my half of the species loses all rational thought when a good-looking man's in the room, I happily accept these boy-crazed women as jurors when my cops are hot.

Ray covered some of the same ground as the initial witnesses, describing the mood of the crime scene and Kendra's appearance when MCT first arrived. Then we talked about what happened after he and Jack separated from Chuck and Mike.

"When you saw Kendra Martin at the hospital, did you reevaluate your assessment of her injuries?"

"In some respects." He explained that Kendra's appearance substantially improved once the hospital staff cleaned the blood from her, but she was still in obvious pain, evidenced by severe bruising on her face and body, a large laceration across her nose and left cheek, and noticeable discoloration around her neck.

"After you initially spoke with Kendra Martin, did you have an idea in your mind about what had happened to her that night?"

"Yes, based on what she told me and my partner, Jack Walker."

"After the initial interview, did you speak to Kendra again about what happened to her that night?" I asked.

"Yes. After some additional investigation, Detective Walker and I spoke to the victim again when she was still in the hospital."

"Were her statements consistent with respect to certain sexual acts committed against her that night?"

"Yes."

"Was she consistent in describing the physical abuse that occurred that night?"

"Yes."

I could sense Lisa contemplating whether to object. Ray's answers were technically hearsay, even though they didn't reveal what it was that Kendra actually said to him. The answers were enough to reveal that Kendra had been sexually and physically assaulted. But Lisa stayed in her seat, and she was right to. If she objected in front of the jury, they might think she was trying to keep information away from them, and it was information they were going to hear anyway once Kendra testified.

I continued the pattern of questioning, establishing that Kendra's statements were consistent with respect to the most material facts.

"Were there some inconsistencies between the two statements?"

"Yes."

"Did Kendra have an explanation for these inconsistencies?"

"Yes. She admitted that she had omitted certain truthful information and had included some untruthful information in her initial statement to us."

Now, that one was definitely hearsay, since he was repeating something Kendra had said outside the courtroom and asserting it as truth. But the information helped the defense, so Lisa wasn't about to object.

Ray then walked through the portions of Kendra's initial statement that were not true, being careful as we had discussed never to call them lies. He explained that Kendra initially said she was in Old Town to go to Powell's Books and did not know how heroin ended up in her system.

"And Kendra admitted later that those statements were not true?"

"That's correct."

"Now, Detective, do you know what the defendant has been charged with?"

"Yes, I do. Attempted Aggravated Murder, Kidnapping in the First Degree, Unlawful Sexual Penetration in the First Degree, Rape in the First Degree, Sodomy in the First Degree, and Assault in the Third Degree."

"From an investigative standpoint, did the facts as Kendra Martin stated them in her initial interview indicate that those charges would apply in this case?"

"Yes."

"So, in other words, if someone had asked you right after you initially interviewed Kendra Martin what the suspect might be charged with, those are the charges you would have anticipated?"

"That's right."

"Would your answer to that question have changed after you learned Kendra Martin's actual reasons for being in Old Town and how the heroin ended up in her system?"

"No."

"Why is that?" I asked. "After all, the victim in the case changed her statement."

"She did change some details in her statement, but her

statements with respect to what the suspects actually did to her did not change. The charges would still be the same."

Ray wrapped up his testimony by describing the change in Kendra's demeanor from the first interview to the second. He was well-suited for this role. He actually managed to make Kendra's mood swings weigh in her credibility's favor. As he explained it, Kendra was initially very agitated. But once they made it clear that they were there to find out what happened to her and who did it, she was cooperative and focused. When they interviewed her again and indicated their concerns about her initial statement, she seemed embarrassed and worried that her honesty would hurt the case. Once she amended her statement, she seemed relieved.

After Ray was excused, I called Dr. Malone to the stand. I was worried that the bailiff might actually have to wake the poor guy up in the hallway, but apparently not. Moments later, Preston Malone strode confidently to the witness stand. I guess it's true that residency trains doctors to perform well regardless of the sleep deprivation.

Dr. Malone took the oath and explained his credentials to the jury. Pretty impressive. Undergraduate degree in biochemistry from Pomona, MD from Johns Hopkins. Played the viola in the Portland symphony in what he generously termed his "spare time." Damn. If I thought he had room in his schedule, I might've called him for a date.

We walked through Kendra's medical records together, with Dr. Malone explaining the cryptic notes that detailed the physical trauma that Kendra experienced. Knowing Kendra like I did, it was hard to listen to. But it was critical that the jury hear it.

"Dr. Malone, you have described what you have called tears to the wall of Kendra Martin's anus. After your physical examination of Kendra Martin, did you form an opinion as to what caused those tears?"

"Yes, I did."

"And what is your opinion?"

"You must understand that the anal wall is extremely sensitive to pressure. Most people experience detectable trauma simply from a standard bowel movement, so it's not unusual to detect some irregularity in what we call the 'anal wink.' In fact, I have seen patients report to the emergency room with voluntarily inflicted injuries in that particular area that are, as you might imagine, extremely abnormal."

A couple of the jurors shifted uncomfortably in their seats.

"And how would you describe Kendra Martin's injuries?"

"Severe. Even compared to very young sexual abuse victims, the trauma was incredible. There were no signs of lubrication, either chemical or natural. The only thing I can compare it to is an episiotomy, in which we enlarge the vaginal opening for childbirth. Of course, the patient is anesthetized for that procedure. Given the degree of injury this patient sustained, I would have expected her to need at least two weeks' healing time. It was only because of this particular patient's emotional resiliency that she was able to go home the following day."

"And were you able to form an opinion about what type of object created Kendra Marin's internal injuries?"

"Yes. With voluntary pressure, for comparison, it's not unusual to see perforations in the anal wall, but they tend to be superficial, and the use of lubrication minimizes the damage. In Kendra's case, the injuries were abrupt. Someone had subjected her to quick and intense pressure in specific areas. Moreover, I found several wooden splinters in her skin. This, as well as the degree of tearing, led me to conclude that she was penetrated abruptly and repeatedly with an unfinished wooden stick at least an inch and a half wide and seven inches long."

I pushed my hair behind my right ear as I looked down at my notes for a reminder of where I was and what I was trying to get out of this witness's testimony.

I hadn't discussed these questions with Dr. Malone, but I sensed that he had a nonobjective investment in the case. I chose my words cautiously to get the answer I wanted.

"During your medical residency, have you ever seen a patient as seriously injured as Kendra Martin was from the hands of another person?"

"No, I have not. Of course, I've had patients die, but it's always been from either natural causes or from some sort of weapon." Then he looked at the jury as if he'd been trained to do this. "But, as little sleep as I sometimes catch during my work in the ER, I had trouble sleeping after I treated Kendra Martin. Without a gun, without a knife, someone had physically ruined this child with his bare hands."

Several years from now, after tending to and losing scores of other patients to the hands of sadists, Dr. Malone might be able to offer unbiased, affectless testimony in a case like this. But, for now, he had crossed over from a detached observer into our side of things, and he wanted Frank Derringer to go away. I felt confident enough to wander into unventured territory with him as my witness.

"In your experience as an ER physician, do you develop a sense of a patient's chances for survival when they come to you for treatment?"

"Sure. The hardest part of being a doctor in the emergency

room is that we often get patients for whom it's too late to do anything. We lose a lot of people whose chances have passed before they even come to us."

"And, in your opinion, in light of your review of Kendra Martin's condition when she arrived for treatment, what would have happened to her if she had not been found in the Gorge and brought to you at Emanuel?"

He paused before responding. "I remind myself daily that I'm not God, that I don't know this world's truths any more than anyone else. But in my medical opinion, Kendra Martin's lucky those kids happened across her. Another couple of hours out there would have killed her. She was crazy high on heroin, but that, in and of itself, would not have killed her. It did, however, decrease her chances of surviving. She was losing a lot of blood from her anal injuries. Her blood pressure and pulse were low, which further reduced the rate of oxygen distribution through her body. And it was cold outside. I'm confident that if she were left overnight, she would have died."

I needed to write myself a reminder to keep this guy's name and number for future testimony.

When we were done talking about Kendra's physical injuries, I directed his attention to the effects of drug use. He started out by explaining that, although Kendra may have used heroin frequently enough to develop a physical addiction, she did not have the track marks that give away any hard-core addict.

"We've heard testimony earlier, Doctor, that Kendra Martin was 'popping' heroin when she used it voluntarily. Are you familiar with that term?"

He indicated that he was and explained that *popping* was the street name for shooting up with a subcutaneous injection. Relative newcomers to heroin could inject the dope just beneath the skin and still get a good high from it. Once they were hooked and needed a bigger high, they'd need to inject straight into a vein.

He explained that, on the night she was attacked, Kendra was under the influence of heroin that had been injected directly into a vein. To prevent her from overdosing, he had injected her with Narcan, a narcotic antagonist. Within a few minutes of injection, Narcan completely reversed the narcotic effects of heroin. Used on someone dependent on the narcotic, an antagonist could trigger extreme symptoms similar to withdrawal. It helped explain the severe mood swings and general nastiness that Kendra displayed toward the police that night.

Finally, Lisa had a cross-examination ready. It wasn't unexpected. Malone had to concede that heroin had adverse effects upon a user's memory. It was an obvious point, but jurors always listened more carefully when it came from a doctor. Fortunately, I had plenty of evidence to back up Kendra's ID, so I wrote the day off as a win for our team.

To reward myself for my great day in trial, I picked up some Pad Thai at Orchid Garden on my way home. Two hours later, I was lacing up my New Balances. The peanuts weighed me down for the first mile or so, but after ten minutes I started to work out my stride and could feel the endorphins kicking in. Seventeen minutes after I started, I finally reached my two-mile turnaround point at the Rose Quarter, home of the Trailblazers. I know a lot of runners who claim to reach a meditative state when they run. I'm not one of them. I get bored, and my mind wanders. As I finished my lap around

the stadium and began heading back up Broadway toward
my neighborhood, I was laughing to myself about the joke
at work that the DA's office needed a separate sports celebrity
unit. A better name for Portland's NBA team would be the
Jail Blazers.

And it wasn't just the basketball team. After the local ice
skating princess gained infamy for having had her rival
slugged in the thigh with a stick by a very fat bodyguard, she
supposedly settled back into her hometown for a quiet and
humble retirement, disturbed only by the occasional bout of
celebrity boxing. The reality is that she partied like hell and
had restraining orders against her ex-husband and the four
ex-boyfriends she'd gone through since him. Apparently all
these people hung out at the same handful of cowboy clubs
and trailer-park bars, and the princess called the police to
enforce the restraining orders every time she happened to
run into one of her exes. Throw in the state's mandatory
arrest law for restraining-order violations, and you've pretty
much got yourself a case to be reviewed every Monday morning, all involving a woman whose name always invites some
kind of media attention.

This line of thought got me through another half a mile
or so. I was passing the Fred Meyer parking lot, about a mile
from my house, when I noticed the car: a brown Toyota Tercel at the back of the lot, close to Broadway, far beyond
where a shopper needed to park at this time of night. It was
too dark to make out the face of the person inside, but I could
see the ember of a cigarette burning near the steering wheel.

It could be anyone. Maybe Fred Meyer made employees
park at the back of the lot. Or maybe the guy was waiting for
his wife to get off work. Or he could be sneaking out of the

house to get a few drags of nicotine in his car. Then there
was the possibility that the guy I saw at the zoo was out to
finish me off, having already trashed my house, kicked my
dog, and knocked me out.

I couldn't make out the license plate. I thought about running through the lot to get a closer look, but I couldn't think
of any way for just my eyes to cross the street while my body
stayed a safe distance away.

So I kept running and tried not to be obvious as I looked
up and down Broadway to make sure I wasn't being followed.
When I was a couple hundred yards past the lot, I saw the
car pull out onto Broadway in my direction. When it stopped
for a red light, I ducked into a convenience store on the corner and pretended to peruse the tabloid headlines until I saw
the car go through the green light and disappear into the
other traffic down Broadway.

I eventually got up the nerve to run home. Well, not that
much nerve. I took a route that involved running an extra
couple of miles and jumping over my back fence.

After locking myself inside my house and setting the
alarm, I went straight to my handbag to find the license plate
number I'd scribbled down at the zoo. I looked on both sides
of all the bills, but I couldn't find it. I must have spent it.

Given the turnaround of cash in a register, the likelihood
of it still being wherever I'd spent it was next to nil. Orchid
Garden was most recent, so I gave it a try.

The employees were closing the place down for the night.
They looked alarmed when I started banging on the door to
get their attention, but after I flashed my DA badge, a pimply

bespectacled girl let me in. I pled my case to an eighteen-year-old kid who wore a tie with his striped shirt to denote his authority as the night-shift manager, and he finally let me fish through their singles.

After all that work it wasn't there.

"I told you so," the tie guy reminded me. "I told you, when we take your money, it goes in the top of the drawer, so it's the first one paid out."

Like I needed him to explain that to me. I thanked him anyway and went home angry at myself. Now I had no idea if the brown Tercel had anything to do with any of this.

I managed to fall asleep, but my pager woke me up shortly after the wee hours had kicked in. I recognized the number as Garcia's cell, so I returned the call. He could tell from my voice that he'd woken me and apologized.

"I wasn't sure whether to call you, but I'm down here at juvie with Haley Jameson. She got popped for loitering to solicit."

Portland's loitering-to-solicit ordinance was enacted just last year after the city ran into problems proving prostitution cases under the state statute. In practice, the only way to prove an agreement to exchange sex for money was to conduct sting missions using undercover officers posing as either prostitutes or johns. It was an expensive and time-consuming process, and the sting missions had gotten out of hand. To avoid the stings, the regulars all started insisting on free samples before they'd negotiate the date: "Let me touch your cock so I know you're not a cop." What real john's going to turn that down? For obvious reasons, though, the bureau prohibited officers from engaging in sexual contact with suspects.

The beginning of the end for sting missions was when an

officer decided to get clever, put a nine-inch rubber replica in his pants, and whipped it out on an unwitting prostitution suspect. Actually logged it into evidence after the bust. PPB didn't like it, so they started hiring non-police informants to conduct the stings. When the weekly scandal rag disclosed that Portland's finest were paying losers to get hand jobs, the entire vice unit almost got shut down. The result, fortunately, was the adoption of a loitering-to-solicit ordinance. Everyone wins: Police get to stop the street-level prostitution that no one wants in their neighborhoods without having to conduct stings, and the johns and prostitutes take a lesser punishment from a city ordinance instead of a state statute.

As Tommy described it, Haley's loitering pop was pretty typical. Time of day, red-light neighborhood, flagging down cars with men in them. It was usually enough.

"She saying anything?" I asked.

"Nope. She's making it real clear that it's nothing new and she knows the only thing that's going to happen to her is mandatory counseling that she'll never attend and assignment to a foster home that she'll immediately run away from."

"I don't see a lot we can do then, Tommy."

"Agreed. I only called you because she brought up your name. As tough as she's playing, I think she'd like to get out of it if she could do it without any work on her part. She told me Kendra said the female DA on her case was alright, and that if we had told her that day in February that you were a friend of Kendra, she might not have been such a bitch."

"Did she say when she talked to Kendra?" I asked.

"Not exactly, but it sounded recent." I knew I shouldn't have believed Kendra when she said she hadn't been staying in touch with Haley. "Anyway, since she brought up your

name and is apparently hanging with your vic again, I
thought I should call you. You want me to cut her loose?"

I thought about it. It would do Kendra some good to see
the consequences of the life she'd left behind. "Screw her.
Unless she's willing to give us something useful for vice, put
the case through."

"I figured as much but thought it was your call. I'll
give her my card and tell her to call me if she wants to share
any info?"

"Go ahead, but I don't see it happening."

I had a hard time falling back asleep.

| 9 |

The next day of trial continued uneventfully. Things move along surprisingly smoothly when the defense never objects or cross-examines your witnesses. Lisa's silence initially made me nervous, because I suspected she was reserving the hardball for Kendra. I was wrong, though.

After Jack Walker's testimony, Kendra took the stand and walked the jury through her life story. Two female jurors wiped away tears when Kendra talked about what Derringer had done to her.

To my surprise, Lisa took the high road on cross. She didn't roll over, but she didn't rip Kendra apart, either.

The entirety of Lisa's cross focused on Kendra's heroin use; she did not discuss prostitution activity at all. And even her questions about the drugs did not seem like a character attack. Instead, she zeroed in on the effects that heroin may have had upon Kendra's perceptions that night. Even I had to admit that her questions were fair.

After Kendra testified, I called Andrea Martin to the stand, primarily to humanize Kendra by showing the jury that she had a mother. Her testimony, which was limited to Kendra's recovery, was uncontroversial, and Lisa didn't cross-examine her. Andrea had to leave for work once she left the stand, but Kendra stayed for the rest of the day.

Pleased that Kendra had testified with relatively minor trauma, Chuck, Grace, and I took her to the Spaghetti Factory for dinner right after court got out. Nothing tops a hard day's work like a big plate of carbs followed by spumoni ice cream.

Most of the dinner conversation focused on the trial. Kendra wanted to know how I thought it was going and what it meant that Lopez hadn't been tougher on her. I tried not to get her hopes up, explaining that the defense attorney appeared to be going through the motions so that Derringer got a fair trial. I didn't voice my growing anxiety that Lopez was hiding something up her sleeve.

"Well, I don't think there's anything fair about it. He gets to sit there and glare at me while I have to talk to a bunch of old people I don't know about what he did. It was really embarrassing for me, and then he doesn't have to get up there at all. He just gets his fair trial? What about mine?"

I wasn't going to try to defend the system on this one. "You're right, kiddo. The rules aren't always fair. But you're playing by them, and I think things are going well. You did a great job today. I think those old people who don't know you *did* know that you were telling the truth."

Kendra held my eye for a moment, but then turned her attention to playing with her water glass. I was grateful when the waiter broke the awkward silence to top off our coffees.

When he left, the silence returned, and Grace invited Kendra out to the dock behind the Spaghetti Factory to look at boats. I considered proposing that I take Kendra instead; I'd been wavering about whether to broach the subject of her renewed contact with Haley Jameson, despite my warning.

I thought better of it, remembering the summer that our fathers forbade Grace and me from hanging around the school whorecake. Left to our own devices, we would have tired of her in a couple of weeks. But parental pressure backed us into a corner and we were stuck with helium heels for months. Plus, right now Kendra saw me as part of a system that was treating her unfairly. A walk with Grace could be just what she needed.

So I let my opportunity to talk to Kendra alone slip by and volunteered to wait around for the bill. Chuck offered to keep me company.

Once Grace and Kendra were out of earshot, he spoke up. "Hey, something came up at work today, and I wanted you to hear it from me and not from the news. It's probably nothing, but I know what the media are going to do with it. And that's going to bring up some stuff that's been bothering me already."

"Just tell me. What is it?"

"I guess the *Oregonian* received an anonymous letter today from someone trying to exonerate Landry and Taylor. Whoever wrote it claimed to have killed Jamie Zimmerman."

"Jesus. Where the hell's that coming from?"

"Some crackpot. Who knows? Could just be someone who wants attention, like those people who turn up and claim to be serial killers. Given the politics around here, it could be some nut job against the death penalty. Someone trying to make a point, now that it looks like the state might actually move on some of these death sentences. All I know is it's bullshit."

"And I think people will see it the same way. It's going to take a lot more than some anonymous letter to a newspaper to reverse those convictions."

"Honestly? I'm not even worried about the conviction. I went through this crap already a few years ago. Landry's attorney tried to make me out to be some rough rider, framing an innocent old lady to help my own career. It made me sick to my stomach when the best way to make the case was for that prick O'Donnell to argue to the jury that I didn't need to frame people, I could just milk my daddy's name to the top of the department."

I had never considered how rough the publicity from the Zimmerman case must have been on Chuck. And now it looked as if he was going to have to go through it all over again.

"I assume the department's investigating the letter?"

"Yeah, at the highest levels. The Chief met with your boss today, and they decided to assign Walker and Johnson, since they know the details of the original Zimmerman case. But Mike and I are off."

"I'm afraid to ask why."

"Like you need to ask why, Sam? Shit!" A family next to us turned their heads at the noise of Chuck's raised voice and his slap against the tabletop. He nodded at them and tried to whisper. "They obviously think that if anything went wrong in that investigation, it had to do with me. And Mike's my partner. So we're off, and I'm going to be the center of every-body's fucking conspiracy theory again."

There were actually good reasons for segregating Chuck from the investigation, even if the DA and the Chief were convinced—as I was sure they were—of the truth. But, for the second time tonight, I thought better of trying to defend the way things sometimes work.

"Chuck, I'm so sorry. Look, you know Ray and Jack are on your side here. They are *not* going to set you up. You know how much they believe in that case. Remember? I thought Walker was going to climax talking about Taylor's lethal injection."

I smiled, and Chuck shared it with me. "No, you're right. If they were trying to fuck me, they'd assign IA to it or bring in the Justice Department. Yeah, Walker and Johnson will handle it right."

It was quiet for a while. "Man, Sam, I've been stewing about this for hours, and you manage to calm me down. How do you do that?"

"You give me too much credit. You're not taking into account all those times when I'm the one who can rile you up like no one else."

I paid the bill, and we went out to meet Grace and Kendra. "OK, guys, it's probably time we called it a night." I put my arm around Kendra. "This chica's got school mañana."

She didn't look too happy about that one. But we finally managed to get her into Grace's car. Once again, Grace was a lifesaver. The last thing I needed was an hour-long car ride.

Chuck and I made small talk about Kendra while he walked me to my car. I could tell he wasn't ready to be alone, so it didn't surprise me when he asked if I wanted to catch a movie.

I looked at my watch. "Can't. Vinnie awaits, you know. Piss him off, and he seems to forget about his doggy door. Never know what I might find on my rugs."

I think he actually tried to hide his disappointment, but he looked worse than Vinnie does when I take away his Gumby baby. I caved.

"Why don't we rent something? Vinnie'd probably like to see you. But I get to pick."

He countered with his own conditions. "No subtitles. No cartoons."

Hard bargain, but it was a deal.

A warning to the wise. Don't rent one of those friends-who-fall-in-love movies with an old lover you've sworn off as just a friend. Around the time Harry asked Sally if she wanted to partake of a piece of pecan pie, I made the mistake of pointing out that the film's only flaw was how implausible it was that they didn't figure out earlier that they belonged together.

"Yeah?" Chuck said. "Well, take a look at us. Some people might say that we should've figured out a few things ourselves by now."

It was the first time either of us had ever acknowledged out loud the potential to be more than friends again. I might like directness in every other aspect of my life, but I didn't think I liked it in this context.

"No mistakes here. We were made to have a beautiful friendship," I said with my best Bogart impersonation.

"Nope, not this time, Sam. Whenever I move a little closer to you, you pull out something goofy to help you scoot away. Cut it out with the *Casablanca*. I'm serious about this."

"Well, maybe you missed your chance to be serious. If you were serious, and you thought we were meant to be together, you wouldn't have dumped me."

He laughed out of exasperation. "Sam, we were kids back then. And I didn't want to dump you, as you put it. But I also didn't want to move down to California to learn how to be some corporate drone."

"Then you could've come with me and done something else," I said. I stood up and started heading toward the kitchen, but he took my arm and pulled me back down.

"You wouldn't have been happy, Sam. You had this idea in your head about what your life should look like, and back then I just didn't fit into it."

"Well, what makes you think you'd fit into it now? Maybe you'd start to feel like I was trying to change you again, and we wouldn't want that, now, would we?"

"I'd fit in, Sam, because you *don't* want to change me. We like each other just the way we are. The problem has been that you won't admit it. You won't accept that you like everything about me."

"Including your modesty?" I said, trying to laugh.

"Be serious for just a moment, OK, Sam? You know I match every part of that conflicted personality of yours. You like that I have this crazy job. You like that part of me is still a big kid. And you'll never admit it, but you love that I do what I want, even when it meant letting you down."

This time, when I stood, he let me. I went into the kitchen, poured a glass of water, and sat down at the table.

He came in after a few minutes. "When you found out your mother had breast cancer, you came to me, not Roger. And, today, when I heard about the letter to the paper, you were the one I wanted to talk to. We don't have to work out

everything in our history and our future right now. But don't
pretend you haven't thought about this, Sam. I'll go if that's
what you want, but I really do need you tonight."

It wasn't until the door closed that I realized I didn't want
him to leave yet. And that it was important enough that I was
willing to figure out the rest of it later.

He was still on my front steps when I opened the door.
He came back in, and we didn't talk again for the rest of
the night.

Given my long-standing commitment to keeping things
with Chuck platonic, I would have expected larger reper-
cussions from the night's activities. But the sky didn't fall,
lightning didn't strike, and I didn't even regret it in the
morning.

The truth was, I hadn't felt that good for months. Whether
it was just the aftereffects of the great sex remained to
be seen.

And it had apparently taken Chuck's mind off the Taylor
investigation. He hadn't even watched the local news before
we went to sleep.

Unfortunately, reality set back in quickly. While I scurried
around the house picking up the various items of clothing
strewn on the path between the front door and my bed,
Chuck grabbed the *Oregonian* from the porch.

The story about the anonymous letter was a long one and
had made the front page of the Metro section. Putting aside
my outrage that the press had gone forward on the basis on
a single anonymous unconfirmed letter, I could acknowledge
that the story was actually fair. It raised the possibility that

Taylor and Landry were innocent, but it also quoted experienced criminal investigators who were familiar with the common phenomenon of false confessions in high-profile cases. Some even suggested it might be a publicity stunt by a death-penalty opponent.

Although the paper did not reprint the letter itself, I was surprised by the amount of detail revealed about the letter's contents. The typewritten letter was mailed from Roseburg, a logging town a couple of hours south of Portland. According to the report, the letter described with dispassion the grizzly details of the final hours of Jamie Zimmerman's life and her horrible death. Its anonymous author claimed to have been playing pool at Tommy Z's when he saw Jamie Zimmerman running her tongue across her parted lips, watching him while she did a nasty dance in front of the jukebox. She made it clear what she wanted when she graphically simulated fellatio on the last of many bottles of Rolling Rock he bought her.

I looked up from the paper. "Tommy Z's? Did that come up in the investigation?"

Chuck nodded. "Truck stop slash biker bar in southeast Portland. It was reported during the trial, though, so anyone could know about it. Margaret Landry said Taylor picked up Jamie there. We found witnesses who placed Taylor at the bar around the time Jamie disappeared, and Jamie was known to hang out there sometimes."

I went back to the article. The author claimed that Jamie danced for a couple of songs and then walked over to him and said she noticed him because he looked dangerous. After some token small talk, he drove her back to his apartment. In the privacy of the apartment, the dance she began at

Tommy Z's evolved into a strip tease and a lap dance. After the two began to engage in what the article paraphrased as "consensual intercourse," what might have been merely a desperate exchange of bodily fluids between two pathetic lives took a violent turn. According to the author, a drunk Jamie started laughing during the act itself, mocking her anonymous lover about the size of his manhood. The man hit her repeatedly, telling her to shut up. The author wrote that he initially wrapped his hands around Jamie Zimmerman's throat to silence her taunts. But when her eyes started to bulge and she began tensing her entire body in an effort to free her throat from his grasp, he realized he wouldn't stop; that he had never felt such power and gratification as through her suffering.

When I'd finished reading, I looked up at Chuck. He read my thoughts. "You're going to tell me it could be worse, right?"

I nodded.

"I know this kind of stuff happens in death cases and it's something I've got to deal with, but I'm telling you, Sam, I just don't have it in me. At Landry's trial, the entire defense was based on an attack against me as a cop and—a person. That guilty verdict, and the verdict against Taylor: I saw those as vindication. I haven't even been able to deal with my feelings about Taylor's execution, because I can't separate my feelings about the execution itself from the stress I was feeling about the publicity that would go along with it. I knew that somehow this would come back around to me."

I stood up and took him in my arms. He held me tightly, and I could feel his body begin to shake. "Dammit, Sam, I didn't do anything wrong." I stroked his hair and ran my hand along his back, whispering shushing sounds in his ear.

Then I led him back to bed to comfort him the only way I could think to.

Chuck was scheduled to testify at the trial that morning, but we went to the courthouse separately to make sure we weren't seen arriving together. I hoped that concentrating on his testimony would take his mind off the letter.

Chuck was a great witness. The description of the search of the car could have been one of the moments when I lost the jurors, but Chuck's personable style helped keep their attention. He explained that he had not located any blood or other physical evidence of an assault in the car, but that the car looked like it had new paint, carpet, and upholstery. Transitioning into the work order from the auto detail shop, I asked, "Were you able to determine, Detective Forbes, whether your initial impression was correct?"

"Yes, I was."

"And how were able to verify that, Detective?" It felt good when we made eye contact, but I looked away so as not to get distracted.

"During the search of the car, I located an invoice from the Collision Clinic, an automobile detailing shop at Southeast Eighty-second and Division."

I showed him the invoice and he verified that it was the paper he had found during the search. I said to Judge Lesh, "Your honor, the parties have stipulated that the contents of the invoice are in fact accurate."

Judge Lesh turned to the jury and delivered the standard instruction for stipulations like these. "Members of the jury, the parties have agreed that it's unnecessary to call someone with firsthand knowledge about the contents of this exhibit to testify. Essentially, they have agreed that the document is exactly what it appears to be and that what's written on it is true."

When the judge was finished, I turned back to Chuck. "What does the invoice indicate?"

"It shows that Frank Derringer paid eight hundred dollars for new paint, upholstery, and carpet for the vehicle."

"And does it indicate when the work was completed?"

"Yes, it does. The work was done the day after Kendra Martin was abducted."

I paused to make sure that the jury understood the implication. Then, for the truly dense, I followed up. "So, one day after the assault on Kendra Martin, and before you were able to search it, Frank Derringer paid someone to replace the carpet and upholstery on the interior of his car?" Chuck agreed. "And one day after the assault on Kendra Martin, Frank Derringer paid someone to change the appearance of his vehicle by painting its exterior?" Yes, again. "And he paid eight hundred dollars for this work?" Yes.

"Detective, are you familiar with the *Blue Book* for automobile prices?" Yes. I pulled out the photocopy of the relevant page from the *Blue Book* and asked Chuck to refer to it. "Based on that, Detective, what is your estimate of the maximum fair market value of Frank Derringer's vehicle, prior to the work he had completed at the Collision Clinic?"

"Twelve hundred dollars."

"And what is your estimate of the fair market value after he paid eight hundred dollars for the work at the Collision Clinic?"

"Fourteen hundred dollars."

Lisa was predictably gentle on cross. Yes, Chuck admitted, some people spend money to improve houses and cars, even if they might not get the money returned. And, yes, he conceded, it may have been worth eight hundred dollars to Mr. Derringer to have a new feel to his car. When Lisa finished her questioning, reserving the right to recall the witness later, I didn't see any need to redirect. Instead, I caught Chuck's eye as he left the witness stand. I was right. Testifying in a solid case with an easy cross had taken his mind off the Zimmerman debacle.

The trial was trucking along smoothly. I began to suspect that my paranoia about Lisa's strategy was exactly that—paranoia. Perhaps she had simply concluded there was no reason to knock herself out trying to save Derringer. She didn't even try to attack the accuracy of the fingerprint evidence when the criminologist, Heidi Chung, called a match based only on six points. Her only questions concerned the timing of the latent print found on Kendra's purse. Chung conceded the point that must always be given up on fingerprint evidence: Although she could state with confidence that the defendant had left his fingerprint on the victim's purse, there was no way to determine when the print had been left behind.

On redirect, Chung explained to the jury that it was *never* possible to determine from physical evidence alone when a fingerprint was left behind. All the physical evidence could do was confirm that the suspect had touched that item at some point prior to the print's discovery.

Through the end of my case-in-chief, the only witness Lisa cross-examined in any detail was Dave Renshaw, Derringer's probation officer. She didn't get far.

The sole purpose of Renshaw's testimony was to show that when Renshaw saw Derringer's private parts a few weeks before Kendra was assaulted, they were still covered with hair like most other people's privates. Lisa tried to rattle Renshaw's testimony by pointing out that he didn't actually examine Derringer physically and was not looking specifically at that physical feature. In the end, though, there was no way to get around the obvious: A shorn scrotum stands out.

The only other line of questioning she had for Renshaw concerned Derringer's probation record. Renshaw admitted on cross that Derringer had kept all their appointments, stayed in regular contact with him, and maintained regular employment. Lopez even went through a list of the various temp jobs Derringer had worked since he got parole: day labor, grill cooking, stockrooms, inventories.

I could've objected on the basis that Lisa's questions called for inadmissible character evidence. She was, after all, trying to establish that Derringer had been keeping his nose clean, which had nothing to do with the issues in the trial. But any objection would invite a bullshit attempt to justify the evidence in front of the jury. Lisa would probably argue something to the effect that the evidence contradicted the State's theory that Derringer planned the abduction ahead of time or was associating with a possible accomplice. I figured any minimal benefit she got out of the questioning was a reasonable price to pay to avoid giving her an opportunity to make a speech for the jury.

As it turned out, Renshaw was a pro who could diffuse Lisa's points on cross without my assistance on redirect. After Lisa had established that Derringer had reported all address changes, met all appointments, spoken regularly with Renshaw, and worked full-time on parole, she asked one question too many: "Isn't it true, Mr. Renshaw, that Mr.

Derringer complied fully with the conditions of his parole?"

"Sure, counselor. I guess you could say he was a model parolee—except for the fact that he kidnapped, raped, sodomized, and tried to murder a thirteen-year-old girl."

I think I saw Lesh smile as Lisa leapt to her feet to object. Her objection was sustained, but the exchange kept Lisa quiet for the rest of my case-in-chief.

| 10 |

I had spent the week presenting my case to the jury, witness by witness. Building a prison for Frank Derringer with evidence, each piece stacking upon the last like bricks. Now I was ready to sit back and watch Lisa Lopez struggle to save face. I wanted it. I wanted it bad. I tried not to look smug and amused, which I was, when she stood on Thursday afternoon for her mid-trial opening.

"Ladies and gentlemen of the jury, my point is a simple one." She put her hands on Derringer's shoulders. "This man, Frank Derringer, is innocent." A simple statement, but it caught the jury's attention.

Lopez walked to the front of the jury box and continued. "Ms. Kincaid has done a fine job of presenting evidence the way she wants you to hear it. But what I want you to hear, and what you will conclude to be true, is that Frank Derringer finds himself on trial for a crime he didn't commit because a troubled and confused young girl who has led a very sad life mistakenly identified him as she was coming out of a heroin-induced haze."

Although Lopez conceded that Kendra "may have been subjected to horrendous acts," she went on to remind the jurors of the presumption of Derringer's innocence and the oath they had taken to evaluate the evidence dispassionately. But she wasn't just arguing that there would be a reasonable doubt about Derringer's guilt. She was using the word *innocent* repeatedly. The defense's position wasn't just that Derringer was not guilty in the legal sense because the State couldn't make its case, but that he was factually innocent. Jurors feel better about acquitting someone they believe is innocent, but Lisa's strategy was risky. It's harder to prove innocence than to establish reasonable doubt.

Lisa's quiet, contemplative tone became more urgent as she talked to the jurors about Derringer's alibi. Then she shifted her theme. "By the end of this trial, you will realize that Kendra Martin is a victim, but my client is as well. In fact, I believe that we will prove to you that both Mr. Derringer and Miss Martin are victims of the same wrongdoing."

I tried to maintain my typical trial composure, looking as bored as possible while the defense presents its case. But for the life of me, I couldn't figure out where Lisa was going with her statement.

"The wrongdoing that has brought Kendra Martin, Frank Derringer, and all of us together began about four years ago. Four years ago, Portland police officers found the body of another troubled young girl named Jamie Zimmerman in the Columbia Gorge. Jamie wasn't as lucky as Kendra. She was murdered—strangled—after being raped and beaten. Like Miss Martin, Jamie was a drug addict who supported her habit through occasional prostitution. Like Ms. Martin, she was raped and sodomized. Police found Jamie's badly decomposed body less than a mile from where Kendra Martin was located. Ms. Kincaid mentioned that whoever committed this crime took Kendra's purse. Well, guess what, ladies and gentlemen? Whoever killed Jamie Zimmerman took her purse too, and it was never recovered.

"Those are enough similarities that you're probably thinking to yourself right now that the two crimes might be connected. You'd certainly think our police would at least look into it, especially when you learn that the same detectives who testified in this case investigated Jamie Zimmerman's murder."

I was seething. How the hell did Lopez think she was going to get away with blindsiding me this way? I didn't know every detail of the Jamie Zimmerman investigation, but I knew enough to recognize that Lopez was trying to take advantage of that case's recent revival in the media to confuse the jury. I also knew that she had never bothered to mention to me that her defense had anything to do with the Zimmerman case.

There was nothing I could do, though, without playing into Lisa's hand. Any outburst from me would only add dramatic emphasis to her opening statement. So I sat there quietly while Lisa told the jurors about Margaret Landry and Jesse Taylor and their protestations of innocence, the recent letter to the *Oregonian* confessing to Jamie Zimmerman's murder, and a supposed conspiracy among Portland police to conceal the truth.

"Because a jury didn't hear the truth about that case three years ago, innocent people were convicted. I don't want you to make the same mistake. I don't want you to convict an

innocent person. So I'm going to make sure you get all
the evidence. You're going to hear not only how the police
messed up the Zimmerman case, but also how those same
detectives have bungled this investigation. They don't want
to admit that they missed a killer four years ago, and they
don't want to admit that they've got the wrong person again
now.

"Let me make something clear to you. I'm not required to
prove who killed Jamie Zimmerman. That's supposed to be
up to the police and the district attorney. But I think it's
important that you at least know about that case, because it
sure looks a lot like this one, and it's sure starting to look like
whoever did it is still out there.

"In the end, the evidence in this case may present more
questions than answers. We may never know who killed
Jamie Zimmerman, but I have a feeling you're going to suspect that it's not Margaret Landry or Jesse Taylor. I also have
a feeling that you're going to suspect that whoever killed
Jamie Zimmerman assaulted Kendra Martin. But one
answer you will have for certain: Kendra Martin identified
the wrong man, and Frank Derringer is innocent."

So my paranoia had been warranted. Lopez had a trick
up her sleeve after all. But what Landry and Taylor had to
do with Derringer's defense was beyond me.

Judge Lesh apparently agreed. When Lisa finished her
statement, he turned to the jury and calmly excused them to
their waiting room for a break. Then he sat back, crossed his
arms, looked at me, and said, "Before I flip my lid up here,
let me confirm, Ms. Kincaid, that Ms. Lopez never informed
you that she would be introducing anything having to do
with the murder of Jamie Zimmerman. Is that right?"

"That's correct, your honor. I'm forwarding to the court a

copy of the witness list I received from the defense before trial. I received no notice from Ms. Lopez that she would be springing the possibility of a serial rapist at trial, and she obviously reserved her opening statement so she could drop this bombshell as late in the day as possible."

Lesh looked at the witness list and shook his head. "Alright. That's pretty much what I figured. Ms. Lopez, give me a good reason why I shouldn't declare a mistrial right now and then send a letter down to the Bar suggesting that they look into this little stunt you've pulled here."

Oh, petty vengeance can feel so good. If I could've stuck my tongue out at her without anyone noticing, I would have. In fact, this was good enough to warrant a big wet raspberry, but I settled for my best poker face.

Lisa feigned ignorance as she rose from her seat. For someone like me—who roots for Sylvester to eat that damn baby-talking yellow bird—it was hard to take. "I apologize if I've done something inappropriate, Judge Lesh, but I believe I have complied with my obligations toward the State. I'm not required to do the State's work, your honor. All I have to do is disclose my witnesses, which I did, and I'm entitled to reserve my opening."

Lesh wasn't buying it. "You mean to tell me that the people on this list are going to raise the specter of a serial rapist who attacked the victim in this case and also killed Jamie Zimmerman three years ago?"

"No, your honor. Those witnesses serve a legitimate purpose—"

Lesh cut her off. "You mean the legitimate purpose of throwing the prosecutor off track?"

Lisa was on the edge. She was getting defensive. "Your honor, if Ms. Kincaid was thrown off track, that's not my fault. I do intend to question those witnesses. They don't know about the Jamie Zimmerman case, but the State's witnesses do. And Oregon's discovery rules are clear: I can call any witness named by the State without having to declare my intention to do so ahead of time. It just so happens that the same investigative team in this case handled the Zimmerman investigation."

I cut in. "I find Ms. Lopez's choice of words interesting. It seems to me that if these two cases didn't 'just so happen' to involve the same detectives, we might be hearing about some other old case that the MCT handled. This entire tactic seems manufactured to spring something at trial and catch the State off guard."

"I'm inclined to agree," Lesh said. "Ms. Lopez, you may be in technical compliance with the discovery statute, but you have certainly violated its spirit. It would've been nice of you to tell Ms. Kincaid what was going on here."

Lisa worked her jaw and looked for words. "With all due respect to your honor and to Ms. Kincaid, my job isn't to be nice. My job is to defend my client. I sincerely believe that Mr. Derringer is innocent. If I had trusted Ms. Kincaid to believe my sincerity, I would have gone to her in the hopes that she would dismiss this case and reopen the Zimmerman investigation. But from the minute she walked over to the Justice Center to handle the arraignment on this case personally, your honor, Ms. Kincaid has made it clear that she wants to hammer my client. So I weighed my options and decided on this one."

I started to defend myself, but Lesh didn't see a need for it. "Ms. Lopez, I'm letting you know right now that both you and Ms. Kincaid have appeared before me several times since I've been a judge, and up until today I've never had reason to question either of your ethics. Your attempt to impugn Ms. Kincaid's integrity has failed with me. I hope you understand that. Now, here's what we're going to do. I have deep suspicions about your intent, Ms. Lopez, in holding your cards so close to your chest. But it looks like you have stayed within the letter of the law. So for now you're not in lawyer jail. Consider yourself lucky."

When a slight smile registered at the edges of Lisa's mouth, Lesh leaned forward. "Not so fast, Ms. Lopez. Your strategy will have its consequences. You can't have it both ways. You're going to have to make your case with the State's witnesses and the ones disclosed on this sorry witness list. I won't let you parade a couple of convicted murderers in front of this jury, and I won't let you bring in anything you can't get through those witnesses. With that in mind, I suspect that much of what you said in your opening statement is hearsay. At the end of the trial, I will instruct the jurors that they should disregard anything you said in opening that wasn't actually proven through evidence during the case. With that said, it's time we brought these jurors back in, so we can get on with this trial."

I rose to address him. "Your honor, the State requests a continuance. I need time to research this defense. I'd like two weeks to investigate any possible connection between this case and the Zimmerman murder. I assure the Court and Ms. Lopez that if we determine a connection, we'll proceed as necessary from there."

I could tell from the way that he tilted his head and smiled that he sympathized, but he wasn't going to give me any time. "I understand that you've been put in a jam, but you don't really think you're going to find a connection between these cases. What you want is time to disprove a connection so you can nip this defense in the bud. Trust me, I understand that desire.

"But Ms. Lopez is right. The defense is not obligated to disclose its theory ahead of time, only its witnesses and any alibi defense. Basically, she's allowed to drop these little bombshells. I suspect it's one of the things that make being a defense attorney entertaining. If she really wanted to screw you over, she could've waived opening altogether and hid her cards until testimony."

He told me he'd give me some leeway during rebuttal to recall witnesses, but it was little consolation.

As an alternative, I moved to exclude any evidence relating to Zimmerman's murder, at least until I had a chance to file a written motion to exclude Lopez's defense. In my urgency to point out that Lisa had been a complete bitch in failing to disclose the defense's theory, I had almost forgotten to question whether the evidence supporting Lopez's theory was even admissible. Any connection between this case and the Zimmerman murder was tenuous at best, so I had a good argument that, even if the Zimmerman case was minimally relevant, any relevance was substantially outweighed by its potential to distract and confuse the jury.

I think Lesh skipped that part of the analysis as well and now saw the opportunity to get this mess out of his courtroom. The problem was, we were venturing into a risky area of the law. Trial courts routinely get reversed on appeal if they completely prohibit a defendant from presenting his theory. On the other hand, as long as the trial judge lets the defendant present his theory, the court has tremendous latitude in excluding evidence that might support it. The fact that I understood the nebulous distinction between the defendant's theory and the evidence used to support it made me think I'd become a complete asshole.

Luckily, Lesh understood the relevant distinction too, so I wouldn't have to try to explain it.

"I can tell you right now, Ms. Kincaid, that I'm not about to keep the defense from arguing that someone else might have committed this crime. But, I'm no Judge Ito either, and you're correct to point out that the defense doesn't necessarily get to put on whatever evidence it wants. So, here's what we're doing. Ms. Lopez, either you agree to a continuance or you call the witnesses you named on your discovery list before you start calling cops to the stand to talk about the Zimmerman case."

Lisa objected. Big surprise. "Your honor, it's highly unusual for the Court to dictate the order in which evidence is presented."

"Well, it's also highly unusual for an attorney to pull the kind of stunt you've pulled this morning. Think of this as another repercussion of your strategy." He had noted Lisa's objection but then forced her to make her choice.

"I have no interest in a continuance, your honor. Mr. Derringer is eager to go home."

"Very well then, Ms. Lopez. No mention of Jamie Zimmerman, Margaret Landry, or Jesse Taylor again until I've ruled on these issues. Now we're taking a twenty-minute recess so we can collect our thoughts."

Forcing Lopez to work her way through the boring stuff first helped me in a couple of different ways. Obviously, the detectives and I could use some time poring over the police reports for the Zimmerman murder to get up to speed, and I could prepare a motion to exclude evidence about the case. But even if the evidence wound up coming in, Lesh had provided a more subtle kind of assistance. In the time it would take Lisa to get through these other witnesses, the jury might forget the drama of her opening statement, and the defense might lose its momentum. Along the same lines, it would be hard for Dan Manning to write a great story when he had no trial testimony to back up the opening statement yet.

For those reasons, I decided I wouldn't object to testimony relating to Andrea Martin's arrest for criminal trespass at the Lloyd Center Mall, although it was blatantly inadmissible. It was better to let Lisa present that kind of innocuous evidence and hope the impact of her opening statement wore off before the sexy stuff started. Plus, I might have a better chance of getting Lesh to exclude the damaging evidence if I didn't throw a fit over this chippy stuff.

A twenty-minute recess wasn't much, but at least I could update my investigators so they could start working on it while I was in trial.

I almost knocked Dan Manning on his ass as I was rushing out of the courtroom. He looked like a high school kid who just won a swimming pool full of beer and a squadron of cheerleaders to share it with. I could see his willingness to be sucked into Lopez's defense. It was, after all, a great story. But I didn't have time to set him straight and I suspected it wouldn't work anyway. So instead I almost knocked him on his ass.

To save valuable time, I pulled out my cell phone rather than fight the courthouse elevators to get back to my office.

My first call was to Alice Gernstein, the paralegal in our

major crimes unit. I gave her a quick rundown of what was going on and asked her to pull the files from the Landry trial from archives and put them on my chair and to order the trial transcripts. As it turned out, she had already pulled the stuff for O'Donnell. He had prosecuted Landry and Taylor and was now part of the investigation into the new letter to the *Oregonian*. Alice said she'd make copies for me. I also asked her to tell O'Donnell that I was going to need to talk to him soon, since he'd handled the Zimmerman case.

Next, I called MCT. I was lucky. Chuck was out interviewing a witness, but Ray and Jack were both in. They put me on speaker and I told them what Lisa had unloaded in her opening.

It was a great opportunity for catty chat about my nemesis, but I told them I had to make it quick. They had already refreshed themselves on the Zimmerman case, since they were working on the investigation into the anonymous letter. I warned them that Lisa might call them back to the stand to testify about the case.

"Do you have anything yet on the letter?" I asked.

They were silent. I could picture them looking at each other over the speakerphone, wondering how to tell me that I was outside the official circle of knowledge. Walker handled it. "This thing's really hot, Sam. O'Donnell and the lieutenant are going nuts over it, this being the first execution and all. If anything leaks—"

"Hey, forget it. I only asked because it would obviously be a lot easier to defuse this Lopez stunt if we could show that the letter was a hoax. If you don't want to tell me—"

I heard the line get picked up off the speaker. Walker spoke quietly into the handset. "Look, don't count on getting anything on the letter. No prints. No DNA on the envelope or stamp. Typewritten on plain paper and dropped in a mail-box by the side of a road." Great. No help for me, and no help to Chuck. "And Sam," he said. "No one knows, not even Chuck. I just didn't want you getting your hopes up."

I hung up feeling let down. It would be easiest if I could tie up any loose ends that Lopez pulled free about the Zim-merman case, but apparently I couldn't count on that. I would need to convince the jury that Derringer was guilty, even if they developed doubts about the guilt of Landry and Taylor.

When court resumed, Lisa called her first witness, the star with the alibi—convicted felon Derrick Derringer.

His testimony was predictable. Lopez did her best to make him sound respectable. He owned a home in southeast Port-land and worked night shifts at one of those quickie oil-change places. As expected, he swore under oath that his loser brother had been at his house on the night Kendra was attacked. According to Derrick, his brother Frank—a few months on parole and ready to set off on a new law-abiding lifestyle—had walked the mile and a half to his house to hang out. They wound up watching a *Saturday Night Live* repeat. He remembered that John Goodman was the host because he did a brutally accurate impersonation of the woman who had sold out the former president's mistress to the indepen-dent counsel. I wasn't impressed. Last time I checked, John Goodman hosted that show a couple times a month. And it still wasn't funny.

Fortunately, I was ready with a tough cross for Derringer's brother, and Lisa did little on direct exam to blunt the effect in advance.

With permission from Judge Lesh, I rose and approached Derrick Derringer for questioning. The fact that the witness was the defendant's brother was enough to give him a motive to lie, but fortunately that line of questioning was only the beginning of my cross.

"Isn't it true, Mr. Derringer, that you've had some run-ins with the law yourself?"

"Yes, ma'am, I have."

"Now, do I have this right? You have three felony convictions in the last ten years?"

"I believe that's correct, ma'am."

Lisa had done a good job of warning Derrick not to get defensive about his criminal history. When a witness with a problematic background owns up to his problems, some jurors will actually give him points for it. I hoped Derringer's brother's record was bad enough to speak for itself—whether he admitted the convictions or not.

I asked him about his felony record, and he conceded that he'd been convicted of armed robbery and then of two separate incidents of forgery in the first degree. In a perfect world, the guy would still be in the pen for the robbery alone. He walked into a Subway sandwich shop just before closing and left with just $67 from the cash register. The cashier was a sixteen-year-old kid who'd started working at the shop a few days earlier. After Derringer discovered that there were only small bills in the register and that the cashier had no access to the safe, he made the kid get on his hands and knees on the floor in front of the safe. He stuck a gun in the kid's mouth, forced him to make three tries at opening the safe despite his protestations that he didn't know the combination, and then dry fired the gun when the safe didn't open.

After the kid pissed his pants, Derringer got down on his

knees in front of him, grabbed him by the hair, and mocked him while he cried. As he grabbed the small bills from the register, Derringer told the kid, "Hey, just be glad you're not a chick, man, or you'd really be having a bad day."

Unfortunately, the Rules of Evidence being what they are, all the jury got to hear was that Derrick Derringer had been convicted of armed robbery. Just doesn't have the same effect.

When I finished asking about his felony convictions, I got to the good stuff.

I pulled out a thick case file from my leather legal brief-case, opened it, and asked him, "You've offered in the past to testify on your brother's behalf, haven't you?"

He took the bait and tried to avoid what he knew to be the issue. "I'm not sure what you're referring to specifically, ma'am, but I have been saying since this unfortunate event occurred that I'm willing to tell the truth about what happened to establish my brother's innocence."

What a fucking idiot.

"I'm aware that you've been what you call 'willing' to testify for your brother in this trial, but I was referring to a trial two years ago in Clackamas County where your brother also was the defendant. Do you recall that, Mr. Derringer?"

Of course he recalled it, he said.

"And in that trial, Mr. Derringer, didn't you offer to testify that your brother had been with you when the crime of which he was accused occurred?"

He had to admit that one, too.

"Did you eventually testify in that trial?"

"No, I did not," he said.

"Were you in the courtroom when your brother testified in that trial?"

Derringer looked surprised. I think Lisa expected me to get this evidence in through a DA or a cop instead of through her own witness. I guess she and Derrick Derringer didn't know that the DA who tried that case must've gotten bored during Frank Derringer's testimony. The prosecuting attorney had made a note in the file that Derrick Derringer was in the courtroom during his brother's testimony and looked irritated when his brother admitted having sex with the victim but said that it was consensual. Clackamas County had happily made the file available for me to use.

"I'm not sure whether I was there for the entirety of his testimony, ma'am."

"Well, let me ask you this. You were there when your brother admitted under oath that he was present at the scene of the incident that was the subject of that trial, right?"

He finally gave up what I was looking for and conceded that he'd heard his brother admit to being at the scene of the crime.

"And, let me get this right, before your brother testified under oath that he had been at the scene of the crime, you had been willing to testify—also under oath—that your brother had been with you on the same day and at the same time as the crime occurred?" This was the stuff that made being a trial lawyer fun.

"Yes, ma'am."

"And in *this* trial, you're saying that your brother was with you at the same time and on the same day as *this* crime occurred, is that right?"

"Yes, ma'am, but—"

I cut him off. "No further questions, your honor."

Lisa tried to rehabilitate him as a witness, but what could he say? He claimed he was confused in the previous trial about the night in question, which might be better than admitting to an offer to perjure. I was pretty sure the jurors saw him for what he was, though. Considering the crap Lisa had pulled, I got through the afternoon pretty well.

By the time we were done with Derrick Derringer, it was a little past five, so Lesh was more than ready to call it a day. Lesh is one of the hardest working judges in the courtroom, so you can usually count on him to have trial every day, even Fridays, which most judges view as golf day. But this evening he announced that he had a funeral to attend the next day and that we would not reconvene until Monday. The delay would give me some extra time to file whatever papers I planned to submit in support of my motion to exclude the evidence of the Zimmerman case.

When I reached the eighth floor, I went straight to O'Donnell's office. Luckily he was still in.

"Thank God you're here. Did Alice tell you what's happening in Lesh's courtroom?"

"Yeah. I figured you'd want to talk as soon as possible, so I told the guys to go running without me."

I was glad enough not to hear him say *I told you so*. But missing an opportunity to run on a sunny day in Portland is huge around the DA's office, where running is essentially our religion. I suspect I got my job more for my mile times than my educational pedigree. "Thanks. I need the help. I know close to nothing about the Zimmerman case, and Lopez is dumping it with no notice right in the middle of the Derringer trial."

He looked at his watch. "Unfortunately, the Zimmerman case was pretty fucked up, and this anonymous letter just makes it look worse. It'll take awhile for you to get up to speed, and I don't have long."

A date, no doubt. Good to know the head of the major crimes unit had his priorities straight. "Well, start by giving me what my detectives can say and where they might be weak. The only good thing about Lopez springing this thing on me is that she boxed herself in on witnesses. She's basically got to get the defense in through my witnesses. I've got Walker, Johnson, and Forbes. They were all involved in Zimmerman, right?"

"Yeah. I can tell you right now that, if you've got a problem, it'll be Forbes. Let me give you some background." He explained what I already knew, that Forbes got involved in the case by happenstance when Taylor's probation officer, Bernie Edwards, called him in to follow up on Landry's reported suspicions.

He then filled in the details leading up to Landry's confession. "You got to understand that when Edwards and Forbes went out to Landry's, they were already pretty sure she was full of shit. It was basically a CYA house visit in the event Landry actually knew something. It was about a month after Zimmerman's body was found, and the *Oregonian* printed a short Crime Watchers column with a picture of the vic and a bare-bones description of the crime, asking people to call in if they knew anything. Landry told Edwards and Forbes that she read it and started thinking that maybe Taylor had something to do with the murder.

"She said she remembered Taylor coming home drunk unusually late around the time of the crime and taking a shower, which was not typical for him at night. When she woke up in the morning, he was doing a load of laundry already, which was also strange. She said that about a week later she overheard Taylor talking on the phone, saying something about how someone named Jamie had flipped out on him. She assumed Jamie was a guy at the time, so didn't think too much of it. But, according to her, she put all this together when she read the article and then called Edwards."

I took a second to process the information. "Huh? Even if she was telling the truth at that point, why would she connect Taylor to a murder based on that?"

"I know. It didn't make sense to Edwards or Forbes either. They shined her on a little bit and then left. But then Margaret figures out that they're blowing her off, so she calls Edwards the next day and tells him she was poking around in Taylor's stuff and found a matchbook from Tommy Z's that said *Jamie Z* with a telephone number on it. Edwards runs a reverse trace on the number and it comes back to Jamie Zimmerman's mother's house."

"Did Jamie live with her mother?" I asked.

"As much as she lived anywhere for any substantial period of time, I guess. Before she was killed, she'd been out of her mom's house for about six months. Hey, I know what you're thinking, and, trust me, Edwards and Forbes thought it too. They figured she looked the number up in the book or something. But Jamie's mom had a different last name—I can't remember what it is now—and the paper never printed it. That phone number was a big piece of evidence for us down the road, when Margaret was backing out of her confession. We looked at the case up and down, and we just couldn't figure out how she could've come up with that number other than through direct contact with Jamie."

"So what happened after Landry came forward with this name and phone number?" I asked.

"Like I said, Edwards does the reverse trace and figures

out it's Jamie's mother's number. My recollection is that Forbes contacted MCT at that point to let them know what he and Edwards had and to see whether Margaret could've gotten the number from the paper somehow. The case was getting cold, so MCT had cut the investigation down to one team—Johnson and Walker—and they weren't working it very actively. In any event, they decided the Landry lead was worth following up on, so they went out and interviewed Taylor and confronted him with the *Jamie Z* matchbook.

"Now, you got to understand, Jesse Taylor is an absolute freak. Tell you the truth, I don't know how a guy like that even lives to be thirty-five. Unless his whole presence is an act, the guy doesn't know which end is up. Never knows what's going on. Talks in circles, non sequiturs. Drinks himself into a blackout about every day. Basically a gigantic human id."

"But a court found him competent for trial?"

"Don't they always?" O'Donnell's smirk was irritating, but I tolerated it for the sake of the briefing. "So, when Walker and Johnson do the interview, they assume Taylor's playing dumb, because they can't imagine that someone's actually as stupid as this guy really is. Taylor denies anything having to do with the murder. But then Walker and Johnson confront him with the matchbook. He says that for all he knows, he might've met Jamie Zimmerman and gotten her number. He can't really say because he can't remember anything that happens from one day to the next."

"Sounds like a real winner."

"Hey, who the hell else would be shacked up with some sixty-five-year-old cow? Old Margaret's not exactly a looker." He could tell from my stare that I didn't have time for this right now, so he resumed his summary. "Based on Margaret's info and Taylor's wishy-washy statement, we got a warrant for his house and his car."

"I thought you said he shared a house with Landry. She wouldn't just consent to the search?"

I should've known not to let my guard down and ask a question of O'Donnell. Predictably, he used it as a chance to belittle me and make himself look knowledgeable. "You know how it goes," he said, even though I obviously didn't. "Court says a roommate can only consent to a search of the parts of the house they actually share. You and I know that a couple living together and banging each other shares every part of the house. But come trial, wives and girlfriends who consent to searches have a tendency to say, 'Oh, by the way, Judge, that cupboard where they found the murder weapon? That's his cupboard; I'm not allowed to go in there.' Result? Weapon is gone. Maybe in the dope unit, you guys don't give a shit about that stuff, but we don't risk it on major cases. We go for the warrant."

I ignored the comment. As long as O'Donnell was giving me helpful information, I didn't care about the insults. "Did they find anything useful?"

"Depends on what you call useful. For a second, they thought they'd hit the jackpot. See, as far as the police could tell, Jamie was wearing these gold hoop earrings that her friends said she always wore. Dead girl turns up without her earrings, you don't really know what that means. Could've fallen out; she might've taken them out, who knows? But it was definitely something the police were keeping their eyes out for during the search. So what do they find in Jesse Taylor's toolbox but a pair of gold hoop earrings, about two and a half inches in diameter, just like the ones Jamie was always wearing.

"Problem was, Jamie's mom sees them and says there's no way they're the same ones. Seems Jamie got the earrings from her dirtbag father a couple years earlier—one of his only visits to her, according to the mom. Anyway, he told Jamie the earrings were fourteen-karat gold, trying to push himself off as a big spender. So Mom, to prove a point and bust any hope Jamie had that her dad was a mensch, dragged her into one of the jewelry stores at the mall one day to prove the earrings were fake. Turned out they actually *were* solid gold. The mom figured Jamie's dad must've ripped 'em off from somewhere. The earrings the cops pulled out of Taylor's toolbox were fake."

I was thinking out loud. "So Landry read about the earrings in the paper, bought some like them, and planted them in Taylor's toolbox?"

"No way. We never released the information on the earrings, just in case the perp took them as a souvenir. Johnson went back and read every article and watched every newsreel on the case, and there was nothing about the earrings. So, yeah, the theory was that Landry was planting evidence, but she was planting it on a guilty person. Happens, you know—look at Mark Fuhrman and O.J.'s bloody glove. We figured Taylor had to be involved at that point, because how else could Landry know about the earrings?"

"What did Landry say about the earrings?" I asked.

"That was one thing about Margaret. All the way up until she was indicted, she was quick to admit her lies. She'd say, real matter-of-fact, 'Oh, that. Well, yes, you're right, I wasn't exactly honest with you on that one.' She always replaced it with some other lie, but each time she dug herself a little deeper, giving us a little more of the truth." O'Donnell smiled and shook his head, recalling the case, then suddenly seemed to remember he'd been talking about the earrings. "Same thing applied with the earrings. She admitted planting them right away once she was confronted."

"Did she say how she knew Jamie wore earrings like that?"

"Not until someone asked her. That's how everything worked with her. She said she saw the earrings listed on her copy of the warrant when the police went to the house to execute it, and she happened to have a pair of earrings that fit the description, so she snuck into Taylor's toolbox and put them there. We knew it was bullshit right off the bat. First of all, the list of potential evidence in that case was long, like it is in any homicide. The earrings were mentioned on one line six pages back.

"Second, the only description in the warrant was for gold hoop earrings. If Landry had planted real ones, we never would've known they weren't Jamie's. The mom says they were identical—same diameter, same width of the metal.

"And finally, I was there when the police executed the warrant. Don't get me wrong, here. Those MCT guys are as dim-witted as any other Keystone Kop, but I was there and they at least know how to execute a fucking warrant. Margaret Landry was not wandering around the house planting evidence while we were there."

I'll never understand why some people have to temper any comment that could possibly be construed as a compliment with an insult. I suspect they think it makes them look knowledgeable. I think it makes them look mean. If I was lucky, O'Donnell would never feel compelled to rise to my defense.

"So the only way she could've known to plant those particular earrings would be if she had seen them," I said.

"Exactly. In fact, of all the details Margaret provided that corroborated her confession, it was the earrings that most convinced me of her guilt. On a lot of the other facts, she tried to say at trial that Forbes had coached her. But the earrings were such a perfect match, she couldn't explain how Forbes could've coached her about a pair of earrings in that kind of detail. And she admitted planting them. I hammered on that in my closing argument, and I'm convinced that the jury agreed there was no way for Landry to get around those earrings."

"So what happened when you found out the earrings weren't Jamie's?" I asked.

"That's when this whole thing changed. I made the call to send Forbes back in to talk to her. He was a rookie, but he'd developed a good rapport with her, and we needed to know what the hell was going on. Forbes told her that was it—we were going to stop working with her. She started crying, saying that he had to believe her and she knew Taylor did the girl. Forbes did a good job, actually. Stayed tough, told her he didn't want to hear any more from her, you get the drift. So then Margaret blurts out that she knows Taylor did it, because she saw him. Gives the whole confession right there, so no one but Forbes was there to hear it."

"How big of a problem was that for the case?" I asked.

O'Donnell shrugged his shoulders. "Hell, in retrospect, it was a problem. He seemed like a kid, didn't have a lot of experience, and held too many pieces of the investigation together. The defense made it sound like Forbes was a climber using this case to become a star in the bureau. Fortunately, the defense didn't realize that Officer Forbes was none other than Charles Landon Forbes, Jr. I think the jury figured out that a governor's son doesn't need to manipulate an investigation to get where he wants to go in city government."

"What about physical evidence? Anything to corroborate the confession?" I asked.

O'Donnell shook his head. "Zilch. Zimmerman was missing for months before the body was found. No DNA, no hair, no fibers. We were lucky to have a firm ID and cause of death. Her license was in her pocket, and we used dental records to confirm it. ME called the strangulation based on damage to the small bones in her neck." O'Donnell looked at his watch. "Hey, I hope this has been helpful, but I really gotta run."

"Shit, I was hoping you could tell me more about that confession. You around tomorrow?"

"Nope."

Asshole didn't even pretend to explain. The big boys around here take off on dry days for golf, and the DA pretends he doesn't know about it. I guess I'd gotten the maximum amount of help a person can get out of Tim O'Donnell in a day. Actually, this might be it for the month.

"Alright, I can probably get the rest from Forbes. Thanks for the help."

As I was walking out of his office, I heard O'Donnell mutter behind me, "Hey, you should thank me for not finishing the rest of the story. Now you've got an excuse to be alone with Chuck Forbes after hours."

I spun around and glared at him. "What the hell is that supposed to mean?"

"Hey, fire down, Kincaid. I thought you had a better sense of humor. The staff up here goes nuts over the guy every time he's in here. I was just having some fun with you—thought it wouldn't hurt you to spend some time with the guy."

I decided he was telling the truth. He didn't know anything. "That's something I don't joke around about. I don't date people at work, especially cops."

"Alas, Kincaid. It's our loss."

As I started to walk out of his office, I stepped back and asked, "Oh, by the way, do they have anything yet on that letter? It would help shut Lopez down if I could show that we got the right bad guys in the Zimmerman case."

Looking down at his desk, he studied an open magazine. "Letter's still at the crime lab. If we find out who sent it, I'll let you know."

I imagined myself saying, At the lab, my ass. I hear the lab got diddly. Instead, I nodded. "I'd appreciate it."

"Now get back to your trial," he said. "Let me know how it turns out. Bad enough that you took it to begin with. You better not crash and burn."

I tried not to let his gloating piss me off, since he did stay past his normal five o'clock punch-out to help me. But his help was something of a mixed blessing. Now if my case went down in flames, he could say he filled me in on what I needed to know about the Zimmerman case and had warned me from the start. No pressure.

| 11 |

Lisa was giving a statement to Dan Manning outside the courthouse when I walked out of the building. I wished I'd gotten to him first. No doubt he was already envisioning this case as his first Pulitzer, or at least a true-crime paperback and a made-for-TV Sunday-night movie.

While Lisa spun a story involving sex, double crosses, and justice delayed, I was left to make a lame and predictable statement that the defense was reaching for tall tales out of desperation and that I trusted the jury to weigh the evidence impartially and ascertain the truth. Not exactly headline material.

Grace met me at the door of her loft apartment in the Pearl District with a big hug and an even bigger glass of cabernet. I had called ahead from the office, so she knew I was in a bad way.

When she was quiet after I finished relating the events of

the past few days, I looked at her with exaggerated disappointment. "Grace, as my lifelong best friend, you are under a standing obligation to feed my outrage. Right now, for example, you should be stringing together a litany of insulting names for my archenemy, Lisa Lopez." Nothing. "Here, I'll get you started: Snake. Slime. Skunk. Skank. I'm only on *s*. You want to start with the *t*'s?" Still nothing. "Grace?"

She woke up from her daze and looked me in the eye. "Before I say anything about your case, I just want to clarify something. You're back with Chuck?"

I rolled my eyes and did my best to voice exasperation. I sounded like Kendra. "You don't have to say it in that tone, Grace."

"Well, Sam, it's pretty much the tone you seem to reserve for him."

"And that's usually after a couple of martinis when I'm angry at him for breaking my heart. This time feels different, Grace. We've both grown up a little, and he's doing more than just trying to flirt his way into bed with me. He's really opened up to me about this trial and the Zimmerman case, and he's great with Kendra—"

She interrupted me. "What? You think because he brings CDs and Happy Meals to your witness that you're going to have little babies together and live happily ever after? Jesus, Sam, Chuck's a nice guy, but look at the twits he goes for. Not to mention the fact that he makes your life chaotic, and you hate chaos."

"Maybe some chaos would be good for me."

That made her laugh. "You're kidding, right?"

When I didn't smile at that, she rubbed my forearm, which was resting on the table. "Oh, Sam, I'm sorry. You do what's right for you, and I'll support whatever that is. Just be careful. I'm worried about you."

"Yeah, me too, but I want to do this." I changed the subject. "So, can we move on to the trashing of my nemesis now?"

She smiled, but I could tell she was feeling serious. "It just seems strange," she said.

"There's nothing strange about it, Grace. Lisa Lopez is completely scummy slime and has absolutely no ethics. She'll do anything to win, even for a dirtbag like Derringer."

"But you said yourself that she sat there passively through your entire case."

I tried not to reveal my impatience. "Right," I said slowly, "but now it turns out she was doing that so she could hide her ridiculous theory until the last minute, when I'd be caught off guard."

"But, Sam, look at the big picture. When did she think of this? The anonymous letter to the *Oregonian* wasn't printed until the middle of your case. If she got the idea from the letter, what was her plan before then? It seems too coincidental that she just happened to be putting on a lame defense and then decided in the middle of the trial to capitalize on this anonymous letter thing."

I could see where she was headed. "Right," I said. "I've thought about that too. It explains why she seemed up to no good ever since the start of the trial: she was planning to tie the case to the Zimmerman murder all along, and the anonymous letter happened to come up right before her opening."

"Which is also a major coincidence," she said.

"It's really not, Grace. Think about it: the Supreme Court announced it was upholding Taylor's sentence right before my trial started. Lisa heard about it and saw a convenient defense. The anonymous letter was also a reaction to the court's decision, probably by some death penalty opponent or someone just looking for attention. Two totally unrelated decisions, but both pretty predictable in hindsight. Taylor's the first real test of Oregon's death penalty; it was bound to attract some nutjobs."

Grace nodded in agreement, and I moved on to bad-mouthing Lisa Lopez as we finished the bottle of wine. As usual when I visited Grace, I left feeling better than when I arrived.

On the way home, my cell phone rang. The caller ID read PRIVATE. Real helpful. Maybe if I hadn't answered, I would have at least had a recorded message to give the police.

"Long dinner, Kincaid. Were you and that hot little friend of yours doing a little eating out up there? If I'd known, I might've followed you up."

The voice was vaguely familiar, but too muffled to place. "Who is this?"

He was already gone.

I spent the weekend reviewing the Zimmerman file behind locked doors. Between checking out every sound, double-checking my alarm, and periodically turning off the lights to look out my windows, I didn't feel even half prepared when I headed back to court on Monday morning.

One thing had become clear to me, though: There was no doubt that the entire case against Margaret Landry and Jesse Taylor turned on Landry's apparent inside knowledge. Either she had something to do with the murder or someone had told her these details. No wonder the defense had turned the focus to Chuck.

As furious as I was about Lopez's dirty tricks, the fact remained that there was no evidence tying the assault on Kendra to the Zimmerman murder. I also had what is known in the legal world as a buttload of evidence against Derringer—Kendra's ID, the shaved pubic hair, the detailing of his car a day after the assault, and the fingerprint. It would be harder work than it first appeared, but I still had a solid case.

Also, the weekend media coverage was better than it might have been under the circumstances. Manning's piece appeared as a sidebar to a follow-up story on the Zimmerman case and anonymous letter. The feature story didn't contain any new information, just a summary of the case against Landry and Taylor and an update on their status in prison. She was a model prisoner who counseled young women; he was a headcase who spent most of his time in solitary.

Manning's sidebar couldn't add much. Just that a defendant was claiming during his trial that whoever killed Jamie Zimmerman had committed the crime of which he stood accused. Seeing the assertion in black and white, without any evidence to support it, made me see how truly lame it was.

At 9:30 A.M. on Monday, when Lesh took us back on the record, I settled into my chair for what promised to be a long morning.

Jake Fenninger was Lisa's next witness. Fenninger was the patrol officer who popped Kendra last Christmas when she was working up in Old Town. Kendra had already talked about the arrest on direct during my case-in-chief, but Lisa's hands were tied. She couldn't get into the Zimmerman case until she plowed through the witnesses she had included on her defense witness list, most of whom had nothing to say other than that Andrea Martin might be a trespasser. Compared to them, Fenninger was riveting.

Lopez walked Fenninger through his background before he started to get hostile. Fenninger was another New York transplant. He'd worked in NYPD's infamous street crimes unit before joining PPB a few years ago. Considering where he got his training and the fact that his dad was reportedly a hard-line Irish detective from the throw-down school of the NYPD, Fenninger was a pretty good cop.

I suspected he'd moved west to escape the pressures of being an old school cop and sincerely wanted to do the right thing on his beat. Unfortunately, I think he still bought into Giuliani's propaganda that a "zero tolerance" approach to street crime was for the good not only of the community but also of the suspect. It can be true in some instances, but Fenninger had gone too far with Kendra.

Once Lopez had gone through Fenninger's background and current duties with PPB, she turned to Kendra's Christmas arrest.

"In your role as a patrol officer in Old Town, did you have the opportunity to encounter Kendra Martin on Christmas of last year, Officer Fenninger?" Lisa asked.

"Yes, ma'am, I did."

Like most cops, Fenninger probably figured that using "ma'am" and "sir" in his testimony might counter the stereotypes some people have of police. They forget that anyone who's been stopped for speeding has heard the same polite tone and still wound up with a whopper of a ticket.

"And how did she come to your attention that day?"

"I was patrolling in my vehicle and noticed a girl on the

corner of Fourth and Burnside. She came to my attention because, quite honestly, just about anyone walking around close to midnight in Old Town on Christmas is probably up to no good, but she looked like she was only fourteen years old or so. I figured she was probably a street kid out working."

"And what do you mean by 'working,' Officer Fenninger?"

"Prostituting herself. Exchanging sex for money."

"So what did you do about your suspicions?" Lisa asked.

"I first saw her when I was headed west on Burnside, so when I got to Fifth, I took a right turn, headed north to Couch, turned right again, then headed south on Fourth so I could watch her from my patrol vehicle."

"What did you observe?"

"I saw the girl wave to a few cars that drove by on Burnside. A couple of cars stopped, and she talked to them through the passenger window. All the cars that she had any interaction with were driven by what appeared to be men who were alone."

"Did you draw any conclusions from that?"

"Yes. Given the time of day, the fact that it was Christmas, the neighborhood, and the activity that I observed, I believed that the girl was loitering to solicit prostitution." Fenninger testified that he arrested Kendra for the ordinance offense and then searched her and her purse, in what's called a "search incident to an arrest."

Lisa held up a plastic bag with Kendra's purse in it, which I had marked as evidence during my case. After looking at his police report to refresh his memory, Fenninger confirmed that it appeared to be the same type of purse Kendra had been carrying last Christmas. He found heroin residue in the purse and added a charge for drug possession.

Instead of booking Kendra as a prisoner, he wrote the charges on a ticket and took her to juvenile hall to have her processed as a runaway. It was a nice thing for him to have done for her.

Lisa asked him whether he seized the purse as evidence. Fenninger said he should have, but that Kendra started crying, saying it was a Christmas gift from her mother. So he shook the residue into a baggie instead and let her keep her purse. Jesus, no wonder the juvie DA had dumped the case. Even the arresting officer seemed to think it was chippy.

I didn't have much for Fenninger on cross. "Officer, do you know who assaulted Kendra Martin last February, two months after the arrest you've testified about? . . . Do you know anything about where Frank Derringer was when Kendra was attacked? . . . In fact, have you ever even *seen* the defendant before today?" No, no, and no. I thought the jury would see that Lopez had no legitimate reason for calling Fenninger.

Next was Kerry Richardson, the so-called loss prevention officer at Dress You Up, who was called to testify about Andrea Martin's trespass arrest at the mall. The testimony was completely irrelevant and inadmissible, but I didn't mind letting Lopez waste time with evidence that wasn't going to hurt me. Andrea hadn't been an important part of my case anyway. She only testified about the extent and duration of Kendra's injuries, facts that were established by other evidence too.

Richardson testified that he was sure he saw Andrea conceal something inside of a shopping bag back in November before she left the store. He told the store manager, Geraldine Maher, and the two of them confronted Andrea in the mall. However, they didn't find any stolen goods on Andrea, and Richardson hadn't actually seen Andrea steal anything. So instead of trying to prosecute Andrea for shoplifting, he had asked Maher to issue a trespass warning, telling Andrea she'd be arrested if she came back into the store. When he saw her again in January, he called the police.

My cross was quick.

"Was Ms. Martin convicted for shoplifting merchandise in November from Dress You Up?" No. "Was Ms. Martin even *arrested* for shoplifting merchandise in November from Dress You Up?" No. "Do you have any information to provide to the jury regarding whether Frank Derringer raped and attempted to murder Andrea Martin's daughter, Kendra, last February?" No.

I couldn't help but give a look to the jury after I finished my cross of Richardson, just to make sure they got the point. I'd never seen such a desperate defense.

My confidence began to feel misplaced when Lopez rose for redirect. "A point of clarification, Mr. Richardson. You testified that you couldn't actually see what Ms. Martin stole in November, but that you were left with the impression that she was concealing something, is that correct?"

"Yes. Like I said, she was carrying a large shopping bag and it looked like her hand passed over it and she stuffed something in there, but I couldn't actually see what it would have been."

Lopez used the old trick of looking at Richardson curiously, like she'd just realized something for the first time. "Interesting. You say that it looked like she 'stuffed' something in the bag, not that she merely 'dropped' something. Why is that?"

Richardson thought a moment. "Well, just the way her arms moved. It was like she was struggling with the bag."

"As if the object she were placing in the bag were relatively large?" she asked.

This was getting ridiculous, so I piped up. "Objection, your honor. Leading and vague."

"Sustained."

This shows why I rarely object at trial. Once the leading question has been asked, the damage has been done if there's a rapport between the questioning attorney and the witness. Even though my objection was sustained, Lopez followed up by asking Richardson, "What size would you estimate the object to be that you thought you saw Ms. Martin conceal in the bag?"

Richardson's response was predictable. "Relatively large. Bigger than a pair of earrings or something. Maybe a shirt or something bulkier like that."

Lopez then moved to the table at the front of the courtroom where the physical evidence that had been introduced lay. She picked up the plastic bag containing Kendra's purse. "I'm showing you a purse that has been marked as State's Evidence Three, which prior witnesses have identified as Kendra Martin's purse, a gift from her mother Andrea. Is it possible that you saw Andrea Martin hide this purse in her bag last November in Dress You Up?"

"Sure, it's possible."

After Richardson left the stand, Lopez called Geraldine Maher, the store manager who barred Andrea from Dress You Up. I had expected Lopez to continue her questioning about the supposed theft incident, although I couldn't see why it would matter if Andrea stole the purse she gave Kendra from Dress You Up. But Lopez had something else in mind.

"Ms. Maher, as the manager of Dress You Up, are you

generally knowledgeable about the merchandise that you stock in the store?"

"Of course. We're a fairly small store, so I take pride in knowing our inventory well." Never put it past a retailer to take advantage of any opportunity to get in a free plug.

Lopez picked up the purse again. "I'm showing you a purse that's been marked State's Evidence Three. Has Dress You Up ever stocked a purse like this one?"

"Yes. We've carried that purse. I believe it's an Esprit."

Lopez pretended to check the small cloth label sewed on the side of the purse. "Correct indeed, Ms. Maher. You do know your inventory." The Home Shopping Network banter was killing me. What was going on here? Lopez continued. "Could this purse have been on your shelves last November, when Kerry Richardson thought he saw Andrea Martin steal something from the store?"

"Yes. We would have gotten that in around June. I think we may still have a couple in the store. It's a relatively popular style."

"So you had this style in stock last October, is that correct?"

"That's right. June of last year until at least the after-Christmas sales, and we may have one or two left still on clearance."

"Ms. Maher, do you recall contacting Staffpower Temporary Agency to count Dress You Up's inventory last October?"

"Yes, I do. We do inventory twice a year, in April and October. I've been using Staffpower for a few years now."

At that point, Lopez handed me a piece of paper I'd never seen before and then approached Geraldine Maher with a copy of the same document. Defense attorneys are not

required to show their documentary evidence prior to trial.
As I scanned the paper to make sense of it, panic set in. But
there was nothing I could do, and I was left watching Lopez
go to work.

"Ms. Maher, I'm showing you a document I've marked
Defense Exhibit One. What is it?"

Maher responded, seemingly as oblivious as I was about
where this was going. "It's a letter from Staffpower notifying
me of the individuals they hired to conduct our inventory
last October, with the amounts to be paid to each of them
for their work. We pay the lump total to Staffpower to dis-
tribute and do wage withholding, but this acts as a sort of
itemization of the amount."

Lopez continued. "Please read for the jury the sixth name
on the list."

There it was. Even Geraldine Maher was surprised. "Oh,
it's Frank Derringer, or at least according to this."

"And do you have any reason to doubt the accuracy of
that list?"

"No, I do not. If it says that a Frank Derringer worked on
our inventory, then I suppose he did."

"And, to be clear, an inventory requires the person doing
the counting to handle the merchandise, is that right?"

"Yes, generally. They'd need to move stock around to
count it properly."

That was enough for Lisa. "No further questions."

Lopez had just managed to defuse my most compelling
piece of evidence, Derringer's fingerprint on Kendra's purse.
Renshaw had already testified that Derringer had worked
various jobs, including inventories, through temp agencies.
And now Geraldine Maher's testimony gave a plausible
explanation for how Derringer's fingerprint ended up on

Kendra's purse, if the jury believed that Andrea either bought or stole the purse from Dress You Up.

Judge Lesh denied my request for a recess, so I tried my best to control the damage. "You testified, Ms. Maher, that the handbag marked as State's Exhibit Three is a popular style of handbag, is that right?"

"That's correct."

"Where would I go if I wanted to buy a handbag just like that one?" I asked.

"Oh, any number of stores. Like I said, we've got a few left, but so would most of the major department stores and other women's boutiques that carry that brand of purse. It wouldn't be hard to find one."

"So Dress You Up is the not the exclusive seller of that purse in the Portland area, is that right?" I asked.

"Far from it." Good.

"Can you tell from looking at State's Exhibit Three whether it originated in your store or in any one of the many other retailers who stock it?"

"No, I cannot."

"And you never actually saw Andrea Martin steal anything from your store, let alone this purse, did you?"

"No, I did not."

"So the purse marked as State's Exhibit Three could have come from any number of stores other than Dress You Up?" She agreed. There wasn't much more I could do for now.

During the break, I called MCT from my office. Ray Johnson picked up. It took me awhile to explain the connection that Lopez was trying to draw between Derringer and Kendra's purse.

Ray wanted to make sure he got it right. "So one of Derringer's temp jobs was doing inventory at Dress You Up?"

"Right."

"And Lopez was able to show at least a possibility that Kendra's purse came from there?" he asked.

"Right," I said. "A possibility. We know that the store carried the purse and that Andrea gave it to Kendra. Lopez was able to show that Andrea was in the store a month before Christmas, and there's at least a possibility that she stole something the size of a purse when she was there."

"So what you need," he said, "is something showing that the purse came from another shop."

"That's the idea," I said.

He clicked his tongue while he thought. "Alright. Walker and I are still tied up on this Zimmerman letter, so I'll check with Forbes and Calabrese. Someone will do it, though, and we'll let you know what we find out."

When I got off the phone, I noticed Tim O'Donnell waiting for me in my doorway. He looked annoyed that I hadn't noticed him during my phone call.

"Hey, Kincaid, how's that trial going?"

I didn't see any point in lying. "Pretty crappy, actually. My best evidence was this guy's print on the vic's purse. Turns out he had a temp job doing inventory, so he's claiming an alternative explanation for the evidence."

"Bummer," he said. "Anything new about the Zimmerman connection?"

I couldn't tell whether O'Donnell actually gave a rip about my case or if he was faking it to find out if there was anything he needed to know for his investigation into the anonymous letter.

"I've got until tomorrow morning to file papers to exclude any evidence relating to the Zimmerman case."

O'Donnell looked concerned. "Have you talked to the boss about making that motion?"

"No," I said. It hadn't dawned on me to consult the District Attorney himself about my trial. In our large office, it was rare that we had any direct contact with the boss, let alone on individual cases.

"Well," he said, "this is something Duncan would want to know about. He's feeling the heat on this Zimmerman thing. The last thing he needs is for one of his deputies out there trying to prevent a court from hearing evidence supposedly exonerating Landry and Taylor."

"But, Tim," I said, "Lopez isn't trying to exonerate Landry and Taylor. She's trying to get Derringer off by confusing the jury and trashing MCT. That evidence has nothing to do with my case."

"Sam, I'm trying to help you out. How about joining the rest of us in the real world? I don't get it. You're so fucking smart, but you're acting like some rube on misdemeanor row who can't see the politics here."

I knew the politics, but I hadn't connected them to my case. Duncan Griffith ran for DA as an opponent of the death penalty who'd make sure that the law was at least enforced evenhandedly against the truly reprehensible. In short, he got it both ways. The libs liked him because he talked the talk against the death penalty, but no one came after him on it, because he said he'd enforce the law.

O'Donnell had more advice. "Jesse Taylor is the first scheduled execution this state has seen in decades. And we put him on death row, Sam. This is the center of the storm.

If he turns out to be innocent, Duncan's got—well, he's got a major problem. The only way he's going to make it through is if he's one of the good guys making sure we know who killed Zimmerman. If one of his deputies looks like she's part of a cover-up, he's toast. If you don't go to him with this, I will. The Zimmerman case was mine, and this shit that's going down now is a hell of a lot more important than some loser like Derringer."

"Yeah? Well, that loser basically tortured a thirteen-year-old girl and then left her to die. I don't see much of a difference between him and Jesse Taylor."

He looked frustrated, but at least his response seemed earnest. "Sam, I wasn't saying Derringer was a good guy. Hell, maybe I was too quick to write it off as an Assault Three. But be pragmatic. The boss's political exposure on this Zimmerman thing is huge. You at least need to tell him before you try to keep Derringer from getting into it in your trial."

He was right. "I'll talk to Duncan when I get out of trial today." He started to walk away, but I couldn't leave it at that. "You know, Tim, you could be a little more careful about how you handle things, too. I don't think it would help the boss's political image if the newspapers heard that the head of his major crimes unit short-shrifts thirteen-year-old sex-crime victims and tells jokes about incest."

O'Donnell rolled his eyes at me. "You want to make it around here, you're going to have to tame those emotions. This isn't personal, Sam."

The truth was that I didn't know why I'd snapped at him. He was being helpful, but I couldn't bring myself to tell him I appreciated it. "We done here?" I asked.

"Yeah. Come get me when you're out of trial. I want to be there when you talk to Duncan."

I couldn't see any reason for him to baby-sit me when I talked to Duncan, other than to show his authority, but it wasn't worth fighting about. He was the supervisor of major crimes, had prosecuted the Zimmerman case, and was heading the investigation into the anonymous letter. With all those legitimate reasons for him to be part of the conversation with Duncan, I wouldn't be able to convince him or anyone else that he was only stroking his ego.

I couldn't concentrate after O'Donnell left my office. So instead of staring at the Derringer file with my last remaining minutes of the break, I ran out to the burrito cart in front of the courthouse. The combination of fat and spice was just what I needed before going back to court.

Unfortunately, the bliss was short-lived. Lopez called her next witness, a guy named Travis Culver.

I stood up to speak. "Sidebar, your honor?" Lesh nodded, and Lisa and I approached the bench. It was my sidebar, so my turn to speak first. "Your honor, it was my understanding that Ms. Lopez would be prohibited from calling witnesses other than those included on the defense or prosecution witness lists. Mr. Culver was not listed as a potential state witness, and the defense did not include him on its witness list, either. I don't even know who he is."

Lesh sounded concerned. "I thought I'd made myself clear, Ms. Lopez."

"You were quite clear, your honor," Lopez said. "I assure you that the defense is complying with your order. Mr. Culver is the custodian of records for the Collision Clinic, and the person holding that position was in fact included in the state's list of potential witnesses."

"Right," he said. "That's the auto detail shop. The parties stipulated to the admissibility of the invoice, which is"—Lesh fished around for his list of exhibits—"State's Exhibit Five. So if we've got the stip, why is Mr. Culver here?"

"Because," Lisa said, "he has relevant testimony that goes beyond the stipulation of the parties."

There was nothing I could do. Anticipating the need to lay the foundation for the Collision Clinic, I had indicated on my witness list that I planned to call the business's custodian of records. As a result, Lopez was allowed to call that person without notifying me in advance. If his testimony was irrelevant, I could object after the questions were asked, but there was no way to find out in advance what he intended to say.

We retook our seats, and the bailiff called Travis Culver to the stand. Culver's coiffure was the classic white-trash mullet. If you're not familiar with the name, you're familiar with the look: a short regular cut in the front, but with length in the back reminiscent of the great eighties hair bands. Also known as the shlong, since it is both short and long. Truly versatile. Culver finished off the look with jeans that had a brown undertone from wear and dirt, and a NASCAR T-shirt commemorating a race-car driver killed a few years back.

Lopez started by showing Culver the Collision Clinic invoice. Culver confirmed that he owned the business, had filled out the invoice, and had given it to one of his employees, who then cleaned, painted, and reupholstered Derringer's car. The work was done the day after Kendra was attacked, and Derringer paid Culver eight hundred dollars cash.

"Mr. Culver, we've heard testimony suggesting that the work on Mr. Derringer's car only enhanced the market value of the vehicle by a couple of hundred dollars. Do you agree with that?" Lopez asked.

"Yeah," Culver said, "that's about right. On a car like that, guy might get a quarter, maybe half, of his money back on resale, so what's that? About two to four hundred dollars, I guess."

"Is it unusual for a customer to spend that kind of money in your shop? Money that won't be reflected in the market value of the car?"

"Nope," he said. "Auto body and detail work hardly ever pays off. Some guy bumps you in traffic and dents the back of your car. Might cost twelve hundred dollars to fix, even though the dent doesn't lower the market value by that much. Fact is, I stay in business because people want their cars to look nice. This car here was in good shape mechanically, but it looked like—" He avoided the expletive. "Well, it looked bad. Now it looks a lot better. Real clean inside and out. Lots of people willing to pay eight hundred dollars for that."

"Another thing I notice about this invoice," Lisa said, "is that the work was completed on a Sunday. Do you normally work on cars on Sundays?"

"No, we're usually closed," Culver said. Now, that was interesting.

"Why was the work done on my client's car on that Sunday?" Lopez asked.

"Well," he said, "he had come in earlier that week to talk about getting the work done. We were actually supposed to do it the Friday before, but I had to call and cancel on him. A couple of my guys were out, so we were behind on the cars in the shop that week. So I told him we'd do it on Sunday. I do that sometimes to keep us from getting backed up."

"So, if I understand you correctly, Mr. Derringer arranged

to have his car overhauled several days before you actually completed it. In other words, he didn't call you that Sunday morning to get the work done in a rush. Is that right?"

"Right," he said.

"And, in fact, he had originally planned to have the work done two days earlier, on that Friday, correct?"

"Correct," he said.

There went my theory that Derringer had gotten the work done to cover up physical evidence.

Lesh must have felt sorry for me, because he saved me from having to cross-examine Culver empty-handed at the end of an already humiliating day. Even though we were only halfway through the afternoon session, he called it quits. Apologizing to counsel, the jurors, and the witness, he explained he had an afternoon obligation and that we'd have to resume the questioning of Mr. Culver the following morning.

The problem, of course, was that nothing was going to change overnight. As hard as I'd tried over the years, I still hadn't found a way to alter reality. Someday I was going to figure it out. Unfortunately, I wasn't able to do so before returning to my office.

O'Donnell had left a note on my chair. *Don't forget. Get me before you talk to Duncan. TOD.*

When the two of us arrived at Duncan's office, I could tell that O'Donnell must have called ahead, because Duncan didn't seem surprised to see us. I wondered if the two of them had already agreed on how this would end.

Duncan Griffith is one of those men who manages to look young even though his hair is full-on white. He somehow maintains a year-round tan in Portland, Oregon, and I'd wager a bet that the teeth in what seemed like a permanent smile are capped. He was as pleasant on this day as he always appeared to be.

"Ah, my two favorite deputies. Come on in, you two. Make yourselves comfortable." Griffith gestured to a setting of inviting leather furniture.

The law offices depicted on television are for the most part outlandishly unrealistic. Instead of the mahogany shelves and fully stocked bars enjoyed by fictional prosecutors, I, for example, work off a yellow metal desk with a corkboard hutch, and when I'm lucky I can scrounge a Diet Coke off one of the secretaries who has a mini-fridge. Duncan Griffith's office was an exception, however. The walls were lined top to bottom with volumes of the state and federal case reporters, and dark leather sofas welcomed whatever guests were fortunate enough to gain entrance into the inner fortress.

I'd only been invited here twice before, once for my job interview and once during my second week with the office. I had quickly learned that calling a sandbagging defense attorney a scum sandwich on shit toast wasn't within the range of what Duncan Griffith defined as acceptable deputy DA behavior.

He was being much nicer to me now than during that last visit. After Tim and I were seated, Griffith leaned back against his desk and crossed his arms in front of him. "So, Sammie," he said, "the *Oregonian* tells me that the Zimmerman matter has come up in this rape case of yours. Where's that stand right now?"

I gave him a quick overview and told him I thought that Judge Lesh was receptive to a motion to exclude any evidence relating to Zimmerman's murder.

Before Tim could open his mouth, Duncan said, "You're

a good lawyer and an aggressive prosecutor, Sam, and I
appreciate you going after this guy a hundred and ten percent. But we all need to keep our eye on the ball here. The
greater good. As an office, we need to get to the bottom of
this Zimmerman thing and make sure we've got the right
people. We're talking about the death penalty here. A man's
life is at stake."

"I realize that, sir, and I understand that our office is
involved in the investigation into the anonymous *Oregonian*
letter. But that case doesn't have anything to do with mine.
The defense is trying to take advantage of the publicity sur-
rounding the Zimmerman case to confuse the jury."

Duncan still hadn't stopped smiling. "I understand that,
Sam, but remember what I said. It's about the greater good.
If you file that motion, the front page of the newspaper's
going to say that you're trying to squelch a man's attempt to
get to the truth. And I won't have you dragging us into a
cover-up."

O'Donnell had clearly primed the pump. Griffith was
regurgitating the spiel that O'Donnell had given me earlier
in my office.

"What exactly are you telling me to do, sir?" I asked.

"Don't make this adversarial, Sam. All I'm telling you to
do is allow this defense attorney to have her say. You might
need to do some rebuttal, let the jury see that the two cases
are unrelated. Tim, you can get her up to speed on the Taylor
file, right?"

Tim nodded. "We've already gone over it, sir."

"Good," Griffith said. When I didn't stand up at his sign
that we were dismissed, he continued. "No one's telling you
to play dead here, Sam. You know my rule of thumb in trials

is to always stay above the fray. If the defense attacks the police, let 'em do it. Never helps your case if you look like you've got a personal stake in the outcome. Trust me, your jury's going to have more faith in you this way. And, in the long run, this office benefits."

"The greater good," I said.

"Exactly."

I felt neither great nor good after I called Lopez and Lesh to tell them I wouldn't be filing a motion to exclude Derringer's defense. I felt depressed.

Lesh's response had been simple. "Hey, it's your case. Thanks for letting me know."

Lopez, on the other hand, couldn't just accept the gift for what it was. She was convinced I was somehow tricking her. As a result, what should have been a thirty-second courtesy call turned into a fifteen-minute inquisition about my intentions. Hell, if I was lucky, maybe she'd at least lose a little sleep that night wondering what I had in store for her in the morning. Truth was, I was seriously considering cutting whatever plea I could get if things didn't turn around.

I called MCT to see if they'd had any luck tracking down Kendra's purse, but no one answered. I tried Chuck's pager and entered my cell phone number in case he didn't call right away.

I was burnt out and dying to leave, but I checked my voice mail before heading out. Among the usual junk was a message from Dan Manning. "Samantha, it's Dan Manning from the *Oregonian*. I was calling to see if you had any response to today's events at trial and the alleged connection between your case and Jamie Zimmerman. Also, I'd like to talk to you about whatever role you might have in the Zimmerman investigation. Give me a call."

I wrote down the numbers that he rattled off and hit the button to save the message as a reminder, but I couldn't summon the energy to call him back. Besides, what was I going to say? *I'm getting my ass handed to me in trial and am going to have to cut a deal, but I think he's guilty anyway?* Not exactly spectacular spin.

The Jetta and I were crossing the Willamette River over the Morrison Bridge when my cell phone rang. I recognized the number as Kendra's and answered.

"You rang?" It was Chuck.

"You're at Kendra's?" I asked.

"Just pulled up. I guess you called Ray, trying to track down where Kendra's purse came from?" he said.

"Yeah. Did he tell you why?"

"Not really," he said.

I struggled to think of the quickest way to describe what had been a draining day in court. It's not easy to explain how the momentum of a case can shift with just a few hours in trial. I had to jerk the steering wheel back into line as I realized I'd been zoning out on the lights reflecting off the river. I waited until I was over the bridge and had merged onto the I-5 to launch into it.

"The case fell apart today," I said. "Lopez brought in a guy from the Collision Clinic. Turns out Derringer arranged to have the car work done before the attack and the shop couldn't get it done until that Sunday, so our theory about doing it to get rid of the physical evidence is gone."

Chuck tried to assuage my concerns. "I don't think that

part of the evidence was that important, Sam. It made a nice icing to the cake, but you should be alright without it."

"You're right that it wasn't the heart of the case. The problem is that putting a theory out there and having it torn apart by the defense is a lot worse than if we'd never floated it in the first place. It gives the defense the momentum. And losing that piece of circumstantial evidence makes the fingerprint even more important," I said.

"I still don't know what the problem is there," he said.

I filled him in on Derringer's temp job doing inventory at Dress You Up. "Without the print, all we've got is Kendra's ID and Renshaw's testimony about the pethismograph." I had a tough time holding back tears as I heard myself admit how bad things had turned in just one day. "That's why I really need to know where Andrea got that purse. How's it looking so far?"

"It's a long shot. I finally got hold of Andrea at work. She's not supposed to get calls at the restaurant, so she was distracted and I was having trouble explaining to her why it was important. Add the fact that she freaked at the mention of Dress You Up, going off about how they falsely arrested her—well, you get the picture. Anyway, she thinks she bought the purse at Meier & Frank. If not there, one of the other big department stores, not Dress You Up. Problem is, she doesn't have any credit cards and usually just pays cash."

"Any chance she's still got a receipt?" I asked.

"That's what I'm doing now. She says she usually just throws them out, but sometimes she tosses them into a couple different drawers around the house. I'm going to go through them. If I don't find anything, I'll swing by the restaurant on the way home so she can sign a consent form for me to get her old checks from the bank, just in case she happened to pay by check. Other than that, I can't think of anything else."

Neither could I. "OK, let me know if you find anything."

"You going to be OK tonight, Sam?" he asked.

Darn blasted tears were back again. "I don't know. It's just too much, you know?"

"Then let me help you. If you need follow-up, I'm free."

What I really wanted was company. "Will you stay with me tonight when you finish up?"

"Definitely. Easiest request I ever got from a DA. I'll call you on my way out."

"And can you bring some pancakes?" I added. "The Hotcake House makes them to go."

| 12 |

It was almost midnight by the time Chuck got to my house, and we were both exhausted. Not too exhausted to talk about the case while I devoured my pancakes, or to have as good a round of hot and steamy sex as a post-pancake lull will allow, but we were pretty exhausted all the same.

Chuck had looked through the junk drawers at the Martin house, but, as Andrea had thought, there was no receipt for the purse. Andrea signed a release for her account information, and Chuck was going to check with the bank in the morning for any checks that might match with the purchase. He was also going to contact Meier & Frank to make sure they stocked that purse before Christmas. That would at least verify Andrea's recollection, and I could recall her to the stand along with a Meier & Frank rep in rebuttal.

I must've killed the alarm the next morning, because I overslept. Even though I let my hair dry in the car and parked at the expensive garage across from the courthouse, I didn't have time for Starbucks. Now I'd be having my ass handed me in trial with bad hair and office coffee. Terrific.

When I ran into my office to grab my trial notebooks, I was greeted by a nice big Post-it note on my chair: *Sam— Where are you? Don't bother calling Lesh—he knows you'll be late. Get down to Duncan's office ASAP. TOD.*

Now what? I grabbed my notebooks and took the stairs down two flights to Duncan's office. I'd doubled my total number of visits there in just two days. Not good.

When I arrived, Duncan's secretary waved me in and hollered, "Samantha Kincaid's finally here."

Duncan sat alone at his desk. "Tim took off. Have a seat," he said.

"Sir, I'm sure this is important, but I'm still in trial," I said, gesturing down with my head at the stack of books I was carrying for court.

"Please, Sam, just have a seat. We called Lesh earlier."

I did as he said.

It was the first time I'd ever seen Duncan Griffith without a smile. He looked worried. And mean. "Why didn't you tell me yesterday you had a rotten case?" he asked.

My heart started to race as I struggled to collect my thoughts. Why was he asking about my case again when we'd resolved everything yesterday?

"First of all, I don't think it's a rotten case. The defense has had some surprises, so it's no slam dunk, but I've still got a good enough case to fight. Second, I was under the impression that we met yesterday about the case as it relates to the Zimmerman issue. I didn't realize that you wanted an update about the general status of the trial."

"Sam, that kind of answer does squat for me right now."

I blinked and felt my lips separate but nothing came out. "Excuse me?" I finally said.

"Jesus, Kincaid." Griffith shook his head at me. "Tunnel vision. A real tunnel vision problem. You didn't get my point at all yesterday, did you?"

"Yes, sir. Keep the eye on the ball. The big picture. The greater good." Usually, I can manage to sound earnest even though I know I'm being snide. This time, I just sounded snide.

"Damn it. Yes, the strength of your case matters when your bad guy's telling everyone who will listen that he's the innocent victim of the Keystone Kops and that some serial rapist is on the loose. It matters even more when there's another guy on death row saying the same thing, and a little old lady serving a life term backing him up. Jesus. You made it sound yesterday like your guy was just taking advantage of the publicity with Taylor. Now I've got to find out from the papers that there's something to it."

Shit. I hadn't read the papers this morning, and I'd blown off Manning's call last night. I decided it was better not to interrupt Griffith's diatribe with information that made me look even more inept and uninformed.

"Jesus, I started with the softball, Kincaid, when I asked you about your case. The bigger question is why the hell you didn't bother to mention your little tryst with Chuck Forbes. You sat here in my office and acted like this was a routine case with some incidental mention of the Zimmerman matter. Now I've got this." He picked up a folded *Oregonian* from his desk and slammed it down for emphasis.

When in doubt, bluff. It usually works. "Sir, I'm not sure

how it would have been relevant during our meeting yesterday for me to start discussing my personal life, whatever that
may be."

"And you still think that today?" he asked. Again with that
damn newspaper.

My only choice was to 'fess up. "I'm afraid I didn't get a
chance to see the paper this morning yet, sir. Like I said, I'm
in trial, and I was running late."

Griffith stared at me for a second. Then he started
laughing.

"Oh. Well then, let me have the pleasure of being the first
to introduce you to the story that may very well end your
career and mine. Please, be my guest. Go over to the sofa if
you'd like. It's quite comfortable, and, I guarantee, that's
quite an article. It might take awhile."

I thought about rewarding the sarcasm by lying on the
sofa as he suggested, but I wanted to keep my job.

I unfolded the paper to a banner headline that read, DOES
PORTLAND HAVE A SERIAL KILLER? A smaller line beneath it
explained, *Letter from "The Long Hauler" Supports Theory
Linking Current Sex Trial to Murder of Jamie Zimmerman*.
There was a large photograph of a smiling Jamie Zimmerman, with smaller booking photographs of Taylor, Landry,
and Derringer. The text below the pictures explained that,
despite claims of innocence, Taylor was on death row and
Landry was serving a life sentence for the rape/murder of
Zimmerman, and that Derringer claimed that whoever
killed Zimmerman must have committed the crime he was
accused of.

I had to read the article quickly, since Griffith was obviously growing impatient:

Like the letter first disclosed by the *Oregonian* last week, the one received yesterday arrived in an unremarkable white envelope bearing a Roseburg postmark. The writer again claims that he—and not Jesse Taylor and Margaret Landry—strangled Jamie Zimmerman. In this new letter, however, the writer maintains that Zimmerman's murder was just the beginning in what has become a string of grisly murders, scattered throughout the Pacific Northwest and previously believed to be unconnected. He also claims responsibility for a brutal rape that is the basis of the trial of Frank Derringer currently being held in the Multnomah County Courthouse.

Calling himself the Long Hauler, the writer identifies himself as a long-haul truck driver from Oregon whose travels across the country have made it easy for him to kill five women undetected.

I was surprised by the graphic detail reprinted verbatim in the paper. At one point, the author explained that killing Zimmerman had ignited an insatiable desire in him to kill. Six months after he strangled Jamie Zimmerman, he couldn't withstand the temptation anymore, so he picked up a prostitute at a truck stop in Ellensburg, Washington, and strangled her with a leather belt while he orally sodomized her. I kept reading.

Explaining his self-declared pseudonym, the writer says, "All the good ones had a name. Son of Sam, Boston Strangler, Green River Killer. Unless you think of something better, you can just call me the Long Hauler."

In addition to detailed descriptions of the murders of Jamie Zimmerman and four other women, the writer also describes his involvement in a violent sexual assault upon a victim he refers to as "the girl who was dumped in the Gorge last Feb[ruary]." He claims that, as he had done prior to and since Zimmerman's murder, he went with a friend to look for a prostitute to share.

He says, "I knew we were going to kill the girl when my friend couldn't [achieve an erection]. He started working her over and it brought out the urge in me. Maybe the Gorge is my lucky spot. That couple took the fall for me after I did Jamie, and now the cops think some other guy did the other girl. I guess the bad luck is that this time she lived. (Ha-ha.)"

The writer's description of the incident closely matches the crime for which Frank Derringer is currently on trial. Derringer is accused of raping a thirteen-year-old girl and leaving her for dead in the Columbia Gorge with an unidentified accomplice. During his trial, Derringer has claimed to be the victim of a mistaken eyewitness identification. Because of similarities between the offense and Zimmerman's murder, Derringer has suggested that the crimes were committed by the same person or persons.

I reached the end of the front page text of the feature story and opened the paper to jump to the continuation. Apparently, the writer gave detailed descriptions of the five murders, but the *Oregonian* was declining to publish any potentially identifying information until law enforcement officials verified its authenticity.

An exasperated sigh from Griffith reminded me that I was supposed to be rushing. I closed the paper back to the front page and looked up at him.

"I'm sorry, Sam. Was I disrupting your reading?"

"I was getting through it as quickly as I could," I said. "So the paper agreed to keep the details quiet until we figure out if this guy's for real?"

Griffith didn't hide his annoyance. "Yeah, IA's trying to find any cases matching up to what this guy says. But I wouldn't concern yourself with that right now."

I wanted to ask him why the bureau's Internal Affairs Division would be investigating a potential serial killer, but I could tell Duncan wasn't in the mood to answer any more of my questions.

"What are you willing to tell me about this thing with Forbes?" Duncan snatched the paper from my hand and gave it a couple of hard creases, exposing a smaller sidebar on the front page, then handed it back to me. "That," he said for emphasis.

Dan Manning was a little shit. That was all I could think when I found myself staring at the headline:

DA–DETECTIVE RELATIONSHIP CLOUDS DERRINGER CASE

The deputy district attorney prosecuting Frank Derringer is involved in a romantic relationship with a lead detective in the investigation of the murder of Jamie Zimmerman and the rape of which Derringer is accused, the *Oregonian* has learned.

Samantha Kincaid of the Drug and Vice Division of the Multnomah County District Attorney's Office is handling the current trial against Derringer, who is accused of raping and attempting to murder a teenage girl last February. The defense has raised the possibility that the crime was committed by the person or persons who murdered Jamie Zimmerman three years ago.

The *Oregonian* has learned that Detective Charles Forbes,

Jr., of the Major Crimes Team of the Portland Police Bureau, has spent multiple nights with Kincaid at her home since the beginning of the Derringer trial.

Forbes is a member of the team that investigated the case against Derringer. He was also a central figure in the prosecutions of Jesse Taylor and Margaret Landry, who have been convicted of Zimmerman's murder. Forbes, the son of former Governor Charles Forbes, was the only witness to statements by Landry that incriminated her and Taylor in the murder.

When contacted for comment, Lisa Lopez, Derringer's lawyer, raised concerns about the objectivity of the District Attorney's Office. "Mr. Derringer has been trying to tell the police and the District Attorney's Office that there is something seriously wrong here. One girl is dead and another one brutally assaulted," Lopez said. "While the real assailant runs free to write taunting letters to the media, the Portland Police Bureau's Major Crime Team is so eager to close cases that they're going after innocent people like Mr. Derringer. If the prosecuting DDA is having a romantic relationship with this particular detective, I have real questions about the fairness of the process."

Ms. Kincaid did not return calls requesting her comments.

Little shit didn't begin to describe the enormousness of Manning's shittiness. He had clearly called late in the day and left an innocuous message, betting I wouldn't call back. It always sounds better when the media can say that someone didn't return calls.

"Duncan, if I had known, I would've returned his call. He

didn't say anything about this angle. You can listen to the message if you want to. I saved it."

"Oh, that's great, Sam. That's really going to save my neck here. 'Hey, *Oregonian*, I want a retraction. Yes, my deputy's banging this rogue detective, and yes, your reporter tried to call her about it ahead of time, but it's really *unfair* that he wasn't clearer about his *angle*.' "

I guess it did sound a little whiny.

"Is there any way to deny the story, Sam?" he asked. He had calmed down considerably and asked the question in a way that suggested he'd already come to accept the answer.

"No, it's accurate," I said, still failing to comprehend how my personal life had wound up on the front page of the paper and inside Duncan Griffith's office.

Duncan walked around his desk and took a seat behind it. Maybe he thought I'd blame the desk and not him for what he was about to do. Maybe he just wanted a shield in front of him in case I became hysterical.

"I'm taking you off the Derringer case. O'Donnell already notified the defense and Judge Lesh this morning that the office was looking into the information published in this morning's paper and that some changes might be forthcoming. I'm going to put O'Donnell on the case. I expect he'll be able to get an adjournment while we figure out what the hell's going on. O'Donnell may need to consult with you on the file, but you are officially off any case involving MCT. Do you have any others?"

I wanted to walk out. No, I wanted to throw stuff at him, break a few valuables in his impeccable office, and then walk out. Unfortunately, I also wanted to keep my job. The reality was that I could still do more good in this rotten office without the Derringer case than I'd do at some private law firm fighting over money for energy and tobacco companies.

"The Derringer case is my only MCT file," I said.

If someone had asked me the night before, I would've said I'd do just about anything to rid myself of the case: I was going down in flames and about to grovel for a plea. Now I wanted nothing more than to keep my hand in the mix, at least in some small way.

"Duncan, I think it would be a good idea if O'Donnell and I met with defense counsel together to cut a plea. If the defense thinks I'm totally out of the picture, they'll think they've won. They won't want to deal."

"Can't do it, Sam. You're out. And I'm going to make it damn clear to O'Donnell not even to attempt to pressure a plea until IA tells us where we are with this guy's letter. We got lucky that the *Oregonian* withheld the specifics. That letter includes extremely detailed descriptions of those murders. If IA verifies it, we've got a major wing nut on our hands. 'The Long Hauler.' Jesus Christ, what a fucking nightmare."

It's frustrating when people don't listen to you, but it's downright infuriating when you know you're right.

"Why's IA involved?" I asked. "I thought Walker and Johnson were leads on this."

Griffith shook his head. "No. Too much at stake now. The first letter, anyone who read up on the Zimmerman case could've written it. Looked like it wouldn't lead to anything, so the bureau thought it was good enough to keep Forbes off it. If it turns out Landry and Taylor are actually innocent, your boyfriend's in deep doo doo. Starts to look like Landry was finally telling the truth when she said Forbes was feeding her the details."

"But go back to what O'Donnell told the jury. Why would Chuck do that? The governor's son can get through the ranks without framing people."

"See what I meant about bias, Kincaid? You're smart enough to see that the whole governor's son angle cuts both ways. You could also say it puts pressure on him to be a star, to stand out as his own man, make it big in a way that no one could say it was because of the old man. And hey, he probably thought she really did do it. He wouldn't be the first cop to bend some rules to make a case stronger to get the bad guys."

It did look different from that angle. Given what I'd seen good cops do to help convict the guilty, why couldn't I believe that Chuck might occasionally do the same? Even in high school, Chuck had resented the inherent unspoken separation from his peers that came with being the governor's son. If that pressure had been bad as a teenager surrounded by the offspring of lawyers and doctors, what had it been like with rookie patrol officers? If Chuck felt in his gut that Landry had been guilty and wanted to bring down a freak like Taylor, might he help her along with a few details to shore up her story?

As I walked out of Duncan's office, I could barely stomach what I was thinking. He was right. I couldn't be objective.

Since my regular caseload hadn't included MCT cases before the Derringer file came along, you'd think life with my run-of-the-mill drug and prostitution cases would have felt like a return to normalcy. Instead, it just felt anxiety-ridden. I didn't think anything would feel normal to me again until the bureau finished its investigation and I could finally find out what others decided about the future of Frank Derringer and Chuck, not to mention me.

Chuck had been suspended from all MCT investigations and put on temporary assignment to patrol. Since detectives don't work patrol, the police union was filing a grievance, claiming that Chuck had essentially been demoted without a hearing. The union's interest was to make the bureau's staffing as inflexible as possible, so the bureau has to hire new bodies whenever it has a shortage in any single area. The bureau was fighting the beef, claiming that the change was a simple reassignment, since Chuck's salary hadn't been docked. Chuck, of course, wasn't given a say in any of it and was back on patrol, angry but cognizant of the fact that he could have been suspended.

Personally, I'd rather be suspended. Maybe if I'd boinked the entire Major Crimes Team, I'd be one of those lucky public employees who got suspended for a couple of years with pay until a lengthy investigation resulted in my return to full employment with no discipline other than an extended paid vacation. But sex with just one detective left me where I was, back with my drug and vice cases.

Lopez had agreed to an adjournment. True believer that she was, she wouldn't have acquiesced unless she thought the delay would help Derringer. Based on that, I tried telling O'Donnell that the time was ripe to approach the defense with a decent plea agreement. But he refused, reminding me that the boss had ordered him not to pressure a plea until the police determined whether the Long Hauler was for real.

O'Donnell had continued to surprise me with relatively

decent behavior. He agreed that I'd handle communications with Kendra and Andrea about the case. Even though I suspected he did it to save himself the work of victim handholding, I was grateful that Kendra wasn't going to have to hear about the turn of events from someone other than me.

The night after I'd been kicked off the case, I had taken Kendra out to dinner and did my best to explain why the case was being set over. I wanted desperately to answer all her questions about what was going to happen, whether Derringer was still going to go to jail, why some "stupid" letter had to affect her case, and everything else she asked me as she played with her food. All I could do was tell her not to give up hope. We'd have to wait and see.

We both kept up a good front, but the signs of demoralization were clear in her untouched plate.

Now that the case was over, there wasn't much of an official role for me to play in Kendra's life. I talked to her about enrolling in the LAP teen program. Learning Alternatives to Prostitution was intended for court-mandated treatment of criminal defendants, but anyone could enroll. I'd already contacted them, and a counselor had told me she could get Kendra a volunteer tutor to help her with school and Kendra could participate in weekly group therapy sessions. Sometimes the "therapy" took the form of activities like painting and gardening, but those might be just the things Kendra needed to reenter life as a somewhat regular thirteen-year-old.

Now, Monday morning. I reminded myself that I was supposed to be acting like a lawyer. I spent the afternoon returning phone calls and covering grand jury hearings. One guy I indicted definitely earned the dope-of-the-day award, if not the year. The defendant marched into the lobby of Southeast Precinct to report a fraud and pulled fifteen ounces of heroin and a scale from his gym bag. Turns out the seller charged him for a pound. Outraged by the one-ounce shortage, the defendant thought the police would help him get what he called "reparations."

Ordinarily, this would have carried me through the day. But even the reprieve from crank calls, break-ins, head cracks, and brown Toyota Tercels wasn't enough to make me appreciate my return to the mundane. I couldn't keep my mind off the so-called Long Hauler and his claim of responsibility for the attack on Kendra. Something just didn't feel right about it. I needed to get more evidence against Derringer, so I could trash him no matter what the Long Hauler's story turned out to be.

I decided to take a little detour on the way home from work. I wouldn't even say that I decided to do it; it was more like my body willed me. Right after my usual merge onto the I-5 from the Morrison Bridge, I noticed the exit sign for the Lloyd Center mall. I reminded myself of how good I'd been about following Duncan's orders. I thought of the trouble I'd be in for snooping around, the way O'Donnell's nostrils would flare in anger if he found out, and the possibility that it was all a waste of time anyway. The next thing I knew, I was parking my Jetta outside of Meier & Frank in the Lloyd Center parking lot and walking into the handbags department.

Now, if this had been a premeditated case of meddling into affairs that were no longer mine, I would have checked Kendra's purse out of the evidence locker and taken it with me to the counter. But since this was impromptu meddling, I was left describing the purse to the nitwit at the counter.

Nitwit was about seventeen years old. Her blond hair tumbled out of the knot at the back of her head like a fountain designed by someone on a heavy acid trip. From the bottom up, everything she wore was irritating: platform sandals that made my feet wince, jeans slung low enough to reveal a navel ring and bony hips, and a tight belly shirt that evidently operated like a tube of toothpaste, pushing all her bodily fluids into her head and retarding the firing of her synapses.

My badge, ID, and lengthy explanation of what I was looking for and why were apparently lost on her, because she seemed to think I was browsing around for a new handbag.

And, of course, everything she said ended with a question mark. "We don't really have any bags by Esprit right now? But we have, like, a ton of black leather purses, OK? We have some really cute Nine West purses over here? And there's some on sale over there? But I really like these Kate Spade ones?" I was beginning to think she was an evil robot, programmed to prattle on about purses until her frosty-pink lip gloss dried up.

I explained it to her a few more times. I wasn't interested in buying a new purse. I was from the District Attorney's Office working on a criminal investigation and needed to know whether they carried a certain black leather purse by Esprit last autumn.

After the fourth try, Nitwit clued in and the frosty lips started moving again. "OK, like, I totally didn't understand that before? You want to ask about something we had, like, way back in November? I so didn't work here yet?"

I finally uttered the magic words that should have been my first. "Is there, like, a manager or something?"

Sweet lord, a woman in her thirties was never such a relief! Her name tag identified her as JAN, SENIOR SALES ASSOCIATE. All that mattered to me was that she'd worked there for two years and spoke that increasingly endangered language known as grown-up.

"OK, let's see . . . black leather handbag by Esprit. Around November." I was nodding as she thought out loud. "Yeah, we had a line of leather bags by them last year. They normally do more canvas and novelty bags. What kind of strap did it have? There was one that was more like a backpack, one that had a shorty little handbag strap, and then a couple with shoulder straps."

I told her it had a regular shoulder strap and then did my best sketching it on a piece of scrap paper she gave me.

"Yeah, that looks like one of the shoulder strap ones we had." She walked around the counter and pulled a bag out that was on display. "Does it look kind of like this one, but with seams on the side and without this little buckle here?"

"That's *just* what it looks like," I said, surprise in my tone. I couldn't believe anyone could distinguish among purses in such detail, but I guess others would marvel at my ability to distinguish Grey Goose from Smirnoff.

"Do most of the people who were here last fall still work with the company?" I asked.

She looked up in the air like she was thinking and counting. "Yeah, not everyone, but mostly."

"And what are the chances one of them might remember selling that particular purse to someone if I get you a picture of the person?" I asked, my smile revealing that I knew it was a long shot.

"Boy, pretty slim. That was six months ago." She could see my disappointment register. "Hey, it's worth a shot, though. Tell you what, you give me the picture and I'll make sure everyone takes a look at it."

"Great." I thought about the easiest way to get a picture of Andrea to Jan and slipped into thinking aloud myself. "OK, I can get a booking photo of her from January, which should be pretty much how she looked last November."

Solid, reliable Jan looked alarmed at the mention of a booking photo, and I laughed. "Oh, don't worry. She's not a hardened criminal or anything." Of course, the truth is that hardened criminals come to the mall and buy regular, boring things from stable, reliable people like Jan every day, but I didn't see the need to tell her that. "It's actually kind of a long story. A security guard at Dress You Up excluded her from the store. It was really more of a misunderstanding, but they had her arrested a few months later when she came back."

Jan tilted her head. "God, that rings a bell. I sold a purse to a woman, and I remember she was red hot about some security guard at Dress You Up. The guy had accused her of shoplifting, and even though she told them to look through her stuff and they didn't find anything, he kicked her out of the store. Didn't apologize or anything. You know, that would've been around November."

I had to refrain from throwing my arms around solid, reliable Jan. It had to have been Andrea. She must've bought the purse the same day she had the run-in with Kerry Richardson at Dress You Up.

"And this woman bought the Esprit purse we've been talking about?" I asked.

"I have no idea. I just remember the thing about the security guard."

"What about the woman who bought the purse? Was she about thirty-five? Brown shoulder-length hair? About my height?" I was doing my best to describe Andrea, whose appearance was most notable for being nondescript.

Jan shook her head. "I don't know. Like I said, I just remember that conversation. Maybe if I saw her picture—"

I dashed back to my car and drove over to Northeast Precinct. It was only a couple of miles, but pesky things like lights, cats, and frolicking children kept getting in the way of my car. The forty minutes it took me to print Andrea's booking photo from X-imaging and take it back to Jan felt like an eternity.

Jan looked carefully at Andrea's picture and said, "Yeah, I think that's the woman. I remember her now." It wasn't the best ID in the world, but it was a hell of lot more than I had a few days ago.

I was too excited to go home to my usual routine, so I picked up Vinnie for a visit to Dad's. In the car, I checked my cell for messages. There were two from Chuck. I'd been avoiding him since the shit hit the fan in Duncan's office. Hell, I had to face him eventually. I left a message to meet me at Dad's if he felt like it.

Dad was so happy to see me he didn't even complain about Vinnie tagging along.

Going to Dad's is a major treat for Vinnie. Dad's yard is large enough that there were still some bushes that Vinnie hadn't managed to pee on yet. Vinnie would sniff around back, seeking out unsoiled ones to violate. Add the Milk Bones that Dad keeps around to control Vinnie's breath, and Dad's house was the Vinnie equivalent of a Yankees–Mets game.

By the time Chuck showed up, Dad and I had fed Vinnie, gone to the market for the "grocks" as Dad called them, and put a dish of baked penne in the oven.

Dad took great pleasure announcing Chuck's arrival before he headed back to the kitchen. "Sam, your man's here and he's got wine."

Chuck was lingering by the door. As I went to kiss his cheek, he grabbed me around the shoulders and pulled me close. I couldn't tell if he noticed that my response was awkward. I let myself be held; it felt good to rest my head against his chest and feel his arms around me. But I couldn't quite bring myself to return the embrace.

Maybe he picked up on my reticence. As he finally let go of me, he settled for a kiss on the top of the head. "Hey, you. I brought your favorite."

It was an Australian shiraz-cab blend, perfect for someone like me who can't handle a full-blown cabernet. I forced a smile as we headed back into the kitchen. "Thanks. That was sweet."

Dad gave Chuck one of those half handshake, half shoulder-grab things that guys give each other instead of hugs. "Hey, big man, how you holding up?" he asked. I was glad Dad had kicked off the conversation. I was still resisting the urge to pull Chuck outside and grill him until I was absolutely positive, beyond any doubt, that he had fully disclosed everything he knew about Landry's confession.

"You know, patrol's not so bad. It's kind of a nice break from the heavy stuff." From some guys, this might've sounded like saving face, or maybe just making the best of a bad situation. From Chuck, it sounded sincere.

Me? I was just trying to make the most of a bad situation.

"Same here. Too many of those MCT cases and I would've started to lose my faith in humanity. I'd hate to wind up like O'Donnell one of these days," I said with a shudder.

"Yeah, I know what you mean," Dad said. "Back with the Forest Department, you know, we never really had to do anything like what you were doing at MCT. Just some trespassing, drunks, a few fights. Enough to make life exciting, but the most you ever brought home at night was a funny story."

When Dad talked about his career, he tended to leave out his years as an Oregon State Police detective. He joined the Forest Department when I was a toddler. He and Mom decided the hours were more regular, the pension was better, and he was less likely to get shot in the forest than in OSP. Dad liked to say he was grateful for the switch, but I always sensed he missed the excitement of his early career.

"So, Lucky Chucky, what kind of stories you got for us tonight?" I asked, grateful that Dad had never asked for the etymology of the nickname.

Chuck shook his head as he poured three glasses of wine. "Nothing, really. Been pretty slow."

I could tell there were a few possibilities, though. Maybe not full-out, pee-your-pants knee slappers, but enough to make him smile. "Oh, c'mon," I cajoled. "There's no way you've been on patrol all week without something happening. You have a civic responsibility to share your telltale stories with bored retirees and drug deputies."

"OK, there was this one guy. He was weaving his BMW all over the place through a school zone, right when kids were starting to come in. Windows tinted nearly black. When I pulled him over and he rolled down his window, I could see he was yapping into his cell phone. Must've been what distracted him. I was planning to give him a warning and send him on his way, but he refused to get off the phone. Kept telling me that he billed his time at four hundred dollars an hour and I was keeping him from his work."

"So you wrote him a ticket?" Dad asked.

Chuck smiled. "Better than that. I impounded the BMW."

"You did what?" I said.

"I towed it. Oregon Motor Vehicle Code section 815.222: illegal window tinting, a towable violation. Includes applying any tint that limits light transmittance to less than fifty percent. My best guess is he should be getting it out of the impound lot right around now," he said, glancing at his watch.

Dad was laughing, but I wasn't. "I can't believe you did that. It's a total abuse of your authority. That's why people hate cops, Chuck."

Dad and Chuck exchanged a glance before Chuck spoke up. "It wasn't just an attitude problem, Sam. He nearly hit a kid and didn't even care. I was trying to show him some perspective."

"Sounds kind of like something you'd do, Sam," Dad said, laughing.

Maybe, but it still bothered me that Chuck thought it was funny.

He insisted on making sure I got home OK. I had half a bottle of Pinot Gris in my fridge, so I poured a glass for each of us to finish it off.

He finally raised the subject we'd been avoiding. "One of the guys called me a couple of hours ago. Word is, IA's got something on the Long Hauler."

I looked at him with surprise. "Guy seemed like a pro. First letter had no prints, not even DNA on the stamp or envelope."

"I assume the second letter's the same," he said. "I didn't mean they figured out who he is. But the stuff in the letter, it's for real. They found four unsolved homicide cases that match the other girls this guy says he did."

"But is it stuff he could've gotten from papers?" I asked.

"I don't know. He also said he left something of Jamie's in the Gorge. IA's got a bunch of Explorers out there combing through the forest looking for it."

Explorers are high school students who want to become police officers. They make for a handy resource during fishing expeditions. They don't mind hiking around in the mud as long as they get to wear a uniform, they're a hell of a lot cheaper than police officers on overtime, and they aren't fat yet, so they can do helpful things like climb hills and fit through small spaces. On the other hand, if you want an idea of how reliable they are in their searches, the DC police used them to search Rock Creek Park for the body of that poor missing intern a few summers ago.

"Do you know what they're looking for?" I asked.

"No. I'm surprised I heard anything. IA's being quiet about this, and I of all people am not supposed to hear a word. But, you know, the guys look out for each other."

It bothered me that he didn't say who shared the information. Was he actually worried I'd be angry at one of the MCT detectives for leaking information to him? If the gap between cops and DAs seemed that wide to him, maybe he was in a place I would never truly understand. As it stood, I realized I knew little about Chuck Forbes the detective. Perhaps I had been too quick to assume that his hands were squeaky clean.

I turned on the TV to catch my favorite talking-head show, *Hardball*. I still don't know how a guy who looks like a fifty-year-old surfer dude had the balls to think he'd get away with a motto like "Let's play hardball," but Chris Matthews seems to have pulled it off. Maybe if Griffith fired me, I could get Matthews to hire me as a talking head. It would be an easy job, and it seemed like an inevitable stop on the road for anyone at the middle of a media frenzy. Yes, the congressmen did it. So did the missing kids' parents. So did that guy who used to play a detective with a bird on TV. They pretty much always did it.

Chuck and I didn't say much during the show. The silence was interrupted occasionally as we vented about the new terrorism warnings that were issued every time the president's ratings were slipping. But we said that all the time.

I don't know when I decided not to tell him about solid reliable Jan, but I took the fact that I didn't want to as a bad sign, one he apparently picked up on. Once Chris Matthews got through telling us what he really thought, Chuck announced that it was time for him to head home. I didn't try to stop him, and he kissed me on the top of my head again when I walked him to the door.

| 13 |

Things started moving forward the next morning.

The media had gotten wind of the search in the Gorge and were clamoring for more information. That meant I could probe O'Donnell for information about the search without tipping him off that someone on MCT was talking to Chuck about the investigation. I stuck my head into his office door and asked him for an update.

"I'm beginning to think you suffer from selective deafness, Kincaid. You . . . are . . . off . . . the . . . case!" O'Donnell pantomimed the words with his hands to mimic sign language. I would definitely not be inviting him to my next Charades party. He sucked.

I reminded him that I was still supposed to be coordinating communications with Kendra and her mom. I had prepared a white lie: Andrea Martin was clamoring for answers and he either had to fork over some information or explain

it all to her himself before Channel 2 did. A pissed-off victim
is every prosecutor's worst nightmare. A weepy interview on
the local news saying they've been left out of the loop and
victimized again by the system rings true to every viewer
who's ever been ignored by a bureaucrat.

As it turned out, I didn't need to resort to my bluff, because
O'Donnell actually caught himself being an asshole and apologized. "Sorry, you're right. I snapped because this case is
getting to me. Have a seat," he said, clearing some notebooks
from a chair for me.

He picked up the phone, indicating with his thumb and
forefinger that it would be a short call. "Hey, Carl. It's
O'Donnell. Did you double-check with all the crime labs yet?"
He gave the frequent "yeahs" and "unh-huhs" that aren't very
helpful when you're eavesdropping on one side of a conversation. "Well, we gave it a shot. This guy's one lucky son of
a bitch."

"Bad news?" I asked as he hung up.

"Understatement of the century," he said, rolling his eyes.
"C'mon, I gotta go over all this stuff with Duncan. You might
as well come."

"I thought I was off the case," I said, imitating his mock
sign language. He laughed, and I had to as well.

"Damn, you can be a pain in the ass. Just come on, OK?"
he said, walking out of his office. If O'Donnell kept this up,
I might actually start to like him.

Duncan was on the phone when we walked in. He gestured for us to have a seat. I was doing a lot of this today.

O'Donnell leaned forward so the two of us could talk
quietly while we waited for Duncan to finish his call. "None
of this goes to Forbes, right?"

The request was reasonable under the circumstances. I nodded.

"OK. We found four unsolved homicides through the Northwest Regional Cold Case Database. One in Idaho, one in Montana, and two in Washington. All of them women, all either prostitutes or promiscuous. So far, the details match the Long Hauler letter to a T. We're dealing with a grade-A psycho."

"What kind of details, public information or concealed?" I asked. In any murder investigation, law enforcement always held back certain details. It kept the bad guy from knowing what investigators had, and it could help down the road if a wanna-be confessor tried to jump into the mix.

"Stuff no one else could know. Position of the bodies, personal items that were taken, whether specific items of clothes were on or off. I told you, the guy's for real."

"Just on the four new cases? What about Zimmerman and Martin?" I asked. It sounded funny to label Kendra by her last name, but O'Donnell was sharing information. It was better not to remind him of my personal attachment to the victim.

"Them too. On your case, he gave us the exact intersection they pulled Martin from, everything they did to her, that they threw the purse in the trash. The paper didn't have those details."

"No, but it all came out in trial," I said. I was playing it cool, removing the lid from my latte and blowing in the cup, like we were talking about running times or stock performances.

"Are you saying you saw a suspicious serial-killer type sitting in on your trial?"

He was right. I would have noticed if someone had been watching. "Any possibility that Derringer did it all and then wrote to the paper as the Long Hauler when he got caught on the Martin rape?" Clearly Derringer was benefiting from these letters, and given what he did to Kendra, he certainly had it in him to rape and kill other women.

But O'Donnell was already shaking his head. "Doesn't look like it. No way he could've sent them himself. The jail reads all outgoing prisoner mail. There's always the possibility that he could sneak a letter to a visitor or something, but it doesn't look like he could be the guy. We've already got him solid in Oregon during two of the out-of-state murders. He had a parole meeting with Renshaw during one of them and was doing time on the Clackamas County attempted sod for another."

It looked like we had a serial killer on our hands. "Any other cases in the Cold Case Database that match?" I asked. The computerized data bank was a partnership among law enforcement agencies in the Pacific Northwest and included details of all unsolved homicides.

"Nope, nothing obvious," he said. "Our guy's MO seems to be street girls, strangled and dumped outside so it takes awhile to find them. Looks like he copped to all of them in his letter."

Duncan hung up the phone. "Governor's office," he said, by way of explanation. "They're all over me. Jackson's under pressure to pardon Taylor and is looking for something to hang his hat on. Fucking pussy. He won't admit it's because of the death penalty. Doesn't want to lose eastern Oregon."

Bud Jackson was a Portland liberal who managed to win a statewide race only by sending his wife, the daughter of a prominent local ranching family, on the campaign trail throughout conservative rural Oregon.

"If he can say Taylor might be innocent, he could do the pardon and save face." Duncan stopped, seeming to register my presence for the first time since I sat down. "This OK with you, Tim?" he asked, tilting his head toward me.

"Yeah, I'm going to need some help with the Martin family. I was just giving Sam what we got out of the letters."

"Well, it's nice to see you two sharing the sandbox again. So where are we this morning?" he asked, folding his arms in front of him. "I see we weren't able to keep the Gorge search quiet."

"No, sir, we weren't," O'Donnell said, laughing at the obvious understatement.

"They find anything?" Griffith asked.

"Yes, miraculously." Tim turned toward me. "To get you up to speed, Kincaid, the Long Hauler said he threw Zimmerman's purse from his car past a bend in the road up the Gorge, about a quarter mile from the freeway, so we sent the Explorers out there yesterday to dig around along the road out there." He turned back toward Griffith. "They spent all day searching yesterday, but no luck. The bureau was about to call everybody in, but they wanted to make sure they didn't screw it up. Don't want to pull a Washington, DC—have some old guy's dog dig it up next year from right under their noses. Anyway, the detective supervising the search pulls out a park map and talks to every Explorer to make sure he marks off where they've searched. Turns out there's a monster patch of blackberry bushes no one wanted to touch. About a quarter of a football field, four feet high. Now most people would've let it slide, thinking no way a purse can get in there."

I nodded. Blackberry bushes are dense and woody. You can't get through them without a hatchet. I knew from the countless golf balls I'd lost to them that a purse thrown on a blackberry bush would bounce off.

"But this guy is ex-military, total sphincter boy. He checked with the parks department and found out they started letting those bushes grow two years ago, meaning they weren't there when Zimmerman was killed. So he gets everybody clearing out blackberry bushes all night. They found it early this morning," he said, sounding more excited. "They actually found Jamie Zimmerman's purse, and it's pretty much where the guy said it would be. Still has a bunch of stuff in it. Cigarettes, makeup, and, most critically, a fake ID issued to one Jamie Zimmerman. A detective told me he got chills when he found it. Her real ID was in the pocket of her jeans along with a condom and a lipstick, and we figured that was all she carried. We never even knew to look for a purse."

"So we've got him tied to everything now," Duncan said. "Jesus, five dead women, Sam's vic, God knows how many others. Do the police have any leads on this guy?"

"No. Whoever he is, his luck is unbelievable. Crime lab says there's no DNA on either letter. The Cold Case Databank entries for all four of the other cases indicated there was too much deterioration for testable DNA samples, just like with Zimmerman. I had IA call the hometown police agencies to verify the computer information, and I heard from them right before I came down. Nothing."

"Were there any other strangling cases in the database without DNA evidence?" I asked.

O'Donnell paused. "No, just the ones from the letter."

"What's the FBI doing?" Duncan asked.

"They're interested but haven't taken over yet. They've got a profiler studying the cases. Can't give me a time line on when they might have something."

Duncan gave a dismissive wave. "Useless anyway. Let me take a wild guess. Guy in his mid-twenties to forties, loner, no meaningful relationships with women, with a job or life-style that takes him through the Pacific Northwest. Likes to type letters and call himself the Long Hauler. Yeah, real science."

He looked down at his desk and picked up a file.

"Alright, folks, here's what we're going to do. We're dumping the case against Derringer." Duncan put up a hand to silence me before any words came out of my open mouth. "No, Sam, we're dumping it. Your evidence has gone to shit. You've got nothing but the vic's ID. Now, I know you've got a personal interest in the girl, and it's admirable. It really is. But the girl was coming out of a heroin OD. Plus you've got a nearly identical crime committed by a different person— same type of victim, same location, both with missing purses. Oh, and don't forget that the different person is confessing to both crimes. You don't have enough to prove your case beyond a reasonable doubt. Hell, Sam, you don't even have probable cause."

"Duncan, the man's a convicted sex offender with shaved pubic hair. That, combined with the confession—"

He interrupted me. "You know damn well the jury can't hear about the sex offense. Plus we had that defense attorney in here a couple days ago about that, because the shaving was bothering me too. I can see why you butt heads with her," he said, smiling. "What's her name again?"

"Lisa Lopez," I said.

"Right, Lopez. Real firecracker, that one. But she made a

good point. She says Derringer shaved his privates because
he was due for a second pethismograph the Monday after
the assault. I guess the wires pulled at him on the first one.'
Duncan and Tim both made faces like even the thought was
painful. Wusses. They should try a bikini wax. "We confirmed it with the PO—what's his name—"

"Renshaw," O'Donnell reminded him.

Griffith nodded. "Renshaw checked his calendar. Derringer was due in on Monday, just like Lopez said. She couldn't
find a way to bring it out at trial without letting the jury know
her guy was a pervert, so she had to leave it out. Anyway, all
you've got left is the ID, Sam, and it's not enough."

But I had more than that. I had solid reliable Jan. I told
them about my visit to Meier & Frank. Surely it would be
enough. It meant that the fingerprint was back. The print
had always been the best evidence. So why weren't they
excited?

"No dice, Sam," O'Donnell said, shaking his head. "I saw
your note in the file that the mom thought she got it from
Meier & Frank. Just to be safe, I called Staffpower, the temp
agency that Derringer worked for?"

I nodded.

"They faxed this over," O'Donnell said, handing me a piece
of paper from his file. "Turns out most stores do inventory
before the holiday shopping frenzy, and a lot of them use
Staffpower. Derringer did inventory at Meier & Frank last
October also."

The paper he'd handed me was a list of all of the jobs
Derringer took through Staffpower last year. In the two
months before Thanksgiving, he must've worked inventory
for half the stores in the mall.

"You could've saved yourself some time if you'd talked to

ne before you went running around Meier & Frank on your wn after you got taken off the case," Tim said.

"I didn't 'run around,'" I said, making air quotes with my ands. I was seething. And I *hate* air quotes. "It's on my way ome and—"

Griffith put a hand up to silence us. "Sandbox. Remember, ids?" Tim and I stopped. Duncan was right. It didn't matter nymore.

"Sam, you'll explain the situation to the family?" Griffith sked.

I nodded. Yes, I would have to. I couldn't pretend any onger that the case was winnable. It rested entirely on Ken-ra's ID. Eyewitness ID is always questionable, but I had a hild victim who had suffered a horrific assault and was nder the influence of heroin. And if I couldn't maintain that he case was winnable, I couldn't argue with the decision to lismiss it. I hated the thought of breaking the news to Ken-ra, but I couldn't stomach the idea of anyone else doing it ither.

"What do you want to do with Taylor and Landry?")'Donnell asked.

"That one's trickier," Duncan said, pressing the pads of is fingertips together to make something resembling a fil-eted crab, an annoying male gesture that seemed popular in he power corridor. "Juries heard the evidence and found 'aylor and Landry guilty. Even now, the evidence we've got n them isn't so bad, a lot better than we've got on Derringer. 'here's no way around the phone number and earrings that .andry planted on Taylor. But now we've also got ironclad roof that the Long Hauler is involved."

"We've basically got proof beyond a reasonable doubt of wo separate theories," I said.

"Right," Griffith said, "unless we buy Landry's explanatio[n] for how she knew so much. So if we say she didn't do it, we'r[e] basically admitting that a cop helped her with the set-up o[f] Taylor and then lied about it on the stand. I want to be care[-] ful here."

He turned to Tim. "Call the FBI. See if they'll make [a] polygrapher available to us. Then see if Landry and Tayl[or] will agree to polys. You'll have to discuss the questions wit[h] the FBI examiner, but what I really want to know is whethe[r] they did the Zimmerman girl, and whether they know th[e] Long Hauler."

The results of a polygraph examination aren't admissib[le] in court, but the examinations are used by law enforcemen[t] all the time. Sometimes you hook a suspect up to one so he'[ll] confess after he fails it. The failed poly doesn't come int[o] evidence, but the confession does. Polygraphs also help clea[r] someone you already want to cut loose, based on you[r] instincts: the missing kid's parents, the dead woman's hus[-] band, the suspects who become suspects merely because o[f] their status. If you don't have any other reason to suspec[t] them, a passed poly lets you stop looking at them and mov[e] on to less obvious theories. Griffith would feel more co[n-] fident about exonerating Landry and Taylor if they passe[d] polygraphs first.

"Isn't there also the possibility that someone connected t[o] Landry or Taylor wrote the Long Hauler letters?" I asked. [It] couldn't be Landry or Taylor themselves. As O'Donnell ha[d] pointed out, outgoing prisoner mail is strictly monitored.

"I thought that was a possibility with the first letter," Ti[m] said, "but I can't see it with this new one. First of all, I don[']t think Landry knew about Zimmerman's purse, or she wou[ld] have mentioned it when she was trying to set Taylor up fo[r] the fall. More importantly, whoever wrote the Long Hauler letter had to know not just about the Zimmerman murder but the four other murders, plus your case. No way some friend of theirs could cook this up. But, like Duncan said, we should make sure with the poly that Taylor and Landry aren't somehow wrapped up with the Long Hauler."

"So there's the plan, team," Duncan said. The filleted crab fingers were gone and the capped smile was back. "Sam, you take care of the dismissal on Derringer. Any calls from the press, you give 'em some bullshit about new evidence produced by the defense. Don't tie it to the Long Hauler, or we'll get even more pressure to cut Landry and Taylor loose. And talk to the victim today. The family needs to be on board for this. Let them know we're going after this guy and her case won't be forgotten. Tim, get me those polys. I need to get back to Governor Jackson."

So that was it. The case was gone, and I was the one who had to dismiss it and deliver the news to Kendra.

Part of me wanted to call her immediately. Get it over with. Rip the bandage off. But she was in school, so I worked my hardest to keep my mind occupied, trying not to think about how much the case's dismissal would hurt her.

I used the morning's custodies as an excuse not to complete the dismissal order for Derringer. And not to call Chuck. He'd already left me two messages asking why I'd been so cold the night before. As much as I knew that I'd eventually have to answer that question, it was the last thing I wanted to think about right now. So, I stayed cold and worked on custodies.

Today's custodies were typical. Thirty-two new cases,

almost all of them identical. Knock and talk, traffic stop, jay walking ticket. Something small—usually a ruse—starts the encounter between police and someone who looks like they're up to no good. Sometimes the no-goodnik consents to the search. Sometimes it's a pat-down for officer safety reasons, or maybe the officer claims exigent circumstances. Whatever the basis, the search always occurs, and the police find either heroin, coke, or meth. I timed it out once and figured I spend an average of seven minutes to review and issue the typical drug case. Nothing to be proud of, but, like I said, they're all the same.

When I finished up, I changed into my running gear and headed out into the drizzle. The loop around the downtown and eastside waterfronts of the Willamette is almost exactly three miles. I ran hard, trying to chase visions of Kendra and Chuck from my head, and I finished in twenty-two minutes. Not quite as fast as our current president, but I work a lot harder at my day job.

Back at the office, I bought myself some more time, drafting a procrastinated response to a motion to suppress. But I couldn't ignore the clock's reminder that my time to write the dismissal order for Derringer was running out.

It's surprisingly easy to make a criminal case go away. I prepared a one-sentence motion and order stating that the case was dismissed in the interests of justice in light of exculpatory evidence produced by the defense at trial. Lesh signed and filed it, and I faxed copies to Lisa Lopez and the jail. Derringer would be out in a couple of hours.

By the time I finished, I was pretty sure that Kendra would be home from school.

After a couple of minutes of small talk, I told her I wanted to come out to talk about the case. The tone of my voice must have given her an idea of what was coming. "Go ahead and tell me," she said. "God or Edison or whoever invented the phone for a reason, you know."

This wasn't going well. When I insisted on driving out, I got a "whatever" in response. I signed myself out on the DVD board, grabbed the file, and made it to Rockwood in record time. When I knocked on the door, I heard what I recognized as Puddle of Mudd blasting from Kendra's CD player. In my neighborhood, that kind of volume would trigger a call to police. In Rockwood, it was background music.

She apparently didn't have any plans on answering the door for me. I banged on it and pressed the bell for a full two minutes before walking around the back of the house to knock on her bedroom window. "I know you're in there, Kendra. I'm not leaving until you open the door." I rapped the bottom of my fist against her window with the beat of her music for a couple of songs until she finally turned it off.

A few seconds later, I heard her holler from the front door in a singsong voice, "I don't know how you expect to get into the house if you're not here when I open the door." I sprinted around the house like a famished cat responding to a can opener, before Kendra could change her mind. When she didn't say anything about making me wait, I pretended like she hadn't.

"You really didn't have to drive all the way out here, you know," she said, sitting on her bed and going through her CDs, probably searching for the one most likely to give me a headache.

"I know," I said, even though it wasn't true. "But I wanted to see you. You hungry?"

"You trying to give me an eating disorder or something?

French fries and a milkshake don't make everything OK, Sam."

Since when? "Fine," I said. "I want to talk to you about the case, though."

I started by showing her the *Oregonian* articles about the Long Hauler. Andrea didn't subscribe to the paper, and I suspected Kendra had never seen the articles themselves. "What are these?" she asked.

"Please, just read them, and then we'll talk."

She took them from me and spread them out in front of her on the bed, but I could tell she wasn't really reading them.

"Do you mind if I get a glass of water from the kitchen? I'm kind of thirsty," I said, backing out of the room. I got another "whatever" in response, but it gave me a way to leave her alone in her room with the articles for a few minutes. When I returned, she was clutching a pillow on her lap and staring at the photographs on the front page.

"I could've sworn it was him," she said.

"You're not sure anymore?" I asked.

She held the paper up to her face, staring at the photograph of Derringer. "I still think it looks like him, but it can't be him, can it?"

I should've given Kendra more credit. I had been clinging to our theory of the case because I was too stubborn to admit we were mistaken. Here she was, five minutes after reading the article, accepting the unavoidable conclusion. We had the wrong man.

"No, Kendra, I don't see any way it can be him. I know that the newspaper only says the Long Hauler letter had details about your case, but it actually had a lot of information that no one could have had without being one of the men who did this to you."

"So does everyone think I'm a liar now?" she said.

"No one thinks you lied about anything." Looking at her, knowing she was doubting my faith in her, made me want to cry. "We know you told the truth about what happened to you, but you might have made a mistake about who did it. You shouldn't feel bad. You had just been through a horribly traumatic experience. Plus, there was a lot of other evidence pointing to Derringer. Even if you hadn't identified him, we would have wound up focusing on him anyway after his fingerprint came up on your purse."

"My mother did *not* steal that purse," she said.

"I know that. It looks like it came from Meier & Frank. The problem is that Derringer worked there too."

Kendra gave what I thought was a growl of exasperation into the pillow. But when she didn't lift her head, I realized she was crying. I held her and patted her on the back. There was nothing to say.

Once the tears had stopped and she was breathing regularly again, she wanted details on where the Long Hauler investigation stood.

"Well, you already knew that a girl named Jamie Zimmerman was killed a few years ago. Her body was found in the Gorge, not too far from where"—I didn't know how to refer to what happened to her with her: Not too far from where you were dumped? were found?—"from where the ambulance picked you up. Like the paper says, a couple named Margaret Landry and Jesse Taylor were convicted of killing Jamie, but they claim they're innocent. You knew that Derringer's attorney was suggesting in your trial that whoever did the bad things to you had also killed Jamie. With these letters, it's starting to look like one person, someone other than Margaret Landry and Jesse Taylor, killed not only

Jamie but four other women. And he's claiming he was one of the people involved in what happened to you."

"Will the police be able to find out who the Long Hauler is?" she asked. I wanted so much to assure her that they would, that we'd nail him and justice would be served. But I learned a long time ago that you should never make promises to victims unless you don't mind breaking them.

"I know they're trying. They've got the FBI involved. The police chief and the DA are making this a top priority. The feeling is that if the guy's writing letters to the newspaper and naming himself, he's escalating."

I could tell from the way she looked at me that she didn't know what I meant.

"The suspicion is that he'll start to kill even faster," I explained. "That he'll come up with a signature or something now that he's interested in notoriety."

"Oh, so that's why they want to catch him, to keep him from getting to anyone else. They don't actually care about the people he already hurt," she said.

"Hey, you know that's not what I meant. Kendra, the man has killed five women. Of course they want to catch him. I was just trying to tell you how much this matters to the police."

She was quiet while it all sank in. "I guess I wasn't really thinking of it like that. That guy *killed* other people. And he meant to kill me." She looked dazed. "I knew you'd charged him with attempted murder and all, but I never thought of it as someone trying to kill me. That I'm lucky I lived through it."

"Shows you're a survivor, kiddo. You're tougher than him; you beat him."

"Do the police know anything yet?" she asked.

"Well, enough to think that this guy did the things he said he did. The paper didn't mention all the details, but the letter included pretty specific descriptions of all the attacks. The information he provided about what happened to you and Jamie was accurate, and it's stuff he couldn't have taken from a newspaper or something. Also, the police have found unsolved homicides that match the other murders."

"Did they find anything when they searched the Gorge?" she asked.

"Yes, I was going to get to that. Again, the paper didn't publish this detail, so it's important that you keep this between us for now. But the Long Hauler told police he'd taken Jamie Zimmerman's purse and thrown it off the side of the road in the Gorge. Using that information, the police were able to find the purse, and it's absolutely Jamie Zimmerman's. It even had her fake ID in it."

"I guess that's another thing that makes her case like mine, huh? That he left us in the Gorge and took our purses?"

I hadn't thought about that before. Lisa Lopez had had the prescience to argue that Kendra's case was just like the murder of Jamie Zimmerman, but what exactly had she said about it?

I went out to the Jetta to grab what had grown into several volumes of files on the Derringer case. I knew I'd seen the trial transcripts in a binder somewhere. After Duncan turned the case over to O'Donnell, O'Donnell must have ordered them so that he and Duncan could get up to speed. Something was nagging at the forefront of my brain, something someone had said during the trial. I flipped through the transcript pages frantically. It was going to be lost if I didn't find a trigger to pull it forward.

Then I spotted it.

"What's going on?" Kendra asked.

"Wait a second, Kendra." What else had I missed? I started from the beginning of the file and reread everything. When I was finished, I knew exactly where I had gone off track. It wasn't just what someone had said at trial. I'd also missed the Tasmanian Devil.

I looked up at Kendra. "Tell me more about Haley."

I looked for her first outside of the Pioneer Place Courthouse, the waterfront, the Hamilton motel, all the places I could think of. I finally found her at midnight, standing on the corner of Burnside and Fourth Avenue. She had her thumb out and looked like she'd just shot up.

I stopped the Jetta in front of her, and she walked over to the passenger side and opened the door. Guess she couldn't see through the tinted windows at night.

"Hey, Haley. Want a date?" I said.

"What the fuck are you doing out here?" She looked around. Not seeing any police, she said, "Nothing you can do to me without a cop around."

All those *Law & Order* shows had done some serious damage to my image out there. Now that everyone understood that whole "separate but equally important parts of the criminal justice system" thing, no one is afraid of being arrested by prosecutors anymore. Sometimes it's just a matter of reeducation.

"Not today, maybe. But I can go drive my little Volkswagen back to the courthouse, type out an affidavit, and have an arrest warrant for you in the system by tomorrow morning. It's not like it takes the cavalry to find you or anything."

She thought about that for a while. "Yeah, well, I can

handle another loitering pop. Nothing but a thing at juvie." Her eyes were barely open. It's probably hard to care about being arrested when you're pumped full of heroin.

"I'm not talking about juvie this time, Haley. I'm talking Measure Eleven time."

She might not know the details, but anyone on the street as long as Haley knew the gist of Measure 11. It meant being charged as an adult and getting real time. The threat was enough to fire her up as much as could be expected in her current state.

She pretended to laugh. "You ain't got shit on me. Now you better move along, bitch. I got work to do."

I suppressed the impulse to mow her down with the Jetta. I would've opened a six-pack of Fahrfegnugen on her ass over the c-word, but under the circumstances I could handle the b-word.

"I'd be careful about how you choose to work, Haley," I said. "From where I sit it's called promoting prostitution, not loitering. And promoting prostitution for a thirteen-year-old lands you under Measure Eleven."

"Pimping? Lady, you got me confused with some Cadillac-driving, purple-velour-wearing, platform-shoe-stomping dude." She was laughing uncontrollably now, rattling off some more descriptors I couldn't understand.

"Haley, listen to me. You're in major trouble here, and I'm not fucking around." My tone got her attention. "You arranged dates for Kendra in exchange for a cut of the fee. You set her up at the Hamilton, knowing she was using the room to work. You sold her condoms when she ran out, again at a profit and knowing she was using them for prostitution. Plus, you knew she was only thirteen years old. All I have to do is go down to the Hamilton, and I suspect I'll find several other girls who'll say you do the same things for them. Guess what, Haley? That's promoting prostitution, even if you don't wear purple velour."

"That's bullshit. I was helping her out, is all. Safer to work at the Hamilton than out of cars. And, big deal, I hooked her up with a few guys who liked younger girls and who I knew were all right."

"Too bad, Haley. I'd heard you were smart. At this point, I'd advise you to shut up until you've talked to a lawyer, because what you just said amounts to a confession to a Measure Eleven charge."

I rolled up the window and hit my turn signal like I was going to pull out into traffic on Burnside. I was beginning to think she was going to let me leave when I heard the tap on the window. I rolled it down again.

"So what do you want?" she asked.

"Now that's more like it. Get in."

| 14 |

When I finally got home it was nearly two in the morning.

Chuck's Jag was in my driveway, and Chuck was asleep in the backseat. I tapped on the window, and he reached over his head and unlocked the front door.

"This piece of crap chose my driveway to break down in?" I said.

"Cute. Where have you been?" he asked, sitting up and pushing his hair down from sleep.

"Another late one," I said.

"A late one where? I've been leaving you messages all night."

"Sorry. I got busy. I would've called you tomorrow."

"So, again, where have you been?"

Shoot. He'd learned something about interrogations over the years. "Working. Griffith told me I had to dismiss the case against Derringer, so I went out to Rockwood to break the news to Kendra."

"You were at Kendra's until two in the morning?" He sounded appropriately skeptical.

"I had some follow-up. I'll tell you about it later. Right now I'm exhausted." I headed toward the front door.

He grabbed my arm as I was walking up the steps to the porch. "Dammit, Sam. What kind of follow-up? Where the hell have you been?"

I pulled my arm from his grip. "Jesus, Chuck. The stalking routine really isn't becoming. Is this jealousy? Do you actually think I was with someone else?"

He shook his head.

"What?" I asked.

"You scared the shit out of me. I thought something happened to you."

"Well, nothing happened to me. With Derringer's charges dismissed, he doesn't have any reason to try to scare me off anymore, so stop worrying. I told you, I'll talk to you tomorrow. Please respect that."

"Don't do this, Sam. You were distant last night, you blew off my calls all day, and now you're out till whenever and won't tell me where you were. I know you. The only thing I have to compete with is your job, so something must be happening on the case. What's going on? My guys tell me the governor's cutting Landry and Taylor loose. You tell me you've dismissed the case against Derringer. So why were you out so late?"

I looked at him but didn't say anything.

"You don't trust me, do you, Sam?"

I knew I should say something, but I didn't. I couldn't get my mouth to work.

I finally spoke up when he started walking toward his car. "Explain it to me, Chuck. How did Landry know so much about Jamie's murder if she wasn't a part of it? And if she was a part of it, how come she passed a polygraph while some guy tells the *Oregonian* where the police can find Jamie's purse? Explain it to me. Come inside and talk to me about it."

He turned his head just long enough to say, "You're really unbelievable, Kincaid. You don't know me at all."

I stopped myself from pulling out my cell phone as I watched him drive away. Part of me wanted to apologize; another part wanted to scream at him.

Instead, I decided to get to sleep so I could wake up and work on what I'd learned from Haley.

Two days later, my ducks were finally in a row.

Sneaking around hadn't been easy. Once the charges against Derringer had been dropped and the news had been broken to Kendra, my role in the matter was officially over. I was taking a big risk by jumping back into it again without notifying Duncan and O'Donnell.

I had reserved a block of time in front of the grand jury without indicating a specific case name. Anyone looking at the schedule would just assume I was presenting several drug cases together. Actually, I was trying to indict Derrick Derringer.

Getting an indictment's much easier than getting a conviction. The grand jury's only role is to decide if there's enough evidence against the defendant to warrant a trial, and in practice grand jurors "true bill" almost every case presented to them. Because the grand jury doesn't actually determine the defendant's guilt, the proceedings are considerably less formal than at trial. No judge, no defense attorney. Just the prosecutor and seven trusting grand jurors. We rarely even kept a record of grand jury testimony in state court, but I'd gotten a court reporter for this particular session. At least if I got fired, I'd have a transcript to show for my hard work. It wouldn't be a great trade, but it was better than nothing.

"Members of the grand jury, today's proceedings will not be typical of the hearings you have experienced so far as grand jurors. By now, you have figured out that most criminal cases are cut-and-dry. The prosecutor says hello, calls in a police officer or two, and asks for an indictment. No one gives you the other side of the story, the evidence that complicates the picture, what the defense will say at trial.

"Today, I will ask you to indict Derrick Derringer on charges of obstruction of justice, perjury, statutory rape, and conspiring with his brother to rape and murder a thirteen-year-old girl named Kendra Martin. This will not be a straightforward story. You will learn, if you do not already know from the news, that the State has already dismissed charges against Derrick Derringer's brother, Frank Derringer, for raping and attempting to murder Kendra Martin. To complicate things further, someone has written anonymous letters to the *Oregonian*, claiming that he and an unnamed accomplice, and not Frank Derringer, are responsible for the attack on Miss Martin.

"I'll be honest with you. I am currently unable to offer a single theory that explains both the evidence against Mr. Derringer and his brother, and the anonymous letter that would appear to exonerate the Derringers. I suspect that you will also find it difficult to reconcile the evidence against

Mr. Derringer with some of the State's other evidence. That's why your role today is so important. At the end of the presentation of the evidence, I will ask you to decide for yourselves whether the evidence against Mr. Derringer warrants an indictment, regardless of the exculpatory evidence."

I started with a thorough overview of Frank Derringer's trial, the Jamie Zimmerman case, and the Long Hauler letters. The rules of evidence do not apply during grand jury proceedings, so I didn't have to use live testimony to establish this background. Instead, I offered it in summary form, using the white board to make a list of the central characters in the case and the important points for them to remember. I ended with the discovery of Jamie Zimmerman's purse.

The jurors looked exhausted by the time I was done. An elderly woman across the table raised her hand. She gestured to her notes with her pen while she spoke. "Um, maybe I'm confused or something," she said, "but it sounds like whoever wrote these letters killed Jamie and the other women and also raped that poor little girl. And you're saying that you don't see how these other people—Margaret Landry, Jesse Taylor, and Frank Derringer—could have written the letters, so it sounds like they're all innocent. Have you told us anything about Derrick Derringer yet?"

"Not yet. The evidence I have just summarized for you is the background of a larger investigation that relates to the case against Mr. Derringer. What you've heard so far suggests exactly what you've stated. Like I said, you may find it difficult to reconcile all that information with the evidence you will hear today. So I want you to consider the remaining evidence in light of the background I've given you and then decide whether to issue the indictment."

There were no more questions, so I called my first witness, Haley Jameson.

Haley walked in with an attitude. I would've been disappointed in her if she hadn't. She slumped down into the witness chair at the center of the room and looked up at the ceiling as I had her spell her name and take her witness oath.

"Where do you live, Haley?" I asked.

"Varies day to day. I been in a bunch of foster homes, but mostly I just crash with friends. Stay at a place in Old Town called the Hamilton."

"And how do you pay for things like your hotel room at the Hamilton, food, things like that?"

"I got immunity, right?"

"Right. As we've discussed, you're testifying today with my promise that nothing you say will be used against you."

"Mostly I date," she said. "Sometimes I'll sell some pot to friends or something to pick up a few extra bucks."

"When you say that you date for money, are you referring to prostitution?"

She rolled her eyes and sank into her chair a little deeper. I was starting to worry she might slide right off.

"You need to reply to my questions with a verbal answer, Haley. The court reporter is transcribing everything."

"Yeah. I meant prostitution," she said.

"How long have you been working in prostitution?" I asked.

" 'Bout three years," she answered.

"And how old are you now?"

"Sixteen."

A couple of the grand jurors shifted uncomfortably in their seats as they worked out the math.

"Do you know Frank and Derrick Derringer?" I asked.

"Unfortunately," she said. "Can't be on the street as long as I have without running into them."

I had made the connection when I reviewed the file at Kendra's. I had printed out Derrick Derringer's PPDS record so I could cross-examine him about his prior convictions, but I'd never seen the need to pay any attention to the basic identifying information, like hair and eye color, height, and, most importantly, tattoos.

I pulled out one of the photographs that Kendra had given me the first time I met her, the one showing Haley and a couple of girls with a man whose face wasn't shown but whose tattoo was. I'd retrieved the photographs from Tommy Garcia before I'd gone looking for Haley.

"Haley, I'm handing you a photograph that appears to show you with a man and two other girls. Will you please tell the grand jurors what's going on in that picture?"

"Uh, it's pretty obvious, isn't it?"

"Humor us," I said.

"Well," she said, looking at the picture, "a few of us were partying with a guy, and someone saw a disposable camera lying around and started taking pictures."

"Whose camera was it?"

"Kendra's," she said.

"Kendra Martin?" I clarified.

"Yeah. Kendra wasn't actually there. She'd been in my room earlier, hanging out, and left it behind."

"Are the other girls in the picture also from the Hamilton?"

"Yeah, on and off, like me," she said.

"Who's the man in the picture, the one with the tattoo of the Tasmanian Devil?"

"That's Derrick Derringer."

"How do you know him?" I asked.

"Like I said, hard not to know him," she said. "Him and his brother cut in on a lot of the girls' business out there. They take a share from you, or all of a sudden bad things start happening to you."

"Do you give any money to Frank and Derrick Derringer?"

"Yeah, I got to give 'em half of what I make. For a long time, they were leaving us younger girls alone as long as we'd do other stuff for 'em. Now they want both. Like that night we took the picture, we did the group thing for him, but then I had to keep giving him money on top of it."

"So you have had sexual intercourse with Derrick Derringer?"

"Duh," she said.

"The court reporter, Haley," I reminded her.

"Yes. I've had sexual intercourse with him."

"To your knowledge, did Kendra Martin pay any of the money that she earned to Frank and Derrick Derringer?" I asked.

"Nope. She hadn't been working long enough to really know who they were yet. She seemed to think she was too good for a lot of it and was real careful to stay on her own."

"What did the Derringers think of that?" I asked.

Haley and I had gone over her testimony carefully before I'd given her the immunity deal. I was still worried, though, that she'd back out on me.

"They were pissed. All the girls knew Kendra was out on her own. A couple times, we told her to come around when we knew Frank or Derrick were coming by. You know, we'd say we knew these guys and we wouldn't be getting paid but needed to do it anyway. I figured she knew the score, but she kept blowing us off while we were still getting stuck with them. It was pissing a bunch of the girls off too, and they started telling Frank and Derrick that they weren't going to go along if Kendra wasn't."

"How did the Derringers react to that?"

Haley looked at me and then the door. For a second, it seemed like she considered bailing, but she stayed put. She was going to need some prodding.

"Haley, I asked you how the Derringers reacted to that."

"All I know is, I saw Derrick the day after Kendra got messed up. He said that me and the other girls should take a lesson from her, that that's what happened to girls who didn't have someone watching out for them."

"Did he ever tell you directly that he or his brother was involved in the attack on Kendra?" I asked.

"No, just that we should take a lesson from it."

"Did you say anything in response to that?" I asked. I could tell she was considering clamming up again, but then she gave up.

"Yeah. I was pretty messed up at the time and mouthed off to him. I told him he'd better be careful because Kendra had a picture of him."

"Are you referring to the photograph that we just discussed?"

"Yeah. I saw the pictures after Kendra got them developed. Derrick freaked when I told him and started shaking me to find out what I was talking about. I told him I was just fucking with him, that the picture didn't show his face or anything. But then he made me tell him where Kendra's mom lived at so he could try to get the picture back."

I paused to tell the grand jurors about the key missing from Kendra's purse and Andrea Martin's suspicion that some items were out of place in the Martin home. I also showed them reports documenting the break-in at my house, explaining that the photographs had been in Tommy Garcia's possession until a few days ago.

"After you gave him Kendra Martin's address, did you ever talk to Derrick Derringer again about the photograph?"

"Yeah. He told me I better get that picture back from Kendra. I've been calling Kendra trying to do it, but Kendra will only talk on the phone with me. She won't meet me anywhere, so I've been trying to avoid Derrick." I mentally apologized to Kendra for doubting her.

"Haley, I want to show you another photograph now." I handed her the DMV photo I had pulled of Travis Culver and reminded the grand jurors that Culver was the owner of the Collision Clinic who had testified at Frank Derringer's trial. "Do you recognize this man?"

"Sure, that's Travis," she replied.

"Do you know his last name?"

"Not before you told me. Street don't really care about last names," she said.

"How do you know Travis?" I asked.

"Regular out there on the street. Dates. You know."

"You mean he picks up prostitutes?"

"Yeah. The younger the better, it seems. I used to see him a lot more about a year and a half ago. Guess I got too old for him and he moved on."

"Have you seen him at all since Kendra Martin was attacked?" I asked.

"Nope," she said. "Seems like he stopped coming around about that time."

The grand jurors didn't have any questions, so I thanked Haley for her testimony and excused her.

* * *

Next up was Travis Culver. I'd slapped the subpoena on him the day before and received a call from an attorney within the hour. Lucky for me, Culver had called the attorney he uses for the auto shop, a guy named Henry Lee Babbitt who hung a shingle outside of his house and called it a law office.

Since Henry Lee's usual fare was wills and uncontested divorces, he was useless as a criminal defense lawyer. To begin with, I had to walk him through the way grand jury subpoenas work. Culver'd be subject to arrest if he failed to appear. Although he had the right to refuse to respond to questions if he believed that the answers might incriminate him, he had to show up, and he did not have the right to an attorney during the grand jury proceedings. At most, Henry Lee could wait in the hall outside the hearing room; Culver could ask for breaks if he wanted to consult with his attorney at any time. You can see why the defense bar says that grand jury proceedings are a prosecutor's best weapon.

Henry Lee's request for an immunity deal was further proof of his abject ignorance of criminal procedure. A good defense lawyer will find out what the prosecution knows before even considering the possibility of a deal. To do otherwise tips your hand. Henry Lee had tipped his for good. I had told him only that I wanted to talk to Culver about his testimony in the Derringer trial. In return, Henry Lee had given up his client in the form of a hypothetical.

"Let's say hypothetically that I had a client who got wrapped up by some bad guys into an ugly sexual incident, thinking the whole thing was consensual?" he said. "And then what if, hypothetically, when it turned out that the

young woman hadn't in fact consented to this little encounter, the client got blackmailed by the bad guys into a
cover-up?"

Henry Lee had watched way too many bad TV shows, and
now I had even better questions for Travis Culver.

Culver looked terrified as he took the chair in the middle
of the grand jury room. He was sleep-deprived and dis-
heveled, and I could smell the fear in his sweat as he passed.

At least Henry Lee had given him one piece of good advice;
Culver invoked his rights as soon as we got past his name
and address.

"Do you know Frank or Derrick Derringer? Isn't it true
that you overhauled Frank Derringer's car on a Sunday, on
short notice, to get rid of physical evidence? Do you use the
services of teenage prostitutes? Did you and Frank Derringer
rape and beat Kendra Martin and then leave her to die in the
Gorge?" That last one was what you call a compound question, but no one was there to object to it, and Culver wasn't
going to answer anyway, so what the hell?

I kept going. "Isn't it true that you paid Derrick and Frank
Derringer to stage a sexual assault upon a young girl for your
pleasure? And that when, unbeknownst to you, the violence
turned out to be real, they threatened to reveal your identity
unless you cleaned out the car and offered false testimony in
Frank Derringer's defense?" Another horrendously compound question, but it worked. Culver was clearly thrown off.
I wish there was a way for the court reporter to transcribe
the look on a witness's face. This one said, *How the hell do
you know all that?* I wanted to respond, Your stupid attorney
pretty much told me, but I didn't.

Culver looked like he was thinking about answering the

question but then gave me the standard response. "On the advice of counsel, I refuse to answer on the ground that it might incriminate me."

When I thought the grand jury had the gist, I excused Culver and brought in my final witness, Lisa Lopez.

"On behalf of the grand jurors and myself, thank you for coming, Ms. Lopez. I know how busy you are. You were the public defender assigned to represent Frank Derringer, is that correct?"

"Yes. As you and I have discussed, it is highly unusual and extremely questionable that you have brought me here by subpoena, and I have appeared only on your assurances that you are seeking an indictment against Derrick Derringer, and that my testimony will not be used to secure new charges against my client, Frank Derringer."

Securing Lisa's presence here at all had required substantial maneuvering. When I had explained the situation to her at her office, after hours, she had immediately balked, citing attorney-client privilege, work-product privilege, the duty of loyalty, and the duty of zealous representation. She seemed offended when I responded, "Ethics, schmethics," so ultimately I'd had to convince her that helping me out was both ethically permissible and morally required. After lengthy negotiations, she finally accepted service of the subpoena and promised not to rat me out to my boss. The deal was that I'd ask only a few questions, which we agreed upon beforehand. In response, she would provide the exact answers we'd rehearsed in advance, including the long-winded caveat she'd just provided as an introduction to her testimony.

I continued the questioning as planned. "In your defense

of Frank Derringer, one theory you presented at trial was that the crimes against Kendra Martin were committed by whoever killed Jamie Zimmerman, is that right?"

"Yes, that's correct."

"Ms. Lopez, I'm handing you a transcript of your opening statement in the Derringer trial. Please read for the grand jurors the highlighted passage."

She read from the transcript:

"The wrongdoing that has brought Kendra Martin, Frank Derringer, and all of us together began about four years ago. Four years ago, Portland police officers found the body of another troubled young girl named Jamie Zimmerman in the Columbia Gorge. Jamie wasn't as lucky as Kendra. She was murdered—strangled—after being raped and beaten. Like Miss Martin, Jamie was a drug addict who supported her habit through occasional prostitution. Like Miss Martin, she was raped and sodomized. Police found Jamie's badly decomposed body less than a mile from where Kendra Martin was located. Ms. Kincaid mentioned that whoever committed this crime took Kendra's purse. Well, guess what, ladies and gentlemen? Whoever killed Jamie Zimmerman took her purse too, and it was never recovered."

I saw some of the grand jurors flip back into their notes, asking themselves the same question I'd asked myself three days ago. "Ms. Lopez, how did you know that Jamie Zimmerman's purse was taken and never recovered? The police were unaware of that fact until just days ago."

"I refuse to answer on the ground that the information is protected by the attorney-client privilege and the work-product privilege," she responded.

"Ms. Lopez, you understand that the attorney-client privilege protects only information obtained in the course of communications between you and a client, is that correct?"

"That's correct, counselor."

"The work-product privilege, on the other hand, applies to *any* information you obtain during the course of working as an attorney on behalf of your client. In other words, it covers not only communications between you and your client but also information you derive from research or interviews of third parties. Is that a fair summary of the privilege?"

"Yes, counselor."

"It would be a violation of your professional ethics, wouldn't it, Ms. Lopez, to assert a privilege that you did not actually believe covered the information requested from you?" I asked.

"That's correct. I would not assert a privilege unless I had a good-faith belief that the privilege applied to the requested information."

"I want to be very clear here, Ms. Lopez." I paused for emphasis. "I have asked you how you knew that Jamie Zimmerman's purse was taken from her when she was killed. And you are refusing to respond not just on the basis of work-product privilege, but also on the basis of attorney-client privilege. Is that correct?"

"Yes, it is," she responded.

"I understand and respect your position, Ms. Lopez. Thank you for your time," I said, excusing her.

When I announced that I had no further witnesses, the grand jurors' questions began to fly. Was I arguing that Frank Derringer had killed Jamie Zimmerman? How could that be, when we knew for certain that he didn't kill at least two of the other women described in the Long Hauler letter? Did I think Derrick Derringer was in on it? What should they do about Travis Culver? Did this mean that Detective Forbes coached Margaret Landry's confessions?

"I am asking you to indict Derrick Derringer on the following charges. First, statutory rape based on Haley Jameson's testimony that Derrick Derringer has had sexual intercourse with her. She is only sixteen years old, and the photograph you saw corroborates her testimony. Second, obstruction of justice and perjury for offering false testimony on behalf of his brother, Frank Derringer. Third, conspiracy to rape and murder. He may not have been present at the time that Kendra Martin was attacked, but you have heard evidence suggesting that the Derringer brothers conspired to rape and kill Kendra Martin to send a message to other girls on the street that they'd better make their payments, one way or the other.

"I am not presenting any charges relating to any of the murders described in the Long Hauler letter, including the murder of Jamie Zimmerman. Nor am I requesting charges against Frank Derringer or Travis Culver." Double jeopardy protected Frank Derringer from being charged again with the attack on Kendra, and Culver couldn't be indicted by this grand jury, since he'd been brought here under the compulsion of a subpoena. "I understand that it is difficult to reconcile my theory of the charges against Derrick Derringer with some of the extraneous evidence. The question for you to resolve is whether, despite those complications, you believe a jury could find Derrick Derringer guilty beyond a reasonable doubt."

I had blocked off the rest of the grand jury's afternoon so they would not feel pressured in their deliberations. I gave them my pager number and asked the foreperson to beep me when they'd reached a decision.

I passed Tim O'Donnell in the hallway on the way back to my office.

"Hey, Kincaid, I was just looking for you. Where you been all morning?"

"Went over to JC-2 for a couple of arraignments. Crazy over there," I said, looking down to make sure that everything was tucked away neatly in my file.

So I wasn't sharing the sandbox anymore. Big deal. Playing well with others isn't all it's cracked up to be. Besides, technically speaking, I had done everything I was told to do. Frank Derringer was free, and my actions had in no way jeopardized the exoneration of Margaret Landry and Jesse Taylor.

As it turned out, O'Donnell still thought we were sharing.

"Just got back from OSP," he said, taking a bite of the bagel he was carrying around. The Oregon State Prison was nastiness incarnate, but O'Donnell was probably well past letting it affect his appetite. "Landry and Taylor passed their polys. FBI guy says no signs of deception to the three key questions."

The polygrapher had asked Taylor and Landry whether they abducted or killed Jamie, wrote the Long Hauler letters, or knew the Long Hauler. Passing the polys helped clear the way for their release.

For a second, I thought I felt a pang of guilt for not telling O'Donnell what I'd done, but I decided it was hunger brought on by watching him eat his bagel. The moment passed when he started chewing with his mouth open.

"So what happens next?" I asked. As far as I was concerned, what happened next was a big fat indictment against Derrick Derringer, but I kept that to myself.

"Duncan's on a call to the governor now," O'Donnell said. "The only question is whether to get Landry and Taylor out through the courts or have the governor pardon them. Looks like a pardon, though. The courts will take too long, and there's no guarantee we could even get them out that way without an error at trial."

Believe it or not, what's known as a "mere" showing of innocence is not a legal basis for setting aside a lawfully obtained conviction. Instead, the defendant has to point to an error during trial that affected the result of the case. Illegally seized evidence introduced? Public defender fell asleep? Then you might have a chance at reversal. But if the procedures were lawful, it's pretty much impossible to set aside a jury's guilty verdict, even if you subsequently demonstrate your innocence. Respecting the finality of the guilty verdict is the only way to keep the courts from being flooded by convicts' endless claims of innocence. Without a procedural error, Taylor and Landry had a better chance of release through the governor's intervention than in a court of law.

"Is Jackson willing to issue the pardon?" I asked.

"Looks like it. We've talked about a stipulation of police misconduct as the trial error, but Duncan and Jackson are worried about a beef from the police union," he said.

"Was Landry polygraphed about that? What did she say about Chuck?"

"Nada. The polygraph only covered the ultimate issue of factual innocence. The examiner was worried about adding too many questions."

The greater the number of material questions you put in a poly, the higher the risk of either false signs of deception or inconclusive results. So much for using modern technology to find out if the man I'd been sleeping with was lying his ass off.

"Oh, and the FBI finished its profile. Pretty much what we expected," he said.

"Any theory as to why the guy wrote the letters now, after all these years?" I asked.

"Probably because of the media attention. He might not have come out on the Taylor stories alone, or maybe he would've waited until after the execution. But the theory is that the combo of the Taylor and Derringer stories was too much for this guy to resist. The profiler compared it to the Unabomber sending out his manifesto after Tim McVeigh stole his thunder."

"So how come we haven't heard anything from him since?" I asked.

"FBI says that's the kicker," he said. "Usually, a communication like that is followed up with a body or at least more taunts. It's possible there's another one out there, and he's waiting to see if we'll find it on our own. Another possibility, of course, is that this guy's got his own way of operating. Wait and see, I guess. Anything else on your end?" he asked.

Oops. Now I was going to have to be a hypocrite on that whole lying thing. "Nope," I said, mentally crossing my fingers. "The victim understands what's going on. The family won't be making any statements to the media. They just want to be kept in the loop." The truth was that Kendra and her mom were so grateful for Kendra's continued anonymity that they'd never contemplate making a statement to the media.

But seeing as how I was already lying to Tim's face, there was no real harm in letting him think the Martins might embarrass him publicly if he dropped the ball.

I might not play well with others, but I was getting pretty good at faking it.

My pager finally buzzed as I was taking a plea in Judge Weidemann's courtroom.

"A problem, Ms. Kincaid?" Weidemann inquired, peering down over his half-moon glasses. I was surprised that he was paying enough attention to the proceedings to notice that I'd glimpsed down at the device clipped to my waistband.

"No, sir," I responded. "Just waiting for a grand jury decision, your honor."

"Not too much suspense to be found there. Who's today's ham sandwich?" he responded. The defendant and his attorney, Frankie LoTempio, got a laugh out of that one. A running joke among criminal defense lawyers is that grand jury proceedings are so one-sided that grand jurors would indict a ham sandwich if asked to by the prosecutor. The way I saw it, if prosecutors were doing their jobs and only asking for indictments that were warranted, grand jurors *should* be indicting all the cases given to them. I doubted that Weidemann and LoTempio wanted to hear my view, though.

"Well, seeing as how they're the grand jurors and I'm a judge, let's finish up here before you head on up to them, if that's acceptable to you, Ms. Kincaid?" Weidemann asked.

"Of course, your honor," I said, reminding myself once again that displays of ingratiating deference come with the territory when you're a trial lawyer. The rest of the sentencing was predictable, given Weidemann's Solomon-like approach. I recommended an upward departure from the sentencing guidelines, mentioning a few facts I'd noted in the file that were mildly aggravating—some packaging materials, a tattoo hinting at a gang affiliation, the defendant's choice words for the arresting officer. Then LoTempio cited a few lame reasons for requesting a downward departure from the sentencing guidelines. In the end, Weidemann applied the guideline sentence. The sentencing guidelines provided 99 percent of all drug sentences and left little discretion for the judge. Weidemann, though, had to feel like he was doing something important, so everyone who appeared before him played along.

When we finished, I ran up to the grand jury room on the seventh floor and knocked on the cracked door before pushing it open. "You all done?" I asked.

The foreperson, a seventy-year-old man in a T-shirt that said I STILL LOVE MY HARLEY handed me the slip of paper. A single check mark told me they had true-billed the requested indictment by a unanimous vote.

"Some of us wanted to know if we'd be able to find out what happens in the paper," he said.

"Oh, I think you can count on that," I said.

"Go get 'em, Tiger," he said. "And watch out for yourself."

Maybe grand jurors are a prosecutor's conspirators after all.

I had wasted no time getting the paperwork for the indictment to Alice Gernstein. I thought I'd have to sneak it through while O'Donnell was in court, but I got lucky. His legal assistant mentioned that O'Donnell had left early to head down to his fishing cabin. The superstar of office paralegals,

Alice had Derrick's warrant in the system by the following morning.

As it turned out, the rush hadn't done me a damn bit of good, because three days later, Derringer still hadn't been picked up.

The plan was to find Derrick without tipping him off to the warrant. Once he was in custody, I'd arraign him, confess my sins to Duncan, and let the chips fall where they may. The arrest might force my boss and the bureau to come up with a theory that explained all the evidence, not just the evidence they liked.

I didn't say it was a great plan, just a plan.

The plan was looking even lamer now that I couldn't get even the first step off the ground. I'd called in my markers with four different pals in the Southeast district, but they hadn't seen Derringer at his house or work all weekend.

At one point, I picked up the phone to call Chuck, but I quickly replaced the handset. Since the showdown at my house, I must have done this at least a dozen times.

Grace was always good at strengthening my resolve, so I asked her to meet for lunch at a bistro that was halfway between the salon and the courthouse. Once we'd placed our orders, I filled her in on my plan.

She wasn't pleased. "You realize, don't you, that you may very well get fired over this."

It didn't sound like a question, but I answered anyway. "I sort of figured that if Duncan tried to fire me, I'd use the grand jury transcripts as leverage."

"And how, exactly, will the transcripts give you any leverage?" she asked.

"The press looks at the JC-2 calendar every day to see who gets arrested. When Derrick finally gets arrested, the media will start asking questions, so Duncan will at least have to keep investigating the Derringers and find out how they're involved with the Long Hauler. If he tries to bury it and get rid of me, I could hint that I might release the information presented to the grand jury."

We were momentarily distracted by the arrival of our food. Or, to be more accurate, by the arrival of our extremely attractive waiter. Apparently having sex on a semiregular basis over the last month had altered my cognitive priorities.

"I thought grand jury proceedings were secret," Grace said, as we both admired our waiter's extremely attractive departure.

"They are. Doesn't mean Duncan won't worry about the threat. Prosecutors have been known to leak grand jury information when it helps them. Look at Ken Starr," I said.

"So your big plan is a bluff?"

"I'm not sure about that, Grace," I said. "I think I'd actually do it at this point. I mean, they convicted Landry and Taylor based mostly on the fact that Landry knew things no one but the killer could know. Now those same defendants are being released, and Frank got his case dismissed, because the Long Hauler knows things no one else could know. But it turns out that Frank had information too. How could he have known Jamie Zimmerman's purse was stolen unless he was involved somehow? And the Derringers' involvement in teen prostitution is just too coincidental. I think Duncan will have to pursue it once I force the issue with Derrick's arrest. If he tries to ignore it, I don't have a problem with making sure that the press doesn't let him."

"And what does Chuck think about your plan?" she asked.

"He doesn't. I haven't told him."

She raised a perfectly plucked eyebrow at me.

"Look, I realize that I might've had more pull with Griffith if I hadn't been fooling around with Chuck." I paused. "To be honest, Grace, I don't know what to think. I mean, I seriously doubt that Chuck coerced a confession out of Margaret Landry, but what if he did? That cocky independence of his could translate into some questionable police tactics."

"Or he could be a perfectly honest cop, Sam. I thought it was that cocky independence that appealed to you in the first place."

"No, I know. I just want to make sure that my judgment's clear on this one."

"That's so unlike you, Sam. You're always so quick to say you're a good judge of character. That every egg's good or bad, and you can tell right off the bat."

"That is what I always say," I confirmed. "But what did Roger turn out to be?"

"Well, blow me over. You're beginning to sound like someone who's willing to accept some gray areas in her life."

I half smiled.

"And how's Lucky Chucky taking it?" she asked.

"He's not—I mean, I haven't exactly explained it to him. In fact, we're not actually speaking at the moment, I don't think. Which is a bit inconvenient, because I want him to go pick up Derrick Derringer."

There went that eyebrow again.

"And I miss him," I added.

| 15 |

Before I left for the day, I checked in with my Southeast Precinct pals to see if they'd had any luck, but there was still no sign of Derrick Derringer. It's hard to arrest someone when you've asked the few uniformed patrol officers working on it not to do anything that might tip the suspect off, like knock on his door or ask for him at work.

I thought again about calling Chuck on my way home, but I held myself back. I'd thought the evidence through backwards and forwards, but it kept coming back to him. Either he'd coerced a confession out of Margaret Landry, or somehow she'd managed to squeak through the polygraph while someone else wrote letters to the *Oregonian* in an attempt to exonerate her—someone who had access to details about unsolved crimes.

But something was bothering me about the letters too. It seemed peculiar that the Long Hauler had confessed to every strangling case in the Northwest Regional Cold Case Database that *didn't* involve DNA evidence. Why did all the killings happen to occur in the handful of states that cooperated in the database? And what were the odds that *every* strangling without DNA in those states had been committed by the Long Hauler? The perfect correlation struck me as odd. But every time I felt like I was close to putting my finger on the missing piece, I'd come back to the obvious: maybe Chuck just wasn't the person I thought he was.

So I hadn't called him. I decided that if Derrick didn't get picked up tonight, I'd call in sick tomorrow and sit outside his house until he came home.

Maybe if I hadn't gotten so caught up in fantasizing about Derrick's impending arrest scene, I would've noticed when I opened the door that Vinnie hadn't waddled up to meet me. It wasn't until I was locking it behind me and realized I didn't hear the alarm beeping that I registered the déjà vu. Bracing myself for another crack on the head, I heard a familiar voice, the one that had called my cell phone the night I left Grace's. "Welcome home, Samantha."

The good news was I'd managed to find Derrick Derringer. The bad news was he was standing behind me with a very large gun.

"Why don't you join us in the living room?" He waved his gun to indicate that I should walk in front of him.

The bad news got worse. Tim O'Donnell was tied to my Mission-style chair, Frank Derringer sat on my sofa with the remote control, and Vinnie was whimpering, presumably relegated to the pantry again.

I noticed, though, that Derrick was pacing behind the sofa, and Frank was chewing the cuticle of his right thumb.

They were nervous, and I tried to take advantage of it by faking confidence.

"Nice to see you were enjoying a little TV. Anything good on? I try to stay away from the reality shows myself," I said.

Derrick wasn't amused. "Maybe that explains why she didn't listen to you, Tim," he said, glancing at O'Donnell, who looked truly terrified. "Has trouble with reality. Now, if I were you, sweetheart, I'd shut the fuck up and have a seat."

"Stop it, Sam." A puddle under my Mission-style chair and spots on O'Donnell's pants suggested that things had already gotten ugly before my arrival. "This is some serious shit."

Derrick laughed at him. "Figure it out, ass-wipe. This bitch don't listen, not to you, not to anyone. But you had to tell us you'd handle everything, you'd get it all taken care of. But what the fuck happens? Nimrod here," he said, gesturing to his little brother, "gets his case dismissed, and *I* wind up under indictment. Well, I'm through letting you and Frankie fuck this shit up. This shit ends tonight. My way."

"Look, I got you in just like you wanted," O'Donnell whined. "You said you'd let me go if I was telling the truth about knowing her alarm code. Let me out of here, and I won't say a word."

All that money for my super deluxe alarm, down the drain. If I got out of this mess, I'd be smart enough not to use the security code from work as my home password.

Derrick laughed again. "What are you gonna do, Tim, call a judge and say I broke my word? This ain't some plea bargain, counselor. You don't get to walk just 'cause you flipped on someone."

"Jesus, Derrick, I've done everything you wanted!" O'Donnell was practically whimpering.

"No, you did everything *you* wanted!" Derrick was pointing the gun at him now. "I thought the Zimmerman girl was behind us, and now dumb fuck here goes and does it to some other girl, and you say you'll take care of it again, but I'm the one who winds up getting fucked in the ass."

O'Donnell was blowing it. The Derringers had been showing signs of doubts about their plans, but now Tim was getting Derrick wound up, and Derrick was reverting to his aggressive mode. I had to find a way to make Derrick anxious again.

"Look, Derrick," I said, speaking very slowly. "I don't know what's going on between you and Tim here, but killing us will only make things worse. There's no murder beef on you right now. You kill us, and you're going to feel heat like you never knew before on—what do you have, a few forgeries or something? Don't do this."

It didn't work. Now the gun was pointed at me. And Derrick was still ranting. "Don't you pull that shit with me. You know exactly what's going on here, and that's the whole problem now, isn't it? You couldn't let it alone. You got a major hard-on for this case and couldn't let it drop. Now this dumb-fuck DA's calling me, telling me you got a fucking indictment against me."

I couldn't stop to figure out how O'Donnell knew about the indictment or why he would tell the Derringers.

"Derrick, listen to me. The indictment was a bluff. Grand jurors will indict anyone the prosecutor tells them to indict. I just wanted you picked up so the police would talk to you about the case. I don't have any evidence against you or your brother." I could tell he was beginning to tune in, so I talked a little faster.

"Here's what we're going to do. Tim, as a supervisor at the

District Attorney's Office, you are on official notice that I am hereby resigning from my position as a deputy district attorney. Derrick, give me some money. A dollar, whatever, and tell me you want to talk about your legal problems. Attorney-client privilege will protect everything you say to me, OK? Let me talk to you about this."

Derrick was looking at me, not saying anything.

Frank couldn't keep quiet any longer. "Derrick, give it to her," he said.

"Shut up, Frank," Derrick said. "She's full of shit, and she's gonna die, so I don't give a shit about privilege."

"Think about it, Derrick." Frank was beginning to sound desperate. "Just in case something goes wrong, the judge won't let her rat on us."

"Yeah, well, nothing's going wrong," Derrick retorted, clicking the safety off his gun and pointing it at me. "You're the one who leaves people alive who are supposed to be dead, not me."

"Stop! It's not supposed to happen till after eight!" Frank yelled.

Hearing they'd apparently penciled in my death for a specific time made me dizzy. Luckily, I seemed to have found an ally in Frank. He fished a dollar out of the front pocket of his jeans and asked if that would work for both of them.

"Derrick, do you accept my representation?" I asked.

"Sure, what the fuck? Three times I went down, I wanted to kill my lawyers. Guess I can fulfill my wish."

I always wondered what it would be like to go into private practice. This wasn't what I pictured, but I offered my advice anyway.

"Frank's got a free ride on anything that happened with Kendra Martin. The trial started, so double jeopardy protects him. And there's no physical evidence to link you to anything, Derrick. Not that I'm saying you did anything, because I don't know that you did, of course. And, on Zimmerman, two people have already been convicted, so that pretty much creates reasonable doubt for anyone else the State tries to charge down the line."

He was thinking about it, I could tell. What I couldn't tell was whether his brain was big enough to comprehend it all.

"Nice try," he said, "but you left out my fucking eyewitness over here."

"Your brother?" I asked. "Frank's not going to turn you in, are you, Frank?"

This pissed Derrick off for some reason. He said, "I told you she was full of shit, Frank. Don't pretend like you don't know what's going on, bitch. My first mistake was letting Master Crime Fighter here live when it turned out he was a DA and not some salesman from Idaho like he said. Dumb and Dumber here meet each other in a chat room. So one day Frankie tells me he knows a furniture salesman from Idaho who's willing to pay big for a gang bang on a young'un. We set him up with Jamie, and next thing you know the girl's dead and, lo and behold, the salesman's a DA. Should have killed you then, O'Donnell."

"Frank's the one who killed her, Derrick, not me," O'Donnell said. "He's the one who got out of control. Luckiest thing that ever happened to you was me being on call when her body was found. I got you guys out of that jam, and I've been getting you out of this one."

O'Donnell was getting Derrick riled up again. "That's bullshit, man! You helped *yourself* out on that first one, but now you've been screwing *us*."

"Tim, you were involved in this and then told Landry what to say?" I asked, trying to follow the conversation between the two of them. "That's how she knew everything about Jamie?"

"I don't know how she knew, Sam, I always assumed it was Forbes. But I ran with it and got the convictions, didn't I, Derrick? And, even though we were supposed to be even after that, I've been trying to help Frank out ever since. When he got popped in Clackamas County, it was me who told him to argue consent instead of that stupid alibi. And it got him a damn good plea deal, didn't it? I've been trying to get him out of this one, too. I used information from confidential police databases to write those Long Hauler letters. Even tonight, I've done everything you asked. You wanted me to leave a message for Sam, I did it. I got you the alarm code. I've helped you."

Tim obviously didn't care anymore about lying to me; he was doing whatever he could to save himself before the Derringers killed me. His pleas hadn't seemed to work.

"And now I'm under fucking indictment," Derrick said. "So it's time to put this thing to rest."

"What message? I didn't get any message." I was frantically stalling for time before they could implement whatever plan they had in mind.

"Yes, you did, and the police will find it with your bodies," Derrick said.

Frank went into the kitchen and pushed a button on my answering machine with his knuckle. I heard Tim's voice say, "Sam, it's Tim O'Donnell. I just wanted to make sure we're still on for tonight to talk about the case. If I don't hear from you, I'll be at your house around eight. See ya."

Frank came back in, looking very proud of himself. "See,

Tim tells us that the FBI's waiting for the Long Hauler to make a big splash. So he's going to come here tonight to kill you both."

Derrick laughed. "Yeah, Tim. Thanks for the imaginary friend. It was brilliant. He'll take care of the two of you, and down the road we'll take care of Haley and the Martin girl after we've turned them out for a few more months. They'll just be a couple of dead prostitutes."

"Yeah, maybe the Long Hauler can write a letter about it," Frank added, laughing with his brother.

They were psychopaths, but I had to give them credit. They were smart psychopaths. My head was reeling. There was no Long Hauler. O'Donnell had access to the Northwest Regional Cold Case Database. He'd written the letters, carefully selecting details only from cases that lacked DNA evidence. He'd probably mailed them when he was out of town at his fishing cabin.

"Frank, Derrick," I said. "It doesn't matter that Tim was there when Jamie died. There's a rule that says a co-conspirator's testimony alone isn't enough to convict. Even if Tim testified against you, the State would need other evidence to corroborate the testimony. There isn't any. Anyway, he's the last one who's going to turn you in. It implicates him too."

O'Donnell finally clued in. "She's right, Derrick," he said. "I'd never testify against you, but even if I did, the rule she's talking about would keep there from being any case."

The tag team approach seemed to be working. "You're better off blowing town than killing us," I said. "You commit a double murder, and you're looking at the death penalty. They won't just assume the Long Hauler did it. They'll check for copycats, scour the files we were working on. They'll find the pictures I have of you with Haley. They'll find Travis Culver.

Once the police are done fishing around, you'll wind up on death row. As it is, you can bail."

Derrick thought about it for a few seconds, then shook his head. "Nice effort, but our previous counsel here already gave us some advice. I tried like hell to get those pictures back to be safe, but O'Donnell here tells me they don't show much. Hell, my face ain't even in 'em. As for Culver, he'll be shot during a robbery gone bad at the Collision Clinic."

"Derrick," O'Donnell said, "don't you think the police are going to put it together? A witness, the DA, and the victim in Frank's trial all turn up dead? Don't do this, man."

They needed to see that their plan was starting to fall apart. "The police will find the transcript of the grand jury testimony against you," I said. "They'll draw the same conclusions I did. Right now, there's not enough proof, but with two dead DAs they'll put it together. And the grand jury testimony will be admissible in court if any of the witnesses are dead."

"What grand jury testimony?" Derrick asked. "Tim, you said there was no record of a grand jury testimony. Is there or isn't there? Don't you fucking lie to me!" he yelled, backhanding O'Donnell with the gun.

Tim's head jerked to one side with the blow. When he sat back up, blood was running from a cut beneath his right eye. "We don't have court reporters for normal grand jury sessions, but you can request one if you want to keep a record."

Derrick smacked him again in the same place, bursting the cut open even wider. "*Now* you fucking tell me, man!" He pursed his lips, trying to figure out his next move. "OK, bitch."

I assumed he was talking to me.

"You think you're so smart, but now I know you got a transcript, you're gonna tell me where it is."

"It's at the office," I said.

"That's bullshit," Derrick said. "Tim tells me you been holding out on him. He couldn't find the files in your office and tells me you've been hiding them at home. Only way he knew you indicted me was a secretary. Ain't that right, Tim?"

I looked over at O'Donnell. The right side of his face was swollen and bloodied.

"Alice mentioned it to me," he said by way of explanation. "She recognized the name and thought I should know about it."

In an office where I could never find anyone to help me, I'd managed to find someone who was *too* competent. I should've known Alice Gernstein wouldn't miss a beat.

It was clear that O'Donnell was losing his resolve to fight. It was also clear that I wasn't digesting the new information quickly enough. My first impulse was to be pissed at him for snooping through my office, but then I remembered that this was a man who had helped kill Jamie Zimmerman, sent an innocent man to death row, and led the Derringers to me to save his own ass.

Derrick was behind me now, running the head of his gun along my collarbone, pushing aside my hair to graze the back of my neck. "Tell us where the transcript is, Sam, or I'm gonna have one hell of a time on your buddy Kendra before she dies."

I resisted the urge to tell him I wasn't as stupid as O'Donnell. I knew they were going to kill us and do horrible things to Kendra before they killed her, whether I was helpful or not. I also knew that the promise of those transcripts was the only leverage I had at this point.

Luckily, I'd left my case file in the trunk of my car. "I've got them locked in a safe," I said.

"Good girl," Derrick said. "Now where's the safe?"

"Upstairs," I said, "in the master bedroom."

"Aangh," he responded, like a buzzer on a game show, "wrong answer. I personally tossed this place looking for your little friend's peepshow pictures, and there ain't no safe."

"It's an old wall safe. It's hidden in the baseboard. There's no way you'd see it."

I could picture Derrick searching his memory for the ransacking of my bedroom, doubting whether he would have noticed an irregularity in the oversized baseboards. He threw a note pad and pen at me from the dining room table. "The combination," he said. "Where is it in the baseboards?"

"Directly behind the bed," I said, as I scrawled down three numbers that were all slightly off. If my guess about what was going to happen was wrong, I could always tell them that the safe stuck sometimes.

Derrick snatched the paper from my outstretched hand and gave it to his brother, gesturing with his head toward the stairs. "Here, take these," he said, throwing him a pair of gloves from his jacket pocket. Frank took the stairs two at a time. I heard a few thumps from upstairs, followed by silence and a few more thumps. I tried not to think about Frank Derringer being in my bedroom.

After a few more rounds of thumps, Frank scrambled back down the stairs to the landing. "That bed is fucking heavy, man. I can't budge it."

I had sworn at myself many times for buying a solid maple bed that I couldn't move without the help of a strong friend. But it had just been added to the very short list of things I'd never get rid of. That is, if I lived past eight o'clock.

Derrick was less happy with the news. "Jesus Christ, man.

Can't you do a fucking thing by yourself?" Then he looked around the room, in search of Plan B.

C'mon, pea brain, I thought, watching him ponder the possible combinations. There's only one right answer here.

His eyes eventually fell on me. He gestured toward the stairs with his head and said, "You, go up and help." Yes! Good answer, Derrick, good answer! "Try anything, and Kendra will pay the price," he yelled as I went up the stairs, Frank behind me.

Frank was a lightweight. The bed was approximately four centimeters from where I'd last left it. I walked around to the far side, saying, "If we each take one leg of the headboard and pull back, it's usually the best way to move it."

I watched Frank take his position on the other side of the bed, and then I crouched to my knees to reach beneath the bed ruffle and grab the headboard. As Frank pulled against his side of the bed, I pulled on my side with my right hand. With my left, I reached inside the top shelf of my nightstand and pulled my .25-caliber automatic loose from the tape that held it to the bottom of my drawer. I slid it onto the floor next to me and then pulled on the bed hard with all my weight.

The bed jerked a few feet away from the wall. Frank rose from his side of the bed and saw my gun aimed on him before I'd fired off the shot. If he could've just stood still, the bullet would have hit him dead center in the chest. Instead, he ran for the door quickly enough that it caught him in the right shoulder.

I fired off a second shot but missed and hit the doorframe. Damn. Too much time on the firing range, not enough chasing down wily targets.

Two quick shots rang from downstairs as I followed Frank to the door. By the time I got there, he was almost to the end of the hallway leading to the stairs. I fired another shot. I must've hit him, because I heard a low grunt. I must not have gotten him good, though, because he turned down the stairs, and my next shot ripped through the shameless Warhol knockoff on my wall.

Assuming that Derrick would be waiting for me at the bottom, I took the stairs with my back pressed against the inner wall. I stopped at the last step before the landing, steeling myself to make the turn. The pressure of my heart pounding against my chest was fierce, and I fought to catch my breath.

I poked my head around the corner and then retreated to the safety of the wall again. Keeping my back against the wall, I began moving down the second half of the stairs. Tim O'Donnell was still in my Mission chair, but now blood was oozing from a dark hole in his forehead. From the looks of things, a second bullet had been fired into his groin.

As much as I'd practiced shooting, I'd never made a sweep through a house before, and I didn't know what I was supposed to do next. Without any other basis of information, I instinctively relied upon that most reliable of sources, television.

From the landing, I could see that the front entrance and living room were clear. I swung off the stairs in a half circle to face the back of the house, my gun outstretched in front of me. Still clear.

The living room and Tim's dead body were to my left now as I faced my dining room and kitchen. I reached down slowly, keeping my gun pointed in front of me, and grabbed my purse. If I could just make it out the front door and to the safety of my car, I'd be home free.

As I reached to unbolt the front door, I saw Derrick spring around the corner of the dining room with his gun in front of him. He must've watched TV as a kid, too. What he should've been doing was practicing at the firing range, because he was a piss-poor shot. I heard the mirror behind me crash as a bullet ripped into it.

I fired off two shots as I jumped across the hallway, over the top of my sofa, and into the coffee table. I muffled a cry as pain shot through my left side where I landed against the oak edge. I scurried backward to get myself out of the pool of blood that was quickly forming beneath O'Donnell and my Mission chair. The noise was blocked out by the sound of the back door sliding open, followed by tires squealing down the street.

I don't know how long I lay there, listening to myself breathe, trying to convince myself that I couldn't hear anything else. Even Vinnie was quiet now.

I finally mustered up the courage to crawl around the back of the sofa and sneak a quick peek into the dining room. I'd done right by the firing range. Derrick Derringer was on his back, two bullet holes squarely in the middle of his chest. Apparently, it was OK for me to move while I was firing, as long as my target stood still.

Based on the trail of blood through the dining room, into the kitchen, and out the back door, I guessed that Frank had fled when he saw his brother go down. More blood outside suggested that Frank was long gone.

I freed Vinnie from the pantry as I dialed 911. Then I sat in a ball on the kitchen floor holding him and my gun close to my chest until I heard sirens pulling up to the house and fists pounding on the front door.

| 16 |

When I finally woke up the next morning, my whole body was on fire. I was also sleepy and had a sore throat. By the time the police finally left—around two in the morning—I'd related my entire story three different times. First, I had to tell the patrol officers who responded to the 911 call, so they wouldn't shoot me when I answered the front door with a gun in my hand, two dead bodies behind me, and bullet holes all over the place.

Then I had to give it to Walker and Johnson, who drew the MCT call-out. They offered to page Chuck for me. I guess once your sex life's on the front page of the newspaper, it's considered public knowledge. They apparently didn't know the whole story, because they seemed caught off guard when I asked them to call my dad instead.

Then I had to explain it all a third time to Griffith, who

showed up just as the medical examiner was zipping the
body bag closed around Tim O'Donnell's corpse.

"The Chief called me," he said. "He thought I should know
that two of my deputies were involved in a shoot-out."

By then, my narrative skills had gotten pretty proficient.
The Derringers' involvement in street-level prostitution.
O'Donnell's extracurricular interests, which led him from
what he thought was a staged fantasy with an underage pros-
titute to the murder of Jamie Zimmerman. How Kendra's
assault arose from the same scenario, but this time with
Travis Culver as the not-so-innocent dupe. Culver's lies about
Frank's car. O'Donnell's fabrication of the Long Hauler let-
ters. My night of shoot-'em-up action. I dumped it all on him.
Except the part where I'd given O'Donnell my resignation.

"You should've come to me with this, Samantha," he said.
He looked tired, and, in the light of my kitchen, the wrinkles
that usually seemed distinguished just looked old.

"I thought I did the right thing at the time. I knew
O'Donnell was set on killing the case, and I assumed you'd
listen to him unless I had some leverage."

He stood to leave. "You should give me more credit, Sam.
I'm an independent thinker, and now I'm going to go home
to think." As he headed out the door, he gave me a wave
over his shoulder. "Nice house you got here. See you in the
morning."

I had assumed from his comment that I was supposed to
go to the office this morning, regardless of my sleep deprivation, sore throat, and aches. It definitely beat being dead,
though.

And at least I was safe from the Derringers. At my insis-
tence, Walker had dispatched patrol officers to watch Haley
and Kendra while police began their search for Frank Der-

inger. I thought about doing the same for Travis Culver, but s far as I was concerned, he could fend for himself. The varning call I placed to Henry Lee Babbitt seemed courtesy nough.

Around the time Griffith left, Johnson snapped his cell hone shut and announced they'd found Frank.

"Was he dumb enough to go home?" I asked.

"Wherever he was headed, he never got there. Traffic esponded to a major one-car accident on I-Eighty-four. The ar burst through the railing at an overpass and flipped head irst onto the concrete below. Driver was dead by the time hey cut the car open. They were searching the car for holes, rying like hell to figure out where the bullets in the driver's houlder and ass came from, when they heard the APB for)erringer on the radio."

"His butt?" Walker said.

"Yeah. Looks like that second bullet of yours went straight nto the man's left cheek, Kincaid. Must have hurt like a nother fucker when he was driving on the freeway. He was robably squirming around trying to take the weight off his ony ass when he lost control."

I hadn't been able to laugh with them about it then, but n the morning shower, as I rubbed a bar of Dove on my own eft bum, I could see the humor, and I laughed until I started rying again.

A strange bubble of silence followed me through the ourthouse as I walked to my office. I guess no one knew vhat to say to me. This morning's news had featured vague eports of a fatal shoot-out at my house involving the Der-inger brothers and O'Donnell. The reports didn't explain hat they were all trying to kill me, only that "police were nvestigating."

When I got into my office, I checked my voice mail, hoping for a message from Chuck. No luck. He hadn't called my home or cell, either. I did, however, get a message from Griffith, summoning me to his office.

When I got there, he handed me a piece of paper and asked me what I thought.

It was a letter from Griffith to Governor Jackson, supporting the pardon requests of Margaret Landry and Jesse Taylor. It explained that all currently available evidence indicated that Frank Derringer and Tim O'Donnell had killed Jamie Zimmerman during a rape arranged through a teenage prostitution ring managed by the Derringer brothers. O'Donnell had pursued the case against Landry and Taylor based upon the circumstantial evidence that existed, possibly providing the confidential information to Landry that eventually helped secure the convictions. Then, when Frank and an unnamed suspect assaulted Kendra, he'd done what he could to get rid of the case. When I thwarted his efforts to issue it as a general felony, he fabricated the Long Hauler by using confidential information he found about unsolved murders in the cold case database and then ordered me to dismiss the case.

The memo went on to explain my discovery of the Derringers' connection to the sex industry. After briefing Griffith, I'd obtained an indictment against Derrick Derringer as the first step in an envisioned investigation into the Zimmerman and Martin cases. Unfortunately, O'Donnell had discovered the investigation and tipped off the Derringers. They broke into my house, I heroically saved the day, and Griffith would be pursuing any remaining culprits to the full extent of the law.

It was accurate in the ways that counted, and at this point I really didn't care if Duncan wanted to cover his ass. He was covering mine too, and the end result was the right one. "Looks good," I said. "Will Jackson issue the pardon?"

"It's a done deal," he said. "The governor's office will announce it tomorrow, and Landry and Taylor should be out by that afternoon. We need to talk about tying up the loose ends. We'll have problems going after Culver. You know that, don't you?"

I told him I did, but he still seemed to think he needed to convince me.

"Even if your victim can ID him, we're gonna have the same problems you had with Derringer. No physical evidence. No corroborating testimony, because everything you heard between the Derringers is hearsay. No direct evidence of intent to kill. Not to mention the time that's passed since the offense."

"I know," I said.

"You think this guy's attorney will go for a preindictment deal?" he asked.

"Depends on the terms," I said, "but, yeah. Culver's scared. Now that he knows the Derringers aren't going to kill him, I think he'd like to take his lumps and get it over with."

"Alright. I was thinking of something like Rape Three. Have him do a few years but no Measure Eleven charges. Part of the deal could be a scholarship account for the girl, since this guy's got a business. How's that sound?"

We both knew Culver deserved to go away for good. The Derringers may have pretended that the violence was staged, but it took people like Culver and O'Donnell to choose to believe it. The reality was that Griffith had come up with a deal that was the most we could hope for under the circumstances. Sometimes that's as close to fair as we get around here.

"I'll call Henry Lee with it. He'll be happy to hear he doesn't have to try an actual case."

"Then why don't you take the rest of the day off? I'd say you've earned it."

I turned back before leaving the office. "Tim said he didn't give anything to Landry, that he assumed Forbes did," I said.

"She gets out either way, Sam. Unless you think Forbes is a long-term problem, it's cleaner this way."

"I can't make that call right now."

"I know. That's why I made it."

I started to leave again but stopped at the door.

"Now what?" he said.

"Thanks, Duncan."

"Anytime, Deputy Kincaid."

I ignored the stares again on the way back out of the courthouse. Let 'em think I was in trouble. Tomorrow, I'd be a hero.

I wanted to go home and sleep for the next twenty hours, but there was someone I needed to see.

Like most prisons, the Oregon Women's Correctional Institute had been dumped in the middle of nowhere to avoid public outrage and plummeting property values. The only other buildings within a three-mile radius were two similarly ostracized yet essential enterprises, a casino and an outlet mall. Needless to say, the combination made for an interesting mix of soccer moms, prison families, and senior citizens in RVs.

The guard brought Margaret Landry to meet me in one of

the sterile rooms used for attorney-client conferences. As I had requested, he moved her in leg shackles and handcuffs.

When he brought her into the room, I said, "I don't really think those are necessary, Deputy. Would you mind removing them and leaving us alone? I'm sure Ms. Landry and I will be just fine here without all of this."

If the guard ever got tired of corrections, he should try Hollywood. His best attempt to look worried about my request was pretty realistic. He removed the cuffs and shackles and left us alone.

I'd seen pictures of Margaret Landry, of course, but she'd aged considerably during her two years in prison. Assisted by too many cigarettes and too little sleep, she'd gone from looking well fed and nurturing to haggard and crotchety.

After I introduced myself, she said, "I been dealing with someone in your office named O'Donnell."

I dropped the bomb on her and announced that O'Donnell was dead. To simplify things, I told her that Jamie Zimmerman's murderers had been identified and killed, but not before they had shot Tim O'Donnell. I figured it might be hard to earn her trust if I revealed that a member of my office was a homicidal rapist. She'd get the details from someone else down the road, anyway.

"Because of everything that's happened, you'll be getting out of here tomorrow," I said.

"Where are they moving me to?"

"You can stay wherever you want. Maybe with your daughters until you adjust to things. You're being pardoned, Margaret. You'll be free, with no criminal record."

Her lower lip began to shake, and pretty soon she was crying.

When she'd finally stopped trembling, she lifted her head to the ceiling. I couldn't tell if she was looking for answers or trying to thank someone, but I could tell she hadn't felt however she was feeling for a long, long time.

"I never meant this to happen," she said. "I kept calling the police on Jesse, but wouldn't no one help me. When Jamie's body turned up and I saw her in the paper, I thought I'd finally get that son of a bitch out from under my roof, but they didn't believe me. They told me I didn't have no 'corroboration.' I kept digging myself in deeper and deeper, and next thing I know I'm under arrest myself and can't take any of it back."

"I feel bad for you, Margaret, but you put an innocent man in prison and kept the police from looking for the men who actually killed Jamie Zimmerman."

"Jesse Taylor ain't no innocent, but you're right about that last part. As sorry as I feel for myself, I can't help thinking that them other girls would be alive if I hadn'ta done all this."

I thought about letting her in on the truth about the Long Hauler, but the fact of the matter was, her actions had cleared the way for the Derringers to hurt Kendra and countless other girls. The rest of the story was minutiae.

"The pardon will make it clear that you're innocent, Margaret. When you get out tomorrow, you'll not only be free, you'll have your good name back. It must have been awful for you these past years, having people think you did something so horrible, knowing you were innocent."

Her eyes started to well up again.

"And when you get out tomorrow, everyone's going to hear that you were telling the truth at your trial. They'll know that

that detective, Chuck Forbes, helped you come up with corroboration to set up Jesse."

Mid-sob, she went silent, and I heard her breath catch in
her throat. It was time to ask the question that had brought
me here.

"You knew her, didn't you, Margaret? You knew Jamie
Zimmerman. That's how you knew what kind of earrings to
buy, how you knew her mother's phone number?"

I'd seen the look on her face countless times. It's the look
witnesses get when they want to talk but they're scared, even
though they *know* you already know what they have to say.

"After what you've been through, no one's going to prosecute you for trying to help yourself out a little on the stand.
The only thing that changes here is what people are going to
make of Chuck Forbes, whether they're going to assume he
did something that maybe he didn't do. The choice is yours,
Margaret. You're getting out tomorrow either way."

She was tough, but one more push should do it.

"How'd you know her?"

"She'd come into Harry's Place sometimes when she was
trying to go straight." She started to explain that Harry's was
the teen homeless shelter, but I let her know with a nod that
I was familiar with it.

"I went to Harry's for a while when I was volunteering for
Art Therapy," she said. "They sent us out to different nursing
homes and shelters to paint ceramics, arts and crafts, that
kind of thing. Jamie was such a sweet girl. She stopped com-
ing in for such a long time, and then I saw her in the paper.
They found her body and they were looking for information.
I started wondering who could do something like that to her.
Then I started thinking that I lived with someone who could

do that. A few days went by, and they still hadn't found her. I thought I could mess Jesse up with his parole officer, but then it just snowballed. I thought it would look even worse if they knew I knew Jamie, so I said I got it from that young cop. I'm so sorry. I'm just so sorry."

I left her there crying. I needed the emotional energy for myself.

When I got to my car, I found a message from Ray Johnson on my cell phone. He had run all the names of Frank and Derrick's known associates. Turned out that one of Derrick's old bunkmates was on probation for driving a brown Toyota Tercel with a suspended license. He spilled his guts the minute he heard Derrick and Frank were dead. He owed Derrick money and was repaying the debt by following me around and reporting back to Derrick. Derrick used the information about my whereabouts to break into my house, crank-call me, and feed the *Oregonian* anonymous tips about my sex life. Funniest thing was, a search of the guy's belongings turned up a dollar bill with his license plate number scrawled on it. He must've followed me on one of my many food stops.

I thought the guy deserved a life sentence for helping the Derringers scare the shit out of me and publicly exposing my sex life, but in the end I wasn't sure he'd done anything illegal. Maybe I'd think about it later when my brain started to work again.

For now, all I wanted was to go home and go to sleep. But I had one more thing to do. I sat in my car in the prison parking lot, staring at my cell phone, before mustering the courage to dial.

The sound of his recorded voice was anticlimactic. I did

my best at the beep, but I knew it was going to take more than a phone call.

When I pulled into the driveway, he was waiting on the front porch. I had a lot to make up to him, if he'd give me the chance. It would start with a kiss on the forehead and, I hoped, a very long nap.

Acknowledgments

Judgment Calls is the product of the tremendous support I've been fortunate enough to enjoy throughout my legal career and during my work on this first novel.

I am especially grateful to my colleagues at Hofstra Law School; Multnomah County Senior Deputy District Attorney John Bradley; Michael Connelly, Jonathon King, and Maggie Griffin for convincing me my manuscript would be finished; Jennifer Barth, editor-in-chief at Henry Holt, for her incredible work, intelligence, and creativity; Philip Spitzer, the most loyal and supportive agent on the planet; Scott Sroka; and, above all, my phenomenal family.

Samantha's dedication and humanitarianism are modeled on the hard work I observed among former coworkers at the Multnomah County DA's Office. You know who you are.

Read on for an excerpt
from Alafair Burke's next book

MISSING JUSTICE

Coming soon from
Henry Holt and Company

it's true that dreams come from the id, then my id is not
articularly creative.

The dream that makes its way into my bed tonight is the
ame one that has troubled my sleep almost every night for
e past month. Once again, I relive the events that led to the
eaths of three men.

The walls of the stairway pass as a man follows me up-
airs. I force myself to focus on my own movements, trying
 block out thoughts of the other man downstairs, armed
d determined to kill me when I return.

Time slows as I duck beside my bed, reach for the pistol
dden inside my nightstand, and rise up to surprise him.
he .25 caliber automatic breaks the silence; more shots fol-
w downstairs. Glass shatters. Heavy footsteps thunder
rough the house. In the dream, I see bullets rip through
esh and muscle, the scene tinted red like blood smeared
cross my retinas.

I usually wake during the chaos. Tonight, though, the since returns, and I walk past the dead bodies to my kitchen.
open the pantry door and find a woman whose face I know

only from photographs and a brief introduction two year
ago. She is crouched on the floor with her head between her
knees. When she looks up at me and reaches for my hand,
the phone rings, and I'm back in my bedroom.

It is four o'clock in the morning, and as usual I wake up
chilly, having kicked my comforter deep into the crevice between my mattress and the footboard of my maple sleigh
bed. I fumble for the phone on my nightstand, still ringing
in the dark.

"This better be worth it," I say.

It's Detective Raymond Johnson of the Portland Police
Bureau's Major Crimes Team. A member of the search team
has found a woman's size-seven black Cole Haan loafer in
the gutter, but Clarissa Easterbrook is still missing.

The call came only eight hours after my boss, District Attorney Duncan Griffith, had first summoned me to the Easterbrook home. It was my first call-out after a month-long
hiatus and a new promotion from the Drug and Vice Division
into Major Crimes. I was told it would just be some quick PR
work to transition me back into the office.

So far, the transition had been rough.

When I pulled into the Easterbrook driveway that first evening, I cut the engine and sat for a few last quiet moments
in my Jetta. Noticing Detective Johnson waiting for me at
the front window, I took a deep breath, released the steering
wheel, and climbed out of the car, grabbing my briefcase
from the passenger seat as I exhaled.

I climbed a series of steep slate steps, a trek made necessary by the home's impressive hillside location. Despite the

pring mist, I was able to take in the exterior. Dr. Townsend asterbrook was clearly no slouch. I wasn't sure which was igger, the double-door entranceway or the Expedition I'd arked next to.

Johnson opened one of the doors before I'd had a chance use either of the square pewter knockers. I could make out ices at the back of the house; Johnson kept his own down. at in that car so long, Kincaid, thought something might e wrong with your feet."

At least my first case back on the job brought some fa- iliar faces. I had met Raymond Johnson and his partner, ck Walker, only two months ago, when I was a mere drug d vice deputy. But given the history, however recent, I felt bond with these guys—the gunky kind that threatens to ick around for good.

"You must not have given up all hope, Johnson. You were aiting at the door."

"I was beginning to wonder, but then you tripped some- ing off walking up the path, and I heard a voice somewhere nnouncing a visitor. George fucking Jetson house. Gives me e creeps."

The Easterbrook home wasn't exactly cozy, but I'd take it. eutral colors, steel, and low sleek furniture—the place was twenty-first-century update on 1960s kitsch.

With any luck, Clarissa Easterbrook would turn up soon, nd there'd be no need to disrupt all this coolness.

Johnson caught my eye as I studied the house. "Look at u, girl. You're almost as dark as I am." He grabbed my and and held it next to the back of his. Not even close. John- n's beautiful skin's about as dark as it comes.

"Yeah, but you're *still* better looking."

He laughed but it was true. He also dressed better tha me, more Hollywood red carpet than police precinct line leum. "Griffith dragged you back from Maui just for this?"

"I flew in last night, but I sort of assumed I'd have Sunda to myself before I headed back in tomorrow. Maybe the bos thought it would do me good to get some hand-holding prac tice while we wait for Easterbrook to turn up. You know ease me out of drug cases into the new gig."

"They usually do," Johnson said. "Turn up, I mean. Sh probably went shopping and lost track of time or went ou for a drink with the girls."

"Right, because, of course, that's all women do in thei spare time: shopping and girl talk."

"This is going to take some getting used to, Kincaid, afte seven years of MCT work with O'Donnell."

I didn't react to the mention of my predecessor. "Just do ing my part to lead you down the path of enlightenment, Ray Clarissa Easterbrook's an administrative law judge, not som bored housewife."

"Oh, so it's only women lawyers who excel beyond mall and gossip. Got it. Note to all detectives," he said, as if h were speaking into a dictation recorder, "the new Majo Crimes Unit DA says it's still okay to dis housewives." H dropped the routine and cocked a finger at me. "Busted!"

There was no arguing it, so I laughed instead. "Who's i the back?" I asked, leaning my head toward the ongoing mur murs.

"Walker's back there with the husband and the sister. W got here about a half an hour ago, and the sister showed u right after. We haven't been able to do much more than tr to calm them down. We need to start working on the time line, though. I stayed out here to wait for you. I suspect Dr

Easterbrook's still getting used to having a brother in the house."

It was unusual to have MCT involved so early in a missing persons case, but Walker and Johnson were here from the Bureau's Major Crimes Team for the same reason I was: to make sure that our offices looked responsive and concerned when the missing judge showed up and to triple-check that the investigation was perfect, just in case she didn't.

"Sounds good. I'll do my part for the family and any press, but for now you guys take the lead on interviews."

"Music to my ears, Kincaid."

He began walking toward the back of the house, but I stopped him with a hand on his elbow. "I assume you're keeping things gentle for now, just in case. And absolutely no searches, not even with consent." If Clarissa Easterbrook had encountered anything criminal, everyone close to her would become a suspect, especially her husband. We couldn't do anything now that might jeopardize our investigation down the road.

"I should've known it was too good to be true. All DAs just got to have their say. It's in the blood." I could tell from his smile that he wasn't annoyed. "No worries, now."

We made our way to the kitchen, walking past a built-in rock fountain that served as a room divider. The Easterbrooks had sprung for marble countertops and stainless steel, Sub-Zero everything, but it looked like no one ever cooked here. In fact, as far as I could tell, no one even *lived* here. The only hint of disorder was in a corner of the kitchen, where the contents of a canvas book bag were spread out on the counter next to a frazzled-looking woman. She had a cell phone to one ear and an index finger in the other.

Jack Walker greeted us. With his short sleeves, striped tie,

and bald head, he had enough of the cop look going to make
up for his partner. "Welcome back. You look great," he said
into my ear, as he shook my hand with a friendly squeeze.
"Dr. Easterbrook, this is Deputy District Attorney Samantha
Kincaid."

There are women who would describe Townsend Easterbrook as good-looking. His brown hair was worn just long
enough and with just enough gray at the temples to suggest
a lack of attention to appearance, but the Brooks Brothers
clothes told another story. On the spectrum between sloppy
apathetic and sloppy preppy, there was no question where
this man fell.

He seemed alarmed by the introduction. At first I assumed
he was nervous. I quickly realized it was something else entirely.

"Please, call me Townsend. Gosh, I apologize if I was staring. I recognized you from the news, but it took me a moment
to draw the connection."

It hadn't dawned on me that, at least for the foreseeable
future, former strangers would know me as the local Annie
Oakley. One more daily annoyance. Terrific.

"I'm sorry to meet you under these circumstances, Dr.
Easterbrook. Duncan had to be in Salem tonight, but he
wanted me to assure you that our office will do everything
within our power to help find your wife."

When Griffith called, he had insisted that I use his first
name with the family and assure Dr. Easterbrook that he
would have been here personally if he weren't locked in leg-
islative hearings all week. Other missing people might disappear with little or no official response, but Dr.
Easterbrook's phone call to 911 had ripped like a lightning

bolt through the power echelon. Until the wife turned up, here was Griffith's chance to say "I feel your pain."

And Easterbrook clearly *was* in pain. "Thank you for coming so quickly," he said, his voice shaking. "I feel foolish now that you're all here, but we weren't sure what we should be doing. Clarissa's sister and I have been calling everyone we can possibly think of."

"That's your sister-in-law?" I asked, looking toward the woman in the corner still clutching the phone.

"Yes. Tara. I called her earlier to see if she'd heard from Clarissa today. Then I called her again after I found Griffey was missing."

Walker tapped the pocket-size notebook he held in his hand with a dainty gold pen that didn't suit him; most likely a gift from one of his six daughters, it looked tiny between his sausage fingers. "Dr. Easterbrook was just telling me he got home from the hospital at six-thirty tonight. His wife was home when he left this morning at six."

A twelve-hour day probably wasn't unusual for the Oregon Health Science University's attending surgeon, even on a Sunday. Looking at him now, though, it was hard to imagine him steadying a scalpel just four hours ago.

Easterbrook continued where he must have left off. "She was still in bed when I left. Sort of awake but still asleep." He was staring blankly in front of him, probably remembering how cute his wife was when she woke up. "She hadn't mentioned any plans, so when I got home and she wasn't here, I assumed she went out to the market. We usually have dinner in on Sundays, as long as I'm home."

"You've checked for her car," Walker said. It was more of a statement than a question.

"Right. That was the first thing I did, once I was out of my scrubs: I changed clothes and walked down to the garage. When I saw the Lexus, I thought she must have walked somewhere. I tried her cell, but I kept getting her voice mail. Finally, around eight, I thought to look out back for Griffey—that's our dog. When I saw he was gone too, I drove around the neighborhood for what must have been an hour. I finally got so worried I called the police."

In the corner, Clarissa's sister snapped her cell phone shut and blew her bangs from her eyes. "That's it. I've called everyone," she said, looking up. "Oh, sorry, I didn't realize anyone else was here."

"From the District Attorney's office," Townsend explained. "Ms. . . . Kincaid, this is Clarissa's sister, Tara Carney."

It was hard to see the resemblance. My guess is they were both pushing forty, Tara perhaps a little harder, but they had been different kinds of years. Clarissa was a thin frosted blonde who favored pastel suits and high heels. Tara's dark brown pageboy framed a round face, and she looked at ease—at least physically—in her dark green sweatsuit and sneakers.

She acknowledged me with a nod. "I called everyone I can think of, and no one's heard from her today. This just isn't like her."

"She's never gone out for the day without telling someone?" Walker asked.

They both shook their heads in frustration. "Nothing like this at all," Townsend said. "She often runs late at work during the week, we both do. But she wouldn't just leave the house like this on the weekend. With the dog, for hours? Something must be wrong."

We asked all the other obvious questions, but Tara and

Townsend had covered the bases before dialing 911. They had knocked on doors, but the neighbors hadn't noticed anything. Clarissa hadn't left a note. They didn't even know what she was wearing, because when Townsend left that morning she was still in her pajamas.

Her purse and keys were missing along with Griffey, but Townsend doubted she was walking the dog. She always walked him in the morning, and sometimes they walked him together after dinner if they were both home. But she didn't take Griffey out alone after dark. Anyway, these were ten-minute potty trips, not all-night strolls.

Walker was rising from his chair. "Finding out how she's dressed is a priority." He was shifting into action mode. "If we go through some of her things, do you think you might be able to figure out what she's wearing?"

"*You* would be the one to go through your wife's belongings," I corrected. We had to keep this by the book. "I think what Detective Walker is suggesting is that you might be able to tell what clothes are missing if you look at what's here."

"Right," Walker agreed. "And it would help to get a detailed description out as fast as possible." It would also help us determine if we were all wasting our time. Maybe Clarissa had packed a suitcase and her dog to run off voluntarily with a new man or simply to a new life without this one.

"You either overestimate my familiarity with clothing or underestimate Clarissa's wardrobe. Tara, can you help? I doubt I can be of any use."

I suggested that we all go upstairs together while Tara looked through Clarissa's closet. Johnson offered to stay downstairs in case anyone knocked, but Easterbrook assured him that the house's "smart system" would alert us if anyone approached the door. Of course, Johnson already knew that, so I gave him a warning look over my shoulder to join me as I followed Townsend and Tara up the hammered-steel staircase. No way was he sneaking around here while the family was upstairs, especially in a house with its own intelligence system.

The Easterbrook master suite was the size of my entire second floor, a thousand square feet of spa-style opulence. Townsend led us through a large sitting area, past the king-size bed, and around the back of a partial wall that served as the bed's headboard. I couldn't help but notice that the lip balm on the nightstand was the same brand as my own, the paperback novel one I'd read last year.

The back of the suite contained a marble-rich bathroom adjoining a dressing area roughly the size of Memphis. Townsend wasn't kidding about his wife's wardrobe.

Tara started flipping through the piles of folded clothes stacked neatly into maple cubes. The hanging items looked work-related.

After she'd gone through the top two rows, Tara blew her bangs out of her face again. "She tends to wear the same few things when she's around the house, but the ones I can remember are all here. I just don't know."

Townsend stood in the corner of the closet, seemingly distracted by a pair of Animal Cracker print pajamas that hung from a hook. Tara was seemingly unfazed by the moment's poignancy, or at least she did not let it halt her determination. She was examining rows of shoes stacked neatly on a rack built into the side of the closet. "Well, it looks like her favorite black loafers are gone. Cole Haans, I think. But I can't tell what clothes are missing; she's just got too much stuff."

She walked over to a Nordstrom shopping bag on the floor next to the dressing table. She pulled out a red sweater, set it on the table, and then reached back in and removed some loose price tags and a receipt. "These are from yesterday," she said, looking at the receipt. "Town, these are Clarissa's, right?"

She had to repeat the question before he responded. "Oh, right, she did mention something about that last night, I think."

"Can you tell anything from the tags?" Walker asked.

"No," Tara said. "Well, the brand name, but then they use those silly style names and numbers instead of actually describing the item."

"Did anyone go shopping with her? We could find out what she bought from them," I suggested. I knew I told Johnson I'd leave the questions to them, but I couldn't help myself.

Townsend seemed to wake up for a moment. "I believe she went with Susan—"

"I'm sorry." Walker interrupted, holding up his pen and pad. "What's Susan's last name?"

Tara looked disappointed. "Susan Kerr, a friend of my sister's. I've already tried calling her, and all I got was the machine."

A store clerk would be able to determine from the item numbers what clothes Clarissa purchased Saturday. It wouldn't be easy to get that information at eleven o'clock on a Sunday night, but it was worth trying.

"We'll track someone down from the store," I suggested, looking toward Ray and Jack. "Can't we pull a number for someone at Nordstrom out of PPDS?" The Portland Police

Data System compiled information from every city police report and was the handiest source for accessing an individual's contact information.

Within a few minutes, Walker had the home telephone number of a store manager mentioned in a recent theft case. A manager would not be involved in your average shoplifting case, but this one had been unusual. An employee at one of the local thrift stores had bilked Nordstrom out of thousands of dollars in cash by taking advantage of its famously tolerant return policy. The bureau estimated that every Nordstrom brand dress shirt donated to the thrift store during the last two years had been returned to Nordstrom stores for cash by either the employee or one of her friends.

Perhaps the manager would be sufficiently grateful to the bureau for cracking the case that he'd forgive us for calling him after ten o'clock at night. Walker made the call on his cell to leave the Easterbrooks' line open, just in case.

As it turned out, the Easterbrook phone rang just a few minutes later. I found myself watching Townsend to see how he responded. Did he really expect the caller to be Clarissa? Or did he act like a man who already knew we wouldn't be hearing from her? So far he seemed legit, if dazed. He hadn't made any of the obvious slipups, the ones you see on Court TV: using the past tense, buying diamonds for another woman, selling the wife's stuff, things like that.

Whoever was calling, it wasn't Clarissa. Listening to one side of the conversation was frustrating: "I see . . . Where was he? . . . No, in fact, she's . . . missing"—Townsend's voice cracked on that one. "The police are here now. Yes, that's terribly kind of you, if you don't mind." Some more earnest thank-yous and a good-bye, and Townsend set the phone back on its base.

"That was a fellow who lives a few streets down. He works with me at the hospital. He and his wife were leaving the Chart House and found a dog running in the parking lot with its leash on. It's Griffey."

Walker had reached the Nordstrom manager, who generously offered to meet him at the store to track down what Clarissa Easterbrook had purchased yesterday and was—we hoped—still wearing.

About fifteen minutes after Walker left, a voice similar to the one that announces my e-mails at home declared, "Good evening. You have a visitor." Ray was right. Creepy George Jetson house.

I looked out the living room window to see a man in his fifties struggling to keep up with an excited yellow Lab dashing up the slope to the front door, straining against his leash. A woman of roughly the same age followed.

When Easterbrook opened the door, the lab finally pulled free from his temporary handler, dragging his leash behind him. He leaped on Easterbrook's chest, nearly knocking him over. He was a sticky mess from the drizzle, but you could tell he was a well-cared-for dog. Townsend absently convinced Griffey to lie down by the fountain, though the panting and tail thumping revealed that he was still excited to be home.

A dog like Griffey probably had an advanced degree from obedience school, unlike my dropout, Vinnie. Vinnie was actually expelled. Or, more accurately, I was. When it became clear to the teacher that, despite her instructions, I caved to Vinnie's every demand to avoid his strategic peeing episodes, she suggested that I re-enroll my French bulldog when I felt more committed to the process. Two years later, Vinnie and I had come to mutually agreeable terms. He has a doggie door to the backyard, an automatic feeder, and a rubber Gumby doll that he treats like his baby, but if I don't come home in time to cuddle him and hear about his day, there's hell to pay. Griffey, on the other hand, appeared to do whatever Easterbrook told him.

Easterbrook introduced Griffey's new friends as Dr. and Mrs. Jonathon Fletcher. I guess you have to give up both your first *and* last names when you marry a physician. Dr. Fletcher's looks said *doctor* more than Townsend Easterbrook's. In contrast with the flashy Expedition and high-tech house, I noticed that the Fletchers pulled up in a Volvo station wagon.

Mrs. Dr. Fletcher did her best to provide comfort. "I'm certain Clarissa's just fine, Townsend. A misunderstanding, is all. We just have to find her, and that's that. Now when's the last time you saw her?"

She made it sound like we were trying to track down a lost set of keys.

"This morning," Townsend said. "She was still in bed. I had back-to-back surgeries all day, and when I got home she was gone."

"Well, dear, I'm surprised you even get a chance to operate anymore. Jonathon tells me how busy you are, developing the new transplant unit. Sounds like that's going extremely well."

Apparently Mrs. Dr. Fletcher was so used to her job as conversationalist to her husband's colleagues that she was slipping into autopilot. Understandably, Townsend cut her off.

"Who knows? Still so much to do," he said. Translation: Who the fuck cares about the hospital right now? "I didn't even realize Griffey was gone until a couple of hours ago. When did you find him?"

"Right around ten," Dr. Fletcher said. "A group of us were leaving our function at the Chart House, and this feisty fellow was running around in the parking lot. Initially, everyone assumed he escaped from one of the neighborhood yards or something. But then someone noticed that he was dragging his leash around. Our friend went after him, figuring some-one had lost hold of him. When he checked the tag, what do you know? Our own Griffey Easterbrook."

The Chart House sat just a couple of steep miles down from the Easterbrook home. The elegant restaurant was lo-cated on the winding, wooded section of Taylor's Ferry Road that ran from the modest Burlingame neighborhood in southwest Portland, up about two miles to OHSU and back down again into downtown Portland. Spectacular views of the city made the route one of the most popular spots in the area for walks, runs, and bike rides.

It was not, however, the safest place for a woman alone at night. About a year earlier, two guys from the DA's office were taking a run there after work. They heard what they thought was a couple goofing around behind the bushes, a man wrestling his squealing wife or girlfriend to the grass. Fortunately, the woman heard them talking as they ran past and yelled, "Help! I don't know him." The bad guy got away, but the ensuing publicity called the city's attention to the potential dangers of the area. It was no longer common to find women alone on the path after dark.

The Fletchers' discovery of Griffey there was not a good sign.

Johnson must've been thinking the same thing, because

he decided to revisit what I thought had been our mutual decision not to search the Easterbrook-Jetson home. He pulled me aside while Townsend continued the conversation with the Fletchers.

"I know we're playing it safe, but finding the dog changes the picture. We need to go through the place now while he's still playing victim. If we wait until a body shows, he might lawyer up."

I shook my head. "I still don't like it," I said. "Look at him—he's a basket case. Later on, his state of mind might vitiate any consent we get from him. If, God forbid, her body does surface, we can easily get a warrant, since this is her house. We won't need to have probable cause against the husband."

"And what do we do about the fact that our doctor can move whatever he wants and start dumping evidence the minute we're out of here?"

Johnson's point was well-taken, but it wasn't enough to justify a thorough search this early in the case. Not only could Townsend try to throw out the search down the road, we'd pretty much be killing any chance we had of continued cooperation from him. Hell, even if he was innocent—which he so far seemed to be—he might bring in a lawyer if he thought we were zeroing in on him unfairly. In any event, if Townsend was involved in his wife's disappearance, he certainly could have disposed of any incriminating evidence before calling the police.

I explained my thinking to Johnson and proposed a compromise. "Why don't you offer to take a look around to make sure there's no sign of a break-in? I don't have a problem with you doing a general walk-through; I just don't want a detailed search yet. If you check for broken windows and the

ike, we can at least look for the obvious and avoid any major
fuckups."

"Okay with you if I ask him about it in front of his buddies?"

I gave a quick nod. If Townsend felt pressured to consent
to a search because his friends were around, so be it. Courts
only care about claims of involuntariness if the supposed co-
ercion comes from law enforcement.

Before Johnson walked away, I added, "We should also
get people searching up on Taylor's Ferry. Hopefully by the
time the department has a search plan together, Walker can
tell us what she might have been wearing."

Griffey perked up when Tara came down the stairs, apparently satisfied that nothing helpful was going to come
from foraging through her sister's closet. I'd already been
positively disposed toward her, based on her obvious concern for her sister, and I warmed to her even more when she
found the energy to get down on the floor with her sister's
dog and comfort him with a bear hug.

After a few minutes spent on introductions to the Fletchers and the inevitable words of comfort, Tara grew antsy
again. "Griffey, up," she commanded, pointing him toward
the stairs. "Sorry, I can't sit still. You mind if I throw him
into the tub real quick, Town? He's a little crunchy, and it'll
get my mind off things."

It was clear that Tara's nervous energy was grating on her
brother-in-law; he seemed more at ease once she'd followed
Griffey to the second floor and he could turn his attention
back to the Fletchers.

"I keep expecting the phone to ring, but I'm not sure exactly what kind of call it would be; maybe a ransom demand
or something. Obviously, I want it to be Clarissa explaining

that this is all a misunderstanding, that she went with a friend somewhere and forgot to leave a note, and Griffey just happened to get out. I don't know what kind of call it should be. . . ." At this point, he was just rambling. I didn't point out that the leash suggested Griffey had not simply escaped from the yard but that someone had been walking him. Townsend would have to come to realizations in his own time.

I was beginning to think that a ransom demand would be good news at this point. At least we might get an indication that Clarissa was alive.

"This lifestyle of ours," Townsend said, looking around. "Why does any of this really matter, right? Maybe it just invites problems."

Johnson used the moment as his in to ask permission for the walk-through. Consistent with everything else about the man, his transition was smooth.

He started by asking Dr. Easterbrook if he'd ever noticed anything that might suggest that someone was scoping out the house or following them, perhaps planning a way to get to Clarissa by herself.

"No, nothing at all like that," Easterbrook replied. "You know, this neighborhood is so isolated up here. We hardly see anyone at all on our street who doesn't live here."

"Can you think of anyone who has a conflict with you of some kind? Someone who might be motivated to do something to scare you or retaliate against you?"

"Why would someone hurt Clarissa to get to *me*, detective?"

"Just exploring all possibilities, doctor. Maybe a disgruntled patient from the hospital? A former employee?"

"No," Townsend said, slowly shaking his head. "Clarissa would occasionally get some threats about her cases, but she

lways assumed they were only blowing off steam. Never
nything we gave worry to. No one would want to hurt her.
he's such a good, wonderful person."

"I was just exploring all the possibilities," Johnson re-
eated. "Come to think of it, we should probably take a look
round and make sure there's no signs of a break-in, just in
ase. Do you mind?"

"Of course not, but I'm sure I would have noticed some-
hing earlier. Given the security system, I don't see how any-
ne could have gotten in."

"As long as you don't mind, I'll go ahead and check it out.
o harm, right?"

Johnson sidled off before anyone might want to stop him,
nd the Fletchers seized the opportunity to extricate them-
elves from a situation where they knew they couldn't be of
uch help. As they launched into their good-byes, feeding
ownsend more premature assurances that everything
vould be okay, I caught up with Ray. Truth was, I didn't want
o be alone with Townsend, struggling like the Fletchers to
void all those lame clichés—this will all work out, only a
illy misunderstanding, other completely useless pronounce-
nents suggesting the speaker had any clue as to how the day
vould end.

We hit the basement first. My basement is a dark, damp,
usty wreck of concrete and cinder block that my imagina-
ion has populated with thousands of spiders and their cob-
vebs. The Easterbrooks' had been finished into a laundry
oom and a home gym that had better equipment than my
ealth club. Not only did we not find any bodies, blood, or
uts, there weren't even any windows to check. In place of
he flimsy things that are so often kicked in for basement
reak-ins, the Easterbrooks had glass bricks.

Climbing back up the stairs, we could hear Townsend let
ting the Fletchers out the front door, so we headed up to th
second floor, where Tara had Griffey in a bathroom off th
main hallway. She was fighting to get a dog brush throug
his hind leg. Predictably, Griffey stood compliantly whil
Tara tried to avoid pulling his entire coat off by the roots.

She looked up at us from the tile floor, removing her han
from the brush to push her bangs from her forehead. Th
brush stayed entangled in poor Griffey's coat. "I was jus
wondering whether I should show this to you. I thought h
felt a little crusty downstairs when I was petting him, but i
looks like he's actually got something dried into his coat bac
here."

Johnson knelt down and looked more closely at the sid
of Griffey's hip. Then he reached into an interior pocket o
his suit jacket, removed a latex glove, and slipped it over hi
right hand.

"Do you mind giving us a second, Ms. Carney?"

Tara seemed surprised by the request but left the bath
room, closing the door behind her.

"Looks like clay or something," Johnson explained, "lik
he brushed up against it here on his side."

"Shit. We should have gotten the crime lab over here im
mediately when the Fletchers called."

I was beginning to panic. Why the hell hadn't Johnso
taken care of it? "Wasn't obvious," he said, responding to th
unspoken question. "Until you know for certain what you'r
dealing with, it's hard to know what kind of resources to pu
into it. Take the small chance of any evidence off the dog
plus the likelihood that we're dealing with a runaway wife
and it's a tough call."

It made sense, but it didn't excuse the fact that we nearl

llowed Tara Carney to take what might be our best piece of
vidence so far and soak him in a bathtub.

Johnson flaked some of the beige paste from Griffey's coat
into an evidence bag and marked it with his name and the
ate, using a Sharpie pen.

Shit. What else had we missed? "I think we should go
head and get the crime lab out here and search around Tay-
or's Ferry. Everything about this feels bad."

"Your call," he said, pulling out his cell phone.

This new gig was going to take some getting used to.